Contents

Chapter	
The Storm	1
A Message	4
Awakening	13
Confrontation	29
An Unwelcome Visitor	39
Lord's	55
Gallantry and Villainy	84
The Long Room	98
The Decision	124
The Alpha-Omega Anomaly	142
A Shocking Revelation	161
Pursuit	181
The Beast of Highgate	217
Joseph Mortlock	241
The Book	270
Secret Liaison	290
The Second Lamp	302
The Hunter and the Prey	332

Awakening

The Alpha-Omega Anomaly

C J Hansen

Awakening
The Alpha-Omega Anomaly
Published by
Fisher King Publishing
The Studio
Arthington Lane
Pool-in-Wharfedale
LS21 1JZ
England

ISBN 978-1-906377-44-1

Copyright © C J Hansen 2011

Edited by
Sarah-Georgina Sturdy
Cover design by
Sam Richardson
Photography by
Richard Thomas

All rights reserved. No part of this publication may be reproduced or distributed in any form or by any means, or stored in a database or retrieval system, without the prior written permission of the copyright owner. Permission may be requested through the publisher.

For Mika

The Storm

The storm that night was the worst in living memory. The rain thrashed at the land remorselessly, as though intent on turning the very ground into liquid. Lightning rent the sky savagely and the wind tore fiercely at the trees, breaking mighty branches as though they were mere twigs. It was a wild night indeed.

A tremendous sheet of lightning lit up the whole sky in every direction, bringing a large hill into sharp relief. On the hilltop, silhouetted against the momentarily silver sky was the outline of what appeared to be an enormous, rectangular rock. A bolt of fork lightning struck the top of the rock with a force so terrible it might have split it in two. Then more lightning, brighter yet than any that had preceded it. This time it was unlike any the young girl had ever seen; it was horizontal, almost as though the inky fabric of the sky itself were being torn apart.

As the rain continued to strike the ground like bullets, the hilltop was lit up once more by another flash of sheet lightning, and for the first time the girl made out five figures standing around the base of the rock. Although they were only visible for a moment against the briefly illuminated sky, she was able to identify one distinguishing feature clearly; one of the five figures was considerably taller than the others. Despite being unable to see any of their faces, a feeling of immense danger suddenly gripped the young girl, followed by waves of fear and panic.

More lightning, and for the first time the briefest glimpse of a face, now close-up. She noticed nothing but the eyes, and although it was only for an instant, she saw them with a terrible, daylight clarity. Where there should have been white in the eyes, there was blood red. The irises were black as ink, and these surrounded pupils which glowed faintly with a deep, dark, menacing red. And the eyes were staring right at her. Indeed, not only at her, but they appeared to be looking directly into her.

The six year old girl sat bolt upright in bed with sweat dripping from her hair, screaming in a voice laden with terror and emotion that belied her young age. The girl's mother burst into the room, lighting the darkness with her lantern, and she hugged the girl tightly and tried her best to calm her. "Don't worry my darling," she had whispered, "it's only a dream, nothing but a bad dream." But this had felt too real to be a dream.

"Mother, they're here. He has seen me. He knows me and he knows who I am. Why is he here? He shouldn't be here. He is going to come after me. We are all in terrible trouble!" The words tumbled out through uncontrollable tears, themselves an inadequate expression of the absolute fear she was feeling.

This had not been like other dreams. As the rain hammered against the window, driven by the terrible wind of that storm which was to be remembered as the worst in the long reign of Queen Victoria, her mother held her, hugged her and rocked her back and forth for what seemed like hours, until the storm finally began to subside. As the first grey dimness of dawn began to show itself around the curtain edges, the girl's crying became a gentler sobbing. But one powerful feeling would not leave her: that what she had seen was real. Those figures she had seen should not be here. Whoever they were, they did not belong here. This was not meant to be. And now she and everyone she knew were in the most terrible danger.

Although the fear seemed a fraction less terrible now that the wind had dropped and the grey light had started to filter slowly in from outside, she remained convinced that this had not been a dream. She felt sure that the man whose terrible eyes she had seen, had seen her also. He was real and he now knew of her. He somehow knew things about who she was. And something about the way in which he had looked into her, told her with certainty that one day he would find her.

Even after she had finally stopped crying and her mother had left the room, the feeling lingered and would not leave her as she lay back down in her bed exhausted. Something had happened that night, something terrible, and with that event everything had somehow changed. The world as she had known it in her short life so far would never be the same again.

A Message

The sky was grey, a grey of the purest, deepest shade, the colour of sky for which London was the true and undisputed champion. Anna gazed from her attic bedroom window, across the roofs of the other grand houses with their own splendid, tree-lined gardens and their sloping, slate roofs, topped with tall chimneys that puffed out yet more greyness into the sky. Her line of sight moved further out, to the trees that she knew guarded the canal a couple of miles from where she sat. Oh how she longed to be there, by that canal where she knew her friends would be, as free as the small black specks of birds that she could see circling above it in the sea of grey.

In the last few years, the opportunities for Anna to leave the house and meet with her companions had become increasingly few. She knew that her mother loved her dearly, and she also understood that she had probably given her mother reason enough to worry about her, although through no fault of her own. Nonetheless, she could not quite suppress her slight resentment at having gradually become almost a prisoner in that tall, grand house of theirs.

The last few years had been hard on fourteen year old Anna. Her problems (as those around her would refer to them, although she did not consider them to be any such thing) had started to generate attention about four years earlier, and from that time onwards her life had changed irrevocably for the worse. Anna now understood that there were things about her which were different from other people, but that did not mean she had problems, and as far as she was concerned the only problems lay entirely with those who thought otherwise. However, since these differences had started to become known she had suffered mockery and jibes from other children, whilst the levels of attention and protection from her mother and the housekeeping staff had become increasingly suffocating as her freedoms were removed one by one. She had not chosen to be different, and nor could she do anything about apparently being so. None of what was happening had seemed remotely fair or deserved, but that was life, she had supposed.

As Anna sat motionless with her chin resting on her folded arms, her thoughts lost outside beyond the window, there came a knock on the door. Startled, she quickly span round to her table where she was supposed to be doing the studies set by her mother and said "Yes, come in." For the most part Anna could live with her own company, which was just as well, but being prevented from leaving the house for long periods and constantly yearning for the world outside had made her happy for any interruption, any possibility of new excitement that a knock on the door might bring.

The door opened slowly and a tall, gangly girl a few months older than Anna entered. Her name was Lizzy, and she worked in the house as a maid for Anna's mother.

"Anna, I'm not stopping long and you must promise not to tell your mother or any of the staff that I've been here. Do you promise?"

Anna had always liked Lizzy, but she was also well aware that in recent years the feeling had become less and less mutual. She was intrigued to know what had prompted this sudden visit to the far upper reaches of the house. "Yes, I promise," replied Anna.

"I've got a message for you from that friend of yours, Rebecca," she began. Although Lizzy looked as though she had almost needed to force these words out, they were enough to set Anna's heart immediately racing. Lizzy continued, failing to disguise a look of disapproval on her face (probably because she had not really tried to), "You know I don't much care for her. She's free-willed and headstrong, and has far too high an opinion of herself, that one. But she promised she would make it worth my while if I passed on the message, and there are certain things that she is in a position to help me with, so here I am." Her tone and entire demeanour suggested she was already having second thoughts.

"I probably shouldn't be here," she continued, "and I know the mistress will not approve of this message I've to give you, so you'd better not say anything and I'd better be quick." Lizzy quickly peered over her shoulder at the closed door as if expecting Anna's mother to burst in at any moment, even though they both knew she was out in town.

"The message is that Rebecca and the others in your little gang are all meeting down by the canal tomorrow afternoon for the fête. She said they're meeting in the usual place, wherever that is, although I'm sure you know, around two o'clock. They hope you can make it."

Lizzy turned to leave, but then paused. She had delivered her message, but after a brief internal struggle, she couldn't resist adding some of her own thoughts and she turned back.

"I really don't understand why you and they are such good friends. I mean, you're supposed to be a young lady, although heaven only knows what you ever did to deserve such a position, especially with your... condition. And those friends of yours, well they're rough, they're wild, and they don't work hard to try and earn a respectable living like the rest of us. Someone in your position ain't supposed to lark about with the likes of them, I'm sure of it."

Anna waited. She could tell there was more.

"And as for them, I wonder why they would go to such an effort to have a young lady like yourself for company. On the face of it you're all prim and proper and well-presented, not like them at all. But then you've also got your... your problems ain't you?" There it was – Anna had known that was coming. "Well, I simply don't understand what you all see in each other."

This idea about differences between people because of who they were born as had always annoyed and saddened Anna immensely, but she had known Lizzy since they were both young, and she understood something of the complex feelings which lay behind her direct words. Anna was only too aware of the sense of unfairness with which Lizzy had come to view their supposed relative positions in life. And for her part, Anna completely empathised and agreed with that. She had no more idea than Lizzy did about how they had come to be in a world where somehow, some people seemed to attach a different level of value and worth to their position. She did not understand how or why she had been 'born to be a lady' as she was continually told, and through no merit of her own ought to expect nothing but the finest things in life, whilst it was apparently the destiny of other girls her age like Lizzy to be in her service. This state of affairs made no sense to Anna and it seemed plain wrong, especially when as far as she was concerned there was no single respect in which she felt she was better than Lizzy. Anna had never actually felt herself superior on any level, be it looks, disposition, achievements or talent of any kind. Indeed she had probably never considered herself superior to anyone, and certainly not on the grounds of birth.

However, Anna had never been able to explain these feelings adequately to Lizzy, and lately Lizzy seemed to have come to believe that Anna really did feel herself superior. Anna always felt awkward, and feared that raising the subject at all might be to fan the flames, and might result in making the sense of separation all the more real. Anna had always felt that she and Lizzy could be good friends were it not for this artificial 'class' divide. The irony was that because people seemed to assume incorrectly that Anna considered herself superior to them, they in turn became prejudiced against her for that reason. Anna hated all this, but she had never yet been able to find a way to make things right. However, she decided to try again.

"Oh Lizzy, why does my friendship with Rebecca and the others have to be so hard to understand? Why do we build walls to stop people from enjoying the company of whomever they choose? Becca, the others and I are friends because we like each other. And we base whether or not we like people on how they are, not who they are. We don't see ourselves as different in the slightest." She paused for a moment before continuing, "Lizzy, I know what a good person you are, and I wish we could be friends too."

"Don't be silly mistress Anna, we can't be friends. I didn't choose my station in life, it chose me, and I work hard to make the best of it. You don't appreciate what a lucky and privileged position you're in. You ought to make the most of it, I'm sure I would if I were you. You should live up to your position, and behave in the way expected of a young lady of your background and standing.

"And what's more," Lizzy continued, "I'm not sure I should want to be friends with someone who has your problems. I'm all for charity and for helping the sick and needy, but your problems are different. I know we're not supposed to speak about those things that people say you can see, but if they're true, then it ain't natural. It ain't natural, and it ain't right."

Lizzy looked as though she knew she should probably not say any more, or even have said as much as she already had, but the thoughts she was now sharing had clearly been bursting to express themselves for quite some time now and she could no longer hold them back. "If what you've claimed to be able to see is true, and one thing I'll say for you Anna is that I don't think you're a liar, then I reckon that either you're mad as they say, or else that what you can see is something unholy. Me and some of the others, we don't reckon that you're crazy like most people do, you seem too normal and down to earth for that. But if you have some kind of power for seeing things, we don't reckon that those powers were created by any forces of good in this world, and so they must have come from somewhere else. And you know what we mean by that, don't you?'

Yes, Anna did understand exactly what that was intended

to mean, although she was less sure who these other people were who apparently shared Lizzy's opinion.

"Don't misunderstand me Anna," Lizzy continued, ('a little too late, but never mind!' thought Anna to herself,) "I don't mean to say that you're an evil person, exactly. But I fear that the forces of evil have given you powers, and that evil shows itself to you, makes itself known to you and makes you see things, and that can't be good. Evil knows you, and you know evil. These times are troubled enough, what with all this talk of a beast from hell stalking Highgate and I don't know what else…"

"What? What do you mean, a beast from hell -"

"I'm a good, honest person Miss Anna," Lizzy interrupted Anna before she could finish, "and I don't want no dealings with no workings of evil, direct or otherwise, simple as that. That's another reason I don't think you and me can be friends."

"But Lizzy, please believe me," Anna pleaded desperately, although without any great sense of hope now. "I'm not evil, I'm not a bad person, and what I see isn't born out of evil either. What I can see is just the nature of people, and that nature can be good as well as bad. Indeed, there is far more good than bad in what I see, and I long to see the good in everyone." She dared not go into any more detail than that, harsh experience having taught her that to do so usually resulted in tears, and usually her own.

From a very early age, Anna had been able to see things in other people that others apparently could not. The word that she had found to describe what she could see was their 'aura'. If she chose to focus her sight, her mind and her attention in a certain way, Anna was able to see people's auras and she had come to understand that what she was seeing was some kind of manifestation of their nature, indicating something of their character and personality. The visual appearance of the aura varied from person to person, but it was generally a roughly spherical shape, translucent, and usually some variation of light blue in colour. A person's aura was always located roughly in the area between the top of their head and their chest, but it did not entirely obscure Anna's view of the person's physical form, and in an instant she could choose to refocus entirely on the physical world again. The size, surface texture and purity of the aura's colour were different for each person, and in the years since she had started to harness this ability, Anna had become able to read much about what a person was like by looking at these characteristics. The aura that she had never been able to see was her own.

For a long time Anna had not thought too much about this ability. It had seemed natural to her and no more unusual than being able to see physical objects, hear sounds or smell fragrances. She could not remember a time when she was not aware of people's auras. The development of her ability to see them in more detail had been such a gradual process that she had never been surprised by it, and for a long time she had had no idea that other people could not see what she could. As a young child, the only person she had mentioned auras to was her mother, who had told her that it was not something to be spoken about. Had she reflected on it, it might have struck her as strange that auras were never discussed, but as they were not, Anna had assumed that it was just another of those things which people did not talk about openly. It was not until that fateful Christmas four years ago when she was ten years old that she was to learn, and very abruptly, that others actually did not see these things that she could, and that they were scared by it.

Anna took a moment to refocus her attention onto Lizzy's aura, and she could see the roughly spherical shape which appeared to be floating in the air in front her. In her experience, a pure sky blue aura tended to indicate a good person and a pure heart, whereas the appearance of other colours tended to suggest what might be called flaws in that person's character. It was generally the case that the darker the colour of the essence the less pure that person was, and any presence of any red in the aura in particular usually spelt danger and trouble. Her experience had taught her that auras containing red belonged to people who often caused some kind of harm to others. The size of the sphere also varied considerably from person to person, and although Anna understood less about what this meant, it appeared to correlate somehow with the strength of that person's will and character, and their ability to exert influence on events and the world around them, whether that be for good or ill. In Lizzy's case, her aura remained the same light blue it had always been, indicating a fundamentally good person, albeit with some flaws on the surface which seemed if anything to have grown more pronounced in recent times. These appeared to Anna as areas of undulation and roughness which meant it was no longer a smooth sphere, and slight discolouration on its surface. Anna could not tell what this subtle change represented, but it had coincided with a deterioration in Lizzy's attitude towards her. She wondered what it might all mean.

"In your case Lizzy," Anna continued, "I can see a great deal of good, and I don't think there's anything wrong in my being able to see that. I try to be a good person Lizzy, and I only want good things for everyone." That was almost true anyway, even if there were one or two members of the Marylebone Street Gang who might have tested that principle to its limits. "All I want is for the world to be freed from all the unnecessary misery and complications that we create, and the evil we allow to exist, which ruins so many people's happiness. I swear to you, I mean no harm to anyone and I don't believe the things I can see are a way for evil to speak to me, or to use me. I have only good intentions, I promise."

"I don't know what intentions you may or may not have, I'm sure I don't. What I do know is that you have something about you that ain't natural, and it ain't born out of any good.

When you look at me like you did just then, it's like you're looking inside of me, and it's unnerving. It's... unholy..." Lizzy's voice tailed off, as though she had now begun deeply to regret having started this conversation.

"I knew I should never have come up here. This was a mistake. Mistress Anna, don't you tell a soul I was up here today, not a soul, or anything about our conversation. You promised, and I hope you'll see fit to keep to that promise. And Rebecca had better come good 'n all, asking me to come up here against my better judgement..."

With that, Lizzy backed out of the room, closed the door behind her and scuttled back down the stairs. As Anna turned back towards the window to reflect on another frustrating encounter, her spirits were buoyed by the idea that tomorrow might bring new adventure with her friends. Little did she know, as she laid her chin on her folded arms to gaze back out into the greyness, the true magnitude of the adventure upon which she was about to embark.

Awakening

The following day, London had once again outdone itself in the utter greyness of its sky. However, on this day the sky could have been clear blue, sunset orange or for that matter the most shocking of pinks and Anna would not have cared in the least. For after being confined in her house under watchful eyes for longer than she cared to remember, Anna had managed to slip out of the house unseen. She had had a close call when Maggie the house cook had almost spotted her, but she had managed to avoid capture. She loved Maggie dearly, but even Maggie would not have taken kindly to her leaving the house on her own and would surely have raised the alarm.

Anna hurried down the long, straight, majestic North London street that she knew so well, passing one by one the enormous, imposing houses which lined it on both sides, doing her utmost to be as unremarkable and inconspicuous as possible. Fortunately this was something at which she had become well-practiced. The experience of being different from other people and of constantly being referred to as strange had increasingly made her want to go unnoticed through the world, and through her life. However, today she had an additional reason: to avoid being caught.

Anna's mother had always been overly protective even before the so-called problems came to light. Anna was sure that this was partly due to her father having died when she was young. She understood that she had met him when she was very small before he had died in an accident, but she had no memory of him. Anna was sure that this great loss had made her mother even more worried for the health of her only child than a normal mother would have been. Then, when the 'problems' revealed themselves, things got much worse and her freedom to leave the house had been all but removed. The trigger had been that fateful Christmas, when Anna found herself, albeit briefly and for entirely unjust reasons, locked up in an asylum.

That winter her mother had come down with a serious illness and a very high fever. Anna had been terrified that she might actually lose her mother and she had made, with the benefit of hindsight, the grave error of telling Doctor Evin (or 'Doctor Evil' as Anna would always refer to him from that moment on) that she could see her mother's aura fading, and that she feared her mother was going to die. She had not spoken of auras to anyone since the time her mother had told her not to, but this was important and she had feared that if the doctor did not act quickly it could be too late. However, the doctor had started to ask questions about what she meant, and before long he was spending more time and effort interrogating Anna than attending to her mother. Her mother for her part was ranting deliriously, uttering things about Anna, demons and evil powers, and for reasons that had never been sufficiently explained to Anna, Evin had decided that she was somehow to blame for her mother's condition, and that she was a danger to those around her. He further accused her of having evil visions and ultimately of being insane, and worse still, possessed! It had made no sense to Anna then and it never would, but without her mother's protection, and with her uncle, who she knew would have put a stop to Evin's actions immediately, being overseas there was no one else able or willing to argue against the doctor's orders that Anna be carted off to the lunatic asylum.

And what a dreadful and truly shocking place that was. It was a place and an experience that Anna would never forget until the day she died. The things she saw there shocked her profoundly, and would trouble her waking hours as well as her dreams for many years. It was only when her mother had recovered sufficiently from her illness over a week later that she was able to take control, fight the authorities and use the influence of her own considerable contacts to get Anna freed, but by the time Anna returned home, she had been in that ghastly place for almost three weeks. There had been absolutely nothing wrong with her, but had she been there much longer she felt sure there soon would have been. Had her mother not recovered and had she not been so well connected in society, in all likelihood Anna would never have been freed from that place. It was this thought above all others that most disturbed Anna about the whole episode.

In the meantime, word had got out, not only amongst the household but seemingly to everyone she knew and beyond, that she had been institutionalised. No matter that it was under false pretences, and that Dr Evin was held to account for his rash actions and suspended from practising for six months (a punishment considered scandalously light by Anna, her mother and her uncle when he came to learn what had happened). For those who would not take the time to ascertain the details, which meant just about everyone, there was 'no smoke without fire' and she was now and forever more to be branded a lunatic, whilst the kindest amongst them would simply refer to her problems. Broadly two factions existed: those people who merely considered her to be mad, and those, including Lizzy, who feared that something darker was at play, and that Anna was either evil and in league with the devil, or else that she was being used by him as some kind of vehicle for his evil purposes.

This episode had very quickly taught her that she must avoid the topic of auras wherever possible, such was the reaction that it caused. Soon after returning home Anna did discuss it once more with her mother, but her mother told her that this was something never to be spoken of again unless she gave her permission to do so. To make a bad situation worse, these events turned her already overprotective mother into something more akin to a jailer. Undoubtedly the shock of almost having her daughter taken away from her permanently had had a severe effect on Anna's mother, and Anna did understand that her mother's intentions were good, even though she resented her mother's constraints and occasionally found it necessary to deceive her as a result. From the moment that Dr Evin had determined that Anna should be detained 'for her own good and for that of everyone else', Anna's life had to a large degree become a misery.

There were no longer any reasonable excuses that Anna could use to get out of the house, and so on the occasions that she did leave unattended, it could only be done by slipping out and back again unnoticed. In reality, this was made slightly easier because when her mother was not giving her lessons, Anna was often left to her own devices in her attic room. As long as she was in the house, it was assumed that she was fine. Anna had now successfully achieved the first step of that day's deception, and it was imperative that she avoided drawing attention to herself if she was to maintain it.

Fortunately for this mission, being unremarkable was something that she flattered herself to think she was very good at. She could find nothing in her appearance that she believed anyone would find noteworthy, or certainly in any way attractive. Her hair was brown but lacked any richness of colour, her eyes were neither bright blue nor shiny brown but a muddy colour in her opinion, and her face seemed to her out of proportion when she examined it in the mirror, as did her general shape and size. Plain at best, and unattractive at most honest were the only conclusions she could ever reach regarding the girl who looked back at her from the mirror. Indeed, she worried that the biggest threat to her going unnoticed that day might be that her sheer plainness caught someone's eye and stuck in their mind!

Nonchalant and unhurried on the outside, her mind raced ahead of her towards her destination. The canal was not far away now, but it was not yet in sight. Doubts started to creep into Anna's nervous excitement like unwanted clouds encroaching on a long-awaited summer sky. Was there really a fête happening along the canal today? Would her friends really be there? And would Rebecca's younger brother Timmy be there? She allowed herself this thought only briefly before banishing it again from her mind, but it was still enough to make her blush slightly at the momentary honesty of her own feelings. She did very much hope he would be there.

Anna cast all other doubts aside and began to focus solely on her objective once more. Then, just as she reached the next crossroads, she was knocked clean over by a young man running down the narrow adjoining road.

"I'm m-most terribly sorry!" he stammered as he tried to help her to her feet. "I do hope y-you're not hurt?" Despite his thoughtful words, he was already peering all around him with wide eyes. Anna realised that he could not have been more than a couple of years older than her. What struck her most, however, was the look that she saw in those wide eyes: it was a look of absolute terror.

"Yes, please don't worry, I'm fine," replied Anna, who was fine, and was also very keen to avoid a spectacle of any kind at that moment. "What about you, I do hope you're not hurt?"

"Y-yes, I'm fine too, but I must be going. I'm very sorry, I do hope I didn't harm you," responded the boy who was already starting to run again, continuing to look wild-eyed behind and all around him and then muttering, "Oh Lord, I think he's coming!"

Anna couldn't remember when she had last seen someone so frightened ('frightened out of his wits', she thought to herself), and indeed it could only have been in that asylum that she had seen anyone wearing such an expression of bewildered fear. As was her habit she instinctively shifted her focus to glance at the aura of the retreating figure. It was essentially blue in colour, that of a good person, although it also contained an unmistakable tinge of yellow all around its surface. Over the years Anna had come to know this as an indication of a state of longstanding, almost permanent fear.

Momentarily forgetting her own caution, Anna called out behind the retreating youth. "Whatever you're running from, I wish you luck," and she meant it. The boy was clearly running from someone who held the most enormous fear for him, and Anna wondered what could have provoked such a state and wished she could have helped him. However there was nothing she could do, and besides she had her own mission to worry about. Dusting herself down whilst peering up and down the street along which the young man was already vanishing into the distance at great speed, Anna was pleased to see no one else in sight.

She crossed the road safely and resumed her journey – there was only one more major obstacle to cross now between her and the canal. This was a major thoroughfare, busy at this time of day with carriages and the bustle of city life, and the place where she was most likely to be spotted, either by one of the senior household staff or else by one of the enemy, the Fletchers and their Marylebone Street Gang. Either of these outcomes would mean trouble. If it were the former, her mother would surely find out that she had left the house without permission, and that would likely guarantee her being locked up, probably for the rest of her life if not longer. The Marylebone Street Gang, in contrast, would be only too pleased to see her, for the opportunity to attack, chase or humiliate her and cause her whatever other kind of misery they could. For as far as she could tell, that seemed to be the entire purpose of their existence. If they saw her, she knew she would be in real trouble until she managed to reach her friends. She slowed down as she approached the corner, and then nearly jumped out of her skin when she heard her name called out.

"Good afternoon young Anna, how are you? I haven't seen you in a while. Is life treating you well?"

Anna looked around desperately, and saw a slightly rotund old man with lively eyes, ruddy plump cheeks framed by bushy white sideburns, and a broad beaming smile. His clothes, from his top hat, long black coat, silver-grey waistcoat and green cravat, to his dark grey trousers and black shoes, had all once no doubt been very fine but all now had considerable signs of age upon them. The overall impression was one of a man who had known the finer things in life, but for whom such things were now largely of the past. However Anna breathed a sigh of relief. It was only the kindly old Mr. Warwick, a long-standing family friend who ran the old bookshop on the corner. He had always been very kind to Anna, always showing a special interest in her and taking the trouble to find out how she was. He had sometimes let her play in his shop when she was younger, in the days when she had been allowed such freedoms, and the extremely pure blue appearance of his aura had always told her he was someone she could trust.

"Oh, hello there, Mr. Warwick," she responded. "Yes I'm fine thank you. Been cooped up in the house for too long. I'm sorry to rush off, but I'm late for meeting up with my friends. Mr. Warwick, I know I can trust you. If you see anyone from the house, please, please don't tell them you saw me!"

"Ah-ha, I see. Well I do understand that a young person needs to get out and about sometimes, but Anna you must be careful. The streets can be a dangerous place you know. Still, I expect you know all about that. Very well, I won't breathe a word, just as long as you promise me you will take great care and not get into any trouble. Enjoy your afternoon."

"Thank you very much Mr Warwick, I will."

Anna waited for a gap in the carriages to dart across to the other side of the road as fast as she could, anxious to remain unseen by anyone she wished to avoid. Once there, it was a quick right then left, and she was on the narrow path sloping steeply downwards, parallel to the canal towpath. There were a number of working barges on the water with faded paintwork, dirty from past loads that they had already carried and now laden again with new cargo, puffing smoke up into the air as they moved slowly along the waterway. In addition there was one particularly colourful barge moored to the canal side, painted in yellow with green around the windows and the top of the deck, and with the name 'Canal Queen' written in bright red letters on the bow. Anna wondered if the Rileys were home, a family who lived on the boat whom she had got to know quite well during extensive time spent by the canal in her younger years. However on this particular occasion she had no time to stop and look. She was sure to catch up with them later, but now she was heading for the bridge and nothing could distract her.

At last, she approached the darker stretch of path which lay in the shadow of the road bridge that crossed the canal. At first she could not make anyone out, and with a sinking feeling in her stomach the doubts started to drift across her mind again. Was she too late, or indeed had she been misled about there even being a fête?

Then a voice called out, "There you are! We thought you'd never come. Thought you'd been inside so long you'd lost the use of your legs!" Then, as her eyes grew accustomed to the gloom she could see them, sitting on the raised ridge under the bridge, and on quick inspection she could see that they were all there.

Rebecca Thompson was the leader of the gang, being two years older than Anna and at least several months older than the others. The daughter of the laundry manageress, she was a pretty girl with shiny, dark hair and attractive brown eyes. There were a further three girls in the group. Tessa and Tilly were the youngest and were identical twins, so similar that it took Anna a while to be able to differentiate between them, and Alice was fair-haired with the brightest of blue eyes. Like Rebecca, Anna also considered Alice far prettier than herself, and as was the case with Rebecca, Alice too always seemed to be popular with all the boys.

Then there were the five boys of the gang. Johnny Adams, always the most impetuous of the group, was the son of an ironmonger and a year older than Anna. He had curly brown hair and brown eyes, and was the most athletic of the friends. Then there was Edward, whose mother worked as a maid in one of the posh hotels in town, and who was about half a year older than Anna. He was blond with blue eyes, and quite a bit taller than Anna. Next to him sat Alice's brother Robert, a few months younger than Anna, who had light brown hair and eyes and was rather attractive, or so Anna thought.

Charlie Morgan, the over-sized baker's son, slightly older than Anna with mousy-coloured hair and blue-grey eyes sat next to Robert. As she had arrived, Anna had noticed that both Robert and Charlie looked at her in a way that, if she had not already known a lot better, she might have mistaken for attraction. However she knew full well that such a thing could not be possible where she was concerned, and she was just grateful that they had seemed pleased to see her. It was the final member of the group though, Rebecca's shy-looking younger brother Timmy sat at the end, who Anna had been secretly seeking out since she arrived.

As greetings were exchanged, Anna's glance met Timmy's, but only for the briefest moment before they both looked immediately away again in determinedly different directions, neither of them focusing in the slightest on whatever it was that their eyes met next. However momentary the glance may have been though, it was long enough to send Anna's heart almost crashing through her ribcage. The look was also long enough for Rebecca to notice it. She grinned at Anna, but she said nothing.

Although Timmy always had a bashful expression, and his long, floppy, sandy-coloured fringe made it difficult for his blue eyes either to see or to be seen properly, and despite his clothes being ill-fitting and not in the best of repair, Anna was reminded again just how handsome he was – well, to her anyway. Many were the times when Anna, alone in her room, had wished desperately that she had been born pretty.

She would happily have traded all the other supposed benefits of the life into which she had been born, to have instead the sort of looks which might have made her as attractive to Timmy as he was to her. As it was, she had no confidence in her appearance (or rather, she had absolute confidence in its lack of attractiveness), and she could never convince herself that anyone would be able to see past her plain exterior to discover that she was really a good person inside, someone they could perhaps one day even fall in love with. But this had never quite stopped her dreaming where Timmy was concerned.

This group always spent time together whenever they were not expected to be at school or work and did not have errands to run for their parents. Although Anna's background was entirely different to the rest on the surface, she had been part of this group from an early age. It had been Anna's eldest cousin on her mother's side, Richard, who had first got to know the older members of the group when he used to spend time down by the canal, and it was he who had first introduced Anna to them. Richard and his family had moved to Bath some years ago and only visited London occasionally now (much to Rebecca's eternal disappointment as Anna hadn't failed to notice), but Anna had remained close friends with them all. That Anna came from a well-to-do family never seemed to make any difference to them, probably because it made no difference whatever to her. Unlike Lizzy they seemed to understand that, and like Anna none of them made judgements on the basis of a person's background or appearance; all that mattered was that they were good people and good company. Although she was able to meet up less frequently than the others, especially recently, whenever she did join them it was like she had never been away and she would slip seamlessly back into their banter and pranks in an instant. It was when she had the chance to run free in the streets of London with this group of friends that she was at her happiest. It was really only then that she felt alive.

"You've been away long enough ain't you? I thought maybe you were dead. Thought they might have got tired of keeping you prisoner and decided to get rid of you all together!" joked Rebecca. "Mother been locking you up again has she?"

"She certainly has, and it's sending me insane. I managed to slip out today, but if I get caught then your guess could still turn out to be right!"

"I think you should come and stay with us for a while," said Rebecca. "I know there's folk there who'd be more than happy to welcome you." At that point she flicked her eyes very quickly and subtly in the direction of her younger brother and winked, all done so rapidly that no one but Anna noticed. Of course Anna knew exactly what Rebecca was implying, and she spoke quickly to avoid her face turning too red. "Oh Becca, I wish I could, honestly I do. I can't tell you how good it would be to be free for a while. And your mother's cooking is the best I have ever tasted."

"Well I know she'd love to have you to stay almost as much as we would. Chances of you being released aren't promising though I suppose. At least in Newgate Prison you can go free when you've done your time. I don't reckon they're going to let you out until someone carts you off for their wife – and then your next life sentence will begin! I just couldn't live locked up like you are. For all your finery and comfortable house, I don't think I'd swap places with you for the world."

"I would though, in an instant!" said Anna, and they both laughed as Rebecca put her arm round Anna's shoulder. "I wish someone would explain that to Lizzy though," Anna added quietly, almost to herself.

"Actually I need to speak with you about her, but not now," said Rebecca, then she added in a whisper that only Anna could hear, "maybe that is the answer though. Marriage!" and she shot her brother another rapid glance before bursting into laughter once more.

Anna started to blush again but then joined in with Rebecca's laughter as the group started to move off down the canal side. Everyone now seemed to be talking to her at the same time, updating her on the various events that had happened since they had last met. Although it was almost impossible to hold down a conversation with so many people chipping in and talking at once, she took in their words as though drinking fresh spring water after a lengthy spell in the desert. It was so good to see them all again.

"Have you heard about the Marylebone Street Gang?" asked Charlie, and the mention of that name caught Anna's attention above all the other voices. "We think they're getting into some really dodgy business now. We always knew they were wrong-uns, but now it looks like they're getting involved with some real criminals." This now had Anna's full attention. She and her companions had had many a scrape, indeed fights, with this gang, always instigated by the Maryleboners. Anna had long had a healthy dislike for them, but even though they were rough and liked a bit of trouble, she had never before actually thought of them as criminals.

"Yes," joined in Rebecca, the rest of the group now quieter and focused on this conversation. "We've seen them running errands for some right dubious types, including some that I happen to know have spent time inside. They seem to be carrying packages for them. We already knew that some of the gang's older brothers were going bad, but they seem to be deeper into it themselves now too, meeting with some proper rough characters. There's definitely something going on for sure, something illegal I'll wager, and the Maryleboners seem to be getting themselves right into it."

"We don't know what it is yet, but we mean to find out!" joined in Johnny, and the rest of the group murmured their agreement. Anna's mind began to race as she wondered what kind of business their nemeses were getting involved with.

Then the momentary mood of seriousness was broken, as Tilly cried out "Looks as though the fête's going to start soon. Look, the Rileys' boat has moved off."

Anna looked over her shoulder and saw the brightly coloured barge moving away from its moorings. It would be a short journey down the water to where the canal widened out and other barges were gathering for the fête, which was going to take place by the canal side. Quite often the barge owners who lived or worked around this area of London, and any others who were there to carry cargo to and from the capital, would gather in this wider stretch of water and share food, drink, stories and music late into the night, and especially when a fête was happening. Although neither Anna nor any of her companions were from barge families, nor indeed had any direct connection with waterway life, they had played alongside this particular stretch of canal for so long that they had got to know a fair number of the barge owners, and were always made to feel welcome by them.

"Hello there folks," came the booming voice of the portly Mr. Riley, his words thick with his broad West Country accent. He was beaming at the helm of the Canal Queen. "Good to see you all out for the gathering. Heavens, even Anna's joined us. This must be a special one!"

"Hello Mr. Riley," replied Anna, "yes, sorry it's been a while. I've been kept indoors but managed to escape today. How are Mrs Riley, Bob and Jilly?"

"They're all just fine, in the best of health thank ye kindly. Gone on an errand to buy some supplies for the evening they have, but they'll be joining us shortly."

"Wonderful, hopefully I'll see you all a little later then," Anna replied as her friends waved Mr. Riley off. How late she could risk staying out was something that she did not want to think about at that moment. She knew it couldn't be too long, but that was a problem which could wait.

The group approached the point where the canal started to

widen and the boats were gathering, and one by one they started to climb the stone steps up to the road, from where they would be able to cross the bridge to the side where most of the barges would be moored further down the canal. Anna was at the back chatting with Alice when she noticed that Timmy had stopped before the steps to tie up his boot laces, although curiously they didn't look to have come loose from what Anna could see. She slowed down and let Alice climb the steps first.

As soon as Alice was out of sight, Timmy peered up through his fringe, rose from his feigned lace tying, and then Anna was able to look him fully in the face for the first time that day. She had been stealing the occasional heart-stopping glance at him whenever one had been there for the stealing, but now that she was able to look at him properly she got that familiar feeling in the pit of her stomach, but this time so strongly that she thought she might actually be sick. Though if anything, Timmy looked even more nervous than she felt, and for the first time she dared to hope that he might actually be feeling something similar.

Knowing he had only a moment before they would be missed by the others, Timmy reached inside his ragged old coat, and to Anna's astonishment produced a small bunch of rather battered flowers. They looked somewhat on the rough side (picked rather than bought, Anna guessed), and they were also considerably flattened from their concealment within Timmy's coat, but none of those details could have mattered less to Anna at that moment. No-one had ever given her flowers before, nor had the idea probably ever crossed anyone's mind for a second, but now of all people it was Timmy, with his fist which clenched the flowers trembling slightly, who was presenting her with them!

The thundering of Anna's heart was setting the rhythm for the somersaults her stomach was now performing. In pathetic shape though the flowers were, to Anna they were the most beautiful thing she had ever seen in the whole of her life. What was more, Timmy's aura was shining brightly, pure sky-blue and as radiant as she had ever seen it. That purity, and the kindness that it conveyed, was one of the qualities which had always made Timmy so attractive to Anna for as long as she had known him.

The ability to make observations about peoples' characters through their auras was something which had begun to make Anna uneasy once she had realised that others could not do the same, but she still understood absolutely how to read them and she was in no doubt about the good things that Timmy's aura was telling her about him. At that moment, she didn't think she had ever seen anything quite so vividly blue, so completely pure and so utterly beautiful. Now this person, this boy who she had secretly dreamed about so many times whilst shut up in her room, was giving her flowers! She took them from him slowly with both hands, and on an impulse that somehow managed to bypass the conscious thoughts which ordinarily would have rendered such an action completely impossible, she leant forward and kissed Timmy on the cheek.

The pair of them then stood for a moment, looking at each other in a state of slightly awkward but ecstatic shock. Timmy took a couple of steps back out of the shade of the bridge and was preparing himself to say something he had clearly planned, when the spell was suddenly broken as quickly as it had been cast.

Without any warning, Timmy was suddenly hit from above by a stream of stinking filth! And not a small amount either; there had been enough to cover his hat and the best part of the right hand side of his coat, as well as his fringe and part of his face. This was followed immediately by howls of laughter from a number of voices. Anna was momentarily stunned, and the thought flashed across her mind that this must somehow be her fault, that Timmy should not have been giving her flowers or that she should not have shown her feelings so openly in the way she had done. She felt sick again, but now in a very different way to moments earlier.

"Hey, lover boy, don't look so good now do you?" sneered one of the voices from above, followed by another even louder bout of laughter and heckles. Looking up to the bridge under which they had been concealed, she could see at least five faces that she knew far better than she would have liked. It was the Marylebone Street Gang. Always out for trouble in general, and especially if that trouble involved Anna and her friends, they were in raptures over this direct hit, made all the more entertaining by the excellence of its timing.

Timmy looked stunned and totally humiliated. Anna looked at his clothes, and the stench that now starting to emanate from him confirmed her worst fears. Timmy had been covered from head to foot in horse manure!

As Timmy was naturally so shy, she knew that it must have taken all of his courage to have made the gesture of the flowers, and of course it had been the first time that anyone had ever done anything like that for her. It had been a genuinely wonderful thing for him to have done, possibly the most special moment in her life thus far, and now to have had it ruined so embarrassingly and in such a public place seemed to her crushingly unfair. Timmy's pure heart simply did not deserve it. In the split seconds that these emotions exploded within her, something inside Anna stirred. Or perhaps more precisely, it had awakened. This injustice was not something that Anna was prepared to accept. A wrong had been done, and she needed to act.

Confrontation

Enraged, Anna turned and dashed up the stone steps. When she reached the road, she could see the Marylebone Street Gang, seven of them in all: Doug and Reggie Fletcher, Bobby Watson, Sally Hicks, Davy Green, Billy Gillespie and Mary Pike. At the same time, Anna's companions were now returning, having been alerted first by the howls of laughter and abuse, then by the sight of their bitter enemies. However the rival gang's attention was focused entirely on Anna. Their howls of laughter had grown louder, and now turned to pure mockery at the sight of this small girl with her very proper dress, perfectly shiny shoes and carefully brushed hair coming towards them, and it was true that she could not have looked more different from them if she had come from another world. However, as she fixed her stare on the main offender, a ragged boy she recognised immediately as Billy Gillespie, who was gleefully holding up the empty bucket which had contained the manure, his expression began to change. While his companions continued to laugh and jeer, Anna noticed, as much as she was able through her rage, a small flicker of surprise, and possibly even fear, cross Gillespie's face. He quickly composed himself however, and his look soon returned to its more characteristic sneer.

"Ooh, look who it is," he jeered, "if it ain't little Miss Prim and Proper. Or should I say little Miss Lunatic? Been let out of the asylum to fight your weakling boyfriend's battles for him have you? You'd better scarper or I'll have you too, you loony!"

Gillespie's companions joined in the jeering, which was fast becoming more aggressive. However that same corner of Anna's mind which was still paying attention to such details, noted that for all Gillespie's threatening words he had not actually taken a step forward or in any way physically threatened her. There was something holding him back.

As Anna drew closer, she began to slow her pace, every

stride becoming more purposeful. It was no longer the messages from her conventional senses that were occupying her mind now, but those from the additional sense which she possessed. She looked upon Gillespie's aura with an absolute, clear focus, and far from a pleasant sight it was. It did not wholly exude evil, but it did appear distinctly tarnished and discoloured, as well as slightly disfigured. Anna had seen worse before in some adults, but it was nonetheless clear that Gillespie's aura had already suffered serious damage and that its owner was travelling down that same slippery path. It was most definitely not the aura of a decent person. Anna fully understood that the state of this aura was a reflection of the person that its owner had become, or at least was in the process of becoming, a person who was well on his way to losing his common decency, and with it any sensitivity and respect he may have had for the feelings of others.

Then a thought struck Anna. Was it possible that it was the very act of her focusing on Gillespie's aura that was somehow restraining him? She had had no idea that such a thing could be possible, but as she neared him the realisation grew. In her heightened sensory state she began to feel as though she was actually reaching out and touching Gillespie's aura. Of course she was not physically touching it – there was nothing physical there to touch – but for the first time in her life she felt as though she was somehow able to reach out and touch it *using her own aura*. It was not something she could see, but she could feel the contact!

As Anna approached, Doug Fletcher, the older of the brothers and leader of the enemy gang shouted to Gillespie. "Come on Billy, she's asking for trouble. Let the loony have it!"

Doug Fletcher's goading seemed to shake Gillespie momentarily back into life and he took a step towards Anna, who by now was nearly upon him. No sooner had he taken one step however than he froze again, and his power seemed to drain visibly from him. In her mind's eye, Anna had locked onto Gillespie's bruised and disfigured aura and had started to push it backwards. She steadily increased the pressure she was applying, whilst gently smoothing the abnormalities and moulding its shape some way back towards the perfect sphere it ought to be. At that moment she knew that Gillespie's aura was at her complete mercy to do with it anything she wished, whether that be to bring peace to it or inflict further harm. Indeed, had she chosen to, Anna felt as though she could easily have destroyed it beyond any chance of recovery, such were the enormous surges of mental power that she was now feeling.

Anna had no time to ponder what was happening or what had happened inside her to make all this possible. All that could wait. Despite the odds against her in this confrontation, she suddenly felt in complete control. She continued to apply pressure to her foe's aura until she had restored it to a shape more closely resembling a sphere. Refocusing her attention onto Gillespie's physical form, she was standing now within touching distance of him. Gillespie stood completely motionless and stared at Anna through unblinking eyes with an expression which looked to her almost like awe. Her focus fully returned to her regular senses, she then became acutely aware of the rest of the gang, who were shouting and screaming for Gillespie to do something. Though she had absolute confidence that Gillespie now posed no threat to her whatsoever, years of bitter experience had taught Anna that it was always best not to reveal to others the ways in which she was different from them, and the powers she possessed that apparently they did not. It would only be moments before the gang realised that Anna had done something very strange to their friend, and done so without even laying a finger on him.

Acting rapidly to conceal her secret, Anna shouted at the top of her voice for all to hear, "Gillespie, that's the last time you humiliate one of my friends, or anyone else, do you understand me? I'm going to teach you a lesson, and you're going to remember it!" With that, Anna launched herself upon him forcefully, but still with careful measure and control. She pushed him back against the low wall of the bridge, grabbed the front of his jacket by the lapel with one hand and his belt with the other, and with all her might she heaved him over the edge and sent him into the canal below! She barely had the strength to perform this feat, and had Gillespie offered any resistance there was no way she could have done it. However he had not resisted.

There was a loud splash followed by coughing and spluttering as Gillespie started to flounder his way back to the side. None of the Marylebone Street Gang were laughing now. They all looked as stunned by what had happened as Timmy had minutes earlier when he had disappeared under his shower of dung.

"You're gonna regret this!" shouted Gillespie's girlfriend, Mary Pike, though even she looked visibly shaken, not only by what had happened but by how easy it had been. Anna took a step towards them, with her own friends now squarely behind her, ready for any conflict that might ensue. Anna looked each of the Maryleboners in the eye, and for a second time she felt her aura starting to move out from her, making peripheral contact with those of each of her opponents. This time she applied a lighter pressure, but it was still sufficient to turn the tide of the encounter.

"Now's not the time," shouted the gang leader, Doug Fletcher, looking slightly disconcerted. "Come on, let's get Billy and get out of here. We'll get her another time and then she'll be sorry!"

The gang turned and hurried to the stone steps to rescue their sopping comrade. "You're gonna get it, you know that. You're gonna pay, and you'll wish you had never been born, you loony," were their parting cries. If only they knew how often she had already made that very same wish herself! However, for the first time in her life she felt as though she might actually be able to handle ruffians like the Marylebone Gang, even if their threat did become more than mere idle words.

Anna's friends instantly surrounded her and the mood changed to one of celebration, congratulations and then questions as to how it had all started. Anna updated her eager companions as briefly as possible, relaying to them the manure attack, but of course mentioning nothing about the flowers that had preceded it.

After the group had chatted excitedly for a while, Anna's thoughts began to move on. During the encounter, a number of things had happened that she would need time and space to think through, but before that she needed to see Timmy again, and she somehow needed to engineer the chance to speak with him alone.

Timmy had not yet rejoined his group of friends or even emerged from the canal side. Anna led the way back down the stone steps and saw Timmy sitting further down the bank, some distance away on the other side of the bridge from where his assailant had fallen in. Still half covered in muck, he looked thoroughly miserable and the stench was by now overpowering. He had managed to clean the worst of the mess from his face and hands, but his clothes, hat and fringe remained generously covered. Seeing how downcast he looked and realising that he had apparently not yet even tried to clean any of his clothes, Anna began to worry about how much this incident might have affected him. However, it also gave her an idea.

As he saw the group coming towards him led by Anna, Timmy smiled briefly before seeming to remember his condition and looking away in embarrassment, as though he did not want to be seen. Noticing this, Anna slowed down a little and allowed Rebecca to overtake her.

"Well you're in a right state ain't you? Lucky you've got Anna here to fight your battles for you, is all I can say," she laughed. "You should've seen her Tim, she was fantastic.

She faced them down and then threw Gillespie straight in the canal! I couldn't believe it, it was brilliant, and you should've seen the rest of them, they couldn't believe their eyes either. Scared them all off she did, before I'd even had a chance to have a go at them myself!"

It was then that Rebecca seemed to notice that Timmy was not sharing her joy or amusement in the story, and it was only then that it seemed to dawn on her how badly his pride must have been hurt by the whole episode. That Anna – a girl after all – had fought and won his battle for him was probably not helping. Clearly now feeling for her younger brother, she sat down next to him as the others looked on, made as though to put her arm around him before thinking better of it in his state, and said in a more gentle tone, "Got you bad didn't they? Nothing you could've done about it though. You couldn't have seen them up there, and you couldn't have stopped them. Right cowardly of them it was, but you've taken it real well, not running away or nothing. Just like a real Thompson."

Timmy's expression was complex, as though he felt partly comforted and grateful to his sister for her sympathetic words, but at the same time embarrassed that there had been a need to say them at all, especially in front of their friends. The mood needed to be broken somehow, and Anna seized the opportunity to devise a plan whereby she and Timmy could be alone for a time.

"Well Timmy," she said, "I hate to say this, but I'm afraid you really smell. We can't have you going about stinking like a heap of manure for the rest of the day. There's only one thing to be done. You need a proper wash, and while the canal may not be the cleanest bath in the world," Anna peered at the dark water below, "it's still an awful lot cleaner than you are. Come on, and no arguments."

Anna took Timmy's hand, concealing the thrill that went through her at its touch, pulled him up and directed him further down the canal side. "Right, on the count of three, into the water. No, there's no use taking your coat off, that's the whole point! Now seeing as it's not fair that you are the only one who has to jump in, and also so that I don't get a reputation for forcing boys into canals as a regular hobby, I'll join you. It's only right since I was as much a target for that muck as you were. No, no arguments!"

The others laughed and cheered them on. Timmy himself looked completely nonplussed, but then even he too offered a slight smile. "One, two – don't back out on me now Timothy Thompson, I don't want to be jumping in there on my own now – one, two... three!"

Gripping Timmy's hand, she jumped into the cold canal, with Timmy by her side. The rush of the cold water was a shock, and at first the pair of them found even breathing difficult as their chest muscles tightened. However, as they reached the surface again and their bodies adapted to the temperature they could hear the jovial sounds of their friends, and when Timmy also began to laugh and to splash water at them, Anna knew the worst was over.

"Come on, I'll race you to the other side, where we can dry off," proposed Anna once Timmy had done his best to rub himself clean in the water. That would hopefully give her the chance she needed to speak with Timmy alone.

"All right," said Timmy, and they both swam the short distance to the other side before clambering out, dripping wet. Anna had spent many previous summers playing in the canal with friends and she was both a quick swimmer and perfectly capable of hauling herself out of the water. However, she decided that it might aid Timmy's recovery process if she ensured he got to the other side first, and then let him be seen to help her. He did so, and she thanked him.

The others started to make for the stone stairs again, presumably intending to head over the bridge and rejoin them on their side of the canal, so Anna did not have long.

"Timmy, there's something I want to say to you about today," she started.

"There's nothing I want to talk about," said Timmy, gloom suddenly descending on him once again. "I simply want to forget this day ever happened."

"Well I don't," replied Anna. "And I never will forget it. Timmy, when you gave me those flowers, well, it was the most wonderful thing anyone has ever done for me. I will never forget it Timmy, never, and I wanted to say thank you."

She paused while Timmy silently watched the reflection of the grey sky dancing on the bobbing water of the canal.

"What happened with the manure… yes I know you don't want to talk about it and we don't have to, but it was nothing more than a horrible prank, and I am sure we'll all look back and laugh about it one day. Especially as we had the victory in the end today, and I say 'we', because we are all together, a team, and any one of us would have done the same for any other. I know you would have stood up for me if it had been the reverse."

"Yes, I would have, you know that," said Timmy looking up at her earnestly.

"Yes I do know that, Timmy, of course I do," continued Anna, her heart starting to leap about like a maniac again as she thought about what she was about to say, and to whom she was about to say it. "But I wanted to say, please don't let that experience, or any experience like it, ever change you. Please promise me that you won't. It would be so easy to feel hatred or to want revenge when someone does you wrong like Gillespie did today. But you've got such a pure heart Timmy, I know you have because I can, well, I can sense it. Don't ask me how. It makes you the most special person I have ever met, and it's the greatest quality anyone could ever have. It's something that I love about you." There, she had said it, forcing that particular word out through a barrier built of fear and embarrassment which had always been completely insurmountable until that very moment. "So please promise me you won't change, that you won't start to do things to hurt other people because someone has hurt you. I'm certain that's one of the roads which eventually turns people from good to bad, and explains much about what's not right in the world. Timmy, you're a special person and a very good one. Please don't lose that, regardless of what anyone ever does."

Anna was sure that their friends would re-emerge at any moment, but for some reason that she could not have fully explained, she needed to hear him say the words.

"Please Timmy, promise me. Promise you will remain the same, pure person you have always been and that you won't change, no matter what."

"All right Anna, well, I'm not too sure what you mean to be real honest with you, but if you mean you want me to promise I ain't going to change who I am, then I can do that. I promise, Anna. I don't think I'm really the changing sort anyway."

"Thank you Timmy," sighed Anna with a depth of relief that even she could not fully understand. "And thank you again for the flowers. I will never forget that."

As a sudden thought crossed Timmy's mind, he patted the front of his coat as if searching for something, then peered over the side of the canal. Without a word, he reached over and fished out a single, very limp, very wet yellow flower.

"You put them down when you ran off after Gillespie, so I picked them up and put them back in my coat. Must've fallen out when we went swimming."

Anna found herself unexpectedly having to force back sudden tears, which she somehow managed to do, as she took the one remaining flower back from Timmy. She concealed it inside her sodden cardigan against her madly dancing heart, and gave Timmy one more hasty kiss on the cheek, seconds before the others appeared.

"You feeling better now, after your little dip?" asked Timmy's sister who came into view first.

"Yes, I am actually. In fact I feel great!" he replied, looking about him and grinning.

"Oh really?" answered Rebecca with evident suspicion. Though she pursued it no further, Anna was sure that Rebecca had flashed her another of those knowing smiles of hers. 'Well, if she did, I'm glad she kept it to herself!' thought Anna as she began to float on pure air.

An Unwelcome Visitor

The group all sat on the canal side as Anna and Timmy waited for their clothes to dry. However, in the absence of any sun this was taking far longer than Anna had expected. After a good thirty minutes had passed and her clothes were still wringing wet, worry began to intrude upon her euphoria. Anna sometimes felt as though anxiety was her natural state, the default condition to which she was always destined to return after any short-lived bout of happiness. However the worry which returned at that moment to overshadow her enjoyment of what had just happened was a very real one. Her clothes were still soaked and it could take hours for them to dry completely, by which time it would be getting late and there would be a real danger of her disappearance being discovered. However if she returned home in wet clothes there would be an equal chance of her being found, out and she would be in twice the trouble. She needed another plan, and she needed one fast.

"I must get dry somehow, and quickly too. Do any of you have any ideas?" she asked the others.

"Anna, why don't you come home with us and get dry there?" replied Rebecca. "It's the least we can offer after how you've stood up for my brother today."

"Yes," agreed Timmy, casting his earlier embarrassment at having been helped by a girl aside almost too enthusiastically to avoid suspicion, Anna worried. "You can come home with us!"

"Becca, Timmy, that's very kind of you, but I wouldn't want you to leave the fête early because of me. Also you do live quite a way away. By the time I get there, get dry and get back again I think it might be too late. Thank you again, but I need to do something more quickly."

It was then that she spotted old Mr. Warwick again in the distance beyond the other side of the canal. He appeared to be heading in the direction of his shop.

"I know, I'll ask Mr. Warwick. He's always been very kind to me and besides he's my only hope. I'll ask him to help me."

With that Anna politely declined all further offers of help, bade a fond farewell to her companions (being very careful not to show any special attention to Timmy in front of the others), and headed back over the canal bridge.

On reaching the other side, Anna called out in the direction of the elderly gentleman. "Mr. Warwick! Mr. Warwick! It's Anna. I'm afraid I've fallen in the canal! I'm going to be in a lot of trouble unless I can get dry and back home very soon. Is there any chance you could help me? I'd be ever so grateful."

"Oh dear Anna, whatever have you been doing?" asked Mr. Warwick, appearing for a moment as though he was going to be stern with her, before he suddenly broke into his customary broad smile again and replied, "Of course, I'll help. Come with me to my shop, and you'll be dry and ready for home before you know it."

Relieved, Anna replied "Oh, thank you Mr. Warwick!" and she followed him in the direction of the bookshop.

They were outside the shop in no time. Above the window a dark green sign with large white letters shadowed with black read 'Barton's Bookshop', and in smaller letters underneath, 'Seller of Rare & International Books'. Anna had no idea who Mr. Barton was; she had only ever known Mr. Warwick to work in the place. In a moment they were in the warm interior of the dusty old shop, and Anna followed Mr. Warwick across the shop floor into one of the back rooms. Anna had never been here before, and she noticed with curiosity that contrary to what she would have expected, this room was in fact much cleaner, tidier and altogether more elegant in appearance than the part of the shop that customers would see. It had well polished, expensive-looking furniture, and was lined from floor to ceiling with books that looked more costly and much better cared for than those that were actually for sale in the front of the shop. There was a highly polished and carpeted wooden staircase in one corner of the room, leading to the first floor which was lost in darkness.

In the middle of the back wall of the room there was a large, roaring open fire, which helped explain the warmth of the shop behind them. Mr. Warwick pulled up a big chair next to the fire and invited Anna to sit on it to warm herself. He briefly disappeared, then re-entered with a towel, a robe and slippers for Anna to change into.

He then left the room once more and knocked before reappearing again with a hot drink, some bread and cheese and a rack on which to dry her clothes, before leaving her to change and get dry. He would be in the shop, and Anna was to come and find him when she was ready. Anna wasted no time in getting out of her damp clothing and wrapping herself in the thick robe which, although too big for her, was beautifully warm, before laying her clothes on the rack in front of the fire. They would undoubtedly smell of smoke she thought, but she had a fire in her own room too, albeit much smaller, and if she asked someone to light it for her when she returned she should be able to explain things that way. It was late summer now and the evenings were getting a little colder, so that shouldn't appear too unusual. The yellow flower that had been concealed in her cardigan was the one thing she held on to throughout, as though if she let it go it might somehow disappear, along with the wondrous events of the day.

Once the clothes were laid out to dry Anna sat down and, gazing into the flames as they danced about the hearth, she began to reflect on the events of the day. Her musings naturally turned first to Timmy and the wonderful developments that had taken place. As she looked at the battered remains of the yellow flower in her hand, she had to pinch herself to believe that it had all really happened. Timmy had given her flowers, she had kissed him on the cheek and she had even used the word 'love' – and above all else, it appeared as though he might just have some of the same feelings for her that she had harboured for him for so long! How could that possibly be? What could he possibly have seen in her to make that happen? She had no idea, but the thought made her stomach resume its somersault routine. If it turned out really to be true, it would be everything she had ever dreamed of.

However, there were other things to think about and to try to understand as well. Reluctantly she dragged her mind away from the subject of Timmy to reflect next on the encounter with Gillespie. Some very interesting things had happened in a very short space of time during that brief confrontation, and Anna had felt things that she had never felt before. There had been no doubt that in the immediate aftermath of the dung dumping, after she had seen Timmy's shocked expression as he disappeared under that stinking mess, she had been as furious as she could ever remember. She could not even remember the initial thoughts which had sent her off in pursuit of their attackers – a sure sign that at that moment her rage had held her fully in its control.

By the time she had mounted the steps and reached the top of the bridge to face her enemies though, her condition had already changed. Anna could remember all her thoughts and emotions from that point onwards in clear and extreme detail. Although obviously still very angry, by the time she faced the Marylebone Street Gang she was in control of her rage, and she was able to channel it. Her anger had taken a clear direction and purpose. Then, as she had advanced towards Gillespie, it had almost ceased to be anger at all, but rather a feeling of purposeful power, a determination to right a clear wrong that had been done. Her thoughts had become very quick and clear, and she had felt powerful and in complete control. That was it, *control* – a feeling that she had really never experienced before. It was as though something had clicked into place, and she had somehow taken a first step towards being the person she was meant to be. She could not explain it any better than that, but it had been a very powerful, liberating feeling.

Then there were other points to consider too, namely the experience of touching, pushing and actually going some small way towards reshaping Gillespie's aura, and then briefly touching the auras of his fellow gang members as well. Though she had been able to see auras for as long as she could remember, until that day she had had no idea that it was actually possible to *touch* them. Although she had not been able to see it, she was in no doubt that it was with her own aura that she was touching them. And the effect that it had had! It had overpowered Gillespie, a boy older and far tougher than her, and had rendered him completely defenceless, completely at her mercy. And not only that, essentially, without even exerting a fraction of the power that she was feeling by then, she had been able to face down the whole gang of them, merely by gently nudging their auras back. It had been unbelievable, and it was something that she could not fully understand. She did not know how she had been able to do it, and neither did she know if she would be able to do it again.

She was at once excited and scared by what she had been able to do, and the uncharacteristic confidence she had felt in that moment. She was struck by the power that these experiences appeared to suggest she might possess. She had long known that a person's aura provided a direct indication of their nature and character, so being seemingly able to manipulate Gillespie's aura, and to some degree re-form it... what did that mean? Was Anna actually able to change the way people were? Could it possibly be that she had an ability to take people who had started to turn bad, and somehow turn them back? Would the small changes to the form of Gillespie's aura that she had caused be permanent, or were they only momentary? And if she was able to change people's nature in some way hopefully for the better, did that mean she also equally had the capability to change them in the opposite direction… in the direction of evil? That idea filled her head with new worries.

Following this train of thought further, the next thing that troubled her was the extent of the damage she might have done to her opponents if she had really let go with the full power she had been feeling at that moment. For she had actually been holding herself back and had only acted with a fraction of the force she had felt within her; she feared for the possible consequences of what might have happened had she got carried away. She was just immensely grateful that her feelings of power had been accompanied by such a sense of complete self-control. She hoped fervently, although without any reason to be certain, that this would always remain the case.

She reflected on how careful she had been not to cause physical hurt to Gillespie when she had engaged with his aura. She had had the foresight and presence of mind to ensure that there were no barges on the canal before pushing him over the edge, and she had been confident that he would come to no physical harm. Most fundamentally, she had understood the importance of not overreacting and doing anything disproportionate back to him, or doing anything that would have hurt his pride further and rendered further damage to his aura as a consequence.

And there was something else that she realised. It had been very important that she had not been venting her own anger and seeking revenge for her own sake, or even worse acting to make herself look good by humiliating someone else, even someone like Gillespie. These were all emotions and motivations that she understood and had experienced herself in the events of her short life. But she had come vaguely to understand that to act in such ways to satisfy those emotions would only serve to multiply the wrongs being done. For her to have done so might have had the unintended effect of turning her into a person no better than the one who had done the original wrong, and this would probably be reflected in damage to the state of her own aura, just as she had seen happen to those of others. Such an awareness of the effect of one person's actions on another was probably unusual in someone so young, but that was the kind of person she was, and the particular circumstances of Anna's life so far had given her plenty of time and very good reason to think about such things!

What was interesting now as she reflected was that these thoughts had come to her very clearly and instantaneously on that bridge. Acting to right a wrong and to make things better for the future? Yes, that might be reasonable, depending on the situation. However revenge for revenge's sake and for the satisfaction that that could bring? No, though that could certainly be temporarily satisfying, it would also be potentially damaging to her own aura, and hence ultimately self-defeating. She felt certain that this was precisely the kind of sequence that would lead a person down the path that Gillespie was clearly now travelling on, as evidenced not only by his actions but by the disfigurement of his aura. It was the same path that had led people to make the world a far worse place for everyone than it needed to be. She was aware that the state of a person's aura could change over time and that often those changes, for the better or worse, were caused by good or bad motivations and deeds in response to the actions of others. It occurred to Anna that remaining in control of her own attitude, motivations and actions in the face of whatever came her way could be immensely important in the future, especially if she were ever again to experience the kind of power that she had felt that afternoon.

Rousing herself from her reverie, Anna remembered the time and the need to get home before her absence was detected. Her clothes had dried well enough and she changed as fast as she could, concealing the flower again carefully inside her cardigan, and went to find Mr. Warwick in the shop.

She found him buried in a particularly large, dusty old book and she let him know that her clothes were now dry and that she would be making her way home. Mr. Warwick seemed deeply absorbed in what he was reading, but finally he looked up at Anna, smiled and told her that she was most welcome as she thanked him for the umpteenth time. Just as she was about to turn and leave however, Mr. Warwick's kindly gaze moved from Anna's face, over her shoulder to the front of the shop – and suddenly his jovial expression was transformed into one of alarm! Anna span round to see what it was that could have caused such a change, and through the shop window she saw the tall figure of a man wearing a black top hat and a long black cloak and carrying a silver-tipped cane, alighting from a carriage which had come to a halt on the other side of the street.

The sight of the tall figure brought an instant and complete change in the old man's demeanour, and moving far more quickly than Anna had ever seen him or even thought him capable of, Mr. Warwick swept Anna up in his arm and whispered urgently, "Quickly, you must hide, you can't let him see you. In here, and not a sound. Not a sound, promise me!"

Before Anna could promise anything at all however, quick as a flash the old man opened a concealed door that had looked just like part of the bookcase until that moment, and he half encouraged, half gently shoved Anna through it into a very small, hidden room on the other side.

"I'm sorry about this Anna, but it is absolutely essential that this customer does not see you. I will explain all in due course, but for now you must trust me. There could be enormous danger. Whatever you do, do not make a sound. Not a sound!"

Anna had no opportunity to tell Mr. Warwick that she did surely trust him and that she would be silent though, because Mr. Warwick had already closed the secret door again with Anna on the other side.

'I really need to get back home soon,' thought Anna to herself, but the sudden change in Mr. Warwick told her that this must be something serious, and that she clearly could not go anywhere for now. She wondered what Mr. Warwick had meant by 'enormous danger', although it was evidently something to do with that man. 'I wonder who he is,' Anna pondered

The room in which Anna found herself was not lit, but neither was it completely dark. Light was filtering in from the narrow cracks around the door through which she had just come, and moving very quietly forward until her eye was right up against one of them, Anna could see a portion of the shop beyond. Someone had just entered – presumably the man who had alighted from the carriage – and Mr. Warwick was now addressing him. Anna noticed that he seemed back to his affable old self again, moving slowly and deliberately. Anna thought she could sense just the slightest apprehension in his voice, but there were no other traces of the suddenly more dynamic and excitable Mr. Warwick she had seen but seconds earlier.

"Ah, Mr. Faulkner, how very good to see you again. Welcome, welcome!" he was saying

"Enough of your pleasantries, old man. You know why I'm here so get to the point. Do you have it?"

The other man stepped into Anna's line of vision for the first time, and turned slightly towards her as he was, she now saw more clearly the same man who had been outside in the street. He was very tall, probably roughly in his late thirties although Anna always found these things hard to judge, and had dark, slicked-back hair, visible now that he had removed his hat. His face was adorned with a thin black moustache which curved down around the sides of his mouth. Although her view was restricted, Anna was still able to make out his dark, piercing eyes, almost black in colour, and a stare that seemed to penetrate its target, in this case Mr. Warwick, as though nothing could be hidden under its gaze. Anna supposed he was what would probably be considered handsome by most, but there was a complete absence of any kind of warmth, and in fact there was nothing in his appearance or manner that Anna could find remotely attractive. She could not separate his looks from his cold and threatening air; wariness and fear were the main emotions that this stranger instilled in her.

Mr. Warwick hesitated. It was clear that he felt very uncomfortable under Faulkner's penetrating stare, and his voice became slightly more tremulous.

"Well now Mr. Faulkner, sir. Won't you sit down and share some tea with me before we get on to business?"

"I'm warning you," replied the younger man angrily, "I've exhausted my patience. Do you have the book or not? If you have it, give it to me and I will pay you the sum we agreed, plus a little extra for your trouble. However if you do not have it, even after these weeks of promising me it would be here, then I am going to get very angry. And when I get angry, bad things tend to happen. *Dark* things. Am I making myself clear?"

As the aggressive younger man was speaking, something else came into focus in Anna's mind almost unbidden. She was beginning to make out the stranger's aura, despite her severely restricted view. And what she saw sent a chill of pure fear through her.

That this was not a good man was immediately apparent. Indeed, although she did not yet fully understand everything she could see in a person's aura, she was in no doubt that this was the aura of a man with a greater potential for doing evil than anyone she had ever met in her life. But the aura was also quite radically different from anything in her experience. Firstly it was enormous, significantly larger than any aura she had seen before. In addition, rather than having a relatively smooth spherical surface like most people's, this was a roughly spherical ball of long, sharp, conical shapes, all stemming from a small spherical core. The overall impression was a deadly one, like an enormous, menacing, spiked ball! Its colour was also unlike any she had seen before, and this was something else that shocked her. In stark contrast to the pure sky blue colour of Mr. Warwick's aura, Faulkner's was inky black at its core, merging into dark red at the tips of the spikes. In short, Anna could not have imagined an aura which appeared more sinister, more lethal and frankly more *evil* than this one. She could not imagine what could have happened to this man, or what he himself must have done, to create such a monstrous aura, and she shuddered as she imagined what this might mean about this person's nature now.

"I'm afraid I don't have it yet, Mr. Faulkner sir," answered Mr. Warwick hesitantly. "I'm still going to require some more time. But my contacts assure me that we will acquire it, and needless to say -"

Mr. Warwick was cut off in mid-sentence by a sudden blow to the side of his head from the silver-tipped walking cane wielded by Faulkner. He had moved so fast that neither Anna nor apparently even the old man had seen it coming. Despite her instinctive fear of this tall, dark stranger, Anna felt that same sense of outrage building up inside her that she had felt earlier that afternoon. Mr. Warwick was one of the kindest people Anna had ever met, and whatever this book was that was the cause of their disagreement and whatever might have been promised previously, the young man could have absolutely no justification for this attack

The old man stumbled to one side, recoiling from the blow, and just managed to catch hold of the table to his right in time to prevent himself from falling. Suddenly Faulkner was on him, and he shoved Mr. Warwick hard until his back was against the bookcase on the far side of the shop, sending the table that the old shopkeeper had used to catch his balance crashing over sideways to the floor. Faulkner now had his thick black cane pressed horizontally against Mr.

Warwick's throat, and he was pressing heavily against it, almost choking him.

Anna had to do something. She had a strong sense of the danger that this would involve and that Faulkner would probably be able to swat her away as though she were no more than an irritating insect, or possibly do far worse than that, but she simply could not just stand by and do nothing while he attacked the kind old man in this way. As she was steeling herself to bolt out of her hiding place however, she checked herself as she noticed something. It was very slight and subtle, but something had started to happen to Faulkner's aura.

When he had begun his assault, the appearance of Faulkner's aura had become even more menacing than before – the spikes had become even more pronounced, and their tips had been a brighter red colour, almost scarlet – and he had started to press it against Mr. Warwick's bright blue aura just as he was pressing his cane into Mr. Warwick's throat. However, as Anna was about to make her move, the surface of Mr. Warwick's aura also started to move, almost imperceptibly, in what looked like a very subtle, calming and soothing motion. She wondered what could be causing this and whether Mr. Warwick himself was aware of it. Could it even be, and she caught her breath at the idea, that he was deliberately manipulating his aura in some similar manner to the way she had done on the bridge earlier? But if so, this would mean that there was someone else who understood about auras! Whatever the truth of that though, the effect this subtle movement was having was noticeable. Faulkner's aura had suddenly seemed to lose something of its hardness. It remained spiked, but the tips seemed to have become somehow softer, and its colour too seemed to have dulled. It was as though Mr. Warwick's aura was in fact soothing Faulkner, calming his rage and aggression.

Anna now held herself motionless, gripped by the scene that was unfolding. Although she had been able to see auras for as long as she could remember, she had never seen two coming into contact and interacting in this way before. She reflected again on her own experience with Gillespie, and how she had somehow been able to apply pressure to his aura to the point of rendering him almost powerless, before pushing him in the canal. She felt sure that she had witnessed Mr. Warwick doing something similar, but with a much greater level of skill and finesse, against an infinitely more dangerous adversary. Rage subsiding, she was now utterly intrigued. Could Mr. Warwick also see auras as she could? Did he have powers similar to hers, or indeed far greater? It seemed to her that he must have. And what about this man Faulkner? He had instigated the contact between the two of them, so she wondered if he also shared the ability to 'see'. But if this was so, why had he not seen what Mr. Warwick was doing? However even Anna herself had only just been able to detect the movement when staring directly at it, and such was the subtlety with which Mr Warwick had moved that Faulkner might not have noticed it in his preoccupation with the physical world and with getting what he came for. Suspending all thoughts of intervention now, Anna looked on in fascination to see what would happen next.

Sure enough, Mr. Warwick's subtle influence on Faulkner's aura seemed to have worked. Slowly, Faulkner started to lessen the pressure on the stick held against Mr. Warwick's throat, then finally he allowed him to move. Mr. Warwick immediately collapsed in a chair, rubbing his sore neck and panting hard for breath. Faulkner still loomed large over him, without any air of regret whatsoever but with his rage now somewhat contained.

"Old man, understand me – this is your last chance. You get me that book as you promised, or things will go very badly for you. I don't want to hear any more protests or excuses, I just want the book. I will return soon, and you had better have it!"

With that Faulkner snatched up his hat, and with a sweep

of his cloak he left the shop as suddenly as he had entered it.

Mr. Warwick said nothing more, but he watched the younger man's every movement until Faulkner's carriage had drawn away, out of sight. When enough time had passed to be confident that Faulkner would not return, Mr. Warwick rose slowly to his feet. Holding the side of his head where he had been so forcefully struck moments earlier, he moved over towards the window to make sure his assailant was not coming back, then made his way to Anna's hiding place.

Opening the door to let her out, he said "I suppose you saw what happened Anna? You mustn't worry, I would have expected you to be watchful of everything, though I thank you for remaining concealed."

"Yes, I saw it. Are you hurt Mr. Warwick? Would you like me to fetch some help?"

"No Anna, please don't do that, that will not be necessary. I am quite a bit tougher than I may appear, and aside from a headache which will soon pass, I am fine."

"Who was that Mr. Warwick, and why was he so angry over a book?" Anna wanted to know, her sense of outrage returning as she reflected on what had happened.

"Actually it is not just any book. Far from it in fact, the book that he seeks was once considered to be of the greatest importance." Mr. Warwick paused thoughtfully for a moment before continuing. "His name is Faulkner, and he is not a good man, though I am sure you are already aware of that." Mr. Warwick had now turned to look Anna directly in the eye. "Did you see his *essence*?"

Anna hesitated for a moment, trying to assess whether or not Mr. Warwick was asking her what she thought he was. "Do you mean his aura, Mr. Warwick?" she asked hesitantly in a quiet voice, guessing that this must be what he meant given what she had seen, although she had never heard the term 'essence' before. But yes, that was a perfect word for it. The aura represented everything a person was – their very essence in fact.

"Aura?" replied Mr. Warwick. "Ah yes, very interesting. I can quite see why you would call it that. And yes, that is what I mean. Did you see it?"

Anna paused again, her heart now pounding so hard that she could hear it in her ears. She was about to talk of that subject which had caused her so much trouble in the past, and which she had vowed through bitter experience never to discuss with others again. But now, for the first time she believed that the person she was talking to might not think she was mad, and that he might actually understand what it was that she was able to see. Indeed, might he even be able to explain things to her?

With a great deal of effort she finally replied, "Yes, I saw it. And it looked like the most evil thing I have ever seen."

"Anna, that is because it was. It was almost certainly the most evil thing you have ever seen." Then it was Mr. Warwick's turn to pause for a moment, which felt to Anna like an eternity, before continuing. His kindly old face, lined by time and experience which lent him more gravitas than Anna had previously noticed, wore the expression of someone considering his final options before embarking on a course of action from which, once started, there would be no turning back.

"Anna, the time has come to share some things with you. There are some things that you now need to learn, things about the true nature of the world, things that none but a select few have known of throughout the ages, but which I believe have always been your destiny to understand."

"Your mother, your uncle and I have tried to protect you and keep you safe for as long as we could, until this moment. However things are now starting to come to a head. Today was very close, much too close in fact, and I sincerely hope that we have not waited too long to begin your instruction, but without question the time is now upon us. I will arrange for us to meet again in the coming days, and at that time your instruction will begin, provided you agree. It will be led by your uncle and me."

Then Mr. Warwick suddenly looked her directly in the eyes again, and this time with a look so vibrant and piercing that it seemed to her it should belong to a far younger man – a man of enormous power. "Anna, tell me. Is there anything inside you, telling you that you are ready to start this journey?"

The startling turn that the conversation had taken left Anna momentarily silent. She had been taken completely by surprise by some of the things Mr. Warwick had just said. Yet since Mr. Warwick had begun, a feeling had in fact been growing inside her. With a confidence unknown to her before that day but akin to the feeling she had had on the canal bridge, she sensed that everything that had happened in her life – the bad things that had occurred, the things that had marked her out as different from other people, the things that she had thought only she alone understood and all the many things that she had not yet been able to explain – had all been leading towards this moment.

Looking Mr. Warwick straight back in the eye with a more powerful and unwavering look than she would ever have been capable of before that day, she replied simply, "Yes, I am ready."

Lord's

Anna had been surprised at the old man's suggestion that she meet with her Uncle James, of all people, to begin her instruction – whatever that was supposed to be. She had found it difficult to believe that her uncle could have much to do with the kindly Mr. Warwick at all, for the two of them could not have been more different, or have inhabited more different worlds. It was not that she did not like her uncle, for in truth she did very much. He was the one breath of fresh air ever to freshen the oppressive atmosphere of the old house on his occasional visits, in between the events in his life that sounded infinitely more interesting. It was just that he could not have been more different from Mr. Warwick, or indeed from her mother, his sister-in-law, either.

Anna's mother always seemed ill at ease with the world outside, and was always intent on controlling it, or better still blocking it our all together if she could, preferring her own confined but safe version that she had created behind the closed doors of their house. To the contrary, Anna's uncle wholeheartedly embraced the world and all it had to offer, seeming to live every moment of life absolutely to the full. From the various accounts she had heard, he was always attending or participating in one high profile event or another, be it playing or watching sport, attending concerts or the theatre, or socialising at some high society function, usually well into the night. And of course, all that was when he was not adventuring overseas.

Anna very much liked her uncle and always looked forward to his visits, but that was not to say she entirely approved of him. Perhaps it was her mother's influence, but even at her young age she had the impression of what might be considered slight flaws in his character. It could not be denied that he cut a dashing figure whenever he swept into their home, adding colour and a sense of adventure from the great wide world beyond the front door to their small, trivial lives – before usually sweeping out again as suddenly as he had come. That he was supremely confident was also beyond question; confidence sometimes bordering on recklessness. But it was perhaps his supreme confidence that appealed least to Anna, as it sometimes appeared to contain a streak of arrogance with a slight air of superiority, which Anna instinctively reacted against. But he was also more intriguing than that. Somewhere behind all that met the eye there were greater depths, depths which contained contradictions to that confident and sometimes even insensitive outward appearance. She did not know her uncle well enough to understand properly, and besides she was still a little too inexperienced in life to fully comprehend such things, but it seemed to her that behind the outgoing and highly confident exterior there were other, deeper layers to his character, though beyond this observation she could tell no more.

Of all the places that Mr. Warwick could have chosen for her to meet with her uncle, Anna cursed her luck at the one they had selected. The message had come from her reluctant mother that Jim, the junior butler of their household for the last couple of years, was to take Anna to meet with her uncle at Lord's cricket ground. 'Lord's', the name loomed large in her psyche.

Lord's had been a venerable sporting venue of apparently some repute ever since Napoleonic times. It was also the hub of social activity in Anna's neighbourhood which had turned its tranquil environment (or at least, as tranquil as it was possible for London to be) into a writhing mass of unwanted humanity when thousands of people descended on their little world for a match. She could not deny that Lord's must hold some great significance to attract so many people from so many different parts, not only of London but also from lands much more distant. And such a diversity of people too – young and old, the very rich and the seemingly not so rich, the sober and the far less so, and people with accents from all corners of England and from far beyond its shores.

But on the whole she did not think she approved of the place. It seemed to be like some kind of sporting temple, whose worshippers unfortunately created far too much disruption on match days, much too close to her house. She remembered having been terrified one day as a small child when she and one of the housemaids had been engulfed and surrounded by all manner of people who had flooded out of the ground at the end of a particular match. It was not that anything bad had happened to them, but she had never seen so many people before, and she had felt completely helpless as they had been swept along in the crowd. It seemed to her to be something too big and far-reaching to exist in the middle of her cosy, familiar world; it was the kind of place that belonged farther away, in the heart of the City or the West End where the streets were already hectic and a little more madness would not be so out of place. However, whether she liked it or not, Lord's was but a walking distance from her house, and now she was to go there to meet with her uncle.

What had surprised her most of all was that her mother, who was normally so careful and cautious, had agreed that she should go. As her mother gave Anna the news it was clear that she was less than comfortable with the idea, and it was probably only because Anna was to meet with her uncle that she had consented. But why had she chosen this time, and that place, to loosen the chains? Anna was certainly excited about meeting with Mr. Warwick again and hopefully learning more about Faulkner and auras. Indeed that was a conversation she was most keen to have. But the idea that she was to be forced to endure cricket first before she could have that conversation, well that just seemed like unkind and unnecessary torture.

Perhaps what had intrigued Anna the most regarding the brief conversation she had had with her mother though was that she had said "Anna, your instruction is about to begin. I give you my consent, and you can trust Mr. Warwick and your uncle implicitly. However, I feel heavy in my heart that this time has come so soon, and I ask you to promise me that you will be careful with the knowledge that you are about to gain, as careful as you have ever been with anything, and that you will do your utmost to stay clear of danger. Anna, please promise me."

There had been a slight yet nonetheless unmistakable note of desperation in her mother's voice as she made this request, and of course Anna had agreed, but this had made her even more curious than before as to what she might learn.

Jim's reaction to the news that he was to accompany Anna to Lord's to meet with her uncle could not have been in starker contrast to Anna's. He was delighted. Not only would he have the day off work, but Anna's uncle had also paid for his entry ticket. Jim apparently liked cricket and all that went with it very much, and he was in extremely high spirits when the morning came.

Anna liked Jim, who was a burly man in his mid-twenties, with light brown hair and blue-grey eyes. He did not usually seem to pay much attention to Anna when about the house unless he had a specific reason for doing so, and this suited Anna perfectly. What she liked most though was that, unlike certain others who worked in Anna's house, he did not seem to resent her for her supposedly fortunate position, nor did he seem to share the view that Anna thought herself superior. He simply did his job and was very pleasant to Anna whenever they came into contact, but otherwise he left her alone for the rest of the time. His aura was pure sky blue too, which of course always helped.

For the first time in what seemed like months, London had shed its leaden-grey cloak for the occasion and it was a beautifully sunlit morning. The sunshine, coupled with Jim's irrepressibly good mood, made Anna feel slightly better about having to make the short trip to their famous neighbourhood landmark, which Jim enthusiastically informed her was the 'Home of Cricket'.

Cricket? Cricket? What was the attraction of it she wondered, and why did it need a home? She really had no idea what it was all about or why people were so interested in it – all she had was the vague perception that to watch it must surely be the dullest way imaginable to spend a day. Or indeed a number of days apparently. Despite this though, there was no denying it was a fine day for it. Anna breathed in the air which tasted unusually fresh and clean that morning, borne by a pleasant breeze from the lands to the west. As they walked the street from Anna's home, the midmorning sun was still rising in the sky and it reflected off the leaves of the trees that lined the road in such a way as to make them shine in a spectacular collage of varying shades of light and dark green. The leaves rippling in the breeze appeared like a gently lapping green sea in the air above them, with a cloudless blue sky just visible beyond, through the gaps.

Anna tried not to think of what other more exciting activities might have occupied her rare freedom on such a day, and who else she might have spent that freedom with. Instead she drank in the fresh late summer air and decided to make the best of the time and whatever it might bring. On reaching the end of their street, the sky came more clearly into view between the tree branches, and it was indeed a beautiful deep blue with only a few faint wisps of cloud. How long it was since she had seen it! Anna looked behind her at the road they had just travelled along, at the trees now in their full late summer finery almost touching one another above the middle of the road, creating a wonderful contrast between light and shade in the air and on the ground beneath them. Her road seemed a truly enchanted place at that moment. Something in the beauty of the day and her surroundings stirred a feeling of exhilaration deep inside her, something that Anna had felt before when confronted with a scene of breathtaking beauty. It was a feeling that she had never tried to put into words, and nor would she have been able to at that time even had she wanted to, but it seemed to her to be a feeling that might almost be described as spiritual. It was a deep sense of appreciation and awe for the stunning beauty of nature, even here within this great man-made city, a beauty which far exceeded the creations of man. She was aware that there was something of importance in those feelings at such moments, a sense that she was feeling something fundamental about what it meant to be alive.

Today was not a day to pause and ponder such things for long however, for cricket awaited and Jim appeared intent on making that wait as short as possible. Remembering the cricket and the hoards of people it would bring was enough to snap her back into the here and now with a jolt. She suddenly wondered if Timmy liked cricket. Unsurprisingly it was not a topic which had ever come up in the all too brief conversations they had shared so far, but if he did like it, that might make a difference, she thought. She decided to assume that he did, so as to give her a reason to try to take an interest in this activity that was clearly going to consume a large part of her day.

"It should be a good match today, Anna," said Jim eagerly, hastening their already brisk pace still further as they crossed the road. "Perfect conditions and two good teams."

"Who are the teams?" Anna asked.

"You mean to say you don't know who's playing?" Jim seemed genuinely surprised. "Why, it's Middlesex versus Surrey, a county match and a proper local derby. Surrey are our nearest rivals from south of the river, and nothing's better than beating them. They're a good team though, mind."

"Are you supporting Middlesex then?" asked Anna, presuming that this might be a worthwhile thing to know. However her question was met with a slightly exasperated look from Jim.

"Yes, Anna, I most certainly am. And so you should be too, being that it's your local team and all."

"Jim, I'm afraid I really don't know anything about cricket. I don't want to trouble you, but could you explain it a little, so that I might have some idea?"

"Why yes Anna, I'd be more than happy to. I love cricket," added Jim unnecessarily. "Well, there are two teams of eleven players each, and each team bats twice, either until they're all out or until the last team to bat passes the total score of the other team. Either way, the team that gets the highest score wins."

The pair turned another corner onto a busier street, and they now joined a steady stream of people making their way to the ground. Anna kept her voice low, suddenly feeling embarrassed to reveal to these people just how little she knew about their religion. "How do you bat?"

"Well, when we enter the ground, you'll see a special area in the middle of the playing field, which is called the pitch, or the wicket. Each team takes it in turns to bat on the wicket you see, which means the players of the batting team go out there with their cricket bats and try to hit the ball, which is bowled at them by the other team. That's why it's called 'batting'. Anyway, the batsmen try to hit the ball to score 'runs', which are points, while the bowling team are trying to hit the three pieces of wood stuck in the ground behind the batsman, called 'stumps', with the ball. On top of the stumps there are two more small pieces of wood, called 'bails' – and together the stumps and bails are also called 'wickets'. I must say now I come to explain it, it does sound a little confusing, but it really is very simple. The bowlers bowl the ball and try to hit the wicket behind the batsman. If the ball hits the stumps and knocks off the bails, then that batsman is generally 'out', which means he has finished his turn and must leave the field. So the batsman, as well as trying to hit the ball to score runs, is first and foremost trying to stop the ball from hitting his wicket. Well, they keep going in that way until there is only one player on the batting team remaining, and then it's the other team's turn to bat. Both teams bat twice, and then the team with the highest number of runs wins."

As Jim enthusiastically trundled on through his explanation, Anna's eye was caught by the striking headline of a newspaper being read by a man walking in the opposite direction. It read 'Beast from Hell Strikes in Highgate!' The headline was all she could make of it before the man walked past. Then she recalled that Lizzy had also mentioned something similar a few days earlier. She was now desperate to know what this meant and she wanted to ask Jim if he knew, but there was no way of finding an opening now in his passionate monologue.

"There are also other ways for the batsmen to be out," he was saying, "for example if he hits the ball in the air and then one of the fielding team – that's the team who are bowling – catches the ball inside the boundary – uh…, that means the field of play – before it bounces. But I can explain more of that to you once we're inside."

"Thank you Jim," replied Anna, to whom it had all made some basic sense so far as she had been listening, whilst at the same time of course sounding completely pointless. What she really wanted to know was whether he knew anything of this beast in Highgate, but she hesitated for a moment for fear of appearing as though she had not been listening, and that delay was to prove fatal as before she knew it he was off again!

"There's actually much more to it though," he was continuing, enthusiasm undimmed, "like different ways to score runs, other ways to be out, a range of different ways to bowl and a lot more subtlety, but it'll be easier to explain when you can see it happening. The key aspect that you'll notice over time though is the style and finesse with which the players play the game, and the cunning and the guile that they use to outwit one another. There are sometimes great encounters between the best batsmen with their beautiful stroke play, and the best bowlers with their accuracy and all the variations in the way they bowl. You get some marvellous individual duels too between the top batsmen and bowlers, and it gets really interesting when two top teams come together, like today."

"I see. Thank you Jim," Anna replied simply. It was not because Jim's explanation had not raised further questions for Anna that she did not question him further. It was more that she did not want to pester him with too many basic questions like an irritating little child – that and the genuine worry that if she did he might never stop talking again! As they drew nearer the ground there were by now hundreds, if not thousands of people approaching from all directions, and she fought to quell the slight feeling of panic that this induced in her as she concentrated on ensuring that she didn't become separated from Jim and lost in the crowd. The continuation of her cricket tuition would have to wait until she was safely inside the ground. And for all Jim's enthusiasm, truth be told she was still not in any particular hurry for more!

As they neared the entry gate, the crowd grew more and more dense. Again Anna was struck by the array of people who surrounded her, from affluent gentlemen in their top hats, long coats and waistcoats with shiny golden watch chains, to altogether scruffier looking folk with smaller, flatter hats. What they all did have in common, however, was that they were all considerably taller than she was, causing her to feel increasingly enclosed as the crowd began to funnel towards the gate. Her childhood memories of having been engulfed by that other crowd returned vividly to her, but this time she was able to control the fear, being that much bigger and older, and having burly Jim there to protect her and prevent her from being pushed from all sides. That it was before the match rather than after probably helped too, as people had not yet partaken in a full day of 'refreshments'!

"Mind out for the young lady!" Jim said on a number of occasions when people got too near, and each time the members of the crowd did as they were told. Anna felt safe with Jim there to protect her, and she made a mental note to tell her mother how well she had been chaperoned. Through the crowd Anna noticed a particularly tall man ahead of them, with very dark hair visible under his top hat and wearing a very fine coat. 'Faulkner!' she gasped inwardly and instinctively shrank back, only to be relieved when the man turned his head to reveal a clean-shaven face and much friendlier eyes than those owned by the man she had seen in Mr. Warwick's shop. 'That man has certainly affected me,' thought Anna, laughing at herself but still unable to forget the terrible memory of his aura.

By now there was a palpable feeling of excitement and anticipation amongst the crowd all around them, each group engrossed in deep discussions about the game ahead. Almost in spite of herself, Anna felt her own sense of anticipation start to grow too, as though it were infectious. There was still some time before play was due to begin when Jim and Anna finally took their seats, and as they emerged and Anna was able to see the playing area itself for the first time, she took a sharp intake of breath. For all the hubbub of people moving this way and that around her, she could not help but be struck by the splendour of the scene now before her. They were facing westwards with the sun still only midway through its upward morning journey behind them, and in that morning light the grass of the playing surface was a most luscious green, almost like the great lawn of a grand country house. And beyond that, directly in front of them at the far side of the ground stood the splendid country house itself, or 'the pavilion' as Jim informed her it was called, where the players and the other most important people could be found. "That is where your uncle will be. He's a member of the MCC," said Jim with an air of reverence which suggested that this was something of immense significance, although naturally it meant absolutely nothing to Anna. The building was a suitably elaborate and impressive one though, and appeared quite magnificent as it reflected the morning sunlight. Anna could easily picture her uncle atop one of its balconies, where he would undoubtedly be in his element. The edifice dominated the other spectator areas.

'Perhaps this might not be so bad after all,' thought Anna. 'Even if I can't fathom the cricket, there could be worse places to spend a day, and there's no shortage of interesting people to observe.'

Anna had never enjoyed being part of a large crowd until then, and especially not the sort of thronging one which this event had attracted, but she had always enjoyed watching people from a safe distance. Although she was surrounded by people here, and she was younger than nearly all of them, no-one was paying her any particular attention and it suddenly seemed like the ideal observation point. And there were indeed many interesting scenes worth observing, for there was such a variety of characters, with some groups laughing and joking whilst others engaged themselves in more serious discussion. Quite instinctively she shifted her focus to the auras or essences as she resolved to call them from then on, of those nearest to her. There was the usual mix of the pure and the somewhat less pure, but in general they did not seem to be a bad crowd.

As the space around them filled, Jim started to become more and more agitated, looking all around him. At first Anna thought he was simply excited by the event and trying to take it all in, but it soon became obvious he was looking for someone. Anna wanted to ask, but her usual reticence prevented her. Then suddenly, all became clear.

An attractive young lady who looked to be in her early twenties approached. On catching Jim's eye her face lit up and she came over to them immediately and embraced him! Jim could not have looked happier. He turned to Anna and said "Anna, allow me to introduce Miss Emily Barmby. Emily, this is my mistress's daughter, Anna."

Emily bowed her head politely in Anna's direction and offered a slight curtsy, and Anna returned the gesture. "Delighted to make your acquaintance, Anna," said Emily, and Anna noted the very proper way in which Emily spoke, suggesting that she too might have been 'born to expect only the finest things in life' and other such nonsense, but had successfully ignored those artificial constraints to find a good heart, which she had surely found in Jim.

"Very pleased to meet you," Anna responded, and they both smiled. Emily seemed to relax slightly, and Anna couldn't help but notice the beauty of this young lady. The light brown curls of her hair on either side perfectly framed the pale skin of her face. Her lips were full and curled upwards into a delightful smile, a sight which Anna imagined must have set many a young man's heart racing. However, it was her twinkling light brown eyes that somehow shone in the light which did most to highlight the prettiness of her face, especially when she smiled. Anna shifted her focus for a moment and, as she had hoped, Emily's essence was every bit as pure and as blue as Jim's, though it was actually considerably larger.

Jim lent towards Anna and said in a quiet voice, "Anna, I would appreciate it if you would not mention Miss Emily to anyone in the household. I am very much in love with Emily, but our parents don't yet know of it, and I'd very much like for us to tell people ourselves when both of us are ready to do so. I feel sure I can trust you Anna, which is why I arranged for Emily to meet with us here. You won't say a word about her, will you?"

"No, Jim, I promise," replied Anna, smiling again as she realised that Jim's excitement had not been entirely due to the cricket match after all. Anna had initially been rather surprised by this sudden turn of events, but now she felt strangely happy. Happy for Jim and Emily because they looked so content together and happy also because she had some inkling as to how he must feel. Although even more secret, she too harboured feelings for Timmy that she could not share with anyone, and she now dared to believe that Timmy might even feel the same. Even at her age, she understood all too well how hard it was to have to keep such feelings secret, and to be able to meet with the subject of those feelings so infrequently. So Anna was very happy for them, and she silently wished them every good fortune for the future.

After Emily and Jim had caught up for a few moments, Emily left them again to 'powder her nose' (a ridiculous expression, Anna had always thought) and a question sprang to Anna's mind.

"Jim, why were you so confident that you could trust me? I mean you can trust me, completely, for I will never breathe a word to anyone, but what made you so sure of it? We have never spoken of anything but the most everyday matters before."

Lowering his voice so that only Anna could hear, Jim replied, "I have never needed to speak with you to know it, Anna. I can't explain it simply, but in recent years, well, I have become able to see these things, and I can see that you are one of the most trustworthy people I have come across, despite your young age."

As he spoke he looked awkward at first, but then relaxed again and continued. "To be honest I don't ordinarily speak of these things, but I felt sure you would understand. From the ignorant gossip from certain maids in the house, I've long thought that perhaps you can see things about people in the same way I've started to. I dislike the way they talk intensely, as though you're somehow strange, when if I'm right it's actually a wonderful gift that you have. It's because people are like that that I don't talk about what I can see. Or at least, that's one of the reasons. But regardless of that, I knew I could trust you, because I could see it in your... your nature."

"I understand completely," said Anna, "and you are right, I am able to see the nature of people too. At times it frightens me, but there is little I can do to change it."

Anna fell silent. She was in fact stunned that she had found a second person she knew who seemed to share her abilities within the space of two days. Unlike Anna, Jim had apparently only developed his power in recent years, but it surely could not have been mere coincidence that Mr. Warwick and her uncle had chosen such a person to be her chaperone on the day she was supposed to begin her instruction. As if to confirm her suspicions, Jim added, "You know, your uncle is a fine man, and he has taught me much about what it is that I can see, and how to use this power. He mentioned to me that your instruction was about to begin, which did surprise me given how young you still are, but I believe that's why I was chosen to accompany you today."

Up to that point in the conversation, Anna had been doing her best to remain calm and not give away that her heart had begun to race. However, the impact of this last revelation – that her uncle was presumably able to see essences too – had clearly made a sufficient impression on her for her disguise of calmness to slip, because Jim suddenly added, "But perhaps I've said too much now. I am not permitted to speak to anyone about what your uncle has taught me…"

"Please don't worry Jim, I won't tell a soul. Your secret's safe with me. In fact both of them are!" she added, glancing quickly at Emily who was now returning.

They both laughed, but had to cut the conversation short as Emily returned. Anna's mind was now flying and she longed to discuss the subject further with Jim, but she knew that the necessity for secrecy meant that Jim was unlikely to divulge any more. Even more so now, she longed for the end of the game, even though it had not yet started, so that she could finally meet with her uncle and begin their discussions. She was intrigued beyond words now, and for a while she was lost in a world of her own thoughts.

It was the friendly conversation in which Emily engaged her that finally brought her back from her musings. Emily was delightful, not to mention amusing, company once they had both overcome their initial natural shyness. She had an easy air, which was good for someone like Anna whose tendency towards over-seriousness sometimes needed some tempering. Anna warmed to the young woman immediately, and was sure that Emily was a person whose company she would enjoy.

Anna soon learned that Emily had not originally been at all interested in cricket either, but that she had gradually become so first through her father's influence, and then through that of Jim. Anna laughed as Emily explained that although the concept of grown men expending so much of their precious and scarce energy on throwing and hitting a ball of red leather with sticks was clearly nothing short of bizarre, as it was something that meant so much to the men in her life she had determined to suspend all common sense and attempt to find some form of enjoyment in it. And to her genuine surprise, she had found herself increasingly engrossed by it – so much so that when Jim had told her of the opportunity to meet with him at this match, she could not be quite sure which prospect excited her more, that of seeing her beloved Jim again or that of watching the match! On hearing this, Jim pretended momentarily to be crestfallen before joining in the laughter.

Emily then leant across in front of Jim and whispered in Anna's ear deliberately loud enough for Jim to hear, "And some of the players are extremely handsome too!" Emily grinned at Jim, who returned the smile with mock sarcasm, before she continued, "So beware Anna, and take my advice as an older and more experienced woman. Cricket can become a dangerously attractive addiction. You have received fair warning!" Although Emily's conversation had been extremely light-hearted, Anna decided that at the very least she would give this game a chance.

Finally a distant bell rang from somewhere within the pavilion, and the fielding team followed by the two opening batsmen took the field, all dressed from head to foot in cream-white. Accompanied by Jim's extensive explanations, cricket was evolving slowly from an incomprehensible and irrelevant concept into one which she was at least able to grasp, though if honest one she was still hardly gripped by. She had asked Jim what time she was supposed to be meeting with her uncle, and learned that it would not be until after the game had finished. "And a game is usually about seven hours, give or take," Jim had informed her.

Seven hours! 'Typical Uncle James,' thought Anna to herself, 'making me wait until the end before I can see him. No doubt he has important people to see and entertain, and doesn't want me spoiling his enjoyment of the game!' Turning to Jim, she said "I'm very sorry that you have to look after me all day, Jim."

"Anna, don't be silly. It's my absolute pleasure and not the slightest trouble. And even if it were a trouble, which it isn't, it's my job. Besides I am only too happy to help you and your uncle. He's arranged for my tickets to be here today, and I'm most grateful to him for that. You wouldn't be allowed in the pavilion where he is during play in any case, because it's a special place and only members are allowed to enter. Not to mention the fact that all the members are men. Come to think of it, I'm not quite sure how you're to gain entry even after the match – but I'm sure your uncle will find a way."

"I'm sure he will," responded Anna, who had no doubts concerning her uncle's ability to find a way to do anything if he wanted to, "and thank you again." Jim nodded, and returned all his attention to the men in white on the pristine lawn in front of them.

As the morning's play drew on towards lunchtime, Anna gradually became more and more absorbed by what was going on around her. Some of the people, and most specifically the men, had already started to drink various liquids that she assumed to be intoxicating. Some were doing so surreptitiously from concealed hip flasks, while others were becoming altogether more conspicuous, pouring various red and brown liquids openly into glasses before sipping from them. As they did so, they seemed to be engaging in ever more lively and more animated discussions, making jokes and laughing uproariously, sometimes even when a ball was about to be bowled, much to the displeasure of others in the crowd including Jim. Anna had never drunk more than the occasional glass of alcohol on specific occasions in her house, but she had sometimes witnessed what it could do to others, and wondered at the state some of these spectators would be in come the end of the day, given that it was not yet even lunchtime!

She shifted her focus to view the essences of some of those who were drinking nearby, and she was intrigued by what she saw. In each case, the essence seemed to be glowing a little more brightly, and in some cases the blue at their centres had become slightly more vivid than they had been when she had first seen them. However, in each case the blemishes in the essences – any discolouring or imperfections on its surface – also seemed to be more visible. These changes were only subtle, and it was not that they had altered in their colour, shape or the number of blemishes they contained, it was simply a change in the vividness with which they could be seen. Anna did not know exactly what this meant, but it seemed to her that parts of these people's natural characters and personalities were somehow being amplified by the alcohol they were drinking. This seemed to suggest to her, although she was not quite sure, that these people at that moment were more likely to do greater good than normal, but also had the potential for greater ill. Either change could occur, or possibly both, one after another. She had a clear impression that the temporary change in the essences she was seeing was not necessarily a change for the worse, there was more complexity to it than that, but there was something in their state that was more fragile than normal, and more prone to a sudden shift in either direction. Having not often had the chance to observe such changes, Anna was at once both fascinated and slightly frightened. Anyway, at least she wasn't bored as she had thought she might be, and she had also been treated to a delicious picnic lunch prepared by Emily.

Then something happened on the field of play which focused everyone's complete attention back in that direction. At the end of one over (as Anna had learned was the name for each set of six balls), a murmur spread around the crowd that someone called Higgins was coming on to bowl for the Surrey side. Higgins was a very large, bulky man, with a huge handlebar moustache and enormous shoulders and arms. He was clearly well known to the crowd, although not in a way that could have been described as remotely favourable, judging by the boos, jibes and hisses that began to fill the air.

"You're nothing but a bully, Higgins!" shouted one.

"Get back to the Oval, you animal!" shouted another.

"Get back south of the river, you're not welcome here!" cried another. And there was plenty more.

Anna was fascinated and looked to Jim for an explanation. "Ronald Higgins is the Surrey captain, and there's history between him and Middlesex," he explained to her. "To be honest there's history between Higgins and most teams, but particularly with us. He's considered quite a ruffian you see. Last year when Surrey played here, he broke the hand of our captain, Walter Smythe, who's currently batting at the other end, with a high-bouncing delivery. Then in the return match at the Oval in Kennington, which is the home of Surrey, two more of our players had to retire with injuries caused by his aggressive bowling. The umpire had warned him, and then suspended him from bowling for the remainder of the match following those incidents. I've heard that it got so heated down there that some of the crowd turned ugly, which never normally happens during cricket, and there was nearly a riot at the end of the game. You needn't worry though," he quickly added, probably noticing a concerned expression crossing Anna's face, "people would never get so carried away here at Lord's!"

Anna watched with intrigue as Higgins came in from a long run-up to release his first ball at the Middlesex batsman. It kept low and darted through to the wicketkeeper without damaging anyone. The second and third balls kept similarly low as they bounced up the wicket towards the batsman, one of them passing in front of him as he stood side-on to its direction of travel, and the next one changing direction as it bounced, eluding his swing entirely. The batsman this time had clearly tried to drive the ball off the field but had missed it completely, leaving him looking rather stupid. None of these balls had seemed to place the batsman in any great physical danger though, and Anna started to wonder if all the fuss that the crowd had been making was really justified. However, when Higgins had thundered in for his fourth ball of the over, she suddenly understood. The big bowler seemed to bounce the ball on the wicket closer to himself than he had with the previous deliveries, causing the ball to rear right up towards the head of the batsman, who only realised what was happening in the nick of time. He jerked his head out of the way of the onrushing ball but a split second before it cut through the air precisely where his head had been, missing him by an inch at the most.

Anna was briefly horrified at the thought of what might have happened had the batsman's reaction been any slower, and she imagined the bowler would be similarly concerned and apologetic. To her shock however and no little disgust, she could just make out the oversized Higgins actually taunting the poor batsman, telling him what the ball would do to his head the next time, before he turned back for his run up with a smirk. Various derisive shouts rose from the crowd around her and she even felt as though her own blood temperature was rising at this. It recalled to her mind her feelings when Gillespie had dumped manure on Timmy, and all the other occasions when she had seen a person do something to another that was unfair, hurtful and plain wrong.

"Ban him umpire, before he injures anyone else," shouted one young man now standing not far from Anna. He was one of those who had been sipping from his hipflask all morning, and Anna could see the ruddy shade of his cheeks as he took another slug of whatever its fiery contents might be.

Then it was time for the next ball, and seeing Higgins thundering in again, Anna began to fear that Higgins might indeed imbed this one exactly where he had said he would. It was another short ball, but to her relief this time Anna could see it moving in the air clearly away from the batsman. The latter took a swipe at it with a horizontal bat, but the movement of the ball in the air had deceived him and he was only able to make the slightest of contacts with the upper edge of his bat before it flew into the waiting cupped hands of the player referred to as the 'wicketkeeper'. There was joy from the fielders, and also the many Surrey supporters who suddenly became noisily evident amongst them, having obviously travelled north of the Thames for the event. The rather forlorn-looking batsman trudged disconsolately back to the pavilion.

"Well, that's all right. At least he didn't get injured, or end up with the ball between his eyes," said Anna.

"That is not the point, Anna!" responded Jim, who was now becoming quite animated, though still much more controlled than most of the people around them. "He let Higgins bully him into making a ridiculous shot, and now he's out. The ball before ruffled him completely, it scared him I think, and then he lost his head and swung wildly at the next one. Higgins did him all right, and not just physically either – he out-thought him."

Anna had not expected this reply. It made it sound as though the aggressive bowling and threats of injury to the batsmen were all part of the game, and that winning was more important than the players' health. And what was more, the players themselves seemed to take this view too, judging by the demeanour of the departing batsman who, rather than looking relieved to have escaped with his life, actually appeared distraught. 'Oh well', thought Anna, 'I suppose no-one is forcing them to play this game, and they know the dangers they will face.' She was still far from understanding why anyone would choose to risk such danger simply for a game, but she was becoming increasingly certain that it had something to do with them being male!

The next Middlesex batsman took to the field, assumed his position at the crease and awaited the final delivery of the over. Higgins, having soaked up the adulation of his team following the success of his previous dismissal like a huge, smug walrus, now roared in again at the newcomer. It was the first ball faced by the new batsman, but no quarter was given as the ball once again pitched short and bounced in the direction of his head. With no time to spare, the batsman brought up his hands which held his bat to protect his ducking head, and the ball careered into the fingers of his top hand. The batsman's cry was audible to them all as he let his bat drop to the ground and clutched his left hand to his chest, clearly in great pain. The ball dropped onto the pitch in front of him.

Howls filled the air all around Anna as the batsman sank to his knees, cradling his injured hand. Higgins merely fired him a disdainful, dismissive glare, before smirking again and turning to begin the journey back to the start of his run up. As he did so, Walter Smythe, the Middlesex captain whose own hand Higgins had apparently broken in the same match the previous year, and who had opened the Middlesex batting today, stepped into the path of the larger man from the non-striker's end and began to speak angrily. Higgins did not slow down however. Instead he continued until his moustached face was inches from Smythe's and fired a torrent of abuse back at the home captain. For a moment, Anna feared the two captains might come to blows, but the umpire intervened, shooed Smythe away and ushered Higgins back towards the start of his run-up.

Curses and boos continued to fill the air, and Anna noticed that even Emily now looked serious and angry. Jim, however, remained surprisingly balanced and unsympathetic about the plight of his own team's batsmen.

"It was his own fault, he clearly took his eye completely off the ball. With a bowler like Higgins you simply can't do that – you deserve to be hit. We're in danger of throwing this away if we don't raise our game!"

"But Jim," said Anna, "surely Higgins isn't playing fair. He's trying to injure them to prevent them playing. Surely that can't be right, can it?"

"That's as maybe Anna, but that's what you get with Higgins. We already knew that. He might actually be trying to injure them, but he's certainly also trying to intimidate them, and he's succeeding. All the Middlesex players knew of his tactics before play began – that's why they needed to be extra careful and keep their heads, but he's already got them rattled, you can see it.

"You are right though Anna, the way that Higgins plays in not in the spirit of the game. I only wish one of our players would stand up to him, hold their nerve against him and see him off. That's the best way to teach him. Look – the batsman's going off!"

Sure enough, having faced only one ball, the new batsman was already on his way back to the pavilion, retired hurt. This time the Surrey supporters remained quiet, knowing that removing a batsman in such a way was not to be celebrated.

"What makes it worse is that the umpire called that last

ball a 'no ball'," continued Jim. "Which means that Higgins was too far down the pitch when he bowled that last delivery, so it wouldn't have counted even if our batsman had been out. We get one run added for that, but that hardly compensates us for the damage done. And worst of all it means we still have one more ball to face from Higgins in this over, and the new batsman is going to have to face it. I hope we don't lose another one now."

'This is becoming serious,' thought Anna, 'people are being injured. How long will they allow it to continue before someone has the sense to stop it?'

She was still contemplating all this when a sudden roar rose up from the Middlesex support. Looking up, Anna could see a very young looking man coming out from the pavilion, evidently the next Middlesex batsman. Very young looking, and also extremely handsome unless Anna was very much mistaken!

The supporters rose to their feet to welcome the new batsman as though he were some ancient gladiator entering the arena of battle. Jim also gave a cheer and Emily leaned forward and grinned at Anna, clapping her hands vigorously. The young man's looks clearly hadn't escaped her notice either!

"It's Gregory Matthews," explained Jim. "He's only twenty and still at Oxford, but he's a fine young prospect. He grew up locally, and he has recently broken into the county side during the university summer holiday. He's already had a marvellous debut season. There's still much he has to learn, but he's got the heart of a lion, this one."

Anna watched as the young man took his place at the crease. Unlike most of the players he was not wearing a cap, and his dark brown, swept-back hair which was fairly long on top, ruffled slightly in the breeze. Now he was a little closer, Anna could see that he was even more pleasing on the eye than she had first thought. 'And he has the "heart of a lion" too,' she mused. She had suddenly quite forgotten the disapproval she had felt but moments before, and she was now finally beginning to understand the attraction of cricket!

"I'm not too sure he's ready for Higgins though," added Jim, as Higgins started the run-up for his last ball of the over. "I'm not sure he's got the experience to deal with this."

With those words, the gravity of the situation returned to Anna, and she was gripped by the drama that was now unfolding. She felt slightly embarrassed as she found herself hoping desperately for the health of this young man, who she had only seen for the first time but moments earlier.

Dark clouds had started to drift menacingly across the previously unblemished sky, as though conjured up by the events taking place on the pitch before them. They obscured the sun and lent an altogether more threatening edge to the atmosphere. An eerie silence fell upon the supporters of both teams as Higgins reached his bowling mark, turned and began his run. He was moving very fast now, seeming to be reaching his full pace. Then as the ball left his hand, Anna clearly heard the aggressive bowler grunt loudly, possibly a result of the effort he had put into bowling the ball, but Anna felt sure that it was more designed to distract the new batsman from his first ball.

Once again the ball pitched very short on the wicket, before rearing up wickedly towards the head of Gregory Matthews. It seemed to Anna that the noise Higgins had made had indeed momentarily distracted Matthews, or perhaps it was the light which had now started to fade, or maybe he simply needed some time to settle in, but whatever the reason, Matthews hesitated, and at the speed the ball was travelling it could quite literally have been fatal. Anna gasped faintly as the ball careered towards the young man's head. Matthews had not taken his eye from the ball though, he had not panicked, and though his reaction was late he had managed to move his head partially out of the line of the ball. However he was not quite fast enough to avoid it completely and the ball made grazing contact with his cheekbone. Not enough to break the bone, but sufficient to cut the skin and to cause it to bleed.

Anna was shocked and felt momentarily sick. It was true that Matthews had chosen to face this monstrous bully, nobody had forced him, but surely Higgins should not be allowed to continue to attack the opposition players in such a way. She simply could not believe that such behaviour could be within the rules of any sport. The vast majority of the crowd around her were clearly in agreement, though they expressed themselves in a manner of which Anna would never have been capable. Indeed some of their shouts made Anna wonder if they weren't even more maniacal than Higgins himself!

Smythe directed more angry words at Higgins, to which the latter responded merely by spitting on the ground not far from the Middlesex captain, before the umpire, having seen the damage inflicted by another short ball from Higgins, entered into a lengthy discussion with the big bowler, gesturing more than once in the direction of the pavilion as he did so. Higgins maintained a straight face this time, but Anna could tell even from where she was sat that he felt not an ounce of remorse in his large body for his actions.

"Ban him!" shouted a voice from behind them. "Lock him up and throw away the key!" shouted another man just in front, and to Anna's surprise, this one could not have been a day under seventy years old! However to the dismay and in some quarters derision of the crowd, the umpire took no further action, and that eventful over was at an end.

Anna wasn't sure who scared her more now, Higgins or the crowd of which she was a part. However since nobody was angry with her, and with Jim there for protection, she also felt strangely exhilarated again. Though the reasons for her feeling of exhilaration now were quite different from those of earlier that morning when she had walked down the beautifully sunlit street outside her house, the sensations were nonetheless akin in one respect: she felt alive.

The next over was a complete and very welcome contrast to the aggression of the previous one. A shorter and rounder, bearded Surrey player bowled a series of much slower, spinning deliveries to Smythe from the other end. Anna was informed by Jim that this was 'leg spin', a term used to describe bowling which span significantly into the batsman from the right as the bowler looked at it. These balls might have been slower, but they were clearly no easier to hit as one after another pitched in a different place, and bounced and turned to varying extents. The Middlesex captain tried and failed to make contact time again. The craft of the rather rotund Surrey bowler was plain for all to see, as the ball sometimes reached a fair height, sometimes stayed low, and on one occasion Anna could have sworn that it actually bounced from left to right, the opposite direction to all the others. Anna recalled Jim's earlier words about guile and cunning and the duel between the batsman and the bowler, and when she compared the last thunderous over to this one those words suddenly made perfect sense to her. There was a great deal of art and finesse involved in this over, thought Anna, surprised at how absorbed she had become.

On the last ball of the spinner's over, Smythe was finally able to connect as he hit out at the ball, sending it most of the way towards the pavilion before it was picked up by a running Surrey fielder. Smythe ran one run and then stopped, which meant that it would be Smythe and not Matthews who would face the first ball of the next over from Higgins from the other end of the wicket, much to Anna's relief. However, although Smythe gestured to Matthews to stay where he was after that run, Matthews shouted "Again!", and effectively forced his captain to return for a second run. Both batsmen reached their respective ends moments before the ball reached the wicketkeeper, and they were safely in. 'Safely in', thought Anna, but young Matthews must have known that in taking the second run he would now have to face Higgins again for the next ball. 'How brave,' she thought, but oh how she hoped he would not come to regret it.

The fielders took their positions on the opposite end of the pitch for the next over to begin, and once again boos started to fill the air as the Surrey captain beckoned for the ball to be thrown to him. Anna's feeling of sickness suddenly returned as she looked at the handsome young face of the batsman, scarred and still bleeding from his cheek, as he faced the raging bull now galloping towards him again. Anna was struck by the look on the young man's face. Etched onto it was an expression of concentrated determination, without a trace of fear for what was to come.

Higgins released the ball, another short one, and once again it reared up dangerously towards the batsman. This time its flight was absolutely straight, and Matthews followed it clearly from the moment it left the bowler's hand. With perfect timing and poise, the young man took one step back swung his bat horizontally towards the onrushing ball, and with the face of the bat angled downwards and his eyes focused on the ball right to the point of contact, he made a perfect connection with the middle of his bat. The crack of heavy wood on hard leather echoed across the ground like a rifle shot, as the angle of the bat sent the ball safely to the ground, beyond the nearest diving fielder and away to the boundary rope for what Anna now understood would be four runs. Anna realised that she had not breathed for quite some time, and she took a deep one before joining Jim and the other spectators who were on their feet applauding. She searched Matthews's expression for signs of jubilation or relief, but found neither. Instead, he had maintained the same look of steely concentration, which had not a hint of self-congratulation.

"You beauty, Matthews! That'll show you Higgins, you bullyboy!" was one of the more repeatable cries that could be heard all around Anna. "That's more like it," said Jim, to everyone and no-one in particular, "he's using his head and he's not allowing the occasion to get the better of him. A few more like that and we'll soon see Higgins off!"

Then Higgins turned to begin the long walk back to the start of his run-up, receiving a barrage of abuse from all four corners of the ground. The last ball had been his fastest delivery yet, albeit a dead straight one, and to see it dispatched with such apparent ease by this young upstart he had intended to intimidate, and to such joy and ridicule from the enemy crowd, had clearly not gone down well with him. He was now visibly snarling, and the shot from Matthews seemed only to have fired him up all the more, as though the only thought in his mind was revenge.

Concentrated silence once again swept across the entire crowd, every pair of eyes trained on what would next unfold. Anna's brief euphoria evaporated as quickly as it had come. The look on Higgins's face as he approached the start of his run up was one of pure murder now, as though his sole intent was to run right back down and tear the batsman limb from limb.

"Oh dear, I have a bad feeling about this," muttered Anna in a small voice.

"Yes Anna, I know what you mean," replied Jim, the tone of his voice quite changed. "Did you see the look on Higgins's face? Matthews is a brave one all right, and he's got the makings of a fine batsman, but he might be too inexperienced for this. There's not many around, even amongst the most experienced players I've seen, who could survive the kind of bowling Higgins dishes out when he's in this mood. It's not even legal, most of it. And I must say, I don't think I've ever seen him look quite so riled as he does now!"

Suddenly Anna's heart was in her mouth. Her own fears were made ten times worse by the knowledge that even Jim now shared her sense of danger.

Time seemed to stop as Higgins reached the start of his run-up and slowly began to turn. Anna's senses had never felt more heightened. She gripped the seat in front of her with whitened knuckles as Higgins began to thunder in again.

Gallantry and Villainy

Higgins reached the wicket, and then it happened again – a very loud grunt as the ball left his hand. It was as though he had shouted something at the batsman at the moment he released the ball. Whatever it had been, it seemed to have the same distracting effect as before, as the young batsman seemed momentarily to lose concentration, and he failed to react in time to the short pitching of the ball. This time, although it was pitched short, it did not rise as high as the previous deliveries, instead darting up off the pitch at a slight angle like a bullet, straight towards Matthews's chest! Matthews brought his bat up belatedly to meet the ball, but due to his hesitation and the lateral movement of the ball in the air he failed to find its line. A sickening thud was clearly audible even from where Anna was sitting, as the ball made contact with the young man's ribcage. There was a momentary silence, crowd and players alike stunned by the ferocity of what had just occurred.

Matthews slumped down onto one knee. He dropped his bat, put his left hand onto the grass to keep himself from falling over and somehow managed to remain upright. The grimace on his face was visible even from Anna's distance and she could see that he was in enormous pain. Such was the speed at which the ball had been travelling she could not be quite certain precisely where it had struck, but to escape with no broken bones would have been very lucky, and the consequences could be even worse if the impact had been anywhere near his heart.

The silence suddenly fractured all around them as the crowd erupted in outrage at what had just occurred, and this time Anna was on her feet with them.

"You brute! You monster! How could he do such a thing? This shouldn't be allowed!" she shouted at the top of her voice, though still barely audible amid the general uproar. The crowd were extremely agitated now, and most were on their feet screaming blue murder at Higgins. Looking across from Jim, Anna could see that Emily too was on her feet, shouting things which were presumably equally unladylike, although there was no way of telling above the din. Despite the crowd's noisy discontent, Anna was later to note that no-one from the crowd ever crossed the playing-field boundary rope. It was as if some invisible magic prevented anyone from encroaching on the hallowed turf. ("Well this is Lord's!" Jim was to offer later by way of explanation.)

"Surely he can't be allowed to get away with that?" asked Anna, calming down just a little and turning to Jim.

"Well no, he shouldn't be allowed to," replied Jim, and this time even he could find nowhere else to direct the blame but at the big moustachioed brute. "Aside from the written laws of the game, there are gentlemen's rules in cricket, which is one of the great things about the game. Not only has Higgins broken the gentlemen's rules, and he ain't no gent, no doubt about that, he has probably broken the written rules too and even the legal laws of the land by now. That was nothing more than assault and battery, that was. Anna, I do promise you that cricket isn't normally played this way – at least, not when Higgins isn't playing – it's usually a very gentlemanly pursuit. The problem is, he hasn't got a captain to take him to one side and have a word with him, or better still take him off bowling altogether, because he is the captain! He can bowl for as long as he likes, in whatever way he likes. But this simply isn't cricket. It's a disgrace." However, the look of intense, concentrated fascination on Jim's face as he waited to see what would happen next hardly suggested he was about to storm out in disgust!

The umpire had by now approached Higgins and appeared to be having more severe words with him, but it gradually became clear that he intended to do no more than that – just talk, and then Higgins would be allowed to continue. Higgins had walked over to Matthews very briefly and nodded in his direction by way of acknowledgement, but he had then moved away again as Smythe and the Surrey fielders had crowded round him to see that he was all right. And when the umpire's latest reprimand was completed, Higgins turned away from him and Anna was sure she saw another smirk from the big brute of a bowler.

"I can't believe he's going to be allowed to continue! This is just not right. Something must be wrong here," cried Anna.

"You know Anna, I do believe you're right. Something is wrong. There were a lot of rumours after the game at the Oval, when Higgins was prevented from continuing by the umpire due to this kind of bowling. But it was said afterwards that the umpire himself was then struck off the list and will never be allowed to umpire another match. Rumour has it that Higgins, in spite of his behaviour, still has mighty powerful connections, not only in the game but in politics too. Friends and family in high places, that kind of thing, which is also how many people believe he got and has retained the captaincy, by the way. Well, they reckon he was able to get the umpire himself banned after that game, and now all the umpires know this they're too plain scared to suspend Higgins again. I didn't believe all the talk until today, but here's the evidence right in front of our very eyes!"

"If that's true, the umpire's an absolute coward! He should make a stand for what's right, and bravely face the consequences. He ought to be ashamed of himself and never be allowed to umpire again if he's so weak-willed!" asserted Anna, no longer bearing any resemblance to the shy young girl who had entered the ground just hours earlier.

"I agree Anna. But let's calm down a bit and see what happens next," replied Jim, who if anything now seemed to be more concerned about just how angry Anna herself was getting. But she could not help it. She hated nothing in life more than injustice.

By now, members of the Middlesex staff and officials had

come onto the pitch to see if Matthews was all right, and several of them seemed to be urging him to leave the field. However Matthews, who had forced himself back onto his feet, could not have been making it clearer that he intended to continue, and no amount of coercion was going to persuade him otherwise. Smythe had also been talking to him in a concerned manner, but he finally seemed convinced that Matthews was in a fit state to continue his innings, and the captain returned to his end of the pitch.

"Matthews is a brave one all right. Told you he had the heart of a lion, didn't I, eh?" said Jim, his voice filled with admiration.

"Yes, he is brave," agreed Anna, in a much softer tone, but no less impressed. And then in a lower tone still she added, "I only hope he lives to see the day out."

Finally, the Middlesex staff gave up their attempts to encourage the injured batsman to leave the field, and the fielders took up their positions once more. Anna looked on in grim and fearful fascination as the brave young batsman took his guard again and made ready for the next ball.

Higgins walked back to his bowling mark again, catching the ball in his right hand from one of the fielders as he did so. Though the hail of abuse continued all around him, he now looked the calmest man in the ground. So calm in fact, that as he got closer to them, Anna could see he was actually smiling! What did this man have to smile about? Anna had not thought it possible for Higgins to slip any lower in her estimation, but he was now plumbing new depths.

"Surely he won't bowl any more of those high bouncers will he? Not after that?" Anna asked, turning again to Jim and Emily.

"I'm sure you're right, Anna. Surely even Higgins knows when enough's enough. He's had his revenge and left his mark – now let's hope he starts playing some proper cricket."

As Higgins finally approached the start of his run up,

silence gripped the crowd once more. It was as though everyone was wondering the same thing. 'Surely he wouldn't do it again, would he?'

As Higgins reached his mark and turned to begin his run up, it would have been possible to hear a pin drop – the contrast with the uproarious din moments earlier could not have been more dramatic. Anna's senses felt sharper than she could ever remember, such was the state of tension which gripped her and everyone else in the ground. Once again time seemed to have slowed down and it took an eternity for Higgins to get into his stride. Anna looked at the plucky young batsman, whose marked face had returned to its former expression of resolute determination, but whose stance had altered slightly in response to the pain now evidently searing through his side – the same side that faced the onrushing bowler. And now here he came roaring in, letting the ball rip from his hand. No grunt this time, but sure enough he had pitched it short yet again! The ball tore off the pitch and reared up like a spitting cobra, this time directly at the young man's head. But for all the pain he clearly felt, he kept his eyes fixed on the ball and swayed out of the way of the projectile as it hurtled past his head.

"You animal! Murderer! You beast!" A wall of angry noise decimated the silence once again, redoubled as everyone came to terms with the knowledge that Higgins clearly had no morals, no scruples and not a single decent bone in his body. And this time the umpire did not even speak to him.

"What? Does the umpire only tell him off when he actually hits a man?" asked Anna desperately. Jim said nothing but simply shook his head as though, try as he might, he could offer no further rationale. It was clear that in all his time of watching cricket he had never witnessed anything like this. The only man who appeared unruffled, other than Higgins himself, was Matthews. Visibly still in pain, he nonetheless remained standing tall at the crease, staring straight back at the bowler. And the bowler for his part continued to advance down the pitch directly towards him until he was a couple of feet away, all the while uttering what Anna presumed to be more threats of bodily harm. But Matthews did not back down an inch, nor did he break eye contact. The two of them stood face-to-face for several of the longest seconds Anna could remember, before the umpire finally seemed to remember his job and intervened to usher Higgins back on his way again. Anna could only imagine what Higgins had promised to do to Matthews, but the gallant young batsman had not been intimidated, nor had he responded with any abuse of his own. Instead he had maintained an air of pure calm and concentration as he stared his opponent down.

Anna looked up at the pavilion and wondered where her uncle might be. Of course she could not make him out at such distance, but she was certain that he would be up there somewhere, looking on and holding court with the great and the good. She was sure he would be sharing her sense of indignation, though knowing her uncle she had her suspicions that he would also secretly be revelling in the theatre of it all.

It was difficult to believe that only three balls of this over's six had yet been bowled. Higgins walked back to his mark amidst the raging turmoil of the crowd that surrounded him on all sides, once again plainly smirking for all to see. He turned, tore back in, and this time unleashed a ball that did not even bounce at all, but merely flew straight at the upper body of the young batsman, almost horizontally to the ground! Anna gleaned from Jim's outraged utterances that this was even more against the spirit of cricket than bouncing the ball at someone's head – in his opinion it was not even cricket, and the line into pure assault had been well and truly crossed. However, this time the ball was met not with more venomous derision from the crowd but rather a roar of triumph, as the gallant young batsman had stepped forward and slightly to the left with his front foot, moved his body outside the line of the ball and glanced it downwards, sending it through a gap in the fielders waiting behind the wicket and rocketing towards the boundary rope, skilfully using the bowler's aggressive speed and power against him.

The noise of the crowd was deafening, and Anna joined them on her feet. However she was no longer shouting or even talking, for she was fully engrossed in the confrontation between the two men centre stage. Initially unnoticed by most of the crowd, Higgins had continued down the pitch towards Matthews again, gesticulating aggressively in a way which was clearly indicating to Matthews what the next ball would do to his head. However Matthews was unmoved, showing signs of neither fear nor aggression; he was the embodiment of controlled calm. He simply maintained his gaze, staring straight back into the eyes of his aggressor. This time the brute came within inches of the younger man's face, still shouting and gesturing at him in a way that made Anna briefly think he was actually about to strike him, before several of the Surrey players themselves intervened, and pushed their captain back in the direction he was bowling from.

"Not smirking now is he? Doesn't like it when he doesn't get his own way – a classic bully!" shouted Jim above the cacophony, which had finally turned from ecstasy to wrath again when the crowd had realised what was happening. Anna nodded but did not speak. The duel between these two men, one so apparently gallant and good and one so clearly malevolent, now held her entire attention. Oh how she wished she could have seen their respective essences at that moment, but she could not, for the distance between her and them was too great. Though she could not see them however, she felt sure she knew what their appearances would have revealed about their owners. From what she had seen, she imagined Matthews's to be a wonderfully pure essence, just like Timmy's – and then she started to speculate whether

Timmy might be as noble as Matthews if he found himself in a similar situation. How interesting this cricket had turned out to be, that it brought out the characters of its participants so clearly on the field of play.

Anna was more deeply impressed by the young batsman than she could possibly have expressed, and it was no longer due to anything as superficial as his looks. It was the way in which he handled himself, the way he faced down the aggressive bully and refused to bow to his underhand methods, and above all the way he had maintained his calm, composure and control in the midst of this tumult. She refocused her attention momentarily on the essences of two men in the crowd, who were sitting in front of her and to her right. They had been drinking heartily from their hipflasks since almost the time they had arrived, and were on at least their third by now. In the early stages of their consumption, their essences had appeared to become more vivid, both in terms of the blueness at their centre and in the clarity of their blemishes. However, now the brightness of the blue had diminished somewhat and it was the blemishes which seemed to be even more vivid. It had occurred to Anna earlier in the day that essences seemed to become more fragile under the influence of alcohol, with a greater propensity for good or bad thoughts and deeds than normal, and in the case of these two individuals, fired up as they were by the events on the field before them, the latter appeared the more likely outcome at that point!.

However, they did not appear to pose any particular threat to anyone other than Higgins right then, and she returned her attention to the gallant young batsman. In her mind, she contrasted his calm, controlled determination with the bedlam all about her, and indeed her own anger that she had felt only moments previously – the same anger she always felt when an injustice was being committed. Though she thought her outrage had been justified, she wondered about the effect that it might have on her own essence if it were prolonged. The young man in the middle was now teaching her the best way to deal with and channel such outrage, rather than allowing it to grow into uncontrolled aggression which would surely become self-damaging. Something in what she was seeing in the young batsman reminded her of the sudden, powerful feeling of self control that she had found on the canal bridge. She sensed that what she was witnessing on the pitch before her was something of the same kind, but executed in a much more impressive fashion on a far grander stage.

As Higgins made his way back to his bowling run-up mark in front of them for his next ball, there was no longer any sign of a smirk. His face was now a pure scowl, and Anna shivered slightly as she looked from him to the wide expanse of sky above them, which had by now been covered by a layer of ever darker and more threatening cloud. It was difficult to believe it was the same day on which she had been walking down the sunlit road outside her house – it was almost as though the weather was following the match and changing according to its mood.

Higgins had continued to roar in for ball after ball under that dark sky, and had unleashed one assault after another on his young opponent. On one occasion, Matthews had once again been deceived by the aggressive cunning of the bowler, misjudged the line of the ball as it had shot steeply back up at him from the pitch and had received a glancing blow off his jaw for his trouble. Another ball, delivered in that faltering light together with another of Higgins's loud grunts, had struck Matthews painfully on his upper left arm as he stood side-on to the onrushing bowler. However Matthews had steadfastly refused to be cowed by the onslaught, or to show any outward signs of being intimidated, and as the overs passed the injurious blows from Higgins had become interspersed with more and more scoring shots from Matthews. He had started to find the boundary rope with increasing regularity at various different points around the ground, and in spite of the battering he had been receiving he appeared actually to be gaining in confidence with every passing stroke.

Any trace of self satisfaction had left Higgins's face altogether, replaced now by a constant scowl which grew only uglier and more deadly. In fact he was starting to wear the fearsome look of a man who would not be satisfied until his opponent was carried off on a stretcher – or in a coffin. Despite Matthew's ascendency, Anna's heart had still sunk every time Higgins had run in, and the thought had flashed across her mind that the wickets, which Jim had told her were supposed to be the primary focus of both the bowler's attack and the batsman's defence, had become almost entirely irrelevant to the contest now; the target had become the batsman's body and nothing else. But Matthews had gradually continued to gain the upper hand despite his injuries, and it began to look as though he was actually going to emerge from this fearsome confrontation victorious.

Just when it appeared that Higgins would be disappointed and end this duel as the beaten man, on the penultimate ball of what Jim had predicted would be his last over of this spell, the burly aggressor managed to summon from somewhere what looked to be not only his fastest ball of the day but also possibly his deadliest of all. The venomous delivery had reared fiercely off the pitch and darted treacherously from left to right through the air in the direction of Matthews' chest again. The young batsman had adjusted his footing and manoeuvred his bat desperately into the changing path of the onrushing projectile with as straight a front arm as he could, but the ball had careered at tremendous speed into the fingers of his lower right hand as he held the bat, with a ferocity at least as great as that which had caused the previous batsman to retire hurt.

Matthews had not uttered a sound, somehow holding in the yell of pain that must surely have been bursting from within him, but he had been unable to keep the look of pain from his face as he had stumbled backwards, narrowly missing his own stumps before leaning over heavily, propped up by his bat and cradling his injured right hand. That was it, everyone had thought – surely all was finally lost and he would not be able to continue. Middlesex staff had once again run onto the pitch amidst the howling rage all around, to tend to him and escort him away to safety. However upon seeing them, Matthews had straightened up and waved them away defiantly with his uninjured left hand. Yet more debate had followed, but Matthews had refused to leave the field. As the slightly bewildered staff had turned away in the direction of the pavilion and it had become apparent that Matthews would not be leaving with them, but would instead return to his crease and resume his guard, an enormous roar of approval had swept across the entire ground and the crowd had risen as one to applaud the bravery of the young man.

Tuning her attention back to the crowd for a moment, Anna had noticed that even those spectators who had been supporting Surrey earlier were now also on their feet, applauding the batsman. The knowledge that even in a cricket crowd as fevered and as partisan as this one, a sense of justice and appreciation of courage had been able to win out and cause the opposition crowd applaud the home player, had lifted her heart somewhat. Rather than what was happening on the pitch, it was this behaviour of the spectators which had resonated with what Jim had told her about the spirit of cricket, and she had thought it a credit to the supporters of Surrey. Nobility of the human spirit had triumphed over the particular circumstances of the match and its score.

When the scowling Higgins had delivered the final ball of that over, predictably it had been another violent ball which had bounced dangerously towards Matthews yet again. However this time it was greeted with an almighty crack, and the ball came shooting straight back over the flailing hands of the big bowler and right over the boundary rope into the crowd in front of them having bounced only once. Anna looked back from the ball to Matthews, who was now completing his dead-straight stroke, his front arm and uninjured left hand raised high in the air with his bat moving forward and upwards in a beautiful vertical arc. Not only had he managed to survive one of the most aggressive bowling spells ever seen at the venerable cricket ground, he had somehow come out of it on top!

"What a shot! What a stroke!" Anna was just able to hear Jim yelling from beside her. Every member of the crowd, regardless of the team they supported, were now on their feet again, cheering and applauding in wonder at what they had seen. "I can't believe it," Jim stammered, "to produce a shot like that against bowling like this in these conditions, and after the pounding he's taken and the damage he's clearly suffered to his right hand – Anna I swear I have never seen anything like it! Bravo! You're a hero Matthews!" By now he had raised his voice to a yell, but there was no chance that Matthews could ever have heard him, such was the deafening sound now echoing all around them on every side.

Anna looked back from Jim towards the field of play, and this time saw several of the Surrey players themselves applauding. It was clear that both the supporters and players of Surrey understood the right way to behave on a cricket field, and they understood that what they had been witnessing that day directly contradicted it. And for the first time since he had taken centre stage, Higgins had suddenly started to take on the look of a beaten man, as though the mighty crack of that last shot had been a fatal shot to his own heart. He had thrown his worst into his underhand play, only to learn right at the last that it had not been enough. He picked up his large cap from the umpire and looked at his team for some kind of support and encouragement, but none had come. On the contrary, even those players who had not actually been applauding the batsman had still moved away from him as he approached. Finally he turned to take his place in the middle of the outfield on the left hand side, the standing ovation for the young batsman continuing unabated all around him, and he suddenly cut a forlorn and downcast figure.

Higgins had indeed taken himself out of the bowling after that over, and although he was to return later for three more overs, he was never again able to generate the same pace, line or aggression that he had achieved in that first session. Despite his various injuries, and several more short, high-bouncing balls delivered in his direction, Matthews had continued to gain in strength and had hit the burly bully all over the ground with strokes of ever increasing elegance and timing, of which even Anna could begin to appreciate for the artistry. Smythe had also started to inflict similar damage from the other end, wreaking his revenge for the harm that had been done to him in their last encounter at Lord's, and to his team at that other place they called 'The Oval'. Having had his bowling hammered to all corners of the ground, the brutish bowler had finally withdrawn himself from the attack entirely, a broken man. He did not return again, and both Matthews and Smythe took on the other Surrey bowlers with similar relish.

As euphoria and jubilation replaced fury and indignation, Anna observed yet another subtle change in the appearance of the essences of those around her. Where the natural blemishes in the essences of many had become slightly but still noticeably more distinct as they had reacted angrily to Higgins doing his worst, there was now another subtle change. The blueness that was already there had become more vivid again in many, especially at their cores, and their blemishes and irregularities, although still visible, had become a little duller. There was something in the turn of events on the field of play that had finally come to uplift these people, possibly even to inspire some of them, and this seemed to have been reflected positively in the condition of their essences. Whether or not this would prove to be a temporary or permanent change for them Anna could not tell. She suspected it would be the former in many cases, but still she felt sure that the change could become more permanent for anyone who had been inspired to change their behaviour for the better by the shining example of gallantry that they had witnessed at this famous old ground.

Both Matthews and Smythe went on to make fine hundreds that day in a victory that would be spoken about at the home of cricket for many a long year, and the tearful five minute standing ovation which greeted Matthews's century, during which the Surrey bowler ignored the instructions of his captain and indeed the umpire and waited until the applause was finished before continuing, became the subject of folklore. It transpired later that Matthews had suffered a broken finger in his right hand and severe bruising to his ribs, with one or two suspected to have been cracked, in those early exchanges with Higgins, and many of those who were there would maintain to their dying days that it was the bravest innings they had ever seen.

The Long Room

When the day's play was finally over and the jubilant crowd had begun to disperse, Jim's attention returned to his mission for the day, which was to get Anna safely to her uncle. Jim led Emily and Anna gently against the tide of people who were moving mostly in the opposite direction, and headed towards the pavilion. The entrances facing the pitch were strictly for players and members Anna was informed, and they would need to approach the edifice from the back if they wanted to inquire further.

Upon rounding the building, Jim paused, looked a little sheepishly at Emily and said, "Darling, the pavilion is for members only, and also members are only men, so I don't think you'll be allowed in. I'm so sorry, my dear."

"Don't worry Jim, I already knew that. You know I don't approve of that kind of thing, but I understand the rules and conventions, especially in places such as this, and today is not the day to fight that battle. There are more and more of us who believe that these old rules which govern society are going to change one of these days though – and I believe the time will one day come when even this place will accept women, you mark my words!" Anna noted the sudden sparkle in Emily's eyes as she spoke, and she admired her spirit.

Jim responded, "Well you know I have great sympathy for your cause darling, and I hope you're right. But I don't think even you can bring about that change in the next twenty minutes, so if you could wait outside where there are plenty of stewards to keep you safe…"

Emily laughed, "Yes, of course I will Jim, don't worry. I'll wait for you here. But you're not a member either, and as attractive and well-mannered a young person as Anna is, she doesn't exactly look like a gentleman to me either," she grinned at Anna, "so how are you going to get in?"

"To be quite honest I don't rightly know myself. I

suppose we're relying on Anna's uncle to sort all that out. It was his idea to meet Anna in here after all."

Anna gave Emily one last look, received the encouragement she sought, took a deep breath and began to follow Jim's ascent up the stone steps in front of them. They led to the door of the large building, at once both majestic and imposing, and with each step Anna grew more nervous. The appearance of those around them and the overall atmosphere told her that they were now entering a place of some importance, and from what she had heard and the looks she was receiving, she was far from sure that they were going to be welcomed. Anna disliked having attention drawn to her at the best of times, and doubly so in a place of such apparent significance as this. Whatever happened, she did not want to be the cause of trouble here.

As they approached the double doors at the top of the stairs, a formally dressed man in a top hat, long coat and brightly-coloured red and gold striped cravat prevented any further progress inside. "No ladies or girls allowed, and you are not dressed appropriately to enter yourself sir, either." There was no disguising the slight disdain in the man's voice as he leant slightly forward and continued, looking down his nose, "Are you a member sir?" The look in the man's beady eyes and the angle of his raised left eyebrow indicated that he already knew the answer to that question.

"No sir, I'm sorry, I am not a member. But this young lady's uncle is, and he asked that she be brought here to meet him."

"Oh yes?, And who might her uncle be?" asked the steward, his beady eyes narrowing and his voice steeped in suspicion.

"His name is James Lawrence," replied Jim simply. Anna was not sure if Jim had already understood the transformative effect that these words might have, but at their very mention their inquisitor's demeanour changed entirely.

"Mr Lawrence? Oh I see. Why, you should have mentioned that sooner!" was the steward's response, suddenly almost standing to attention, all suspicion vanished as though it had been a mere figment of their own imaginations. "Please wait here – I shall ask him if he's ready to see you." With that he made off briskly inside the building.

In the couple of minutes it took for him to reappear, several formally dressed men entered and left the pavilion, but much to Anna's relief none seemed to pay them much attention, perhaps not considering it could possibly be their intention to enter the hallowed sanctuary. Of course there was not a woman amongst them. For his part, Jim stood motionless, looking down to avoid the gaze of any of those who passed them. It was as though they were standing on the steps of some kind of holy temple, being passed by priests in whose presence they were not worthy, and Anna suddenly felt strangely torn in her feelings. There was something in the traditions of the place, in the fact that those traditions were adhered to at all costs and in the general reverence that the place inspired, which greatly impressed and even excited her. Despite this though, she was still doubtful. 'I'm sure it's not the fault of any of these people,' thought Anna, 'but how strange it is that we should feel so inferior when we actually know nothing about them, or whether or not their behaviour justifies such feelings. After all, this is only a cricket club!' However, against all expectations, the day's experience had shown Anna that there was a great deal more to this cricket than it being just a game. It was a field of activity through which a person's true character could be revealed, and in which people who displayed not only skill but bravery and good temperaments, could be hailed as heroes and act as an inspiration to others. If the building they were about to enter was indeed the home of those who understood and upheld the values of this intriguing sport, then it was just possible they might be slightly more deserving of blind respect than certain others in society at large who seemed to demand it just as much, but with far less justification. She decided to keep an open mind on the subject.

Anna's musings were soon brought to an end by the return of the steward at the door, whose transformation into a polite and respectful human being was now complete. Addressing Jim, he said, "The young lady may enter to meet her uncle. You may accompany her until she is safely with him." Jim and Anna both offered their grateful thanks and followed the man through the doors.

Once inside, Anna could make little out as her eyes took time to grow accustomed to the relative darkness. The first thing that struck her was the thick smell of tobacco smoke that lay heavily on the air. As they followed the steward, she gradually began to make out the room they were in more clearly. It was a long room, with paintings of cricketers, presumably famous ones from times past, filling much of the wall space, separated only by the odd tall bookcase – filled with books about cricket, Anna didn't doubt. The furniture and décor all looked rather fine and expensive, and altogether this seemed to be a far more refined place than anything which lay outside.

"Anna, I can't believe I'm actually in here," Jim whispered to her excitedly. "You know I'm a keen follower of cricket, but this place is for the real serious cricket watchers as well as the governors of the game. There's nothing these people don't know about cricket. They even decide the rules – it's like the parliament of cricket! I could learn so much from these gentlemen in here, but I know I don't belong. No-one like me ever gets to be a member at Lord's. I can't believe how lucky I am to have been able to set foot in here." Although Anna herself felt that familiar sense of injustice again in hearing his words, she noted that his own tone was one purely of awe rather than any form of resentment.

The conversations that could be heard all around them

were about the match just finished, the underhand deeds that had been witnessed, the epic struggle that had ensued and the heroic conclusion to the day. Important-looking men with grave faces in one group were discussing some very fine details of the rules of the game in the light of the day's events, whilst several other groups were busily dissecting every aspect of the day's performances. There was considerably more laughter amongst some as they shared entertaining anecdotes, but there was one thing which was common to all – a deep and profound knowledge of cricket. 'It's still only a game,' thought Anna, 'and yet clearly it's a good deal more than that. It's part of an entire way of life for these people, and to hear them talk it sounds as though they try to apply the same codes of conduct that they apply to this game to their lives in general.' Anna was still barely able to understand all this, but she vowed one thing – that she would never be quite so dismissive again about this very odd but, she had to concede, surprisingly interesting game.

As they were gradually led into the heart of the room, Anna was better able to make out the individual faces of the men they were being ushered past, and the further they progressed the more those faces began to express their surprise. Surprise and some disapproval, it had to be said. Anna searched desperately amongst the faces for that of her uncle, but without success.

When they finally reached the far side of the room, one senior gentleman with ruddy round cheeks, bulging eyes and a silver-grey waistcoat stretched so tightly across his ample belly that Anna feared the buttons might fire off in all directions, finally voiced what all the looks had been expressing. "Excuse me steward, but what do you mean by allowing a girl into the pavilion, not to mention her inappropriately dressed companion?"

There were one or two grunts of support for this line of questioning, if not for its manner. As always in such situations, Anna switched her focus to the portly man's essence, and was surprised to find it an essentially blue specimen, indicating the character of a fundamentally good man, albeit with some telltale roughness and markings near its surface which Anna took to indicate a certain arrogance, and the intransigence which his words had already suggested. On hearing the man's challenge, Jim looked down towards his feet which had started shuffling as he awaited the steward's reply, and Anna was beginning to brace herself for that scene she had been so keen to avoid when another, more familiar voice spoke up from behind them.

"Sir Cuthbert, I do beg your pardon, but this young lady is my niece and it was I that asked the steward to bring her in here to meet me. I do understand that it goes against our code for females of any kind to be allowed in here – indeed, I don't ever recall seeing one in here before – but I needed to meet with my niece on some urgent family business that could not wait. I intend to hold our meeting in one of the committee rooms at the back, so we will not disturb you. I trust that we may be permitted to make a brief exception to the rules in this case?" The speaker was a handsome man in his mid-thirties, with dark swept-back hair, clear brown eyes that shone brightly, and a smile that had won the hearts of more than its fair share of young ladies in its time, if half the stories that Anna had heard were true.

What Sir Cuthbert had made of this proposition was never to be known however, for just at that moment from the other direction, a small group of men wearing cricketers' whites were making their way through the room towards them, and generating even more attention as they did so than Jim and Anna had. They were Surrey players, and in their midst was the hulking figure of their captain, Higgins. He was carrying a large tankard of frothy liquid, some of which had already applied itself to his long, drooping moustache, somehow making him look even more like a walrus than before. The ruddiness of the big man's cheeks suggested that this was not his first such tankard of the evening either.

Though the language of the finely-dressed gentlemen who were now crowding around the players was restrained, as everything in this place was, they left no doubt as to their opinions regarding the spectacle they had seen earlier that day.

One particularly tall, stick-like man with a long, protruding nose, who was clutching a small glass of dark red-brown liquid, poked a bony finger in the direction of the burly cricketer and said, "You, sir, are nothing but a cad and a bigot. You should never again be allowed to set foot on a field of play and stain the honourable name of our great game with your barbaric behaviour." That seemed to typify the general mood, judging by the murmurs of support and 'hear hear' from all around. Higgins had been ultimately humiliated on the field, and in the process had evolved from a hated enemy to a figure of mockery in the minds of the massed ranks of Middlesex supporters. However, it was clear that the men in this hallowed pavilion had longer memories and far deeper sensibilities regarding the sanctity of the game, and the transgressions of this burly ruffian had evidently gone far beyond the point of jest and merry-making. A line of acceptability had been crossed – or rather, obliterated – and for that there could be no forgiveness.

Higgins might have been humbled in the match, and his team might have fallen to a heavy defeat, but there was something in the barbs directed at him from this cricketing establishment which seemed to make his hackles rise again. A defiant look crossed his broad face once more, and as he jutted out his chin, his long, be-frothed, walrus-like moustache drooped into even more of a frown than before.

"Get out of my way," he grunted, shoving his way past the long, thin, finger-poking man, causing the latter to lose his balance and topple clean over in the process, although Anna could not be quite sure which was the true cause of the tumble, the shove or the red-brown liquid! Higgins continued to march forward, chin first, without so much as a backward glance at the sprawling figure behind him, who was finally helped back to his feet by various outraged companions. As the protests grew more vociferous, Higgins came to a stop again and suddenly let out a huge guffaw. He had clapped eyes on Anna, who was next in his path.

"And what's all this then?" he barked with sudden glee at this opportunity presented to him. "So you allow womenfolk in your club now, do you? And not even a woman come to that, but a little girl? In this supposed 'Home of Cricket'? I knew you'd let your standards drop, but I had no idea of the depths to which you had plunged, allowing little girls to run around freely in here. Mind you, it may be no bad thing, given what a bunch of old women the rest of you all are – needed some younger females in here to even out the ages a little!" Higgins laughed heartily, clearly very pleased with his own joke, and looked round at his Surrey team mates for approval. The latter, however, to a man turned out to be much more conscious than Higgins of their surroundings and of the way one was supposed to behave in the home of cricket, and they refrained from joining in his merriment. Instead they looked as though they would rather be anywhere other than there, or more precisely, anywhere other than with Higgins, and several began to apologise to those around them for their captain's behaviour.

In the meantime, Anna's blood had started to rise again. The sight alone, close-up, of this big bully who had behaved in such an abominable way earlier that day, had already set her off, and his words, especially his dismissive reference to her being a 'little girl' in front of all these presumably important people, was the final straw. As he had been speaking, Anna had focused momentarily on his essence, and she had seen exactly what she was expecting. It was the horribly discoloured and disfigured specimen of a man whose arrogance overrode all other qualities, and whose consideration for the feelings of others had over the years become almost nonexistent. Forgetting for the time being the state of calmness she had learned from watching Matthews deal with this same bully, but trying to channel her anger in the way she had seen him do, Anna's outrage overcame her customary shyness. Before anyone else was able to respond to Higgins's abusive remarks, Anna responded to the large man in a tone which, on later reflection, was to remind her of her own mother.

"Higgins, you are nothing but a big bully and a coward. You should be thoroughly ashamed of yourself for what you did today and even more so for what you tried to do. I was told that cricket was a game played by gentlemen, but I don't believe you have a gentlemanly bone or an ounce of decency in your entire body. I'm so glad that Matthews put you in your place. He is everything you're not, Higgins, a noble hero and a true gentleman. Those are qualities that you will never possess, and he showed us all that bullies and ruffians like you will always lose in the end!" Even Anna herself wasn't quite sure where this little speech had come from, but she supposed it had been building up inside her the entire afternoon.

Higgins's face started to redden and he appeared genuinely stunned that this meek little object of his ridicule moments earlier should take it upon itself to answer him back in such a way. He began to stammer as he grappled with his shock for a response, but his predicament was compounded by the sudden, uproarious laughter and support for Anna's outburst from all around them. It seemed that in the face of a common foe as despicable as Higgins, any disapproval of Anna's gender and age was forgotten. Well, for the time being at least.

Finding his day's humiliation in danger of being completed by a mere child, a girl, here in the very heartland of his enemy, Higgins now seemed to lose all self-control. He threw his tankard to the ground, sending its frothy contents in all directions, and lunged forward threateningly towards Anna. Anna braced herself, and she felt Jim make a move from her side to protect her, but the moustachioed bully coming towards them was able to take no more than two steps before a tall, strong, elegantly-dressed figure stepped directly into his path and stopped him dead in his tracks.

"Lay one finger on her, and know that it will be the last movement you ever make," said Anna's uncle in a voice more commanding than any Anna had ever heard, as he looked directly into the bulkier man's eyes. Higgins stopped unexpectedly suddenly at this intervention. Triggered by a recent memory, her heart now beating very fast, Anna instinctively shifted her focus to the two men's essences. She could see that her uncle's pure blue essence already had a grip upon the other man's, and it appeared that through this contact he had rendered the burly ruffian immediately helpless. So her uncle did have the same power she had! All laughter and other sounds around them had now ceased as everyone trained their eyes on the confrontation, ready no doubt to intervene if needed. However, it was all over in an instant. Anna's uncle loosened his grip on his opponent's essence very slightly, and spoke in the same clear and commanding tone. "Now leave this place where you are not welcome, and never return here!"

Higgins hesitated a moment more, his expression a combination of surprise and confusion, and then he did as he was told. With a gentle, final push from Uncle James's essence on his, Higgins turned on his heel and muttering under his breath, he lumbered his way back through the parting crowd and out of the room, head down, looking only at the ground.

Applause suddenly broke out all around them, interspersed with the occasional "Bravo!" and "Well done, James!"

"And well said young lady!" added Sir Cuthbert, turning to Anna and giving her an approving wink of a bulbous eye before turning away to discuss these latest events with his companions. No-one had any more to say about Anna's female presence in their hallowed meeting place that evening, and Uncle James was able to lead her and Jim to a door at the back of the room, hindered now only by hearty handshakes, slaps on the back and congratulatory comments from all those they passed.

"All in all, Higgins has had a very bad day," remarked Anna's uncle with a large grin on passing through the door and closing it behind them, "and one I don't believe he will forget for a long time. I do hope he has learned his lesson. I do not believe he will disrespect this great game of ours again in quite such a hurry – not here at Lord's anyhow. Would that all instances of right and wrong were so easily resolved, and all men who would cause needless injury and humiliation were so easily dispatched. Alas this is not always so, as you will learn soon enough, but today has been a good day at least. Here's to justice being done and to a momentous Middlesex victory!" With that he raised the wine glass which had been handed to him on their passage through the crowd in a toast, and without letting the small detail that neither of his companions had a glass between them deter him, he drained the contents with great satisfaction. Anna suspected that this was far from being the first such glass he had drunk that day, and yet he appeared still to be well in control.

"By the way Anna, well done for standing up to Higgins out there. I don't mind admitting that you took me completely by surprise at how you dealt with him so effectively, so I can't begin to imagine what it did to Higgins. I've never seen you talk like that before – but I commend you. Made me proud to be your uncle, you did!"

"I hope I didn't offend anyone by speaking so, um, directly," responded Anna, attempting hurriedly to disguise the sudden rush of inexplicable pride which had welled up inside her at her uncle's words. "I mean, I know I'm only a girl and that I'm not even supposed to be in here. I do hope you won't get into any trouble for bringing such an unladylike niece in here!" she laughed a little nervously.

"Anna, so good of you to think of such things, but please do not concern yourself. On the contrary, I would think they might be calling you a chip off the old block, or at least I flatter myself to hope that they might. And you know, the members may have very particular ways and traditions which they protect most fiercely – and most of them are good traditions and kept for good reason, if not quite all – but most importantly they have a very acute sense of fair play. What we witnessed on the cricket field today was not a joke, it went far beyond anything that might be considered funny, and every one of the members here saw it as not only rough play, but as a personal insult to them and to the spirit of cricket. So to hear your words when you confronted that ruffian, and to hear you express so eloquently the things that everyone had felt – well I don't think they could have been more pleased with you. Even that pompous ass Sir Cuthbert seemed to have been won over. And so for what it's worth, you made me very proud. In fact, you know, I think we made a rather fine team out there, which, incidentally, bodes well for the future and the far more serious matters which lie ahead of us." And with that last remark, her uncle's face became deadly serious again.

"Anna, there will be those who will continue to urge you not to act even when you believe something to be right, and not to take chances and to stay out of trouble for your own protection." Uncle James made no mention of Anna's mother, but she was nonetheless the first person who sprang to Anna's mind. "Now they will say those things because they care about you, and because they want above all else for you to remain safe. Indeed, I have no doubt that I will find myself having to say such things on occasion, for those same reasons. That is all natural, and certainly Anna there are various reasons why you must avoid taking unnecessary chances in the near future, which will become clearer in due course. But I say to you that when confronted unavoidably with the need to right a wrong, you should continue to do exactly as you did – to face it and to act. It means more to me than I can say to see that you have that kind of spirit in you. It is exactly that spirit which we are going to need."

Anna felt slightly overwhelmed by this sudden speech and could not take it all in, so she remained silent, hoping for a change of subject to buy her some more time to think.

Turning to Jim, Uncle James said, "And I would like to thank you very much for bringing Anna here today and for making sure she was safe all day. I am very grateful to you."

Anna was completely startled by what happened next, for Jim suddenly lowered himself down onto one knee, bowed his head and said, "Master, it was my pleasure to carry out the bidding of the Order." Anna's uncle however showed not a glimmer of surprise as he gave a brief but formal nod of his head in return. And with that, Jim rose to his feet again and turned to leave the room.

"Thank you for everything, Jim," Anna called out behind him as he opened the door, still bewildered by what she had just seen.

"My pleasure, Anna, my absolute pleasure. Maybe you'll come with me to the cricket again sometime?" He smiled, bade farewell and left.

"Uncle," said Anna as soon as the door was closed, "why did Jim bow down to you? And what is 'the Order'?"

"All in good time, Anna, all in good time. Things will start to become clearer very soon. But all that must wait until we meet with Mr. Warwick. I mentioned that it has been a good day here, but word has also reached me that it has not been such a good day elsewhere. Mr. Warwick sent a message to say that following his last meeting with Faulkner the other day, there have been more encounters with Faulkner's associates. He has decided not to take any chances, and so we are to delay our visit to Mr. Warwick until ten o'clock this evening, to allow him to leave the shop as normal, lose anyone who might try to follow him, and then head back there to meet us. I would have suggested a different meeting place, but Edmund, Mr. Warwick, keeps some books there that are very valuable to us, and he does not want to leave the shop unattended for long."

Anna now found the moment to air some of the many questions which had been collecting inside her head over the last few days "Uncle, who is Mr. Faulkner, and what is the book that he wants? And when you say that Mr. Warwick has books which are valuable to us, who do you mean by 'us'? Is it to do with the Order that Jim mentioned?"

Anna's uncle did not respond at once. It seemed to Anna that he was wrestling with himself, as though he wanted to divulge a secret but, having been sworn to secrecy, knew he could not break the promise. "Anna, your questions are quick and perceptive, and they will be answered very soon. But I would ask you to wait a little while longer."

Anna did as she was told. If her uncle was not yet ready to divulge anything then she certainly could not force him, and she was also anxious not to annoy him like a child. It was a shame that they would have to wait several more hours before they could see Mr. Warwick and discuss things further, but if that was the way it was to be then she would have to be patient. At least patience was one virtue in which she was very well practiced!

There was a knock at the door, and another smartly-dressed man roughly her uncle's age appeared and asked to speak with him. "Anna, please take a seat and wait here," her uncle said. "I have had some food prepared here so please help yourself. You'll be very safe here, and I won't be long."

As her uncle disappeared on the other side of the closing door to attend to whatever business it was, Anna took a seat as suggested in a very well-upholstered leather chair. She glanced for the first time around the room, which was adorned with yet more paintings of cricketers and shelves of books – books about cricket of course. Then she saw the platter of food on the table near her, filled with bread, ham and cheeses, together with a jug of water and a glass. Anna suddenly realised how hungry she was and ate and drank heartily until she had had her fill. She had not felt remotely tired up until that moment, such had been the rush of the events through the day, but as she now finally took time to relax and reflect she was overtaken by a sudden tiredness. Moments later her head was nodding and soon, despite herself, she was curled up fast asleep in the chair.

Anna slept deeply for almost three dream-filled hours. She was still in the depths of that slumber when the sound of her uncle's voice gently woke her. At first she had no idea where she was, and then the memory of the day and her present location came slowly back to her. The room was by now a good deal darker than it had been, lit only by a solitary lamp in the far corner, and she noticed that someone had placed a cloak over her to keep her warm.

"Anna, Anna, it's time to wake up now," said her uncle in an uncharacteristically soft voice. "You have had a good long nap but it is now a quarter-to-ten and our evening's work must begin."

Anna still felt deeply disorientated at waking up in this unfamiliar place and at such an unusual hour, but she was keen not to reveal this to her uncle and rose immediately.

"Is this yours, Uncle?" she asked, holding up the cloak.

"Yes," replied her uncle taking it back from her. "I came back twenty minutes after I left the room, but you were already asleep and I didn't want you to get cold."

"Thank you," she replied simply, and she did appreciate his thoughtfulness. It was not one of the hundreds of characteristics she would ordinarily have associated with him.

Donning the cloak and fastening the sliver clasp at the front, her uncle grabbed his hat, gloves and cane and set off for the door. There was a speed and determination about his movements that told Anna he was now focused on their next mission, and she quickly gathered herself to follow.

They passed back through the long room in which the encounter with Higgins had occurred hours earlier, and the number of people there had now thinned out considerably. By now its air was so dense with cigar smoke that Anna imagined she could have cut it with a knife, and those that remained were in the depths of debate and scarcely noticed their passing. Anna's uncle bade farewell to those who caught his eye, but he did not stop as he swept over to the far corner, down the stairway and off out towards the gas-lit street where a carriage awaited them. Such was his haste, Anna almost had to run to keep up with him, but upon approaching the gates that separated Lord's from the world outside he suddenly slowed right down, held out his arm in a gesture for Anna to also slow her pace, and then covered the remaining ground to the waiting vehicle very slowly and deliberately, taking great care to look in all directions.

Seeing her uncle's sudden change in behaviour, Anna recalled his words from earlier regarding Mr. Warwick's caution, and she wondered if her uncle shared his fears. Stimulated by the night air, for the first time since waking from her nap Anna's senses began to sharpen again as she realised that there could be danger here – particularly if that man Faulkner was in any way involved. She recalled his behaviour in the shop, and the vile appearance of his essence, and whether caused by the distinctly autumnal chill now in the night air or something else, Anna felt a small shiver run through her. She was certainly glad to get safely inside the carriage without incident, and even more so that her uncle was there with her. She was sure that he would be able to deal with any danger that might come their way. She was sure about it, and yet the nagging sense of apprehension which had been prompted by the recollections of Faulkner refused to leave her entirely.

As the carriage pulled away from the famous old cricket ground under instruction from her uncle, Anna peered out of the carriage window at the night scenes of London which now started to slide past. They had not gone far when she saw the lights of a tavern on the left hand side of the street ahead, which had a number of patrons standing outside. As they passed, Anna glanced down the alleyway which led down the side of the establishment and glimpsed the familiar face of a young man who, with a companion, seemed to be trying to take two bundles of books from an older, more smartly dressed but slightly inebriated man who appeared to be resisting them. Just as the scene was slipping out of view, Anna saw the young man push the older man, who was clearly frightened, up against the wall and successfully wrestle the books off him. In an instant they were out of sight, and Anna wracked her brains before the name came to her. "Archie Knowles!" she said to herself, but in a voice that was apparently audible to her uncle, for the latter immediately turned to her and said, "Where?"

Anna was rather taken aback by her uncle's sudden response. Archie Knowles was known to Anna and her friends as he used to associate with some of the older brothers of members of the Marylebone Street Gang. He was a nasty piece of work in his early twenties who was usually up to no good, which was precisely the direction in which Anna and her friends suspected the Maryleboners themselves were heading. However she was very surprised that her uncle knew his name.

"In that alleyway that we just passed. He was taking some bundles of books from another man."

Her uncle did not reply, but looked immediately out of the window behind them to see for himself before sitting back again, apparently satisfied that Knowles had not seen them and was not following.

"How do you know Knowles?" Anna and her uncle asked each other at exactly the same moment. Her uncle smiled and let Anna respond first. "Well, I don't know him. I mean, that is to say that I have never met him or spoken to him, but I know of him. He's a rough one, and we all try to keep clear of him and his friends."

"Hmm, yes, well you're right and that's probably a good policy for the time being. He's one of a few in the area who have gone bad, and have started to get themselves unwittingly involved in matters far more dangerous than they understand. And they may just come to pay a very severe price for it."

Anna could not have been more surprised to learn of this overlap between her own little world and that of her high-flying uncle, but that overlap was not of a good kind. She already knew that Knowles was no good, but the idea that there were things far more dangerous than even he knew about worried her further.

"You say he was taking books from the other man? Very interesting. On another evening I would be tempted to return to find out what was happening, but not this evening. My priority tonight is to get you safely to Mr. Warwick's."

'There seems to be an awful lot of interest in books all of a sudden,' thought Anna, again recalling Faulkner's visit to Mr. Warwick's shop. She looked out of the window now with renewed nervousness for any more signs of danger, but saw nothing else untoward. As she sat back in the carriage, the frightened look on the face of the man from whom Knowles had been taking the books stuck in her mind. Naturally she had no idea of what had been taking place, but she could only assume that the older man had been frightened by Knowles and his accomplice. She fervently hoped he would come to no harm. Then her uncle had suggested that Knowles and his friend were also headed for some sort of big trouble themselves as a result of their actions... so who gained from all this? This seemed to Anna to be a theme she had come across time and again.

"I don't know why people don't try to treat others in a way that they would like to be treated themselves. Well, I mean within reason anyway. It seems to me that when a person does something bad to someone else, it provokes the other person to do something bad in retaliation, either immediately or else after the event, and in the end everyone seems to come to harm and become unhappy. I think life would be much better, for each and every one of us, if people made an effort to act in ways which make others happier, rather than in ways which cause fear, hurt and upset." She had said it aloud, but immediately regretted it. Hearing the words spoken made her realise how childish her thoughts probably sounded, and the last thing she wanted to do was to appear even more childish to her uncle than she likely already did.

Her uncle did not respond at first. Anna glanced up at his face, fearing some variation on the theme of ridicule in his expression, but what she found in the lamplight was something far less fathomable. Then he spoke.

"Anna, what you just said was in many ways incredibly naive." Anna's heart sank. "However, within that naivety, there may be a hidden truth more fundamental than you realise." He paused, suggesting he was now giving her simple words far more consideration than she felt they warranted.

"The problem lies not with your logic. If all people thought as you suggest, and if they were able to act in accordance with those aspirations, then your conclusion might just be right. However you have failed to take into account certain crucial characteristics of human nature, at least as it exists in the world today, which unfortunately lead people to take actions that run contrary to your utopian dream, and render it no more than that – a dream." Anna nodded meekly, hoping her acknowledgment would now bring this conversation to a close.

"But, however unwittingly, you have in fact touched on a theme of great importance here, in particular the point I made about human nature *as it is today*, as you will come to understand in due course. I say unwittingly, but perhaps it is no coincidence that you should say such a thing..." His voice trailed off before he revealed to Anna precisely what that last statement was intended to mean.

This had been a far more serious response than Anna had expected, indicating that her uncle's mood had now changed entirely from its higher spirits at Lord's. There had been more to this answer than the simple rebuke Anna had feared, but having avoided his ridicule once she decided not to pursue the topic any further for now.

It was only a relatively short ride from Lord's to Mr. Warwick's shop, and in no time the driver of the carriage reined in the horses and they drew up on the side of the road opposite the familiar old building with its weather beaten green sign. Anna peered out of the window at the shop, and she noticed how clear the night now was, lit by the silvery light of a moon which was almost full. At last the waiting was over, and she wondered with anticipation what it was that she was about to learn. During the remainder of the short carriage ride her uncle had refused to reveal anything further about the content of the meeting, except to say such things as "All will be revealed soon, young Anna." Anna wasn't sure if it was the evasive nature of the response that annoyed her more or its delivery, which had started to take on a slightly patronising tone. But if it meant that tonight she was going to learn more about essences and the many other things that she had understood too little of so far, then he could be as patronising as he liked. Well, almost.

Anna glanced outside at the bookshop which was lit faintly, both by the nearest gas street lamp and by the moon which was now riding high in the sky. However from inside the shop itself emanated nothing but inky blackness.

Before Anna could alight from the coach her uncle told her to sit back where she could not be seen, then with a sweep of his cloak he left the carriage. From the window, although she was sat back deep inside the carriage as instructed, she could see her uncle whisper some orders to the driver, take a lantern from him, look both ways, then walk once around the entire carriage and horses, looking intently all around him, especially in the direction of the neighbouring canal. Clearly he was ensuring that all was safe, and no doubt that neither Faulkner nor any of his henchmen were lurking in the darkness.

The idea that anyone associated with Faulkner could really be lying in wait to attack them pushed Anna's nerves back onto their edges again, but at the same time the presence of her uncle reassured her immensely, and the fear was mixed strangely with a slight thrill of excitement. Her uncle, who by now seemed to have fully overcome the effects of the wine he had been drinking earlier, was such a confident and dominating character that she found it hard to imagine anyone taking him by surprise and getting the better of him. However she did hope he would not do or say anything too rash which might upset the kindly old bookseller.

When her uncle had finally reassured himself that no-one was lying in wait, he opened the door and beckoned for Anna to follow him quickly. She needed no second bidding and clambered out of the coach in pursuit of her uncle, who was already striding across the road with his metal-tipped cane raised at the ready, looking up and down the street. The large moon above them illuminated the top-hatted figure of her uncle and the street around him with a silver sheen that lent the street scene a distinct eeriness.

Anna followed his glances as best she could whilst struggling to keep up with him. Maybe it was the hour or her state of mind, but this street that she knew so well looked suddenly more ghostly and mysterious than she had ever known it. The gas lamps cast long, twisted shadows on the road and buildings, and the bright moon radiated its haunting glow over the whole scene, while the breeze stirred the branches of the tall trees which lined the canal. Other than the coach driver behind them though, no other human movement could be seen or heard. The street appeared to be deserted.

After several long seconds, they reached the bookshop door and Anna's uncle rapped lightly on it with his cane. They then waited in silence for a few moments, listening for any signs of life within the darkened shop, whilst continuing to look up and down the street. Anna felt herself grow even tenser, which had not seemed possible, the existing levels having already felt close to snapping point. What if Faulkner and his gang, rather than waiting for them outside, had already somehow managed to get inside the shop and were now waiting for them somewhere in the darkness? It certainly seemed to her strange that there was no light whatever coming from the shop window when Mr. Warwick was supposed to be inside waiting for them.

Anna felt an inexplicable fear rising inside her now. Despite her bravery when confronting the likes of the Marylebone Street Gang, in reality they were all people that she could understand, and whom she now had the confidence to deal with. However when it came to Faulkner, there was much more that she did not understand, and what she did understand all seemed likely to be very bad. She was well aware that what she was potentially facing here was in a very different league, the world of adults, and some pretty dangerous ones at that. She looked behind her again but could see nothing but the carriage and horses with the driver sat aloft, who himself was looking up and down the street.

She was on the point of voicing her concerns about what might lie inside the shop to her uncle when a faint glimmer of light suddenly appeared in the window. The door at the back of the shop had opened letting in light from the room beyond, and moving to peer through the dusty window Anna could make out what looked like a slightly stooped figure, making his way towards them from the back of the shop. After what seemed like an eternity, the sound of a bolt on the door being slid back was followed by that of a latch being unlocked, and then the door opened a crack. Anna took a deep breath and braced herself for whatever might happen next.

"It is us," whispered Anna's uncle, and with that the door was opened further until Mr. Warwick's familiar features could be recognised, to Anna's immense relief. Anna's uncle gave a signal to his driver, who returned a gesture in acknowledgment, and without any further hesitation her uncle reached out to usher Anna into the shop.

At first Anna could make out almost nothing in the darkness until gradually, vague shapes started to reveal themselves as her eyes became accustomed to the dim light of Mr. Warwick's lantern. Remembering her previous fear about what might be waiting for them inside, her eyes darted all around the dark outlines of shelves and boxes in the cluttered shop. She could not see any signs that someone might be lurking there, but then again it was impossible to tell, the place was in such a state of disorganisation. Anna made a mental note to ask Mr. Warwick one day just why he did not make more effort to tidy the place – not that she herself minded the dust and mess particularly, but because that way he might at least slightly increase his chances of selling something (which she could not recall ever having actually seen him do!). However, neither the time nor the frayed state of her nerves was appropriate for that particular conversation right then. Instead she simply shadowed the old man, looking around her all the time as she followed his lantern towards the back of the shop.

After one of the more unsettling walks of her life, Anna and her companions finally reached the back of the shop floor, and Anna followed the old shop keeper into that same room which she had visited a few days earlier following her dip in the canal. Having taken the upholstered leather chair offered to her, facing the fire and slightly to its right, she cast her eyes around the room and was struck again by how much the atmosphere in there differed from that of the main shop. Everything from the polished wood that shone in the light of the lantern and the luxurious leather upholstery of the chairs to the orderly, and above all *clean*, condition of the extensive book collection, spoke of a different level of attention, and indeed a different state of mind, than did the shop at the front. Anna started to wonder how the two could be owned by the same person, and what it might mean about that person.

Then something else happened, something which left her truly stunned and speechless. Her uncle had by now turned around to face the old man, who suddenly seemed to be standing up much taller and straighter than he had but moments before, and who now had that same air of a younger man that Anna had briefly sensed during her last visit, although this time it was much more evident. Then her uncle, usually so confident and superior, went down on one knee before him, just as Jim had bowed to her uncle earlier that same evening. He lowered his head and spoke the words "Master, your servant is here."

"Thank you. Arise," was the shopkeeper's simple reply, accompanied by a solemn nod of the head. With that, Anna's uncle rose to his feet again before removing his gloves and cloak and moving to another large, heavily upholstered chair to Anna's right, by the now roaring fire. From the way he flung himself casually into it, Anna would never have guessed he had been down on his knees mere moments earlier. She could not have been more surprised by this turn of events than if Faulkner himself had walked straight out of the roaring fire dressed as a circus clown and had performed them all a little dance. Had what she seen really happened? Had her dashing, indomitable uncle really bowed down at the feet of the portly old shopkeeper and called him "Master"? Although now that she came to look again, it was indeed the kindly old bookseller who had the greater air of quiet confidence about him, and who actually now appeared the more powerful of the two!

It was not that her uncle had changed his bearing in any

way (at least, now that he was back up off his knees!). As he sat in the chair waiting for the discussion to begin, his bright eyes dancing in the flickering light of the fire, he still looked every inch the bold adventurer he had always appeared to Anna. Rather it was the kindly old shopkeeper, who had appeared slightly frail and unsteady just moments earlier, who now looked nothing of the sort. Whilst his face looked essentially the same apart from his eyes, in which the youthful look had returned, his posture was no longer stooped and he was suddenly possessed of a certain gravitas that had been absent before. His presence was altogether more magisterial and, well, masterful now. Anna had begun to perceive that there was more to Mr. Warwick than met the eye since she had witnessed his encounter with Faulkner and had noted the contrasting appearance of the back of the shop to that of the front, but she had not expected this. She had hoped that the evening would bring new discoveries and interesting surprises, but she had not expected them so soon, and certainly not before conversations had even begun!

Re-focussing her attention momentarily, it was then that Anna saw the most surprising transformation of all. Whilst Mr. Warwick's essence remained pure blue, smooth and unspoilt in its surface texture and perfectly spherical in shape, it was now significantly larger – in fact it was almost twice the size it had been! It was considerably larger even that her uncle's essence, which itself had always been of significant size. Anna looked in amazement as she realised she was now looking at the largest essence she had ever seen, bar the single exception of Faulkner's, but his had been so entirely different in every respect that the two did not bear comparison. What surprised her most was not how it now appeared but that it had changed so dramatically from the form she had so recently seen. This was something she had never come across before, and she had had no idea that it was possible for a person's essence to alter so drastically in such a short space of time. She wondered what could have happened to him in the last few days to bring about such a change. Her deep sense of wonder at this old man, whom she had thought she had known so well for years but who now seemed to have qualities and depths she had never imagined, was growing by the moment.

A volcano of questions began to erupt in her mind, but before she could put a voice to any of them the old man began to speak.

The Decision

"Anna, I expect you are wondering why we have asked you to come here to talk to us, why we are being so careful, and what we are going to tell you," began the old man.

"Well, um, yes," replied Anna simply, scarcely doing true justice to her curiosity.

"I imagine there will be some things you have already guessed, and others you have long wondered about. However, some of the things I am going to explain will probably be completely new to you, and may seem difficult to believe. But everything I am going to tell you this evening will be the truth, at least to the best of my understanding, and I hope you can listen with an open mind.

"In addition to myself, your uncle will play an important role in your instruction, should you choose to proceed with it, and as representative of your family he will also be your protector. I am sure he already has your trust, and I hope that in time I will come to earn it too.

"So, let us begin. As we sit here today there is a major struggle fast approaching in which we are all going to be involved, whether we wish to be or not." Mr. Warwick momentarily looked Anna directly in the eye with that piercing look she knew him capable of by now, and which told her that there would be little choice in this. "In fact," the old man continued, "you could more accurately call it a war, and unfortunately it is a war that has the potential to affect the entire world.

"It is unusual for these discussions to begin with one so young as you, since the gravity of what you will learn is ordinarily too much of a burden for a child to carry, and with the knowledge that we are going to pass on to you comes immense responsibilities. Additionally, most people cannot use this knowledge until they reach adulthood. Your uncle, for example, was twenty years old when I began his instruction, and any younger than that is unusual. However, we have reason to believe that you specifically may have a part to play in the approaching struggle despite your young age, and although it would have been better were you older, the time is now upon us whether we like it or not and we must prepare you now for the events that are to come."

Then Anna's uncle spoke for the first time. "Anna, as Mr. Warwick has said, many things that you will hear tonight will seem strange, even frightening to you. Certainly they sounded strange to me. But I have subsequently found everything that I was taught by Mr. Warwick and my other Masters to be true and consistent with my experiences of the world since then. So I would ask that you trust Mr. Warwick completely, listen carefully to what he says, understand as much as you can and be as honest as possible in your responses."

Turning from her uncle to the old man, Anna replied, "Mr. Warwick I do trust you. I trust you because... I can see it." Although she hesitated slightly in saying this, she believed he would understand what she meant.

"Thank you Anna, and yes, actually that is exactly where I would like to start, with that ability you possess which sets you apart from most other people – your ability to see essences.

"As you know already, essence is the word we use to describe a manifestation of a person's fundamental qualities. Their personality, their nature, their predispositions – the essence of who they are.

"As you are aware, most people cannot see essences, and even those who can usually only develop the ability as they reach adulthood or later. Whether this faculty is present in all people but lies dormant in most of them, has been the subject of great debate for many centuries. My own view is that everyone does have this 'sixth sense', but that in most people it is never discovered. In your case Anna, I know that you have been able to see something of other people's essences from a very young age, and unless I am mistaken I believe that you can now see them very clearly indeed."

As Anna listened to Mr. Warwick, she became aware that the palms of her clenched hands had begun to perspire. She was finally about to put aside the years of caution and discomfort in discussing this subject which had caused her so much grief in the past, and she was sure that at last she was going to learn the answers to some of the questions which had long filled her head. But before she responded, she remembered the promise she had made to her mother several years before.

"Uncle," Anna turned to him, "my mother told me never to discuss auras – sorry, I mean essences – with anyone unless she gave me permission. Is it right for me to talk about them now?"

"Anna it is good that you ask, but yes that time has come," he replied. "We have spoken to your mother and there is no need to worry. She understands that the subject of the essence is central to many aspects of the teaching, and she has fully consented to us discussing these things with you."

"In that case, yes Mr. Warwick," she continued, turning back to face him, "yes, I can see essences. I have been able to for as long as I can remember. What I can see appears as a coloured image which gives me an impression of what the person is like, whether they are generally good, kind, strong-willed, weak, modest, arrogant..." At this word she tried, just too late, to stop herself glancing momentarily at her uncle, for a slight strain of arrogance was one of the flaws that she had made out in his essence. She only caught his eye for an instant before looking away again slightly embarrassed, but unfortunately it had been enough for him to notice! However, to her surprise he too looked embarrassed, and not a little uncomfortable. And it was not only her uncle who had noticed the look either. When she looked up at Mr. Warwick, she saw a knowing and amused expression on his face.

"You're not going to be able to hide much from this one James!" he jibed in a suddenly jovial tone, which could not have been in greater contrast to the mood up until then.

"Very amusing," her uncle replied, at first looking anything but amused, before allowing himself a rueful smile.

Anna could see this had not been a serious exchange, but nonetheless decided it best to move on quickly. Looking back up from the floor to which her gaze had momentarily fallen, she continued, "I have always been able to see, uh, essences, but if anything, in the last few years the impressions have become stronger, and I can see them more clearly now than ever."

"Can you tell me exactly what you see when you look at someone's essence?" asked the old man. His tone was still light and friendly, but Anna could sense that he was now very alert and completely focused on what she had to say.

"Well, it looks a bit like a transparent ball, usually floating roughly in the space between the top of a person's head and the middle of their chest. I don't see it in the same way that I can see a face or a body, and if I don't focus on it I won't see it at all. But if I choose to look at it, it's a little like refocusing my eyes on something in the distance, or turning my attention to a particular voice in a crowd or a single instrument in an orchestra – and then I can see it clearly."

"And what does the ball itself look like to you?" he asked in the same light tone, but with burning eyes that revealed his intense focus now.

"They can be different colours, usually somewhere between a really clear sky-blue, such as yours today Mr. Warwick..." she paused, in case he wanted to ask anything more about that, but there was no discernable change in his expression and he merely nodded for her to continue, "... to darker colours, and often a mixture of colours. The closer to sky-blue it is, the purer the intentions of that person tend to be. Darker coloured essences lacking blue, and in particular those containing any red, usually belong to less pleasant people, people who tend to be unkind, cruel, dishonest. You know it's funny, but I don't think I have ever met anyone I liked whose essence contained the colour red."

"Anna, there is nothing funny about what you have just said. Indeed, it may be of greater importance than you realise," said Mr. Warwick. "But please continue. What else can you see?"

"Well, then there is the surface texture of the ball. In some cases, those I think of as the best, it is completely smooth. In most cases the surface has at least some parts to it which are not smooth. Sometimes there is a rippled effect on part or all of it." She resisted the urge to look at her uncle this time, knowing this would have given away that she could see something of that effect in his essence. "In much worse cases they have cracks and crevices; people with essences like that are usually the type who do harm to others in one way or another." She had never tried to explain these things to anyone else before, and she was finding the words surprisingly difficult to come by.

Mr. Warwick remained silent for a moment, his eyes sparkling in the firelight as he exchanged glances with her uncle. Anna was now desperate to ask a question of her own, and she put it hesitantly into words. "Are there many other people who are able to see essences in the same way that I can? I know you can see them Mr. Warwick, and I think you can too uncle after what I saw at Lord's earlier, but when I've mentioned them to other people in the past, they have treated me as though I were mad or have some sort of problem."

"We understand Anna, and you have certainly never been mad or merely imagining these things… but for the time being I would ask you to speak of them only to me or your uncle. It is unfortunate that we did not give you this advice sooner – so much trouble could have been avoided had we done so – but I will return to that shortly. The reason for caution in revealing your abilities is that it is in the nature of too many people to find fault with, and to make trouble for, others who are different from themselves, especially if there are things about them that they do not understand. I would go so far as to say that it is one of the major flaws in the nature of people in the world today. It is not how things should be, and hopefully they will not always be this way, but unfortunately such things are still all too common at the present time. Moreover, we are now entering a very dangerous period, and we have more than people's common ignorance to worry about. We have an altogether more dangerous enemy to fight. So for now, the fewer the people who know about what you can see, the better.

"But in answer to your question Anna, yes, your uncle and I can see essences, although neither I nor your uncle can see them with the same clarity it would appear you can. I can sense the overall colour of a person's essence, and I can distinguish between the different colours it might contain, provided they are clearly demarcated. However I cannot see those colours in detail. Similarly, I can make out the overall shape of the essence, and can see if there are any fundamental markings on its surface, but I cannot make out the more minute detail of the surface that you described. I cannot, for example, see small cracks or ripples, only significant ones. And yet I believe I am able to see a person's essence with greater clarity than almost anyone, including your uncle. Would that be fair James?"

"Alas yes, that is correct," replied Anna's uncle. "Although with my Master's help I have been able to increase my ability to view essences, I have never been able to attain to his level. I can see a rough impression, enough to give me the basic insights into a person's general character, and I can also see the overall shape sufficiently to engage with it effectively and to gain holds quickly during mental combat, which is an essential skill you will need to learn. All very useful, but nothing close to what you are describing.

Anna, I marvel at what you have told us, even if some of your insights do not make for pleasant listening! Another time, when my Master is not around, I will have words with you about your impertinence." He then laughed, much to Anna's great relief.

Smiling, Mr. Warwick continued, "And there are others too who also have the ability to see essences, together with other associated powers, and we belong to a group which has existed for thousands of years, and which in English is called The Order of the Knights of the True Path. The greeting your uncle gave me earlier is one of its little traditions. You will come to learn a lot more about this group in the future. However, no-one that I know of today can see essences with the extreme clarity that you have just described. In former times there have been tales of a very small number of people through history who, we are told, could see essences in great detail, amongst them some great people, but they have been very few and far between across the centuries. You will learn much about the great Knights of our Order who have preceded us through history, and the battles that they fought for our cause in their own times – that will form part of your instruction. Before then though, the one thing I must ask of you is that you never mention anything about the Order to anyone unless we give you permission to do so. Is that clear, Anna?"

"Yes Mr Warwick, I will never mention it," she replied earnestly.

"Very good. Returning to your question then, what is unprecedented to my knowledge is the age from which you have been able to see essences. This ability usually develops only on reaching adulthood, which makes your case all the more intriguing, indeed exciting, for the development of your own powers may yet be far from complete. Even in the cases of the very youngest students I know of from the Histories of the Struggle, even they only first became able to see essences at around the age you are now. This is why we had no idea you would reveal such an ability to the world at the age you did. Had we known, I promise you we would have managed things very differently, and you would never have had that terrible experience when you were ten years old. Of course you were not to know that others could not see essences as you could see them. It would have been most natural to believe that they could, as no-one had explained otherwise."

"Mr. Warwick," Anna suddenly interjected, a nerve unwittingly having been touched, "I'm sorry, but would you mind if I asked another question?"

"Of course not Anna, please go ahead."

"My mother has known about my ability to see essences for a very long time because I talked to her about it when I was very young, perhaps four or five. But she didn't really explain anything to me, she just told me that this was something people never spoke of, and that I should not either. If she had explained that most people could not see essences, I might have acted differently at the time she fell ill a few years ago. Do you know why she didn't tell me?"

"Anna I can understand your question, and I can imagine how emotional this subject must be for you. But I can tell you that your mother has only ever acted out of the deepest love for you, and that she has only ever tried to protect you. The reality is that the Powers that we are speaking about have brought her much suffering in one way or another, even though she herself does not possess them. What she wanted above all was that you avoided unnecessary suffering, ridicule, harm and worry. Whether or not things might have been better dealt with another way is not for me to say. She did what she felt was best for you, and that was her decision to make and hers alone.

"When your mother fell ill it was perfectly justified and right for you to speak to the doctor, given what you knew and did not know at that time. Even though we did not know that your powers were already well developed, we knew enough of your potential to have protected you better against the dangers of the likes of that Thrall Evin…" Seeing Anna's enquiring look, Mr Warwick quickly added, "Ah, my apologies Anna. Thralls are a particular group in the enemy's ranks, or perhaps more accurately they are a weapon that the enemy has turned to use against us. You will learn more about such things when we come to talk about the nature of the Enemy in your instruction.

"But there is something else I would like to say on this subject before moving on." Mr. Warwick's expression became grave as he continued. "The truth is that I only found out about your incarceration in that awful asylum more than a week after it had occurred, and although I was able to intervene swiftly enough to prevent Evin from executing his full, despicable plan, and crucially, before he made your presence known to… well, others whom we did not wish to know of your existence, it still took me far longer than was desirable to free you from that terrible place. For that I can only beg your forgiveness." He bowed his head and upper body in a gesture of remorse.

"Mr. Warwick I do understand and it was not your fault," replied Anna, beginning to comprehend just how many of the puzzling things in her life might now be explained during this discussion. So Mr. Warwick had helped to save her from the asylum! But what had he meant by "others whom we did not wish to know of your existence?" From all his words and tone, it was as though he had been taking on some kind of guardianship over her. As far as she was concerned, she was just immensely grateful that someone had intervened in time to get her out – before her sanity had left there without her, never to return.

Seeing the contrition still on Mr. Warwick's face as he straightened up, Anna responded, "Mr. Warwick the asylum was a truly terrible place, one that I am certain actually causes madness rather than cures it, and I am grateful for whatever you did to help get me away from there. I owe you my life, so it is I who should be giving you my eternal thanks, not you giving me your apologies!"

From the corner of her eye she thought she caught an approving nod from her uncle before the old man replied, "Thank you, Anna. Your kind words mean a great deal to me. It does not lessen my own feeling of guilt, but it means a considerable amount to me to know how well you have dealt with that terrible episode."

Mr. Warwick paused, deep in thought for a moment. Anna wondered if she should say more at that point to reassure him that she was indeed fully recovered from her experience of the asylum, whether or not that was actually true, but a single gesture from her uncle advised her that it was not necessary. Instead she joined the brief silence, waiting for what was next.

"Now," continued the old man presently, "time is drawing on and we must talk of more pressing matters." Anna sat back in her chair, sure she was to learn more about Faulkner. However, once again she was to be stunned by what Mr. Warwick said next.

"Tell me Anna, one night about eight years ago, can you remember if you had a particular dream, a dream that was different from other dreams, one which stayed with you vividly even after you had woken? In case it helps you to remember, the night I am referring to was the night of that terrible storm which wrought so much damage in the south of the country. It even blew the old tree outside this shop clean over into the middle of the road."

Anna knew instantly both the night and the dream to which Mr. Warwick was referring – she needed no help to recall that particular memory. That dream had felt so real and so true that it almost did not feel like it had been a dream at all, and she could still remember it as though it had been the night before.

"Mr. Warwick, how did you know about that? Have you had a similar dream? Though if you had, I doubt you would have asked me if I could remember it, for that was something I will never forget as long as I live, much as I wish I could."

"Yes Anna, a number of us in the Order also had a dream, almost certainly on the same night. But what the others and I saw was not altogether clear, and although more vivid than other dreams it was still somewhat difficult to recall in detail. We all understood that the dream had been significant and that something had occurred, something had changed in our world, and we had an idea what it must mean, but it was difficult to interpret it exactly.

"I sense that you were able to see rather more than we did Anna. I understand that it may be unpleasant to recall that night, but do you think you could tell us what you saw? This could be extremely important in preparation for the struggles that lie ahead."

Anna took a deep breath. This was something she had not been prepared for, and recalling that nightmare began to bring her out in a cold sweat. "Mr. Warwick, you are lucky if you didn't see what I saw. Or rather, if you didn't feel what I felt – the way I felt. My mother said that I cried nearly the whole of the next day, and that is not at all like me. To be honest, the feelings of that dream haven't completely left me even now. It was the most terrible dream I have ever had, except it did not feel like a dream. It felt absolutely real, as though what I saw was really there. And the worst part was not the seeing, but being seen."

She stopped with a shudder, and noticed a look of momentary surprise and concern cross the kindly old man's face. He recovered instantly though, and recognising Anna's distress he said, "Please Anna, take your time. I really would not ask you if it were not so desperately important. Please try to go on if you can, but take as much time as you need."

Anna took a deep breath then continued, "Well there was a terrible storm in my dream too, with dreadful thunder and constant lightning. The wind was wild and the rain was much harder than I have ever seen before. And in the lightning flashes, what I could see was a big hill, and on top of the hill was what looked like a huge, rectangular stone. Then the stone was struck by a savage bolt of lightning, followed by a strange, horizontal sheet of lightning, which actually didn't look like lightening at all. It looked more like a huge tear in the sky.

"Then suddenly I was much closer to the hill, and around the base of the stone I could see a number of dark figures. I couldn't make them out clearly, but there were five of them – four roughly the same height, but one much taller than the others. I couldn't distinguish any more about them so I have no idea why, but from that moment I became filled with panic, awful, uncontrollable panic. It felt as though there was enormous danger there, and that I was very much in danger myself."

Anna stopped to gather breath. Tears had begun to run down her cheeks as she recalled what she had seen with unwanted sharpness. Forcing herself to remember all she could was bringing those feelings back again, and she found herself wanting to burst into floods of tears. But rather than suffer the embarrassment of crying in front of her uncle and his Master, she fought hard to regain control. At the same time, her uncle put his arm around her with a concern and genuine affection that she had never seen from him before, and knowing that he was there and ready to protect her helped more than she would have imagined. A degree of composure returned.

She looked at Mr. Warwick who was leaning forward in his chair, motionless. He had been absorbing every word as though it were the last he would ever hear, and now he appeared to be examining those words, searching for a great secret they contained. Finally he spoke again. "Anna, you are being most brave. I would like you to continue if at all possible, but please only do so when you feel completely ready," he said softly.

Encouraged by their understanding, and by the hope that

they might be able to help interpret what she had seen and somehow reduce the terror that it had always induced in her, she steeled herself to relate the final, most terrible part of her dream.

"The last thing I remember is seeing the face of one of the figures. And I know that it was the face of the tallest figure of the five. Although I have no idea how, I know that's who it was as surely as I know my own face in the mirror.

And all I really saw were his eyes. They were utterly unlike any I have ever seen, and how I hope I never see anything like them again. The whites of his eyes were not white at all – they were blood red. Inside that, where we have colour, it was completely black, like darkness itself. Then right in the middle where we have black, I could see a faint, dark red glow. They were horrible, but in the end it wasn't how the eyes looked that scared me the most. It was that it was not just me looking at him. He was looking at me too. I mean directly into me, inside me, into my very heart – seeing and understanding everything, everything there is to know about me. I suppose he was looking at my essence, but seeing it in extreme detail – in much more detail than I have ever been able to see one.

"But the thing was..." and at this point she could no longer hold back and began to sob uncontrollably, in spite of her uncle's comforting, "...he was evil. I mean really evil. I don't know how I know, because I couldn't see his essence and I can't explain it myself, but in this man was evil beyond anything I could imagine. It is terrifying enough to know that such a man even exists, but it's worse still to know that he knows everything about you. And he could see everything in me, I know it. I could feel it..." The flow of tears had now turned into a torrent. Mr. Warwick broke from his almost trance-like state of focus and joined her uncle at her side to console her. "Don't ask me how I know it, for I don't know myself," Anna forced out the words through her tears, "but in this man was the purest evil I have ever seen or felt, and I can still feel it even now, all these years later."

With that Anna broke down into uncontrollable floods of tears, the like of which she had not cried since the night of the dream, even in the toughest of times she had known since then. It took her two companions some considerable time to bring her back to something like her old self again, but finally her embarrassment caught up with her again. She hated the idea of crying like a small child in front of these two men, whatever the justification, and it was this thought that finally enabled her to regain control.

"I am so sorry, I normally never cry... I'm well known for not crying. It's, it's just...," she sobbed again, "it's just that dream. It was so horrible, and it still is to me. And the most terrible thing is, I know it wasn't a dream. I know that he is out there somewhere. And something tells me that one day, whatever I do, I am going to meet him."

Uncle James put his arms around her again and told her that she did not need to say any more, and how proud he was of her courage. There was a long silence broken only by Anna's subsiding sobs before Mr. Warwick spoke again, slowly and with immense gravity.

"Anna, do not feel embarrassed by your tears. I think I know better than you might imagine how terrifying an experience that dream must have been, and how difficult it was to re-live it. Most adults would not have been able to face such a thing without great distress, let alone a six year old girl. It is remarkable that you were able to withstand it as you did. The more I learn about you, the more I find to wonder at. There is no shame in crying at that memory, and indeed it would have been most unnatural not to have done so. You will come to understand better what I mean by that in a moment.

"But first I will address some of the specific points that you described. You may not like everything I am about to tell you, but in the long-run I believe it will help you to start to come to terms with what you have seen, and to prepare you for the future.

"You are right in what you said. This was not a dream, and what you saw in your mind's eye was real and was happening as you saw it. I also believe you may be right that one day you will meet the one you saw. It may be that ultimately this encounter cannot be avoided. However, please take heart, for we will do whatever we can to delay that meeting as long as possible, and we will do everything in our power to ready you for the encounter should it indeed turn out to be unavoidable."

Anna gathered from this that understanding these things would be to her advantage in the end. But having her instincts confirmed, and by someone who would ordinarily never want to scare her, in many ways made things worse. 'I might as well seek out that man now and get things over and done with,' she thought, although the shudder that went right through her core at this idea told her clearly that she did not mean it!

"Anna," the old man spoke again after another pause, "thank you for telling us what you saw, and for not holding back. You have shown enormous courage and determination in sharing it with us, and I am very grateful to you for it. Your dream is of immense significance, and in fact offers us deeper insights than I had dared to hope for. However, the content of what you saw also presents us with some profoundly worrying revelations. Indeed I would go further and say that they are deeply shocking. I cannot be sure I have interpreted your vision absolutely correctly, but this evening I will share my insights with you if you would like to hear them. It is the least I can do after what we have put you through. Having seen the character and courage you have shown tonight I mean to treat you more as an adult and less as a child, and I will trust you with more information. I see now that we could have approached you even earlier for your instruction, but I hope you will understand that we wanted to preserve your childhood and spare you the burden of this knowledge until you were older.

"Anna, some of things I am going to share are of huge importance, to the very world as we know it. If we are to proceed, I will need you to promise me, with the deepest and most sincere promise a person can make, that you will never discuss any of these subjects with anyone other than myself, your uncle and anyone we specifically tell you can be trusted. Now I do not mean to force you to embark on this journey, that is your choice to make freely, and you may take as much time as you need to think about it. But if you do decide to pursue your instruction then you must always keep the promise I am asking you to make. If you do not, the consequences will be very serious – indeed they could be fatal for us all.

Uncle James, who had by now returned to his seat and resumed his staring into the fire as he had done for much of the evening, now spoke again.

"Anna you are under no obligation to us, and no-one on our side is going to take away your free will. That is one of the things that distinguishes us from our enemies. The conversations that we have begun this evening are setting you on a course which may lead you to incredible adventures and experiences, and open you up to some of the deepest secrets of this world. However, in all likelihood it may also lead you into some of the gravest dangers imaginable. From what I can understand though, I believe it more than likely that those dangers are going to find you whether you choose to accept it or not. So the choice you are making is whether to accept this journey, so that you can be prepared for and influence the timing of when you encounter these dangers. I promised your mother as representative of our family and the brother of your father, that you would not feel pressured. Whatever else you may think of me – arrogant for example," another quick smile, "I hope you know that family is of great importance to me, and I will always do whatever I can to take care of you.

"I was six years older than you when I was asked to make the decision to start my training, and, well, you know me – daring and fearless as I like to think, or reckless and foolhardy as others have been known to suggest – but for me it was an easy decision to make and I did not hesitate. The promise of adventure and the discovery of unknown secrets was enough for me to commit. But you are different from the person I was, certainly more cautious and analytical, though I can see you lack nothing in bravery. So as Mr. Warwick says, please take however long you need to decide. If that means coming back another day with your answer, then that is entirely acceptable."

It was now Anna's turn to gaze into the depths of the fire. The decision being asked of her was evidently one of great significance, even if she did not fully understand all its consequences yet. She had always felt herself to be a bit of an outsider, but now it seemed that the feeling of being different had a reason and that there were other people like her, important and powerful people, and she was being invited to join them. The people asking her were people she respected and trusted too, people she might learn much from and even aspire to be like one day. And she could not deny the appeal, not only of being treated as an adult at last, but of seemingly in some small way having their respect.

It also seemed that this path might answer many questions that had filled her head for so long. And there was the idea of adventure, and above all freedom, which when compared with the sheltered, oppressed life she had been forced to lead up to then, attracted her enormously – she presumed that was her uncle's side of the family showing itself!

However there was one obstacle in Anna's mind, and that obstacle was immense. It was that, somewhere ahead of her on this path that was being offered, lay evil in its purest form, the form of that man from her dream. Such was the unspeakable, irrational terror that this idea held for her that it was almost enough to make her choose any other direction, and to run in that direction for all she was worth. But deep inside she understood that no matter how far she ran, he would pursue her and ultimately find her. In her heart, she knew that this had been the message in her dream.

In the end it was none of these factors alone that proved decisive. The truth was that deep down she knew, and really had known from long before the question was ever put into words, that she would accept this path she was being offered, that she must accept it, wherever it would lead and whatever it would bring, either good or ill. Those things about her that were unusual, and the things that had not even made sense to her, were now somehow starting to fall into place, and all the important experiences that had affected her until then had all been directing her to this very point, and to this decision.

The brief conversation she had already had that evening had confirmed that she was no longer alone, and that there were people here who would understand her, guide her and support her as she fulfilled whatever it was that she was meant to. But even with or without these guides, she understood clearly at that moment, more clearly than she had ever understood anything before, that for better or for worse, this was the course she must take.

"I agree," Anna replied.

The Alpha-Omega Anomaly

"Very well," said the old man slowly and quietly after a long pause. "Then the time has come to explain some things about the world in which we live, as best as we can understand them, which will provide the background to all that we go on to discuss in the future.

"Anna, you already understand the importance of not revealing to anyone what I am about to tell you, other than to those who your uncle or I tell you can be trusted, and you have promised that you will not. On that basis, please take everything I am about to tell you as my most honest and genuine belief of what is true. For some aspects of what I will relate, we have hard evidence through actual experience, while other aspects are more theoretical, more a matter of reasoning, extrapolation and in some cases speculation. In the end, you will need to decide for yourself what you believe and what you do not believe, but please take my words to be what I genuinely perceive as the truth.

"I will begin with some fundamental matters which lie at the heart of everything. And our starting point is this: it turns out that the world in which we live, and the entire universe within which it exists, are not quite how they were... um... meant to be.

"It starts with the very moment of our universe coming into being. Most of the cultures we have ever come across in the world have some way or other of explaining how this occurred. In our culture, the common belief is that a single god created everything, whereas in other cultures and other parts of the world they have different beliefs expressed through different religions. In the end, specific religious belief is, of necessity, a matter of individual faith rather than of proof or rationale. Many of the members of our Order who understand the things that I am going to share with you have a strong faith in the national religion of this country. Many others of the Order in other parts of the world have an equally strong faith in other religions, and amongst all these people you will find a myriad of different interpretations of those religions, based on their own individual understandings and beliefs. Then there are also others in our Order who have no religious faith at all. However, it is not my purpose to enter the realm of religious faith in our discussion. We may come to discuss such matters in the future if we wish to, but such a discussion is not necessary for you to be able to understand what you will learn from your uncle and me during your instruction. It is not my intention to influence you one way or another in matters of your own faith, if indeed you have one, for, and this is the key point, accepting what I am about to share with you this evening is not dependent on any particular set of religious beliefs, or indeed on having any beliefs at all – but neither does it preclude any.

"This may sound like an odd place for me to begin, but I say this at the beginning as it is often difficult at first to divorce the topics I am about to discuss with you from religious teachings, since what I am going to share with you touches upon some of the most fundamental aspects of our existence. However, it is nonetheless entirely possible to separate the two, and indeed we often find it essential to do so in order to make progress. By saying this to you in advance I hope we can suspend such questions for the time being. It is entirely possible for someone of any or no religious belief to understand and accept what I am about to tell you. At most, if necessary for the sake of understanding at this stage, you may consider what I am about to tell you as additional information to your existing views, possibly allowing a deeper interpretation of what you already believe, in much the same way as our advancing understanding of the sciences also enables us to do the same.

"So, however the events which brought about the existence of our universe and of our world within it are explained or interpreted, your uncle, the other members of our Order and I all have good reason to believe that there was a form of 'Elemental Energy' that instigated it all. Naturally, many understand this Energy to have been God as described in the Bible, although again it does not necessarily need to have been, but anyhow we do have reason to believe that there was actually some kind of *fundamental* energy, a driving force which existed before the universe and which was responsible for its inception and the shape of its development. Again, we should leave for another day questions such as whether or not the many religions of the world and their stories of creation are in fact drawing on the same fundamental truths, albeit then interpreting them in widely differing ways, for once again such a debate is not pertinent to what we need to discuss.

"Back to the main point then: what we in the Order understand is that we are all part of the design of this Elemental Energy. However, and this is a point of central importance Anna, at the time of the inception of the universe there was more than one fundamental energy in existence. Whether this second energy was merely a different facet of the first which had somehow become fragmented from it, or whether it had a different origin... well there are many theories, both ancient and modern, that I will not trouble you with tonight. There will be plenty of time for such discussions in the future, but they are not salient to what I will tell you tonight.

"What is important is that this other energy was directly opposed to the Elemental Energy, or opposed at least in so far as it related to our universe, our world and everything that lives in it. Furthermore, we understand that, at the moment of the inception of our universe, this opposing energy also sought to create its own universe, but one according to its own, very different design; a universe which would have been utterly different from the one in which we now live.

"I should add at this point, please do not confuse the

Energies that I am referring to here, and which we have long used in this context, with 'energy' as scientists now talk about it. What scientists observe as energy is something they calculate and can measure, and is of this world and this universe. It is quite different from the forms of energy we refer to as Elemental and Opposing, which are more fundamental, indeed transcendental, and which are not something we can observe directly, or have any means of measuring. However, we do still find it helpful to think of them as another energy form, albeit an unimaginably powerful one and one that has direction and purpose.

"Now, as I mentioned, we understand that this Opposing Energy also sought to create its universe at the same time that ours was created. Whether it actually succeeded in creating another different universe, or indeed other universes, according to its own design in a space other than ours, has been the cause of much speculation and debate among the scientists and philosophers of our Order, but no factual evidence one way or the other yet exists. However, what we do know, and what concerns us most right now, is that the universe in which we live today was not created exactly according to the design and direction of the Elemental Energy. More precisely put, there is an anomaly that exists in our universe and has done ever since the time of its inception.

In some way, the Opposing Energy's influence affected the creation of the universe at the very moment of its coming into being, and certain shadows, or echoes, of the universe which the Opposing Energy sought to create, came to be present in the one that was created. When speaking of this anomaly, we sometimes refer to our universe as having been contaminated by the Opposing Energy, and why we use such a word will become evident presently. But this contamination, although it has always been present, has become more apparent in the era of mankind, and increasingly so as civilization and societies have evolved.

The Elemental Energy's original design, had it not been influenced by the Opposing Energy, would have led to a world which resembled our own in many respects, but in which there would have been a great deal more harmony and mutual understanding and respect between individuals, groups and indeed nations – a world without the unnecessary and ultimately self-defeating aggression, cruelty, jealousy, greed and so forth, which we see all around us today. That is not to say that there would be no pain and suffering, but there would be far less, and crucially there would be much less of the needless human suffering that is caused directly by other people. Similarly, there may sometimes be days when we feel inexplicably irritable and prone to anger, or we may feel deeply unhappy or anxious without particular reason. Often, when there is no obvious cause for such feelings, they are the result of the contamination of the Opposing Energy, disrupting our condition and preventing us from feeling as we should according to the Elemental design. And so in various ways, our world today is not, in fact, The World That Was Meant To Be according to the Elemental Energy's original design.

"Now it may seem natural for us to accept these things as an inevitability of life, since as we are so used to seeing them, they seem always to have been there in one form or another and appear to be beyond resolution. But we absolutely must not simply accept them. Much of the unnecessary pain and suffering is created needlessly by people often for short-term ends, is not logical for the stage of development which human beings have reached, and is often even detrimental to the perpetrator's own longer-term interests, let alone to the development of mankind. These sufferings are preventing an optimal existence for us all, and they absolutely do not form part of The World That Was Meant To Be. What we understand is that jealousy, greed, unwarranted aggression, and so on, the list is long and we will return to it in the future, do exist in our reality, and that they are a direct result of the anomaly that I mentioned – the contaminating influence of the Opposing Energy on the Elemental Energy's original design for the universe.

"Now we believe that these two Energies have been in opposition with each other since before the beginning of our universe. So in our terms a battle has been raging between them for all eternity, and it is a battle which continues today. We have little conception of the full extent of their theatre of battle, or in how many other realms beyond our world and universe they are engaged in this struggle, but we do know that it is still very much ongoing in this world of ours.

"The influences of the two Energies are at play in the world now, every day, even right now as we speak. We cannot see or experience them directly, but we are sure they exist because we can observe their effect. Although they are not a physical presence in our world that we can observe, for ease of visualisation people sometimes imagine these influences as eternal winds, attempting to push and drive us all in one direction or another.

"We consider that everyone in the world is subject to these winds of influence of the two Energies, and there is no place completely sheltered from them. It is also true, however, that there are places where the influence of one is stronger at certain times than the other. To illustrate the point, there are many places in this country which are particularly prone to experiencing the influence of the Energies. For example you do not have to travel too far in a westerly direction from London before you come to a place you may have heard of called Stonehenge. There has been widespread speculation amongst the regular population as to the significance of this ancient site, but we know it to be a place which has experienced the influences of the Energies particularly powerfully at various times throughout history. And there are many other such places, albeit not necessarily quite so well known, for which the same is true, both in this country and of course in other countries too.

"No-one is immune to these influences. However, these invisible winds do not actually have the power to control us or solely to determine what actions we take. In that respect they differ from the normal wind which we can feel outside. No matter how strong the winds of influence are, we do still have free will and we can withstand them, and we are able to make our own decision to move in a different direction, though we can sometimes find this incredibly difficult."

As the light from the fire sent shadows dancing around the edges of the room which was otherwise wrapped in darkness, Anna was now listening transfixed, focussing every ounce of her attention on what Mr. Warwick was revealing. She was desperately scrambling to follow and understand at a literal level some of the concepts which were now flying thick and fast at her, some of which frankly might have sounded completely fantastical to her had they been spoken by anyone who she respected less than Mr. Warwick. Yet at the same time she felt a growing sense of excitement deep within her, or something closely akin to excitement, like a long-awaited realisation which was now starting to stir inside her. She felt like someone who had been struggling all their life to see something that was just beyond the edge of their vision, like an object whose outline had been tantalisingly visible, but whose details had been obscured by a veil of mist. Now, finally, that mist was beginning to dissipate as Mr. Warwick's story began to unfold, and Anna wondered if she might be about to start seeing things as they truly were at last.

"There are enormous implications and complexities to take on board in what I am telling you, and for the time being I am attempting to keep things as brief and as simple as I can," continued Mr. Warwick. "But the next thing that I need to explain is how the Energies, or winds as I have been describing them, interact with our essences which we were talking about earlier, and in doing so influence the decisions we make."

Mr. Warwick paused briefly, picked up the poker propped up by the side of the fireplace, and stoked the orange and yellow blaze that lay within it, sending further, larger black shapes to join the shadowy dance on the walls and ceiling.

"Though ultimately a decision is made by what we regard as our free will, in simple terms, one way of looking at the way we make a decision is to think about four fundamental types of influence which come to bear on that decision.

"Firstly, there is the context in which the decision is made, such as our location and surroundings, any event or incident which has taken place, the companions we are with, and even such simple things as the weather; indeed anything occurring in the world around us at that moment which might exert an external influence on us. Secondly, and naturally this is often influenced by the first point, is our own internal condition, by which I mean our physical and mental condition, our mood, whether or not we are hungry, and so forth; essentially then our short-term or temporary state. Thirdly there are the influences of the Energies, those invisible winds I was talking about, which are constantly moving through us and interacting with our essences, influencing us, prompting us to take one direction or another. Then finally, there is our essence itself – our fundamental personality, our character, our values, our predispositions, all of which can play a key part in the decision made.

"There is clearly a relationship and interaction between all these factors. So for example, our essence will have a bearing on the second factor (our mood, and so forth), but these two are nonetheless distinct, our mood being very transitory and our essence being fundamental, constant and longer-term, although it too can change slowly over time. Most importantly of all though, whilst all of the above factors are an influence on the decisions we make, no single one of them will necessarily be decisive, and in the end we believe we make that decision through our own free will."

Mr. Warwick paused there briefly, as though wrestling

with himself as to how far to take his next point. "At this moment I feel I should say something about our free will. This is actually of central importance to your future instruction, but there is one aspect that I want to get out of the way now. I am sure you will not be aware of it, but there has in fact been an enormous philosophical debate raging for a very long time, not only within the Order but amongst philosophers in the mainstream population too, as to whether or not there really is any such thing as free will. This debate brings into play concepts such as 'predestination', 'determinism', 'libertarianism' and other ideas that I certainly do not propose to go into now. All I want to say now (and we can return to this subject in more detail another time if you would like to) is that at any given time, based on the information that we have available to us, we do not know what the outcome of any given event will be, and hence it is imperative that we act in the way that we believe will bring about the right outcome, whether or not it turns out in the end that this outcome was predetermined or could have been predicted by someone else who had access to more information than us. I will leave this point there for now, but in the future you will come to understand why I have chosen to mention it this evening.

"So," continued Mr. Warwick rubbing his hands together, clearly now warming to his subject, "back to the factors that drive our decisions. What is crucial here is the interplay between the four elements I mentioned. The exact relationships between them are highly complex and no-one has ever been able to map them effectively, although I may tell you, many have tried! However, what I will say with confidence is this: when the influence of either Energy sweeps over us and attempts to move us in one direction or another, the strength with which we feel that influence, and our ability to withstand it if we want to, are deeply influenced by the state of our essence.

"To describe the interactions between our essences and

the influences of the Energies, one analogy people like to use is that of the sailing ship. In the analogy, the ship is the person, the course taken by the ship represents decisions and courses of action taken by that person, their essence is analogous to the ship's sail, and the influence of the energies is compared to the ocean wind. The extent to which the sail, and hence the ship, is caught and moved forward by the wind depends on the shape, material and condition of the sail – some sails of a certain type will catch certain winds more effectively than will others.

"I share this analogy because in the past I have found that it helps pupils to begin to grasp the concepts we are discussing. However, that is not to say it is not flawed in several key respects. For one, it does not convey effectively the fact that a person can withstand the influence of the wind, and can in fact move in the opposite direction – not just 'tacking' as it were in the nautical sense, but to move in diametrically the opposite direction, in spite of the wind. Secondly, in the world of Energies and essences, the influences of the two Energies can attempt to direct us in different directions at the same instant, whereas the physical ocean wind can only ever blow in one direction at a given moment. Plus the analogy only deals with two of the four influence types that I mentioned at the start. So the influences on the essence and the ultimate decisions and actions that people make are altogether more complex than the simple relationship between the wind and the sail of a ship.

"However, provided one keeps in mind its limitations, the comparison can prove useful, even when thinking about the simultaneous effects of more than one influence. An essence that is pure, which you described seeing as a beautifully smooth sphere of sky-blue, might feel the influence of the Elemental Energy like the fully-open sails of a great sailing ship, angled square-on to the wind. A pure essence also feels the influence of the wind of the Opposing Energy, but to a lesser degree, as though that wind were not quite hitting the sail square-on, or the sails were not fully unfurled in respect of that wind. Someone whose essence is flawed on the other hand – uneven, fractured or discoloured as you described it – is far more prone to be caught by the wind of the Opposing Energy's influence, and to be caught more strongly by it, and as a result it is far more prone to be driven to act according to the influence of the Opposing Energy.

"Anna, we sometimes talk about people acting on a whim, or an idea suddenly occurring to us out of the blue. Sometimes those whims or ideas may be trivial and of no consequence. Other times they may be to do something that is good, or they may be to do something that is not good. Sometimes they are the result of one of the first two influences on our decisions that I mentioned. But when these unprompted notions come to us and lead us to act in a certain way that we had not previously planned, it is sometimes the case that at those moments we are subject to the influence of one or other of the Energies.

"From time to time, you may hear someone who has carried out some kind of spontaneous criminal act say "I don't know why I did it", or some such thing. It may be the case that they had been subject to the wind of influence of the Opposing Energy at that moment, they were open to that influence and they did not sufficiently resist it. On some other occasions, we cannot see any directly good or evil outcome to those actions that just pop into our heads, but that is because we do not know the grander designs and direction of the Energies. That does not mean we should not therefore act – it simply means that when we do act, we should do so always keeping in mind what we believe to be the design of The World That Was Meant To Be, which is consistent with sustaining a pure essence. This is a topic to which we shall return in a moment.

"However there is a very important point that I want you always to remember now. We have reason to believe that no matter how disfigured or damaged a person's essence is, and hence how open to receiving the influence of the wind of the Opposing Energy they are, the essence of a person of this world is never immune to the influence of the Elemental Energy and can always still follow its fundamental design to some degree, no matter how faint it may feel. The reason for this is that they were born into a world that was brought into existence at the design of the Elemental Energy, and no matter how far this world deviates from that original design, and how far their own essences become contaminated, we believe that their connection with the design of the world as it was meant to be can never be entirely broken, for as long as they remain alive in this world. This is a crucial point to remember. It may sound reminiscent of some religious doctrines, but it is not necessary to believe in religion for this to remain a source of hope, no matter how bleak times may become."

Mr. Warwick now paused briefly, as though to emphasise the full importance of what he had just said. "Before I go on, there is something I should add regarding the analogy of the winds of influence. In the case of the Elemental Energy, rather than an external wind, I believe it would be more appropriate to say that its influence is something that already lies within every person, at some deep level. And in fact there is enough of the original design within us and in the world all around, for us sometimes to feel what the pure world as originally designed would be like. There are certain situations that arise, and certain non-physical stimuli that we experience, which can trigger in us feelings of euphoria and exhilaration which leave us feeling utterly uplifted and inspired.

"The arts are a common source of such stimuli. Take music for example. As we hope to bring to life for you later on in your instruction Anna, certain music can induce the most profound feelings within us – intellectually, emotionally, even what could be called spiritually (with or without the religious connotations of the term), music has the power to make us feel truly alive and to uplift us to a state more exhilarated than our normal one. Similarly the other arts – painting, sculpture, great literature and so on – also have a similar power to transform our condition for a time.

"But it is not only the arts that can do this – far from it. A mathematician or a scientist, in making a great discovery or breakthrough, can experience elation stemming not only from their feeling of success and the recognition that it may bring their way, but on occasion from the purity of the world as they have glimpsed it through their intellectual pursuits. I believe this to be particularly true for the great mathematicians, who are able sometimes to see purity in things that we seldom have the opportunity to witness in the world around us. And then the beauty of nature itself, for those who properly see it, can touch us at a most fundamental level and uplift us to the heights; its scale and majesty can sometimes do the same; even certain climactic conditions are capable of bringing us a sense of exhilaration, if we're opening to feeling it. But perhaps above all, certain positive interactions and relationships with other people, and I include the phenomenon of love in this category, can lift us to states of heightened being which far exceed our other experiences."

Anna was now starting to hang on every word being spoken, the meaning deeply resonating with her. The old man was describing feelings that she herself had at times experienced but had never been able to express, and a sense of excited anticipation grew inside her as she sought to understand their place in the world of the Energies that was being revealed.

"It is when we are in these uplifted states that you could say we most experience what it is to be uniquely human, feeling things at an intellectual and emotional level to an extent that only humans are capable of amongst all living creatures of this planet. And it is when we are in these uplifted, exhilarated states that we come closest to seeing life as it would be under the original design of the Elemental Energy. 'Living life to the full', depending on exactly what we take this expression to mean, can mean living a life in which we come closest, most often, to experiencing things in this world as they would be if the anomaly I mentioned did not exist and the original Elemental Energy's design had become reality without contamination.

"These are themes to which we will return in the future during your instruction, including what it may mean to be an artist who can induce such uplifted states in others, and what the artists themselves are tapping into in creating their art. But for now, suffice to say that it is in those enlightened moments that the Elemental Energy is most alive and vibrant within us, not like some kind of external force attempting to push us like the wind, but like something awakened within us, at our very cores. At those times we are more prone to think and act in ways that move us and the world around us, closer to that original design. And at those times, we can be at our most immune to the push of those external winds of the Opposing Energy. So in my view there is an important difference between the influence of the Opposing Energy, which operates externally upon us as it were, and the Elemental Energy, which moves us from within.

"However, despite this distinction, this does not mean that even when we have seen and felt that vision of the original design, we will necessarily act from then on in accordance with it. In relation to all the influences I have mentioned, as far as we're concerned we have free will, and the decisions we go on to make at a given moment are not necessarily dictated by any single one of those influences. As a result of the contamination present from the time of the universe's inception, people can make decisions and take actions which contradict the Elemental design, even if they have glimpsed how wonderful it is. In the end, every individual has the potential to resist the influence of either or both of the Energies."

The flames in the fireplace continued their manic dance, but were by now a little lower in the grate. Mr. Warwick paused again, pulled out two more large logs from the basket nearby and tossed them into the centre of the blaze, sending tiny orange sparks flying into the air momentarily. He gave the fire another good prod and stir with the poker, causing the flames to dance higher once again, whilst their shadowy followers continued to mimic their rhythm on the walls all around.

"In order to make the rest of the conversation a little easier, I would like to introduce some new terms to you. Since ancient times, in Europe and beyond we have used Greek script to describe some of the concepts we are discussing. The Struggle between the two Energies was well known to a small number of ancient Greeks, who participated actively in it during their own era, and from whom subsequent generations of our Order have learned much – although in fact the known Struggle even well predates the Greeks, as you will come to learn. I have spoken about The World That Was Meant To Be according to the original Elemental design; since ancient times the Order has referred to this as the Alpha World. Similarly, we sometimes refer to the world of the Opposing Energy's design as The World That Should Not Be, for although that world does not exist, it is still possible that it may come into being, as I will go on to explain. We call this the Omega World. And the world that we actually inhabit today exists in a state somewhere between those two worlds and their respective designs.

"When looking around us at the pain and suffering that seems to be all too prevalent, it may sometimes feel to us as though we are somewhere nearer the Omega than the Alpha World. However, in truth we have every reason to believe that we are in fact very much closer to the Alpha World, although our position on the continuum between the two can fluctuate somewhat, and has done so throughout history as the Alpha-Omega Struggle has continued. But we have some insights into what the Omega World would truly be like, and from our point of view as humans, I will ask you to take my word for it that it would be a truly catastrophic state for us – one in which we could not exist at all. By the way, later you will also come to learn of a place which we refer to as the Beta World, a place which does exist today but which is not properly formed – a twilight world if you will. But we will come to that in good time if you will permit me to defer it for now." Anna nodded silently. She had more than enough to try to absorb as it was, and deferring the introduction of yet another world was just fine with her!

"And now a very key point, Anna – one of the most important of all. We believe that the universe's final state, and our world's position within it, is not fixed or finally determined yet. It is the attainment of that final state and the form that it will take which is the subject of the ongoing Struggle I have been describing. For we have reason to believe that either the Alpha or the Omega World will one day become the reality of our own world. Rather than the world continuing as it is, existing as the Alpha World contaminated by echoes of the Omega and continuing in an unstable state of tension between the two designs, the world will reach a constant state which will always exist from that time onwards, for at least as long as the universe lasts. As far as we can ascertain, there can then be no reversal of that state, at least not as brought about by any entity that exists within the universe. There will be no more contamination of one design in the other, and any inhabitants of the prevailing world will feel no more influence from the other Energy; all creatures will belong to that world and will be in perfect harmony with its state, and will not act in such a way as to move the world away from it.

"What the final victory of either world would mean for the Energy whose design did not become reality is the subject of great conjecture, but it seems certain that the influence of that Energy would no longer be felt in our universe. What is beyond question though is that the outcome of the Struggle simply could not be of greater significance for the men, women and all other creatures that live on this earth, and for all our future descendents who are to succeed us in this world.

"The pure Alpha World would be, as the original design intended, a state in which harmony existed. It would be an existence in which we would each constantly experience the kinds of stimulation and exhilarations that we sometimes glimpse today, but which we can never quite manage to sustain – those moments that I tried to describe a moment ago in which we feel uplifted and inspired. And it would be a world in which the needless suffering and cruelty that are so often a feature of our world today would not be there. However, the Omega World would be one in which neither humans nor any other of the creatures of this world could even exist at all. And what is worse, the transition from our existence today into that state would be more terrible than we can fully comprehend. It would involve the step-by-step destruction and ultimately the elimination of every person and every creature that exists today, together with everything that we have achieved over the centuries and all that we might go on to achieve in the future. What is more, it would be a most painful destruction, possibly to be replaced by very different life forms, or more likely by no life forms at all. Your uncle, I and others like us, we are champions of the Alpha World, fighters in the Struggle whose mission it is to help bring about the Alpha state. We have an immeasurable responsibility to all who exist today and to all future generations to achieve that Alpha state, or at least to move our world closer towards it and to do everything within our power to prevent the Omega World from coming to pass. As I'm sure you can readily appreciate then, the stakes simply could not be higher."

Mr. Warwick paused once more, this time for several moments, to allow time for what he had said to sink in. Anna had remained silent, leaning slightly forward in her chair almost motionless the entire time the old man had been speaking, her eyes following his every expression and gesture, her mind focused with deep concentration on every word. Given how late it must be by now, the torrent of information in which she was being immersed ought to have been tiring her, but it was not. Anna could sense the deep importance of what she was hearing. Some of the concepts shared she had not yet fully taken on board, but others had already started to resonate deeply with experiences she had already had, and were awakening that deeper understanding that had always lain somewhere within her, undiscovered until now.

As she had listened to Mr. Warwick speaking, a large number of questions had been presenting themselves in her mind. It was in Anna's nature continually to question, so it came as no surprise that on this of all evenings she should have so many, but such was her thirst to hear what else Mr. Warwick might next divulge that she decided they could all could wait for the time being. All that was, bar one.

"Mr Warwick, may I ask you a question?" she ventured, to which the old man responded "Of course Anna, please go ahead."

"Well you have told me a lot of very important things this evening, and I am still taking some of them in, but I was wondering just how all this that you have been describing relates to my dream, and to those people that I saw in the dream. They are somehow connected with what you have told me, aren't they?"

Mr. Warwick looked at Anna momentarily then replied slowly. "You are right Anna, they are. I needed to explain all this background to you first to give you the context and grounding, but you are right, it is now time to get to the heart of the matters that are most pressing to us – if you still have the energy for it that is!".

Anna could only guess at the hour, but for the first time in her life she was out of the house this late with permission, and she had never felt more awake. Perhaps that nap she had had at Lord's had helped, but she responded, "Mr. Warwick, yes, please do go on."

"Very well then. So as I have just described, the world in which we live today is in fact balanced on a knife edge, between a much better world and one infinitely worse, one in which our very existence would not be possible. And as I have also already stated, the Elemental Energy and the Opposing Energy are still, right now, engaged in the most titanic struggle, like a deadly, all-transcending chess game dating back to the beginning of time as we know it, finally to bring about the universe that each originally conceived.

"And it is this ongoing Struggle," said Mr. Warwick, now turning back towards Anna, "this eternal war to bring about the Alpha or the Omega state, which brings us back to your dream." The old man was now looking her full in the face, his eyes blazing in the reflected light from the fire.

They had finally reached that point which Anna had been most eager to learn about, albeit also most fearful. She leant slowly back into her chair, tightened her grip on its arms, and held her breath.

A Shocking Revelation

"Echoes of the Omega World are seen in our world not only in the form of people's flawed essences and in the hurtful and destructive acts that some people commit. Intermittently, over the centuries, as far back in history as we have records, agents of the Omega World have appeared in ours in a more direct, physical way – in the form of living, sentient beings. These are more than mere echoes; they are creations of the Opposing Energy, physical manifestations of its design, conscious beings with their own will which appear in our world.

"There are still many things about this that we do not understand, but we are sure that these beings do not take the form that a creature from the true Omega World would. As I have mentioned, it is commonly considered that no creatures could exist at all in that world, and it seems certain that even if they could, such creatures would not take any form that could survive in ours. So we believe that these creatures appearing in our world are transitional beings which exist in a form that is able to survive here, and which exist in order to achieve one specific aim, namely to bring about the final transition to the Omega World." As Mr, Warwick continued, his tone began audibly to harden with every word he spoke next, as though he were fighting now to control the passions that were beginning to stir inside him. "These beings are not of this world, they were not part of the Elemental Energy's design, and they do not belong here. They exist purely to oppose the Alpha World, and they have been the sworn enemy of every knight for thousands of years, since the founding of our order. We call these creatures *Satals*.

"Satal appearances do not occur very frequently, and sometimes long periods may pass without a visitation, though their appearances do seem to have grown more frequent in recent years. When they do appear, they nearly always cause terrible suffering and destruction, for that is precisely their purpose. Satals are physical agents of the Omega World in the same way that we are agents of the Alpha World, and their objective whilst here is to intervene directly in the affairs of the world, to move it closer to the Omega state. Without exception, their means of doing so involves causing disruption to harmony and peaceful existence, be that in the form of hatred between individuals or wars between nations, the creation of conditions in which disease may more readily spread or any other means by which they may wreak misery. The bleaker aspects of the world in which we live that are the result of the contamination by the Omega design are the things they trade on and seek to exacerbate – and the more they succeed, the more we move away from the Alpha World.

"A significant number of the most terrible events in human history have been brought about by the direct intervention of Satals in our world. The stories of the events themselves are known to all, but the general population never sees their true, hidden causes. We will teach you about the history of the Struggle, which will cover some of the more important of these events, and from which much may be learned that is applicable to our own situation and time.

"But what I want to get back to now is your dream. You see Anna, I am almost certain that what you saw in your mind's eye in that dream were in fact Satals. I say this because a number of our Order felt a disruption on the night of that infamous storm – the night that you had your dream. It is difficult to put precisely into words, but it felt to us as though the course of the future had changed direction, and that this was a shift towards the Omega state. However, not one of us saw things with anything like the clarity that you have described.

"From the strength of what we felt, we could guess something significant had occurred – something more significant than in previous such events in recent history. We thought, or more precisely we feared, that not one, but two or three Satals had entered our world simultaneously this time, which has not happened for a number of centuries. That would have been terrible enough, since defeating even one Satal is an extremely formidable challenge, and one that is usually finally achieved only after a lot of pain, misery and death has been inflicted on our world.

"However, from what you have told us this evening, it seems that even our worst fears underestimated the true gravity of what had occurred. It would appear that not two or three, but five agents of the Omega World materialised that night. Five! That would certainly explain the unprecedented strength of what we felt.

"Anna, as this is all new information to you, you cannot possibly comprehend the full implications of what I am saying, but your uncle and I can. Despite all my studies and all that I know about the history of our great Struggle and the fearsome battles that have taken place in the past, I am not aware of any time when we have faced five Satals in our world at one time. If I had time to recount to you now some of the battles that have taken place in the past to rid the world of Satals, you would understand just how terrible, and indeed terrifying, this revelation is. The slight shift in direction towards the Omega state that we felt that night will become an enormous leap if these Satals are allowed to execute their evil work. Indeed with so many, I wonder if this isn't a more fundamental move from the Opposing Energy than we have ever seen before – some kind of major offensive to bring about the Omega World in our own time, for once and for all. It will truly take a mighty, combined effort to bring about the defeat of such a number. And if only that was all we had to deal with here... But there was something else that you said, Anna, something which, believe it or not, may be the worst revelation of all.

"When you said that you saw five figures, you mentioned that one was considerably taller than the others. And you said that it was this taller one to whom you were drawn, and who looked at you. Is that correct?"

"That's right," said Anna, her voice now barely audible. She could almost feel the weight of Mr. Warwick's words starting to bear down on her chest. A feeling of dread began to crawl slowly over her.

"Well," continued the old man, his own voice now reduced to little more than a whisper, "my interpretation, unless I have been mistaken, and oh how deeply I hope I have been, is that this tallest of the Satals was in fact no ordinary Satal at all. It was something far, far worse. I believe that the creature that you saw was a being known as a Gorgal."

At that moment Anna became aware of her uncle again, who had suddenly stopped reclining in his chair with his usual detached air, and was now leaning forward, listening as intently to the old man's every word as she was. In fact he seemed more attentive, more alert and more focused than she could ever remember seeing him. Anna waited silently for the old man to continue. The beating of her heart had become more violent, as though it was about to make a bid for freedom through her very ribcage. She was sure that she was finally about to find out the identity of the image which had haunted her all these years.

"A Gorgal has not been seen in this world for a very long time, in fact for well over a thousand years in the West, and how very grateful we should be for that too." By now the old man was out of his chair and had started pacing the floor in front of Anna and her uncle, his hands clasped behind his back. "Indeed, among our own Order there are now many who do not believe Gorgals have ever existed, although I think that the evidence points rather strongly in the other direction. But certainly there has been no evidence of Gorgal presence in our world for many hundreds of years – and I certainly believe we would know if one had been here.

"Like a Satal, a Gorgal is also an agent of the Omega World. It too is a creation of the Opposing Energy, and is not of our world. But legend has it that the Gorgal represents the Omega World in a far more direct and powerful form. Satals are powerful in their own right as I have said, and are able to bring a considerable direct influence on the course of important events, through the manipulation of situations and of people by various means, so as to shift the world's precarious balance in the direction of the Omega World. Sometimes they have seemed to be aware of the winds of influence of the Opposing Energy and have worked in tandem with those winds. However, a Gorgal's power is of a different order of magnitude altogether, and it has the power to influence the course of history far more profoundly, by actually channelling and driving those winds of the Opposing Energy – if we are to believe the ancient histories that is. This gives them the ability to influence people's behaviour en masse, on a scale far greater than any Satal could. The Histories lead us to believe that the introduction of a Gorgal is the most direct intervention that the Opposing Energy can make to help it bring about the Omega World.

"To return to the analogy of the eternal Struggle between the Energies as being a mighty, all-transcending game of chess, by engineering the appearance of Satals, the Opposing Energy introduces new and deadly pieces into the game, to tip the balance in its favour. However, in introducing a Gorgal, it is playing a piece so powerful that it can alter the course of the entire game, not only by a step but by an enormous leap towards final victory.

"The last visitation by a Gorgal that we know of is believed to have taken place in the East of Asia, in the early part of this millennium. We know of its appearance, and the enormously disruptive effect it unleashed in that part of the world from the Orders of East Asian knights, with whom we have come into increasing contact over recent centuries, and who we understand to have been engaged in the same Struggle that we have, and for at least as long. The effects of that Gorgal's large-scale intervention are still being felt there, as can be seen in the temporary relative demise in strength and influence of the civilisations of East Asia in the last five hundred years. Countries in that region have led the world in terms of civilisation and technological advancement at various times through history, and I have no doubt that they will do so again in the future. But their advancement was set back by centuries as a result of events instigated by that Gorgal.

"The last Gorgal to have been seen in Europe was even longer ago, in the early centuries AD. Before its final defeat, it was able to set in place an irreversible chain of events that led to the decline of the whole of European civilisation, into what are now known as the Dark Ages. That period of relative lawlessness and anarchy lasted for almost a thousand years until the Renaissance. Prior to the appearance of that Gorgal, Europe had reached a relatively ordered state, albeit sometimes still brutal, but with a considerable level of sophistication, knowledge of the sciences, well-developed cultural lives, and so on. These had been spread far and wide by the might of the Romans, albeit sometimes brutally as I say, and they themselves were building on the foundations of civilisation and advancement laid by the Greeks and other even more ancient civilisations of the Middle Eastern lands that had developed and prospered before them.

"Now please make no mistake, there were many aspects of Roman society that appear to us now as being far removed from the Alpha state. In a sense that is good because it shows us how far we have progressed since then. However, we have reason to believe that the organised society and civilisation of Europe before the last Gorgal would have continued to develop on the path away from brutality. European civilisation would then have come together with those of the Asian world and the other continents, and a great advancement of humanity would have taken place. Our world would by now not only be a place far more advanced and sophisticated, but also one more harmonious, idyllic and essentially happy for all, than it is today. In other words, it would be a world much closer to the Alpha state than it is.

"As it is, the devastating effects of the last European Gorgal lasted for many centuries, during which time much of the European world descended into anarchy, bloodshed, disease and misery – a world that was worse than the old Roman civilisation by almost any measure. It was not until the Renaissance that we in the West began to relearn those things that we had known many centuries before but had lost sight of, and eventually we reached a state more advanced than that of the ancient world. In the intervening period, it was the Muslim world of the Middle East and North Africa that had carried, retained and developed the knowledge that had largely been lost in Europe. Their world had been less impacted by the presence of that Gorgal.

"The Histories tell us that it has always required an enormous, almost superhuman effort to defeat a Gorgal. And the consequences during the time that the Gorgal spends here before it is finally vanquished, have each time been disastrous for the world. Disastrous, verging on the catastrophic.

"By the way Anna, legend has told of the appearance of Gorgals in other great continents of the world in the last two thousand years. According to those legends, in Africa and the Americas before the arrival of the Europeans, a tremendous amount of damage and suffering was inflicted on the civilisations there too. There are those who believe that in the Americas for example, certain ancient civilisations may actually have been wiped out due to the malevolent work of Gorgals that appeared in those regions. Unfortunately we have insufficient evidence to corroborate these theories, but my personal opinion is that they could well contain some elements of truth. But the essential point is this, Anna: the Gorgal is by far the most powerful and destructive weapon that the Opposing Energy has available to unleash on our world, and to move it towards the Omega state. And unfortunately for all of us who strive to realise the Alpha World state, it seems that it is now, in our own time, that the next appearance of a Gorgal is upon us.

"However this time, the Gorgal is not alone – it seems that it has been accompanied by four Satals. Once again I am afraid to say that, to the best of my knowledge, throughout history there has never been such a presence from the Omega World in this world at one time. It is not with a light heart that I say I do not believe our world, and the prospects for the Alpha World, have ever before faced a threat of this magnitude. It would seem that the Opposing Energy has played a potentially devastating hand this time."

With that, the room fell silent, as though the true gravity of the discovery were now bearing down and squeezing the very sound from it. Anna said nothing, but she felt it, almost like a physical weight upon her. The implications of the things she had just heard were beyond her capacity to comprehend fully at this point, but no more information was needed to understand the clear and extreme danger that threatened her and all those she knew and cared about. The silence lasted for what seemed like an age as Anna's two older companions looked into their own space, each absorbing the implications of what had just been discussed, and neither feeling the need to add to it for a time. The only punctuation came in the form of a muffled curse, or was it an oath, and the sound of fist pounding into palm of hand from the direction of Anna's uncle – sounds that she took to represent his defiance of the forces of the Omega World.

Finally it was the old man who spoke up again, in a slightly lighter tone which contrasted starkly with the atmosphere that had enveloped the room. "You know though, there is something else that I find very interesting about your dream, Anna. You said that the tall figure was looking right at you. 'Directly into you' were the words you used, I think. That must have been a truly terrifying experience for you, and indeed, one that in itself might have spelt the end for most people. And unquestionably, I'm afraid it means that the Gorgal does know of your existence. That is both frightening for you, and gravely worrying for us all.

"However, of particular interest is that the creature appears to have singled you out. Of all the people it could have chosen, including the great and powerful members of our Order, it chose you. Additionally, at the tender age of just six years old, you seem to have been able to withstand its focus, albeit a brief one and probably at a great distance. For make no mistake Anna, this was no dream. You really did see the Gorgal, and it saw you. It really did look into you momentarily in a way that no other living being on this planet could have done, and I believe that this alone would have been enough to render permanent and potentially fatal damage to a normal person's essence. And I mean the essence of a full-grown adult.

"That it should have sought you out specifically and immediately upon its entry into this world, and that you survived the encounter essentially unscathed, although I do understand that the memory has troubled you ever since, confirms to me something that I have long suspected and fervently hoped – that you are no ordinary person, not ordinary even amongst our Order, and it may just be that you have the potential one day to become a mighty force for the side of the World That Was Meant To Be. My belief is that the Gorgal was aware of this, and that this is why its focus was drawn specifically to you. A strange thing to take hope from you might think, but it sought you out specifically at that time for a reason, and it may just be that somehow, you represented a threat.

"I do not know the full potential of the power that you may come to develop, Anna, but if there is something in you that even the mightiest of the forces of our enemy considers to be a threat requiring their specific attention, then there is something about this awful discovery that also gives me cause for hope. And believe me, at a time like this, we are in dire need of any glimmer of hope we can find."

Anna had started to stir uncomfortably in her chair as the old man shared this latest theory. Ordinarily the things she was now hearing would sound absolutely fantastical and absurd, even to a child such as herself, were it not for her dream. But the man from her dream, and the raw terror that he had instilled, matched the description put to them perfectly. Above all else she was filled with fear by the idea that she might somehow have been singled out by that man as a threat. Whilst it was nice to have it said that she might somehow be special, she had no idea in what way she could be, except perhaps that she could see essences more clearly than others. She had no conception of how she was actually supposed to pose a threat to something so clearly overwhelmingly powerful as this Gorgal. In contrast, she had every idea that a creature with this much power could probably wipe her out at any time in the blink of any eye.

The room had fallen silent again, and had now become very dark, illuminated only by the fire which was once again on the wane. Even the dancing shadows seemed to be stooping lower and moving less frenetically, as though they too now carried the burden of what had been shared that evening. Mr. Warwick sat in his chair in the gloom, now entirely consumed in his own thoughts. 'I'm not the only one who has had a lot to take in during this conversation,' Anna reminded herself. Finally looking up, his face eerily lit by the red glow of what remained of the fire, which seemed to make the lines in his face look even deeper, he spoke again.

"If the stories from ancient times are to be believed – and though they are old, I have no reason to believe that they are without foundation – then it is going to take an enormous effort, possibly unprecedented in history, to counter the Gorgal successfully. So, as part of your training, we must teach you all that we know about Gorgals, and how they have been countered. We do also face a slight complication in the completion of that training… but we will come to that all in good time."

He paused again, and Anna thought she saw a look of sadness in his face. "If only I were a younger man, still in my prime. But even then…" His voice tailed off, and in the red half-light Anna saw a look of real regret as well as concern, etched onto his kind features.

It was Anna's turn to search for something to change the atmosphere, and for a reason to believe that she might be able one day to support Mr. Warwick and her uncle, and to share this new burden with them. It was then that a question returned which had occurred to her earlier in the conversation, and which also happened to be one of the questions that she had pondered most during her life.

"Mr. Warwick, this might sound like a silly question, but can you tell me what my essence looks like? Because I have never been able to see my own, and I have often wondered what it might say about me." Her heart began to race again as soon as she had said this, because she understood better than anyone exactly what the answer to it would mean. In effect she was asking him what kind of a person she was, at the most fundamental level.

"Anna that is not a silly question, far from it. In fact, it is a most natural one to ask, since none of us are able to see our own essences. So I will tell you."

Anna watched with some trepidation as she saw Mr. Warwick change his focus subtly to observe her essence, just as she herself had done with others on so many occasions. "Although I cannot see with the same clarity that you can," he began, "I can tell you that your essence appears to me as a beautiful sphere, coloured in the brightest shade of sky blue. And its surface does not contain a single blemish that I can make out. Which means, Anna, as I assume you will already understand, that you are a very good person with a very pure heart, and that your essence is close to the way all would be in The World That Was Meant To Be. It is not the largest essence, but there is plenty of opportunity for that to develop as your instruction progresses, and your own powers and ability to influence the outside world grow. The power that you go on to develop in the future is in your own hands Anna, although surely we will try to help you in every way we can. But ultimately it will depend on you, how much you want to develop it and how hard you are prepared to work. What I want you to know is that your essence is, and always has been since you were very young, amongst the purest I have ever seen, and a joy to behold for all those of us who can see these things. What it, and you, may become in the future, Anna, is up to you."

This news at least gave Anna cause for relief. She was not quite sure what she would have done if there had turned out to be any red in there! Then the old man continued, "Whatever potential you may possess in the Powers still remains untapped, other than your unusual ability to see essences with such clarity. The rest will come, first through awareness, then with training, and finally with lengthy and continuous practice. This, Anna, if you are willing, is the journey that you will now undertake. It will be a hard journey, particularly for one so young, possibly tougher than you can yet imagine, but nevertheless one for which I think you are ready, based on what I have seen and heard of your character so far.

"However, I think we have covered enough for one evening. Judging by the quantity of wood we have consumed it must be very late indeed, and time to draw this initial discussion to a close. Once again Anna, you must be sure never to mention any of the content of what we have shared tonight with anyone, unless your uncle or I say so. You have already seen the way that people can respond to things that they don't understand, and to people who they think are different from them. This is another consequence of the Omega World contamination I am afraid. You had a very unfortunate experience several years ago when you revealed your ability to see people's essences, and the kind of reaction you would now receive if you were to start talking about what we have discussed this evening would, I'm afraid, be far worse. And of equal importance, it is vital that we do nothing more to make the agents of the Opposing Energy, including the Gorgal wherever it may be at this time, aware of your identity and location. It would seem that The Gorgal already knows more than we would like, but it is my belief that it does not know where you are now, so let's take every possible precaution in order that things may remain that way.

"Mr. Warwick, believe me there is no-one keener than me to stop him… it… finding me. I will do as you say and I will tell no-one."

"Very good," responded the old man. "Now just as a precaution, given all that we have learned tonight James, I recommend that you now stay at your sister-in-law's house from now on whenever possible, starting tonight when you may explain to her why we are so late, and save young Anna here from the interrogation I fear she might otherwise receive!" He gave Anna a wink, and Anna smiled in return.

"There is strong reason to believe that events are now coming to a head, at least in terms of the next battle of this war, and so I would like to have you close at hand when possible from now on James, to protect Anna whenever needed, and also to support me. Apart from anything else, it is even clearer now than before this evening that we need to start Anna's training apace, and as we have already discussed I will need your help with that. For the time being the sessions will take place here in my shop. This approach is not without risk, but until various matters are completed and until I have safely relocated certain items from the shop, I am not prepared to spend long periods away from it. However, we should run the instruction in the evenings, so as to minimise the risk of detection. Provided we take all necessary precautions, remain extra vigilant and never leave

Anna unaccompanied, I believe we will be safe for now."

Ordinarily Anna would have expected her headstrong uncle to resist any suggestion that his much-loved freedom be curtailed, especially in the evenings, but this situation was evidently different. It was a call to duty in the struggle of their lives, and Uncle James could not have sounded more determined in his affirmation. "Of course, Edmund, I will do exactly as you say."

"Thank you, James. However I know you had another trip to the continent planned, and I believe you should still make that trip, but now with an additional purpose. You must make our colleagues in the centres of the Order there aware of the new discoveries we have made this evening, and I shall do the same with our Order within these shores. I will have someone guard this shop while I am away from it. What we have learned this evening is truly fearful, and the sooner the Order is aware and mobilised, the better. Come and see me again tomorrow morning, by which time I will have certain letters for you to take to the key centres of our Order, and I will share with you what I believe the most important points of your discussions need to be. But more on that tomorrow.

Mr Warwick lit a lantern and then turned back to Anna, seemingly fully restored to his affable old self again. "Then I shall bid you both farewell. Anna, as discussed, your training will commence as soon as your uncle and I return from our travels – assuming, of course, that you are still willing to proceed with it after this evening. Make no mistake, the study will be extremely hard, mark my words!" He shot her a questioning glance, in response to which she nodded her confirmation immediately. But her face had started to betray the first traces of a fresh worry, as she began to wonder if her mother would really accept that she was to receive all this instruction, and the increased freedom that it implied. "Mr. Warwick, how...uh... are you sure my mother will really accept my taking on this instruction that you have talked about? I mean, I know you said that you have spoken to her, but still…"

"Anna, you needn't concern yourself with that. Your uncle will accompany you back to your home tonight, and he will inform your mother as to what we have agreed. I will also speak with her when there is an opportunity, but she has already accepted that the time for this has come. That doesn't necessarily mean she's about to slacken the rest of your ties though!" He laughed, then added, "Now, time to go."

As Anna prepared to leave, she began to reflect on the full implications of her mother having given her permission for this instruction. Did that mean she too knew about these Alpha and Omega Worlds, and Satals and all the rest that Anna had just learned about? That thought stunned her again. Had it actually been that her mother's overbearing strictness had in fact been partly to protect her from these things, and from the man in her dream? She didn't feel ready to ask Mr. Warwick any more about that right now, but she determined that, when the time was right, she would need to have a heart-to-heart with her mother, however awkward that might be, to address the questions that were now multiplying in her head. As they reached the front door of the shop, Anna expressed her thanks to Mr. Warwick.

"Anna, you are most welcome, please do not mention it. We are grateful to you for agreeing to this. Now, your uncle will let you know the details of your instruction and when it will start upon his return from Europe." With that, Mr. Warwick led Anna and her uncle back across the shadowy, but thankfully empty shop floor. He was about to unlock the door when something seemed to prompt him to turn back and address Anna one more time.

Looking directly into her eyes in that piercing way which she knew by now meant he was going to say something of great significance, Mr Warwick added, "Anna, please do take heart. The journey you are now beginning is a truly exciting one, one which will take you close to the centre of some of the greatest secrets of our world. It is a journey that only a select few have taken throughout history, but one that is of the greatest importance to all of human kind. It is an exciting moment for any young person, and in all history exceptionally few have been able to begin the journey so young. And in your case, I have a sense that the journey has the potential to be truly spectacular. If you remain brave, if you remain always true to those things that you know to be right, and if you never give in no matter how hopeless things may seem, your journey might just become one of the greatest we have ever known."

It did not seem possible that Mr. Warwick's gaze could have become more intense than it already was, but it somehow did, almost as though, just momentarily, he was looking directly at her soul. For the first time in her life, Anna was able to see an essence without having to make any effort to focus her attention – Mr. Warwick's essence at the moment was the most vivid, pure and bright blue colour that she had ever seen. The old man continued, "I say this because in you I have started to see certain things that I have never seen before. They are still only the earliest of signs, but they indicate the potential in you one day to achieve things beyond those that the rest of us could ever imagine. Anna, if we can complete your instruction successfully, and in time before the immense events ahead are upon us, you may indeed be in store for the most unimaginably exciting of times before your days are done. So take heart!"

With that, the old man opened the door and let her uncle out first to talk to their driver who had been waiting for them, and to check once again that the coast was clear. On receipt of his signal, Anna joined him on the other side of the door. Mr. Warwick bade farewell, closed and locked the door, and then retreated back inside his shop again, his lantern slowly disappearing from view through the window. While her uncle completed a brief discussion with the driver,

Anna stood absolutely still, absorbing the meaning of what had just been said, and more importantly the feelings that had been stirred within her. Finally waking herself from her reverie, she looked across at her uncle to see if he was ready for her to cross the road to begin the journey home. Lit by his own lantern, he crossed the road to join her, and at first his look was as impenetrable as his thoughts were unfathomable. It was clear that he too was in the midst of deepest thought, but he then suddenly broke into a grin and shook his head disbelievingly at her.

"You know Anna, I have known the Master since I was a very young man, and I believe I have become lucky enough to know him now better than most. You would not believe the high esteem in which he is held amongst the Order. Of all the many great people I have had the pleasure of meeting on my travels, there is no-one for whom I hold a greater respect than Mr. Warwick. And yet I believe I have never seen him so impressed, nor heard him speak in such a way, as I have tonight. Certainly not concerning anything I have ever said or done anyway! Anna, you should not underestimate the significance of Mr. Warwick's words. And for my part, I could not be prouder of you, my little niece!"

He shot Anna another grin, which this time she returned somewhat sheepishly, again not quite knowing what to say or think. Without saying another word, Uncle James then ushered Anna through the darkness across the deserted road, opened the carriage door, held it and gestured for Anna to pass through. It was very strange to Anna, indeed faintly ridiculous, but there was almost a slight air of deference in his demeanour as he did so. She had no idea how to react, so she simply followed his guidance and passed through the door, then waited inside for him to join her and give the driver the signal to leave.

On the ride back to her house, Anna continued to digest what she had been told that evening. An insatiable appetite had been created inside her to know more, and very late as it was, she had not wanted that night's discussion to end. There had been talk of hard study, but although she was aware of other children's feelings towards normal school, her case was very different, as indeed her entire life had been.

She had never been allowed to go to school but instead had been taught by her mother and other tutors at home, presumably for her safety and protection. Although she had thoroughly resented the lack of freedom, the lessons themselves had in fact often been fun, and had fired her interest in certain topics in a way that perhaps was not true of her peers in regular school. And the fact that she was able to explore a subject and ask her own questions relatively freely had probably helped. The experiences of her life to date had likely left her more serious minded than most others her age, and for her this offer of instruction was a welcome relief and escape, certainly in comparison to her normal life of incarceration. In fact what she had been told that night she had found utterly fascinating, even if a little mindboggling. There was no doubt that certain revelations had also been truly shocking to her, including all that had related to her dream, but at the same time Mr. Warwick's final parting words had left her feeling unusually calm despite everything, as though she might actually allow herself to believe that she could one day achieve something important in their cause.

In the lessons she had had so far with her mother and tutors, she had developed a growing interest in history, the stories of the great events and deeds of heroes and heroines from times gone by, and the whole story of how humankind had come to be where it was today. She had now just begun to glimpse that there were apparently deeper truths that lay behind some of those stories of history, and this fired her imagination. She could not wait for the instruction to start. But there was something even more significant than that in her feelings. She had started to feel an excitement, deep down inside her, beyond anything that could be explained by the anticipation of receiving instruction. It was a feeling that an understanding of elemental truths which had always been known to her but which had lain dormant, were finally awakening in her. An awakening of her understanding, and with that, of her *Powers*. She still did not really understand what Mr. Warwick meant when he talked about 'the Powers', and she really had no idea what abilities she might possess beyond that of seeing and touching essences, but she had started to feel something new, like an assured confidence that she could start to deal with those things which life had continually thrown at her up to that point. And with that confidence came a feeling of exhilaration, which had begun to grow from those wondrous moments she had shared with Timmy by the canal. Her awareness, her senses and her ability to see essences had all started to become increasingly sharp, and although she could not begin to understand it all, she could somehow feel that her own ability to influence events and the world outside was also growing.

And now Mr. Warwick and her uncle were starting to offer her explanations of what these changes were, and they would be around to guide her in how she could harness them, and to teach her of the grand sweep of history within which all this fitted. Of course they were also highlighting plenty of dangers and challenges that needed to be overcome, but if she were together with these two guardians, she felt as though there was nothing that the three of them together could not overcome. Even, dare she believe it, the dreaded Gorgal from her dream.

That was something she had never felt before, that even the terror instilled by the man in her dream might be something that she could one day overcome and finally banish from her life. Yes, she was ready for her instruction to begin now, whether she was unusually young or not – without question, she was as ready for this as she had ever been for anything in her life. It was as though her life up to just a few days before had all been a terrible mistake and that she was now starting afresh, reborn at last as the person she was always meant to be.

She recalled what Mr. Warwick had said about the influences of the Energies that were constantly at play, prompting us to think and say this or that, to nudge the world in the direction of one or other of its alternative destinies if we were open to their influence. The idea flashed across her mind – had that Elemental Energy's influence been present even in that little room at the back of Mr. Warwick's shop? Had it indeed been that same Energy, vividly alive within Mr. Warwick's essence, which had prompted him to turn back to her before she left, *as if on a whim*, and to speak to her with those words of encouragement before she departed? It was true that she had never seen an essence shine so brightly as Mr. Warwick's had at that moment. The sense that the Elemental Energy might that very evening, have taken a direct hand in the course of events in which she was involved filled her with a deep feeling of awe.

There were to be many times in the future when Anna would look back and wish she could recapture the feelings of that moment – those early feelings of assurance, confidence and deep excitement. As she watched the gas-lit night scenes filter by her carriage window one by one, scenes of London, that immense city in which she had grown up, she saw it now afresh, as though she were seeing it all for the first time. That greatest of cities which had at times scared and hurt her, now suddenly seemed a different place, one which filled her with sheer exhilaration at the possibilities that it, and the wide world stretched out beyond, might now hold for her. Whatever those would turn out to be, and whatever role it might become her destiny to play in the eternal Struggle that was raging across the universe all around her, she knew with certainty which side she would fight on, and she knew that her time had come.

And she was ready.

Pursuit

Since the afternoon at the canal and the events that had followed, Anna had started to view her life differently. True, in most regards it probably appeared little different from the outside since the long night's discussion with Mr. Warwick and her uncle in which so many unexpected things had been revealed, as the routine of her life had then returned to its former pattern of domestic incarceration with disappointing speed after that. Mr. Warwick had excited her with talk of teachings in the ways of this new world which had been opened up to her, and spoken of things never being the same again – and then he had promptly left town! As for her uncle, he had left for Europe that very next evening, although thankfully not before explaining to her mother why she had returned so late the previous evening, sparing her from the jailer's wrath this time. Nothing else had happened since then, and everything now appeared to be just the same as it had always been. It was as though a hidden door to a fantastic and beautiful garden, albeit one that apparently also contained significant hidden dangers, had briefly been opened to her, just sufficiently to spark her imagination and make her long to enter, before being slammed shut again without a key to be found anywhere. It was almost as though the whole episode had been a dream.

However, though life had returned to its former dull path, it was nonetheless subtly different, for something inside Anna had changed. For one thing, despite the sudden and frustrating disappearance of Mr. Warwick and her uncle, Anna still felt sure that what she had heard from them touched on deep truths that were not about to go away, and she knew that they would both return at some point before too long to resume the story. She longed for it to be soon, but she was well-practiced in waiting.

As important to her as anything that Mr. Warwick had or could tell her though, had been the other thing that had happened, by the canal. It was the extremely brief but equally meaningful moments that she had shared with Timmy that had really made everything in her world look different. Until the moment that Timmy had so unexpectedly thrust that fistful of damaged flowers in her direction, Anna had lived her life in the self-assured certainty that no-one she cared about was ever likely to bring themselves truly to feel about her in the same way that she felt about them. She was sure she had not been blessed with the kind of looks that would attract boys to her in the way that she might be attracted to them, and although she had wished with all her heart that someone would be able to see beyond that surface layer, she had never had any reason to believe that this would ever actually happen. Oh how she had dreamt that one day, someone she cared for would see the good, well-meaning and even fun person that she could be inside, beyond the façade, but she had been certain that the shyness which always tied up her tongue and prevented her from revealing the good nature that lay within, would always successfully conspire with her plain looks at the most important moments to snuff out any hopes she might have of romantic happiness. How she had wished for hours on end in the solitude of her room that she had looked more beautiful and been blessed with greater confidence to express herself when she most needed to. However all this longing had, of course, always felt in vain.

But then a miracle had occurred, under that bridge beside the canal. Despite all her self-perceived shortcomings, the person for whom she had stronger feelings than anyone before in her life had somehow seemingly seen beyond all her flaws... and he had given her flowers! And she had kissed him on the cheek, twice! And she had even used the word love, even if a little indirectly. How had she ever managed to utter such a word?

Since it had happened she had relived those moments a thousand times, and every time she reached that point on that well-trodden path of her memory, the familiar, instinctive self-doubts began to jump out to grab her again. Had she said too much? Had she somehow taken a well-meaning but innocent gesture on the part of a friend, and then revealed too much of the depth of her own feelings, and shown them to be completely disproportionate to his? Would that fatal moment of boldness now turn him away forever? But she had left no aspect unexamined in recalling the details of those events, and each time there was one fact which came to her rescue. When the others had rejoined them on their side of the canal, Timmy had replied to his sister that he felt "great", having been feeling so glum but moments earlier. Of course there could have been many reasons for his having said that, but it did not seem to suggest that he was entirely unhappy after hearing her words! That thought at least was enough to keep her hope afloat in the sea of her self-doubt. Oh how she longed to know what it was that he had been intending to say to her just before Gillespie struck, and what he was thinking now.

Although the endless wondering and yearning were painful to endure, having such a hope, such a possibility for the future, was a good deal better than anything she had ever had before, and it allowed her to travel through the mundane life to which she had now returned with a new sense of purpose. The lonely hours in her room were now hours spent in eager anticipation of what the future might possibly hold for her and Timmy, and the long nights were filled with altogether different dreams! Dreams, and also much planning.

Whilst she might not have been able to do anything to hasten the return of her uncle and Mr. Warwick to continue their explanations about the true nature of the world, one thing she could do was to engineer a way to meet Timmy again. She could, and she simply had to if she was going to keep her tiny heart from exploding. She knew she had probably been very lucky to escape undetected the last time she had slipped out of the house without permission, and she knew that she should not rely on such luck again. However, this was simply a risk she would have to take, and then face whatever consequences might follow. Something magical had happened by that canal, at least for her, and she simply had to devise a plan to see Timmy again if she was to retain what remained of her sanity.

So after several weeks had passed since her last meeting with Timmy, Anna had ventured down into the depths of the house when her mother had gone out, fabricated sufficient excuses to survive the various questionings as to why she was heading down to the kitchens, and she had managed to catch Lizzy on her own for long enough to give her a message.

Lizzy's expression had been complex when Anna had asked her to get a message to her friends that she could see them the next afternoon "at the usual place", when she knew her mother was due to be out again. But there had been an unmistakable flicker in Lizzy's eyes when, in her haste, Anna had first of all said "Timmy" before hastily adding "and Rebecca and the others". Anna's feelings that she could not entirely trust Lizzy would not leave her, but at the same time she had no other obvious means by which to get a message out of the house, and so she had gone ahead with her plan.

Having successfully retraced her surreptitious tracks of a few weeks earlier, she waited under the canal bridge in the place they always met. She waited and she hoped that she had not been betrayed. The journey there had been thankfully uneventful; having successfully ridden her luck again in slipping out of the house unseen, there had only been one thing out of the ordinary which had caught her eye on her way to the canal. The poster outside the newspaper stand on the main road towards the canal had shouted 'The Beast of Highgate Strikes Again!' The bold headline had jumped off the paper when she had read it. There it was, that story again. Though Anna could not afford to linger to investigate any further, the headline had stuck in her mind just as it had done on her walk to Lord's. What could this be about?

Before too long though her mission had taken over her thoughts again as she had hastened on, and having reached the meeting place she had looked longingly down the towpath in the direction from which her companions would come, under the sky that was once again blue dappled with fluffy white, rather than slate grey. Two clear days in relatively quick succession! Anna felt as though her luck was definitely changing.

She waited for what seemed like an eternity for any signs they might be coming, of which there were none, and she clung to the hope that they had not yet arrived because she had got there well before the meeting time she had given Lizzy. However her customary worries and self-doubts slowly started to get the better of her again. Maybe Lizzy hadn't told Rebecca she would be there after all, and maybe they wouldn't be coming. Worse, what if Lizzy's unreadable expression had hidden the hatching of a plan to betray her, and to set her up for a trap? What if, rather than her friends, it was the Marylebone Gang who were now on their way to meet her, to wreak revenge for what she had done to Gillespie? Cold sweat began to break on her brow as the worries multiplied. She glanced with increasing anxiety up and down the canal.

Then just as she was starting to think she should make a run for it, her heart jumped as she saw some slightly scruffy forms approaching in the distance. But it was with joy that it leapt, as she had heard the excited babbling in the distance and she knew it wasn't her sworn enemies after all, but her long-yearned for friends. Resisting all urges to run down the path towards them and hug them, and one of them in particular, she remained where she was and did her best to remain calm. The anticipation of seeing Timmy again was forcing the blood into her head with a pounding so fierce that she could feel it in her ears, but she just managed to maintain control and call out in what she hoped was a suitably sarcastic tone, "So you've finally decided to come have you?"

Peering into the gloom the approaching group evidently could not see her at first, but then Rebecca spotted her (it was always Rebecca who saw things first), called out and ran forward to join her on her ledge. They gave each other a quick hug before being joined by the others – Johnny, Edward, Tessa, Tilly, Alice, Robert, Charlie… and there was Timmy. They were all there!

As on all previous occasions, Anna's instincts told her to be very subtle and guarded when glancing at Timmy, in case something in her look betrayed her feelings to the others, and not least to Timmy himself. But a lot of thoughts had passed through her mind since they had last met, and this time Anna allowed herself to look at him fully in the eyes for a few brief but beautiful seconds when he greeted her… and the look was returned! It was still only momentary, but enough to make her stomach turn a full somersault once again. It had been enough to suggest the possibility that she had not been wrong or dreaming in vain, and that he might even possibly have been feeling similar emotions himself since they last met. It was more than she had dared hope for, and she became light-headed for a few moments and lost all sense of what was going on around her. She wondered how the last few weeks had been for him, and whether he had been experiencing the same feelings and speculations as her. Of course she had looked away again very rapidly, and no-one had probably noticed the look between them (although one could never be sure in the case of that eagle-eyed sister of Timmy's). For the next few moments, Anna nodded without hearing and made out nothing of the gabbled conversations that were now taking place all around her, for her mind was racing instead along its own joyous roads.

However three words uttered amongst all the others drew her back into the here and now with a snap. Turning to Johnny, she asked "Did you say 'Beast of Highgate'?"

"Anna, haven't you been listening? I was just talking about it. Haven't you heard the news?"

"Um, well, no I haven't actually. You know what it's like in my house – nothing gets in or out without permission, not even the news! All I've seen are some newspaper headlines. What's it all about?"

"I don't believe it!" replied Johnny, which was met with similarly surprised agreement from the others. "You must be the only person in London who hasn't heard about it. I thought that news would have reached even you in your jail. It's on all the front pages of the newspapers, and it's all anyone's talking about.

"There have been some terrible murders in the Highgate area in the last few days. But it's not only that. There's been talk of the supernatural, of some kind of unearthly beast. Witnesses have spoken of terrible, inhuman cries, like the screaming of some terrible monster, right in the same areas where the victims' bodies have later been found. Two weeks ago, one man reckoned he saw this huge, black, winged creature in the distance in Waterlow Park in Highgate around twilight, attacking one of the victims who was found there later, body all savaged. Reckoned it looked like a demon from hell he did. Then last night another old women reckoned she saw that same creature attacking another poor man down the end of one of the big old roads which leads in the direction of Hampstead Heath, near one of them huge mansions, after it had gone dark. Never seen anything like it in all her years, she reckoned. And sure enough a body was found down there late last night, and a terrible state it was in too. There's lots of other accounts, too. Some of the stories are enough to make your blood curdle Anna, I tell you."

Anna did indeed start to feel a sudden chill in her blood as she listened to what Johnny had to say, cooling it from the steamy temperatures it had been reaching only moments before. The others in the group had also fallen silent to let Johnny update Anna, but now they all started talking at once again, giving her variations on the same theme that each of them had heard. Anna learned that there had been a variety of theories, from a crazed murderer dressed up in a disguise to hide his real identity and to terrify his victims, to Satan himself stalking the streets of north London. What was clear was that no-one, including the newspapers and the police, was sure of the real explanation, and everyone in the group was both appalled and fascinated by this mystery in equal measure.

Then Johnny, always the most impetuous of the group, piped up again. "I reckon we should go up there and have a look around! There's bound to be a load of coppers up there now searching the place, and maybe we can find out some more about what's going on."

"It's a long old walk up to Highgate from here, a good hour I reckon at least, probably closer to an hour and a half," responded Rebecca, although something in her tone suggested she might nonetheless be open to persuasion.

"But it will still be light for at least a couple more hours," returned Johnny, "and besides, I'm sure we can have some fun on the way. I haven't been up to Highgate for ages."

"But it might be dangerous!" countered Tessa. "What will we do if we meet the Beast?"

"Nah, we'll be all right," responded Johnny in a manner so typical of him, Anna thought. "If we stick to the main areas where there are lots of adults around, we'll be fine. Besides, the Beast has only struck at night so far."

The others joined in with their various views, but a consensus quickly emerged. As always, Anna's first thoughts were about the trouble she could get into if she was away from home for too long and her absence became noted. But since her evening with Mr. Warwick and her uncle, and her uncle's subsequent discussion with her mother, Anna felt that although her mother would undoubtedly scold her if she realised she had slipped out without permission, something had now changed, and she would be able to face whatever came her way more easily. At least, that's what she wanted to believe, because more importantly a long walk might provide more opportunities for her to talk with Timmy, who had already stated that he was ready for the adventure. That would be a prize worth enduring any amount of punishment for. "I'm coming too!" she chimed in to the sound of surprised approval from her friends.

"All right then, that's it settled. Let's go." replied Rebecca. The debate concluded, the group set off in a northerly direction. Anna felt alive again, and she told Rebecca how relieved she had been when they had all finally arrived.

"Well of course we came. What made you think we wouldn't? Mind you, I reckon you are right to be wary of that Lizzy. She did pass on your message all right, but she's only helping us because there's something she wants from me. And it's something I'm afraid I can't give her. I think we are going to need to find a new way of communicating, and I'd suggest you be very careful how you deal with her from now on. Can't say any more right now," she concluded a little cryptically, because various others of the group had now caught up with them and they began to bombard Anna with questions. There had been something in this brief conversation that had threatened to trigger Anna's highly-tuned worry reflexes, but the lively conversation with her friends and the joyous freedom of the moment were enough to dispel any such worries for now. She would try to delve further into what Rebecca had meant another time when the opportunity arose again.

For the first half an hour or so the conversations continued amongst the whole group, largely on the theme of the Beast and what it could be. Midway through, something else was mentioned that caught Anna's attention immediately. Once again it was Johnny who was talking when she heard the name 'Faulkner'.

"Who's Faulkner?" she asked, memories from Mr. Warwick's shop of that tall, dark-haired man with *that* essence rushing back into her mind.

"Faulkner's a right nasty piece of work – 'the most dangerous man in London', if you believe the stories." Which Johnny obviously would, thought Anna, as he had always been one for picking up stories and general gossip. "No-one knows where he came from – just appeared on the scene one day they say, and bought himself a big old mansion near Highgate. Dresses in fine clothes like a real gentleman and has the money to match, but by all accounts a man who acts less like a gentleman you're never likely to meet.

"There are some wild stories about him. According to some, most women find him irresistible, as though he puts a spell on them or something, and several have disappeared after having been in his company... and there's those who reckon that's because Faulkner's true identity is a vampire, and that he has killed them to drink their blood!"

Anna certainly did not believe in vampires, but a shiver went through her nonetheless as Tilly gasped at Johnny's story.

Clearly enjoying being the centre of attention now, Johnny continued, "And then there's those that reckon he's into that, what do they call it? Devil worshipping and the like... the occult, that's it. Reckon he performs evil ceremonies and that kind of thing, they do. And now this Beast has started to appear, right up there in Highgate, right near where he lives! Well, it wasn't long before people were putting two and two together and reckoning that it's actually Faulkner who's somehow been summoning that Beast, straight from the pits of hell!"

This brought several more gasps from the audience, as the group continued to make their way northwards. For her part,

Anna was naturally sceptical about any stories of this kind, especially when the storyteller was Johnny, but she could not get the downright evil appearance of that man's essence out of her mind. 'Almost certainly the most evil thing you have ever seen,' Mr. Warwick's words came back to her. It had to mean something, and she vowed next time to ask Mr. Warwick more about Faulkner, and not to forget as she had done last time in the midst of all the other things she had been learning about.

"Where's Faulkner's mansion? Is it actually in Highgate?" Alice asked.

"No, I don't think so. Well I'm not actually sure to be honest," Johnny admitted, "but what they said was that it was on the edge of Highgate, between Highgate and Hampstead Heath I think. Right in the area where the Beast murdered that man last night in fact!"

Johnny was able to hold his audience for a while longer with his stories, but following some further speculation about Faulkner's identity, what his role might be in summoning the Beast of Highgate (which to their credit, thought Anna, more than half the group still did not actually believe really existed), and whether or not they might meet him when they finally reached their destination, the discussion died down. Anna obviously could not tell them anything about what she had seen of Faulkner's essence, and instinctively she decided it better not to mention that she had seen him at all. Unlike Johnny, she was more than happy not to be centre of attention.

Gradually, conversations began to break out among smaller groups, and Anna noticed that Timmy had dropped towards the back of the crowd. Trying to look as nonchalant as possible, Anna also slowed down her own pace, and before long she was walking alongside Timmy at the back.

"So how have you been?" she asked, trying to make her conversation sound natural, knowing that they could still be overheard by the others, whilst at the same time also trying to prevent her heart from leaping out of her chest.

"I've been great thanks," replied Timmy, flashing her a quick, beaming grin. Anna felt her cheeks redden as her heart raced even faster. Then her mind started to fog over, and suddenly she couldn't think of anything to say! She searched for words, but the more she thought the more her mind went blank. Why did this always have to happen, always when she most wanted to make a good impression? The more powerful her feelings, the less able she seemed to string a sentence together. The silence started to deepen, and with it so did Anna's sense of panic that she would no longer be able to think of anything coherent to say, to the person who was the subject of all her dreams. She was about to ruin everything! But then, to her indescribable relief, Timmy managed to come up with something, and he asked her, "Did you get into any trouble last time? I mean after we jumped in the canal?"

Relieved to have a subject other than her tumultuous emotions and frenzied state of mind to focus on, Anna replied, "No, luckily Mr. Warwick let me dry myself and my clothes in his shop, and I made it back home before it got too late, without being seen – so all was fine."

"Good, I'm glad to hear that," replied Timmy. Trying to keep the conversational momentum going for fear that her nerves might otherwise start to freeze her brain over again, Anna asked, "Any more run-ins with the Marylebone Street Gang since Gillespie went for his swim?"

Timmy smiled, clearly now over his embarrassment at having been defended by a girl. "Actually yes, although no more fights this time. Becca and I saw the Fletcher brothers acting very suspicious, carrying some more of them packages and looking all around them like they were trying not to get spotted. So we decided to follow them, and eventually they met up with that thug Archie Knowles who took the packages off them. But then we thought they'd seen us, and with Knowles with them we could have been in trouble so we decided to run for it. Then yesterday, Edward and Charlie saw Bobby Watson carrying another package. They reckon he saw them and then he suddenly darted down an alleyway as if to avoid being followed. So we don't know what they're up to, but there's no doubt they're up to something shady. Probably running errands for criminals, we reckon." Then, as if anticipating Anna's next question, he added "No more sightings of Gillespie though," and then he shared another smile with Anna.

The season had turned in the weeks since Anna had last been out, and it was now a beautiful early autumn day. The late afternoon sun filtered through the leaves of the trees that lined the avenue along which they were now all walking, catching the yellow and orange ones which had started to flutter to the ground in a way that gave the place a slightly magical feel. The colours were almost as bright as they had been the morning of the cricket match, and even more varied now that autumn had arrived. Even the birdsong overhead seemed louder than usual. It felt to Anna as though all her senses were sharper than they had ever been before. Although she had doubtless seen similar scenes many times before, it was as though, since that previous day by the canal, she was seeing the whole world for the first time, and she was struck anew by the beauty of it all. She felt as though she was walking on air – and literally she could barely feel the pavement beneath her feet.

However beautiful the sensations picked up by her external senses may have been at that moment though, even they paled in comparison to the beauty of what she was now feeling within. With Timmy's help she had successfully negotiated the treacherous terrain of early conversation, overcome the usually insurmountable embarrassment barrier, her tongue had been untied and she had now somehow entered into a normal conversation with the one who filled most of her waking thoughts. "I wonder what was in those packages then?" she continued the conversation, focusing on anything but the answer.

"Yeah, that's what we've been wondering 'n all. Couldn't really tell, but the ones we saw were about this big," said Timmy, gesturing to suggest a box over a foot long and high. "Whatever was in them though, they looked heavy and we reckoned they'd been stolen."

"You're probably right. That would explain why they were looking so suspicious, and it wouldn't surprise me at all if that Knowles had any part to play in it."

"Mind you," and Timmy suddenly lowered his voice as he continued, "A couple of people have said that the person they're running those errands for is actually that same person Johnny was talking about earlier – that man Faulkner." At the mention of this, for the first time since they had started talking Anna began to focus more on the content of what was being said than on the mere fact that they were talking. "And what Johnny said about Faulkner was true – I don't mean what he actually said about Faulkner, but that people are talking that way about him – and I've heard some real nasty theories about what might be in those boxes they're carrying. Things for his evil ceremonies and so on. But you know me, I'm not like Johnny and I don't really believe any of that kind of thing."

"No, me neither," said Anna truthfully, but still wishing she could get the image of that spiked black and red essence out of her head. And after her conversation with Mr. Warwick and her uncle, nothing seemed quite as straight forward as it had.

"Anyhow, so Becca, me and the others, we all want to find out what those Maryleboners are up to. We're planning to follow any of them we see from now on, to try and find out some more."

"You will be careful though won't you?" responded Anna without thinking, for the first time saying something a little uncharacteristic that might hint at her real feelings had anyone been paying attention. Immediately she regretted saying it, but Timmy responded, "Don't worry Anna, I'll be fine with you girls around to protect me!" and then they both laughed.

Their brief conversation, which was so much more important to Anna than any of the words it had contained, was then cut short as Alice and Tilly dropped back to ask Anna how she had been. Part of Anna was sorry that she couldn't continue talking with Timmy alone, but her spirits remained higher than the blue sky above as she revelled in the freedom, the company of her friends and the sense that Timmy might just be feeling the same way that she did. The group remained in good spirits, joking and playing pranks on each other as they continued their journey for another half an hour. Just as they were making their way up a steep hill approaching Highgate, Rebecca suddenly stopped dead in her tracks. She gestured to them all to take cover, and looking into the distance, Anna saw two figures on the road ahead of them. Sure enough it was Davy Green and Bobby Watson, two of their Marylebone Street enemies, and each was carrying a package!

Ducking down the nearest side street on the right and then peering back round the corner, Rebecca said in a low voice, "Right, this time we follow them all the way and find out what they're up to once and for all."

"Yes!" cried out Johnny, before immediately being scolded by Rebecca for making too much noise.

"But we've got to be very careful, and we'd better not all stay in one big group or we're sure to be seen," said Rebecca. Taking control as always, she divided them up into pairs and continued, "Johnny and Edward, you go down this street," pointing further down the road they had just ducked into, which ran perpendicular to the one along which they had been travelling, "then turn left at the next junction and head up the hill towards Highgate from there. Go as fast as you can, try to get there before Green and Watson, then wait for us there and let us know where they go next. The rest of us will continue following them up this avenue in separate pairs. Now listen everyone," Rebecca's voice was now deadly serious and she commanded everyone's full attention, "we've got to avoid been recognised. First of all, stick close to the other side of the road, in the shadows of the buildings where it will be more difficult for them to see us. Secondly, each pair must keep separate, since we're less likely to catch the eye that way. Also whatever you do, don't make it obvious you're looking at them. Try to look down as much as possible, only glancing up to check they're still ahead of us and to pick up any signals from me. That way if they do look round they're less likely to see your faces, and to think you're following them. I'm determined to find out what they're doing this time, so no-one must give us away, understand?"

Rebecca's words were so final that no-one would have dared to voice their disagreements even if they had had any. However Anna had no doubt they were all just as keen as Rebecca to learn more about the gang's activities. Johnny and Edward then sprinted off down the side street as Rebecca had directed, and Rebecca and Charlie led the way back onto the main avenue. They crossed the road towards the shadows at the far side of the street, which were now long in the early evening sun, and then turned right again in the direction of Highgate and their prey. Walking casually and looking at the ground and the building that they were passing with only the very occasional glance ahead of them, Anna was impressed with the pair of them – no-one would have guessed that they were following anyone.

Anna was very grateful to Rebecca for pairing her with Timmy (being Rebecca, Anna doubted that it had been pure chance) and they were the next to set off. Keeping a safe distance behind the first pair, they followed their tracks attempting to appear equally nonchalant. Reaching the shaded far side of the street, Anna allowed herself to steal her first surreptitious glance up the hill in the direction of the

Marylebone duo, and sure enough there they were, barely still in sight now at the brow of the hill. Neither was looking behind them, and they appeared to be unaware that they were being trailed. 'So far so good,' thought Anna to herself, looking back with feigned interest at the rather rundown second hand piano shop to her left. As soon as the Maryleboners had disappeared over the brow of the hill and out of sight, she heard a shouted whisper from Rebecca ahead of them, and saw her gesture to them to quicken their pace towards the top of the hill to avoid their targets escaping. Looking quickly behind her over her shoulder Anna could see Alice and Tessa a safe distance behind them now following in their footsteps, and some way behind them, Robert had just started his journey and was crossing the road over to their side together with Tilly, exactly as per Rebecca's instructions. Anna conveyed Rebecca's latest message to Alice and Tessa, who signalled back that they had received the message and would pass it on.

"I hope they don't get away," whispered Timmy by her side as they quickened their pace.

"Yes, so do I," whispered Anna in reply, thoroughly enjoying herself and filled with eager anticipation now at where this pursuit might lead them. Reaching the brow of the hill, Anna saw the outskirts of Highgate before them, with Rebecca and Charlie about twenty yards ahead, and in the distance were Green and Watson, still plainly visible and apparently still none the wiser. Casting quick glances behind her, it wasn't long before she saw the rest of the group also appearing over the brow of the hill.

And so the secret pursuit continued. Just as the Maryleboners approached the end of the avenue, Timmy tugged gently at Anna's sleeve and then subtly gestured towards a large tree in the distance on the corner of the avenue and a large road that traversed its end. At first she could see nothing, but then she grinned as she just made out the figure of Edward, partially concealed in its upper branches.

"I'd never have seen him if I hadn't been looking for him and Johnny," whispered Timmy, and Anna agreed, wondering now where Johnny might be hiding. Although the leaves were turning, the trees still most of their foliage and Edward was surely invisible to the Maryleboners, who were now almost directly below him.

At the end of the avenue, the package-carrying duo waited for a horse and cart to pass, then crossed the road before turning left and disappearing from view in front of a large old church. Rebecca and Charlie ahead of them immediately quickened their pace again, as did Timmy and Anna so as not to lose the trail. Glancing again behind her, Anna saw Robert and Tilly at the back darting down a side street that Anna and Timmy had passed earlier. They had obviously decided to take a different route to intercept their prey further down the street. 'Bound to be Robert's idea,' thought Anna, hoping they would not give themselves away when they emerged.

As Timmy and Anna drew near the corner in the direction in which the Maryleboners had gone and then peered around it, they immediately saw Rebecca and Charlie scurrying down the road looking left and right, but there was no sign of their quarry anywhere. Just then, Edward approached them from behind having descended from his perch and he shouted a whisper, "They went down there!" He was pointing to the next side street on the right hand side, leading down the left side of the large church. Returning towards them, Rebecca hissed in reply, "but we looked in that direction and they weren't there." Then a shrill whistle filled the air momentarily. Looking all around them and then upwards, Rebecca was the first to spot Johnny, perched up behind a mini spire at the left hand corner of the church. 'How on earth did he get up there?' wondered Anna to herself, grinning broadly. Johnny was pointing again in the direction of the street beside the church, and he risked a shouted whisper of his own, "they went down here, and then left again down the next road."

"Good work Johnny!" whispered Rebecca, and this time they all hastened in that direction, forgetting all about being in pairs now. Reaching the corner, Anna came up behind Rebecca who was already leaning forward and peering round it, and on tiptoes Anna peered in turn over her shoulder. Timmy, Edward and Charlie were crowded behind them, Charlie panting somewhat, and all did their best to remain concealed as they looked on. And sure enough there were the targets of their pursuit, walking slowly now, mounting the steps of a large, dilapidated-looking house on the far side of the road.

Anna took in the street they were now looking at. It was not as wide as the avenue along which they had been walking, but the houses were large nonetheless. As she gazed down from one building to the next, she noticed how much duller, darker and decrepit-looking the house that their foes stood outside appeared in comparison to all the others, as though it alone in the street had borne the travails of time and had reached a point of terminal decay. Anna looked around her for a street name, and she saw a sign on the corner of the road opposite. 'Eagle Street' it read, and Anna assigned the distinctive name to memory, just in case.

She watched as Watson rapped on the dull brass door knocker that looked as though it had not had the feel of polish upon it for many a year, possibly many a decade, and then waited in silence for what must have been minutes before the door started slowly to open. Anna held her breath, straining to catch a glimpse of whoever was on the other side. And then she saw him. It was a tall, thin man in a long black cloak, with long, bony fingers that clutched at the edge of the black door. His face was that of an aging man, wrinkled and deathly pale, with large black bags under his black eyes and deeply gaunt cheeks, all framed by thin streaks of long, greasy, grey hair. His appearance gave Anna the overall impression that she was looking at some kind of living skeleton, albeit one with its sagging, leathery white skin still attached. She was too far away to make out his essence clearly, but the deadly expression in his eyes and the snarling downward curl of the pale sagging skin at either side of his mouth as he uttered something to the waiting boys left Anna in no doubt that this was a man of no good intent. What she could make out of his essence clarified her suspicions – she was only able to get an overall impression at this distance, but it was an impression of brown, black and red! Something prompted the word 'Satal' to appear in her mind, and she started to wonder.

The Marylebone pair, usually so full of self-confident swagger, now had an altogether different demeanour, appearing to cower in the presence of this cloaked man. Looking down at his shoes, Watson appeared to mutter something to the man, which the latter met with another snarling utterance before slowly opening the door wider and allowing the now meek duo to enter the murky darkness within. The aging man appeared to push the second boy forward with one withered hand as he followed them inside, and Anna's eye was drawn to the bony fingers of the man's other hand, which was still clutching the door like some kind of hideous, bony spider. On its second finger was a golden ring set with what looked like a very large, black jewel of some kind, visible even at this distance. Just then, the man jutted his head outside the door again, looking first to his right, then starting to move his eyes to his left towards them. As one, the group instinctively ducked back behind the wall, each holding their breath, hoping against hope that those malicious black eyes had not spied them. Seconds later, they heard the distant noise of a door being closed, and holding the others back, Rebecca was the first to dare to peer slowly and carefully back around the corner again. Anna saw her form relax slightly, and then joined her to see that the door with its flaking black paint had indeed been closed, its deathly-looking occupant nowhere in sight.

"He nearly saw us!" said Rebecca, leaning back against the wall and letting out a long breath, as though she had been holding it for quite some time. Looking further down the street, they then saw Robert, Tilly, Alice and Tessa appear at the corresponding corner at the far end. They started to make as if to come down the street to meet with the rest of the group, but Rebecca gestured immediately for them to stop and instead return the way they had come. "Can't see anyone in the upper windows of that old house and the lower ones are shuttered, but I ain't taking no chances all the same," she whispered. In silence, Rebecca, Timmy, Charlie and Anna also retraced their steps some way back along the road by the church, where they were met by Johnny who had completed his descent from his observation point. They waited for their companions, who soon rounded the corner to join them. Then the communal silence gave out and everyone started talking excitedly at once again.

"Did you see that scary old man?" asked Robert of Rebecca and the others. "We'd just got there as those Maryleboners were going into the house, and then I thought he might've seen us when he looked back out again, but I think we got away with it."

"I hope for all our sakes that he didn't see you. That was one person I would not want after me!" replied Charlie.

Prompted by those words, Rebecca quickly retraced her steps back to the road corner again just to reconfirm that no-one was coming after them. She returned shortly to reassure them that the street was still deserted.

"You're right though," she continued, "he was an evil-looking one all right. I wonder what on earth Watson and Green are doing running errands for someone like that."

"Yeah," chimed in Edward, "I mean, did you see them? They looked terrified, not that I blame them. Didn't look like they were there for the fun of it, that's for sure. I wonder if they've got themselves into some kind of trouble."

"Well if they have, it's their own fault," responded Johnny.

"That's as maybe," rejoined Rebecca, "but we haven't completed our mission yet. We still don't know what they're up to, or what was in those packages... and in fact the mystery's only got deeper now."

"Let's wait here until they come out again, and then let's corner them and demand they tell us what they're up to!" cried Edward.

"Knowing them lot, they probably won't tell us though," countered Johnny. "I reckon we have to actually see what they're doing. I'm going to try to see inside the house!" he declared in typical Johnny fashion.

"I don't see how you can," said Charlie. "Look, all the ground floor windows are shuttered from the inside, even though it's still light."

"I know that," replied Johnny, "but I ain't talking about the front am I? I'm going round the back." It wasn't clear from looking, but it seemed possible that they might be able to gain access to the back down the side of the building.

This exclamation created a divide in the group. On one side, Robert and Edward piped up, "Yeah, we'll come with you!" whilst on the other Tilly was saying "Oh no, Johnny, please don't do that," Alice began to warn her younger brother Robert that he'd better be careful and Tessa added, "Didn't you see that man? I'm scared of him."

"He'll have to catch me first though won't he?" was Johnny's defiant reply.

Anna also had reservations about this plan. Ordinarily she would have opposed the idea of entering someone else's property on principle, but she knew that Johnny wouldn't be suggesting it either if this was any ordinary house. It was clear to all of them that this place was probably either occupied by criminals, which would be one explanation as to why the Maryleboners had gone there with their suspect parcels, or else that something even more sinister was going on.

However Anna felt a different fear about the place. The others had all commented on the appearance of the old man, but apart from Tilly and Tessa they all seemed to have already recovered from it. However for some reason Anna could not shake a deep-seated fear in the pit of her stomach, and try as she might she could not rid from her mind the image of that gaunt old man, his skeletal hands and that evil-looking ring on his finger. She realised that this fear was not based on anything specific, but it was still real and it remained. Her mind flashed momentarily back to the stories that Mr. Warwick had shared of the Omega World, that world that should not be, and she wondered again. There had been something of the night about that man... She remembered Mr. Warwick's warning that she should not be found by the forces of their enemy, and her apprehension grew.

Although Johnny had spoken boldly, he still lingered, waiting for Rebecca's opinion before setting out. Rebecca was the oldest and their unofficial leader, and in the end they all deferred to her view. She had not committed so far, but after a pause, she spoke. "Well, usually I'd say we had no business poking around other people's private houses. That's the sort of thing the Marylebone Street Gang might do, or robbers and other criminals. But in this case it definitely ain't no ordinary place, and they're definitely up to no good in there if I'm any judge. And you know what? Much as I don't like those Maryleboners, I think they could actually be in trouble in there. I think they may have got themselves right out of their depth this time. So now that we've come all this way, I think we should find out for once and for all what's been going on."

"So Johnny, Edward and I will see if we can find a way in at the back, and Anna, why don't you come too. After seeing how you dealt with the whole Marylebone Gang last time, I reckon you might be useful in a tight spot!"

Anna smiled, partly pleased to have Rebecca think such a thing, but the larger part of her filled with foreboding that this might bring her face-to-face with that man. However she was no coward and her determination not to let the others down conquered all other emotions. Taking a deep breath she resolved to join them and help in whatever way she could. "All right, let's go then," she said.

"You others remain here and keep a look out at the front of the building, in case anyone leaves – or arrives for that matter," continued Rebecca. Robert, Charlie and most of all Timmy began to protest loudly, but as Alice reproached her brother, Rebecca explained, "If more than four go, we're more likely to get found out, and this way you can let us know if they leave the house, so that we can come back to follow them with you. Robert, if anyone leaves, you give one of them whistles like Johnny did before so we can come back round. If we need help, Johnny will give his whistle again. All right?"

Rebecca allowed no more protests, and Anna set off with her three companions down the road that led back to Eagle Street. They had gone no more than a few paces however when in the distance behind them there came the sudden sound of clattering hooves. Hastily the group all began walking in the opposite direction, dispersing and trying to look as casual as possible as a carriage came careering round the corner and almost hit them! Narrowly missing Charlie as he dived to the cobblestoned street, it continued on, and then swerved into the street where the Marylebone Gang boys had entered the house.

"Hey!" and "What do you think you're doing?" shouted Rebecca and Johnny at the same time as the carriage disappeared round the corner, but the driver, hat pulled down low over his eyes, didn't look round or say a word.

"He was certainly in a hurry wasn't he?" said Charlie, dusting himself off after Johnny had helped him to his feet.

"Yeah, and I bet I know where he was going 'n all!"

replied Rebecca, rushing back to the corner of the street again. The rest joined her to see what was going to happen next, remaining concealed as best they could. Sure enough, the carriage had come to a sudden halt outside the house into which the Marylebone Street boys had entered.

The driver jumped down from the carriage, bounded up the steps and rapped loudly on the door. "He really is in a hurry isn't he?" whispered Timmy to Anna, who nodded silently. She was certain she was about to see that old man again and she shrank back slightly, watching on in grim anticipation.

Moments later the door opened again, but this time it was not the old man. It was a younger-looking man carrying two boxes which looked the same size and shape as the packages the two boys had taken to the house. He was a rough-looking type, but not as downright evil-looking as the other man, Anna thought. Looking left and right, he moved forward out of the doorway and he was followed by first one then the other Marylebone Street boy. Both looked even more downcast than they had when they had arrived, and Anna thought Green even looked as though he might have been crying. And then *he* appeared in the doorway behind them. The old man, looking just as pale and deathlike as the image which was already etched into Anna's memory from their earlier sighting. He was holding a silver-tipped black walking cane with what looked like a silver skull at the top end, around which his skeletal fingers were wrapped like knobbly white vines. And there again was that hideous, black-jewelled ring.

At that moment, Green suddenly tried to make a run for it, darting past the younger man, round the other side of the driver and down the rest of the steps towards the street. But no sooner had his feet touched the pavement than the black caped figure of the old man was upon him, having sprung right from the wall near the top of the stairs! Landing on the boy's back like a giant black spider, he knocked him clean to the ground and then raised his cane before bringing it crashing down on the poor boy's back. Green howled with pain as the hideous old man raised his withered hand and then struck his victim again, then a third time, his lank, greasy hair slapping against the side of his face as he did so. Anna and the others stood frozen to the spot, shocked by the speed and ferocity of the old man's attack. Anna saw Watson now struggling forward to try to help his friend, but he was held back by the powerful younger man who had momentarily cast the boxes he was carrying to one side

Then the old man spoke in a hissing voice which, whilst less of a voice than a hoarse whisper, contained sufficient anger and venom to carry clear to where Anna and her friends were hiding. "You would try to escape, would you boy? You think you can get away? Well let me tell you, there is no escape from us! No escape, you hear me?" Crouching over him, he reached down with his horrible white hands and lifted his victim a foot from the ground by the lapels of his battered jacket, and brought his face to within an inch of his own. With his deathly black eyes piercing those of the now limp youth, his curled, snarling mouth continued, "You belong to us now, do you understand?" His voice then rose, "Do you understand? You come and you go when we tell you that you can, but even when you are away you will never again be free from our will. Now that you belong to us, we will always be able to find you wherever you go – there is nowhere you can hide from us now. Nowhere! The only choice remaining to you now is to do exactly as we tell you. And in our service you may indeed flourish and have all your desires fulfilled..." The old man paused, smiled thinly, then continued, starting in a slightly quieter but even more deadly tone, before his voice rose to a terrible, shrieking crescendo as he completed his next sentence, "But I warn you boy, you dare to cross me one more time, just once more, and I will kill you with my bare hands!"

With that he thrust him back down onto the pavement and stepped away, gesturing to the driver who hoisted up his limp form and dragged him into the carriage. Green offered no more resistance. Watson was already inside the carriage by now, and any thoughts he might have harboured for his own escape had clearly been extinguished. The younger man retrieved the boxes and their contents, a number of old-looking books which had spilled out, and he entered the carriage. With one final quick glance around at the deserted street, the odious old man himself then climbed in, slammed the door shut and rapped audibly on the carriage ceiling as a signal to the driver to depart. The latter instantly did as instructed, quite possibly for fear of a fate similar to that of his young passenger, and geed the horses up to leave at a pace similar to that at which they had arrived. The carriage swerved around the far corner of the street out of sight, and they were gone.

Anna and her companions looked on for a moment in stunned silence, none of them wanting to speak. It was not only that Green had been subjected to such a brutal, albeit thankfully very brief, attack – it was the nightmarish image of that old man which had left them all momentarily rooted to the spot. This time it was Anna who was the first to react, sensing perhaps even more keenly than the others the severe danger their hitherto foes were now in.

"Come on," she shouted to the others, "we have to help them. I think they're in terrible danger now."

"But I want to look inside the house and see what those good for nothings were up to," Johnny was the next to speak.

"No, Anna's right," responded Rebecca sternly. "They may be our sworn enemies, but right now those two are in way over their heads, and their own friends aren't around to help them. You saw what just happened. This could be really serious, and we're the only ones who can help them – so we've got to try."

There was no more dispute, and the group took off as one

down the street in which they had just witnessed the frightening scene. Rounding the corner, Anna was fearful that travelling at the speed that it was the carriage would soon be out of sight, and they would then never be able to trace it. Running down the road,though they were it was still some time before they reached another broad avenue with a view down the hill. The friends looked frantically left and right, but Anna could see nothing.

"Look, down there!" cried Timmy, pointing into the distance beyond the far end of the avenue, to a wide gap between two large-looking houses on the road that crossed the end of the one they were on. And sure enough, briefly visible was the black carriage, before it disappeared behind the next house.

"It's heading in the direction of the Heath," shouted Johnny, running forwards to climb on a nearby wall for a better view. Joining him, they all watched as the carriage, which looked quite miniature by now, continued at its breakneck pace towards its destination. From their vantage point they had a good view down the hillside, into an area of greenery interspersed with enormous houses which were connected by the road down which the carriage was travelling. Finally it slowed as it came to a large set of gates, it swerved once again and then it passed through them. Accelerating once more down what looked like a curving driveway to the right beyond the gates, it disappeared from view behind the green and yellow foliage of the trees.

"I've got no idea what that place is, but it looks like the driveway to a house, so if we can find those gates then we may still be able to find them," said Rebecca.

"That must be a good mile away, probably two, and it will be getting dark soon," responded Charlie, looking a little reluctant.

"Then we've got no time to waste. Come on, let's go!" cried Rebecca, and the friends hared off down the street.

They sprinted at first, and then gradually slowed to a

more sustainable run as they got further down the hill. On the way they passed two separate groups of policemen, presumably in the area on account of 'the Beast'. They all looked on inquiringly as the children sped passed them, but they did not say anything – their business was obviously too serious to concern themselves with the comings and goings of children. However, Anna called out to the others to stop, and when they had all gathered she proposed that they tell the police what they had seen, and get their help in rescuing the two Maryleboners. "I think this is serious, not to mention probably dangerous, and I think we should try to get all the proper help we can."

Following a quick discussion, it was agreed that Anna and Rebecca should go and do the talking, since between them they had the best chance of being believed.

"Excuse me constable," Rebecca called out on nearing the closest group of three policemen. "We have just seen two boys about our age being attacked and dragged into a carriage. We think they've been kidnapped and taken to a house down there." She gestured in the general direction of the gates they had seen in the distance.

The policemen looked at each other momentarily, then one of them asked, "All right, who kidnapped them? What did he look like?"

"It was a horrible old man, he looked more dead than alive, with long white fingers, like a skeleton," Anna chipped in, using the first words she could find to describe the image that still burned in her mind. It was only after she had spoken that she realised how they must have sounded.

But it was too late. "Dead-looking, like a skeleton you say? Here in Highgate in broad daylight? From Highgate cemetery was he? Suppose you've been hearing stories about the Beast, and thought you'd come up here and make mischief did you? Did they put you up to it?" said the policeman, nodding his head in the direction of their companions who were looking on some distance away.

"No sir. I'm sorry, I didn't mean…" Anna stammered.

"She didn't mean he was actually a skeleton. She just said that he looked a bit like one. Look, he had long grey hair, and he had a big black ring on his finger. He attacked the two boys and took them off in his carriage with an accomplice. Now are you going to help them?"

"No, we're not going to help them, because I don't believe there are any boys. Now listen here you two, I'm sure you've been put up to this by your friends, but you ought to know better than to waste valuable police time. My colleagues and I are in the middle of a double shift, ain't been home for fourteen hours we ain't, and we don't take kindly to having our time wasted by young tearaways. Even properly spoken ones!" he added, looking disapprovingly at Anna. "We've got important matters to deal with, what with the murders 'n all, and we don't need the likes of you coming up here and making mischief about it. Now clear off before we take you home to your parents for a good hiding!"

Anna and Rebecca needed no second telling. They apologised and left the irate constable as fast as they reasonably felt they could. As soon as they were out of earshot, Anna whispered under her breath to Rebecca, "I'm so sorry about that. That was the first time I have actually spoken to a policeman, and I think I must have panicked. I hadn't meant to say -"

"I know, Anna, listen, don't worry about it," interjected Rebecca. "It doesn't matter, and I don't think there was anything we could have said that would have made a difference. They're too busy with their investigations of the Beast, and there was no chance that they were going to listen to a group of children like us. We were just wasting our time."

Reaching the group again, Rebecca updated them all. "The police ain't interested folks, too busy they reckon. Looks like we're on our own, so I suggest we get on with it."

Deeply grateful to Rebecca for not recounting the detail

of the conversation that had actually taken place, Anna joined her friends in running down the hill again. They continued for another five minutes before Tessa, who was panting at the back of the group, was the first to shout to the others, "Stop, please, I can't keep up."

Johnny and Timmy, who were by now in the lead, slowed down until everyone had caught up. "All right," said Rebecca, breathing heavily herself, "let's get there as fast as we can, but whatever happens we mustn't get separated now. We must all stay together."

All agreed, and the group set off again, this time at more of a brisk walk. They were soon at the junction of the road along which Timmy had seen the carriage passing, and they proceeded straight down it without stopping. This was a wide road with increasingly large houses spaced further and further apart on either side of the road.

"Doesn't feel like we're in London any more, does it? Look at that place!" cried Johnny, looking up to his left at a huge white mansion, set back from the road with a curling drive leading up to its pillared porch.

"And what about that one?" Charlie joined in, looking down the hill to their right at another magnificent building, even larger than the last one, with even more pillars and a beautiful flower garden flowing down the slope towards it.

"I thought you lived in a palace, Anna, but even your place ain't a patch on these ones," Rebecca quipped. "Bet it makes you feel right poor doesn't it?"

"Yes, I'm shocked!" responded Anna in mock horror, before continuing in a slightly more serious tone, "although it doesn't necessarily mean they're happy, just because they live in big houses."

"Hmm," mused Rebecca, "well I'm sure you're right, Anna... but I think it would still help!"

They passed the last of the houses, and then there were nothing but trees lining the road. Anna noticed the first signs of darkness now, and the worry which had been nagging at the back of her mind for some time moved centre stage. It was getting late and she was nowhere near home. Her absence was sure to be found out this time, but she could not consider leaving her friends and abandoning the mission now.

"We're not too far from Hampstead Heath now, I think," said Alice, and then added after a short hesitation, "Wasn't it around here that the Beast of Highgate was supposed to have attacked that man last night?"

The group fell silent as that thought sunk in. After a long pause, Johnny then spoke up in a quieter voice, "Yeah, actually you're right, it was. In fact I think it was exactly round here. Why aren't there any coppers around here, instead of them all being back there on the high street?"

No-one had an answer, and the silence resumed as they pushed on through the gathering gloom, each consumed with their own thoughts, but all of them on the same fearful subject. Then at last they came upon the gates through which the carriage had passed, on the right hand side of the road.

Now that they were close to them, the gates were even larger and more imposing than they had looked from up the hill. Indeed they were positively intimidating, hinged as they were on huge stone pillars, with a large fence stretching into the distance behind the trees on either side.

"I wonder what this place is?" Anna pondered aloud, her voice now sounding somehow smaller and more timid than before.

There were trees directly ahead, but now they were nearby, in the failing light they could see through the gaps the shape of an enormous house in the middle distance, slightly below them down a slope, with a high roof topped by at least a dozen tall chimney stacks. At the left hand end of the building as they looked rose a short tower with what appeared to be battlements on the top of it. Gothic was a word that Anna thought she had heard used to describe the appearance of buildings such as this sinister looking one.

"Looks more like a castle than a house," said Johnny. "Wait a minute, I wonder if this is where that man Faulkner lives. They said it was a big old place, and this must be right around the area where they said it was. Right near where the Beast struck last night..." Johnny's voice tailed off, then silence enveloped them once more.

Anna had now started to feel that same sense of foreboding that she had felt outside the decrepit old house in Highgate earlier, but this time it was growing more intense. She glanced around at her companions and she could see how on edge they all looked now too. In fact in all the time she had known them, she could not remember seeing them look so tense. Even the usually indomitable characters like Rebecca and Johnny now seemed suddenly quiet and reserved. Everyone was hesitating as they looked through the growing darkness at the imposing gates, up the driveway which curved round to the right before disappearing behind the trees, and then back to the ominous-looking mansion that lay beyond, through the trees below.

"Has anyone noticed how there are no birds singing here?" asked Edward. No natural sounds at all, come to that. I know night's coming, but there have been no sounds of any kind since we came near this place. Something doesn't feel right here." Silence descended again, almost as if to emphasise the point.

Anna was by now lost deep in thoughts of her own. Of course the others knew nothing of the Omega World and the forces of The World That Should Not Be, and nor was she allowed to tell them anything about it, but she was becoming convinced that there was something of that world here in this area. The vicious old man back at the earlier house had already brought that world to her mind, and the last they had seen of him he was entering this place. But the feeling was far stronger now than it had been earlier. Who knew what else might be lying in wait down there? For the first time a new thought entered Anna's mind. 'Maybe there really is a

Beast of Highgate... and maybe it really is 'not of this world'. Maybe it is a creature from The World That Should Not Be...' And the last time the Beast had struck had been right in the area they were now!

As she absorbed these notions she shuddered visibly, to the point that Timmy moved closer to her and put his arm around her shoulder. Without any thoughts of concealment any more, Anna leaned her head against his, which even in the gathering darkness was still plain for everyone to see, but right now she could not have cared less, and neither could anyone else. Whether it was brought on by fatigue from the long journey they had been on that day or whether it was due to the tension that now lay thickly on the air, one by one the companions sank to the ground on the grassy bank outside the gates, paralysed in silence, waiting for someone else to make a move either forward or back. Gradually, everyone started to look towards Rebecca, as they always did when the time came for important decisions. However, so far she had not spoken.

Even though Anna had more genuine reason than anyone to be fearful, possibly prompted by Timmy's support, her thoughts began to change direction. She alone amongst them knew of the Omega World, and she was the only one therefore who had an inkling of the true danger they might now be in. But she had been taught about that world by two very brave men who she felt sure would not be intimidated by what lay ahead of them now, and who would certainly not turn back if someone needed their help, no matter how frightening the situation. They had expressed their confidence in her abilities and her potential, and the time had come for her to start to believe it herself. She had vowed to herself that she would act on the side the Alpha World, and that is what she intended to do. A feeling similar to the one she had experienced on the bridge, and again during her discussions with Mr. Warwick and her uncle, was now stirring inside her, and she knew that now was the time to act bravely, not to run away. However, she was also mindful of the danger that her friends were potentially about to enter, so Anna chose her words very carefully when it was she who stood up and finally broke the silence.

"Everyone, I want you to know that I care about you all dearly, and it would break my heart into pieces if any harm came to any of you. I can't explain to you why, but I have a strong feeling we are right now already in great danger by being here, and if we go ahead through these gates and try to save Green and Watson, that danger could become very grave indeed. A large part of me would like to beg you all to leave now and to return to the safety of home. However, that is a choice that each of us must make for ourselves. As for me, I will not leave those two boys down there alone to their fate. I came here to try to help them, and that is what I intend to do." This time her voice did not sound timid, and it did not waver.

Even in her heightened state of tension, Anna felt her heart skip a beat as Timmy slowly stood up by her side and said, "If Anna goes, then I go too." His voice too was also strong and unwavering. Shifting her focus momentarily, Anna saw his essence shining strongly and brightly, and as pure blue in colour as she had ever known it. Anna felt a surge of pride for him, in spite of the situation. A thought came to her, and she wondered if one, or indeed both of the 'winds' of the Energies of which Mr. Warwick had spoken, were exerting their influence on them all at that very moment. She had no way of knowing, and she could only do what she knew in her heart to be right.

Silence had engulfed the group once more, as all eyes turned again towards Rebecca. And this time, at last, she spoke.

"Well, this is it then. I'm sorry to all of you that it's taken me so long to make my mind up about this. I have a feeling that Anna's right – since we came near this place I have also been feeling the danger in the air. So I've been torn on this, because I know you sometimes all look to me to decide what we should do, and that means I've got a responsibility not to lead you all into trouble. Well, not too much trouble anyhow!" That prompted one or two chuckles, and Anna understood that Rebecca was trying to lighten everyone's mood a little. "But I have to admit that first Anna, and then my own little brother have gone and put me to shame! They've shown all of us the right way to act, to put our own fear for ourselves behind us, and to do what we set out to do and to do the right thing.

"Now that we're here, I can't deny that this place looks a bit, uh, well, daunting. In fact, and this is something I don't reckon I've ever admitted to anyone before, but I also won't deny that I'm more than a little bit scared of what may lie ahead of us in that big old dark house down there. Now that it comes to it, I suppose we're all feeling a bit nervous, and maybe we don't really feel like going through them gates any more. But we said we'd help Green and Watson, and that's what we're going to do. If we think we're frightened, then just think what it must be like for them, and they've got no-one else in the world who can help them now, only us." Anna shifted her focus again, this time to look at Rebecca's essence, and found it to be brighter and bluer than she had ever seen it before, as Rebecca continued, "So come on, we're done thinking and talking. We're going in!"

And with that, Rebecca led the way as the group moved through the imposing cast iron structures in the twilight, and on into the silent grounds that lay beyond.

The Beast of Highgate

At first they moved in silence, Rebecca leading the way, not down the driveway which led off to the right but straight ahead to the trees, through which they could now only dimly make out the house. The slope leading down to the house was not heavily wooded, but there were trees dotted here and there right up to the wide stretch of driveway that passed in front of the house before it swept round the left hand side and behind the house as they looked at it. Unlike the other houses they had passed on their way, there were no flowers here.

The house itself was enormous, with lines of windows on two storeys and wings of the building on both the left and right side, protruding out from the main building towards them. The tower that Anna had seen earlier rose up from the left hand end of the building. The main entrance contained a large double wooden door with a pillared porch roof and a long, wide flight of steps leading up to it from the driveway. Lining either side of these steps was a low wall. Some way to the right of the door was a very large window spanning both stories of the building, suggesting that some kind of large hall lay within.

Despite there being so many windows, there was barely any light emanating from the building at all, which in the current half-light made it impossible to make out any further details at this distance but did serve to add to the dark, brooding presence of the huge structure. The only light visible came faintly through a window above the main door, but even that was only barely visible. "Almost looks like no-one's home," remarked Tilly, although no-one believed that to be true.

"Right, so what's the plan then?" asked Johnny, who, having crossed the threshold into the grounds now seemed to have returned to something of his normal gung-ho self again.

"Well," started Rebecca, who appeared still to be

formulating the plan as she spoke, "first I think we should wait until it's properly dark, which won't be long now. We're going to have a right job on our hands as it is, without letting them watch us strolling up to them. Then, I suggest we move down the slope in stages, moving from tree to tree for cover. Once we get to the building, we'll then need to move right around it, looking for a way in more secret than that big front door down there… We're not exactly the types to ordinarily go breaking into people's houses and none of us have done this before, but I'm sure we'll find a way in somehow. With all them windows, surely one will be unlocked!

"Then, once we're in, we've got to be real quiet and find out where Green and Watson are being held. Once we know what's going on in there, we'll make another plan then."

It wasn't exactly a sophisticated scheme but it all sounded reasonable enough, and no-one had any better suggestions to make. However Johnny then added, "Becca, do you think a couple of us should go first, to check the lie of the land and seek out the best places to try and get in? The fewer of us there are, the less likely we'd be to get caught I reckon. That's what the army infantry does from what I've read. I'd be happy to go."

Rebecca paused in thought for a second before responding, "Johnny, I know what you mean. But overall, now that we've all decided to do this, I think we should all stick together. What I'm worried about is that if the scouts get caught, the rest might not even know about it in this light and, and we might still be waiting while they're being done in. We'll be dealing with adults here, and some pretty nasty-looking ones at that too – if it comes to a fight I think we're going to need all the help we can get. It's not like there are loads of us and we should still be able to avoid being seen, so I say we all go together."

There was general agreement, and then all there was to do for the time being was to wait for it to become completely dark. They waited quietly again for a time, and as Edward had pointed out before, Anna too was now struck by the absolute silence of the place, almost as though nature's regular inhabitants had abandoned it.

After more minutes had passed, Timmy whispered, "I wonder how Watson and Green are doing. They looked pretty terrified even before they went into that house earlier. Goodness only knows what they're going through now, after Green tried to escape."

"Yes, and he got hit pretty hard by that horrible old man, didn't he?" responded Robert in a similarly hushed voice. "He didn't hold back at all in whipping him with that stick of his. But did you see how lifeless Green looked after that? He took a hiding all right, but not on his head or nothing, so I don't reckon he was unconscious. But he could barely pick himself up after that, almost like he was under a spell or something."

Anna said nothing, but she had noticed the same thing, and unlike the others she had an idea of what it was. To her it looked like the same effect she had had on Gillespie on the canal bridge when she had touched his essence and had rendered him next to powerless. Then she had seen her uncle do something similar to Higgins at Lord's two days later. She wondered about that old man, and the more she reflected the more she was convinced that he too had the power to affect others through his essence, although she was certain that someone like that could not be on the side of the Alpha World. She returned to the question which had been troubling her from the moment they had first seen the old man... could he be one of the Satals? Was he even the Gorgal? Something inside told her that he was not the latter though, for evil as the man had appeared to be, she felt certain she would have felt more had she come into such close proximity with that man from her dream. But a Satal? That seemed possible, and that would mean she was now on her way to face one of the most fearsome enemies of the

Alpha World without having completed any training whatsoever. 'Finding the two boys and escaping without being noticed and caught is the only way we're going to get out of this,' she thought to herself.

Her reverie was broken by Johnny, who whispered, "Do you think that that old man is somehow connected with the Beast of Highgate? Or do you think the Beast could even be him, dressed up in some kind of disguise? He certainly looked evil enough to be a murderer, and we heard him threaten to kill Green earlier, and then we saw him come right here, right near where that murder was yesterday."

"You know I've been wondering the same thing," was Rebecca's whispered response. "Anna, you seem to have a sense of the danger we might be facing here. What do you reckon?"

Anna was taken by surprise at being asked such a direct question, and she hesitated for a moment as she prepared her response. She knew she could not speak to them about the Omega World – she had promised Mr. Warwick sincerely that she would never divulge that information without prior permission, besides which it would have been a very difficult thing to explain even if she had wanted to. Choosing her words carefully, she replied, "Well, yes, I have had the same thought, and I do really think it could be him. What I'm in no doubt about is that he is both evil and very dangerous, and it does appear to be a major coincidence that such a man should now be here, so close to where that murder took place yesterday."

"Don't you think that man is Faulkner then?" asked Alice.

"No, I don't think he can be Faulkner," Johnny responded before the others had a chance. "Faulkner's a younger man from what I've heard, and attractive to women too. I can't imagine anyone being attracted to that old monster we saw in Highgate!"

"No, you're right, I'd forgotten about that. But I wonder

what his connection with Faulkner is then, if Faulkner lives here," Alice continued.

"Yes, that what's I was wondering," Rebecca added.

"Well it doesn't surprise me that there's some connection. I bet they make a right charming couple!" Johnny tried to joke, but no-one laughed now, not even Johnny.

'No, I'm not surprised either,' thought Anna. She was not sure what it all meant, but her feeling of foreboding was worsening.

"I wonder if he's actually here right now though," said Edward. "Apart from that one light it don't exactly look like there's many people at home."

"Well if he ain't, and if those Maryleboners ain't either, then we've got nowhere else to look, apart from back at that old house in Highgate town again," was Rebecca's response. "But I don't fancy going all the way back up there again until we've searched this place first. And I think the time has come!"

By now it was almost completely dark, and Anna could now see a beautifully clear, star-lit sky above them, although as yet there was no moon visible. Rebecca rose to her feet and told everyone that the time had come to execute the plan discussed earlier and to run from tree to tree until they reached the last ones between them and the house. Having got there, they were all to wait until Rebecca gave the signal to run to the house wall, from where they would begin to move around the house in a clockwise direction, looking for a way in.

"All right, let's go!" she hissed, and with that she hurried forward down the bank to the next tree, behind which she concealed herself once again. One by one the others followed, Tilly and Tessa choosing the same tree as each other, the rest each going for one of their own. When it came to Anna's turn to run, all the nearest trees were taken so she had a long way to go to get to one. Her state of nervous tension had grown even more intense as the sense of danger returned to the forefront of her mind, and by the time she passed the most advanced of her companions she was running at full speed through the undergrowth. Just as she approached her target tree, her foot caught on a root in the darkness and suddenly she was tumbling before she came crashing down just short of the tree. For a moment she was completely dazed, and then the fear swept over her that she might have given herself away to anyone watching from the house, or even worse, given away her companions. Hauling herself up behind the tree and now wet from the evening dew on the grass, she kept herself completely concealed for a moment before braving a quick look around the side of it in the direction of the house. It remained just as dark and mysterious as before, and to Anna's immense relief there were still absolutely no signs of life.

"Are you all right, Anna?" hissed Timmy urgently, running up to join her from a tree not far behind.

"Yes, I'm fine. I'm so sorry," Anna replied, "but thank you."

"I hope nothing happens to you, Anna. I don't know what I'd do if it did. I don't think I could stand that."

"Thank you Timmy, and me too." That was all that was said, but to Anna it meant everything.

The rest of the secret descent down the slope to the final trees was thankfully uneventful, and once there they all waited for Rebecca's instructions to move down to the house.

"Everyone," said Rebecca in a whispered shout, "when I count to three, I want Johnny to make a run to that corner over there, at the end of the house on the left. It's closer to us than the other end and it looks even darker there than everywhere else, so it's as good a place as any. When you get to the corner, go just round it and find somewhere close where we can all hide and then wait there, all right. Don't go far on your own though – remember, we all need to stay within sight of each other. If anything does happen though, give your whistle signal if you can, or just shout if you need to and we'll all be right there. Then, one by one, I want each person from left to right to do the same and run to join Johnny on my count. Then when you're all there, I'll go last. All right?

"All right, one, two..." and then she suddenly stopped dead. For just at that moment there was the distant sound in the darkness of a horse and carriage starting to move across gravel, somewhere ahead of them. The whole group ducked down low and then froze, waiting with breath held for what was going to happen next.

The sound grew gradually louder, and then in the dim light shed by the brilliant but distant stars, Anna saw a carriage slowly rounding the wing of the house on the left hand side as they looked, on the wide driveway which wound in front of them and then away up the slope to their right. Although it was really impossible to tell in the darkness, certainly from its shape it looked to be the same black carriage that had nearly run them down in the street near the old house earlier that day, before whisking away the two boys. It was moving at a far gentler trot now though, in the direction of the front door of the house. 'That really was close,' thought Anna, 'it came from exactly the direction we were about to run in!'

As the carriage approached the steps to the front door, it slowed up and then came to a gentle halt in front of them. The driver climbed down, mounted the long flight of steps and then gave the door a knock which was just audible from where they were hidden. He stepped back and waited as the group looked on with bated breath, straining to see who would emerge.

After a few moments had passed, one of the two large doors began to swing slowly open, revealing a man standing with a lantern. In its glow, Anna could just about make out the man's features, and she was certain it was the younger man they had seen leaving the decrepit old house earlier. The man took a brief look outside to check nobody was about, before turning back to open the door wider. And then they saw them – the two Marylebone boys they had come to rescue!

It was impossible to tell at this distance and in this light what kind of condition they were in now, but at least they were still alive and able to stand up. And evidently they were about to be shipped off somewhere else too, which would mean that the group's chances of being able to follow them and find them again would be almost nil.

Anna looked around at her companions desperately. Rebecca had evidently had exactly the same thought, and she suddenly hissed a new order to them all. "We can't let them take them away from here. It's now or never. When I give the order, we've just got to rush in and take our chances. We all go together, we do whatever we must to get them boys free, then we all scarper out of here as fast as we can. Everyone's got to look out for everyone else mind, make sure we all get out safe again and then we get back down St John's Wood by any means we can. If we do get split up, let's all meet again in the usual place. Clear? Right, when I say, we all run at them together, but keep as quiet as you can so they only see us as late as possible."

While Rebecca had been whispering, the door had closed again briefly with the boys on the other side of it, as though some kind of final discussion were taking place. However, it soon opened again, and the man began to push the boys forward towards the long flight of steps leading down towards the carriage.

"Now!" hissed Rebecca, and the companions broke cover as one and began to tear through the darkness towards the carriage, though still trying to keep the noise from their feet to a minimum. At first Anna didn't believe they would be able to cover the distance before the boys were forced into the carriage, but then when the trio were midway down the steps, they stopped again and looked back towards the house.

It was a relief to see them stop since it gave the group more time to intercept them, but the relief was short-lived when she saw the reason. A fourth figure had appeared in the doorway to speak to them, and it was the old man! Anna was sure he would notice them as they ran, but it was dark and he seemed to be focused on what he had to say to those who had just left the house. Perhaps the sound of his voice was drowning out the unavoidable sound of their footsteps.

As they burst forward, the fastest runners, Johnny and then Timmy, were moving ahead of the rest, followed by Edward and then Anna herself. The leaders were halfway across the wide expanse of driveway to the carriage when something else unexpected happened. Another figure, a young man Anna thought, suddenly became visible, carrying a large stick and sprinting down the driveway from the right hand end of the building in the direction of the staircase. 'Who can this be and what's he up to?' wondered Anna briefly, although neither she nor the rest of the group slowed up or changed direction at all. Whoever he was, whether friend or foe, help or hindrance, they were committed now and would just have to deal with it when they got there.

The young man was closer than they were and he was running even faster. He reached the steps of the house before they had reached the carriage, and was the first to attract the attention of the group gathered on the steps. The old man was the first to see him, and he instantly howled an order to his younger henchman to "get him". The younger man did as he was told, darted past the Maryleboners and met the new intruder head-on at the base of the stairs. The old man then leapt forward, dropping his walking cane in the process, grabbed both boys by the shoulders and began to manhandle them back towards the door of the house. However, this time both boys resisted desperately, broke free from his grip for a time and delayed him for a few vital seconds, sufficient for Johnny, then Timmy, then the rest of them to round the carriage and reach the steps. The old man howled with startled but terrible rage upon seeing this hoard descending upon them, and scrambled back to grab his cane. At the same time he shouted orders at the coach driver to stop them.

Events then followed with such rapidity that Anna could barely take them all in, as her main focus was on the two Maryleboners and getting them safely away. She was vaguely aware of the driver springing down from the carriage behind her and making it part way up the steps, only to be hit from the side by a combination of Rebecca, Robert, Tilly and Tessa, who through their combined momentum and the element of surprise were somehow able to manhandle him over the side of the stairs into the darkness below. Anna heard his cry as he landed, followed by groaning and cursing. She assumed he had landed badly.

Meanwhile, ahead of her, Johnny and Edward had grabbed the Marylebone duo by their arms and were pulling the startled pair down the stairs, when several more things happened at once. Out of the corner of her eye, she could see that the young intruder had been using his stick and had gained the upper hand over the old man's younger henchman. Leaving him sprawled face down on the ground behind him seemingly unconscious, he was now haring up the stairs. He swiftly shoved Edward to one side and grabbed the arm of one the Maryleboners – Green she thought – but Anna was no longer focused even on that.

Her attention had been drawn to the old man, his face lit up by the lamp that had been discarded on the steps. That face was now twisted into a hideous, venomous snarl as he leapt forward, cane in hand, in pursuit of those who would dare try to escape him. In his terrifying, glistening eyes, Anna clearly glimpsed his intention to fulfil the promise he had made earlier that afternoon – surely to kill them this time. However, as he bore down on them, Timmy had leapt into his way and had knocked him momentarily sideways against the wall on the side of the steps. Doubly enraged, the vile old man swung his cane with all his force and connected with a blow to the side of Timmy's head as he tried to duck. Timmy let out a brief, sickening cry before slumping forward onto the steps, motionless.

All thoughts of the Maryleboners or anything else flew from Anna's mind upon seeing this, and all her attention focused on saving Timmy. Shifting her focus instinctively to the old man's essence for a moment, she was appalled at what she saw. It was very large, but a hideously disfigured shape, with a surface covered in crater-like pockmarks and mainly black in colour, but with large dark red and brown smears across its surface. And sure enough it was already upon Timmy's pure blue essence and beginning to squeeze the life out of it!

"No!" yelled Anna at the top of her voice, and she visualised her own essence being thrust towards that of the old man with all her might. Though she could not see her own essence, she could see its impact well enough, as it smashed that of the old man to one side, away from Timmy's. For a second the old man looked utterly stunned, and even the snarl was momentarily wiped from his ugly features, replaced by an expression of shear disbelief as he looked at the child who had just intervened so dramatically. But the look of menace was gone only for an instant, before being replaced by an even more hideous one of pure evil as he transformed the shape of his essence into a terrible spike and stabbed it forward again towards Timmy's, as though this time intent on killing it finally, ending Timmy's life once and for all.

Seeing this, Anna thrust her own essence forward desperately, moving it between Timmy's and that of his attacker in an attempt to shield it, and then flexing it as hard as she could in her mind to resist the oncoming thrust, as though she were placing a rock in the path of an oncoming blade. She made it just a split second before the terrible blow struck – and it was indeed a terrible, mighty, piercing stab. It felt to Anna for all the world as though someone was pushing a physical spike through her chest. She stumbled forward onto her knees, and for an instant slipped to the edge of consciousness. She had never felt pain like it before, and neither had she ever felt the very life force ebbing out of her as she did now. As her consciousness slipped further, she was dimly aware that this was it, and that if she did lose consciousness altogether that would certainly be the end, for her and surely also for Timmy. It was that last thought that held her, right on the brink of oblivion. She would not let him be killed, not by that hideous old creature, nor by anyone else. Through searing pain, her thinking consciousness began slowly to return. She forced herself to look at the attacking essence again, and she could see that the vile black, brown and red spike which was still inching forward and had almost reached the beautiful blue sphere that was Timmy's essence. Almost, but not quite – not yet. And although she could not see it, she knew that it was her own essence that still lay between them. With all the remaining power she could now muster she mentally clenched her essence as though it were a fist wrapped around the evil, malformed spike, and pushed back against it with all her will. She could not actually move it backwards, but she was finally able to at least arrest its progress forwards, and in taking this grip on it she was also able to lessen her own pain to a degree. Both essences remained where they were, motionless, locked in a lethal stalemate as both their owners tried in vain to gain the upper hand.

And then something happened which stopped every one of the crowd of combatants in their tracks. The air was suddenly rent by the single most horrific, unearthly sound that any of those present had ever experienced. It resembled an ear-splitting human scream, only far more terrible – and far more terrifying. The words 'not of this world' returned dimly to Anna's mind, even in her current desperate state. It was so overwhelming that all fighting momentarily stopped, and even the hideous old man seemed to lessen his attack very slightly to look upwards. Still retaining her grip on his essence desperately, Anna followed his gaze almost hypnotically up to the roof of the old mansion. There, set against the clear stars of the night was the black silhouette of an enormous winged beast, its horned head raised, its jaws open and its wings spread wide. "The Beast of Highgate!" she heard someone yell from below.

The creature seemed to crouch for a moment, then it launched itself from its lofty perch, and the bright, clear stars ahead of it disappeared one by one, as the dark, winged shape slid across them, momentarily blocking them out with its horrific silhouette. Anna watched rooted to the spot as the creature swept over the site of the melee on the steps and dived towards the young intruder who had by now reached the driveway again and was making good his escape up the driveway, taking Green with him. As the demonic beast descended upon him, it once again let out that soul-piercing shriek that nothing born of this world could have created, and this time it was immediately followed by the altogether more human and utterly terrified scream of the young man as he fought to stave it off.

Partly through not wanting to watch what followed, Anna was marginally quicker to recover her senses than the old man, who, although still thrusting forward with his deadly essence, was also looking on hungrily at the terrible scene that was now unfolding below them. Seizing the moment, Anna summoned her remaining strength and pushed back with all her might at the old man's hideous essence again – and this time it moved! Moving fast, she let go of her grip on the opposing essence and then mentally clenched her own again before smashing it against her enemy's, knocking it sideways with all the remaining force she could manage. At the same time, she also lunged at his physical body and shoved his chest as hard as she could. She became aware that below her the old man's legs were also being lifted up – by Timmy, who had risen to his knees and was heaving the old man upwards with all his might! The old man reacted, but just too late to prevent this three-pronged attack from forcing him over the side of the stairs and into a long fall into the darkness below. There was a heavy thud, then no further sound.

Anna helped Timmy to his feet urgently, gave him a quick hug out of pure relief that he was seemingly all right, and then turned her attention swiftly back to the scene below them. To their right as they looked down the stairs, Rebecca and the rest of their group had been running up to help Anna and Timmy in their fight with the old man, but they were now turning and shouting for Anna and Timmy to follow them out of there. Ahead of them was Watson, who was now leading the charge away from the stairs in the direction of the darkness of the trees that lay on the upward-sloping bank beyond the drive. Further away from them, on the driveway some way to the left of the foot of the stairs, lit very dimly by the lamps from the carriage Anna could make out the young stranger, engaged in a desperate battle for his life with the huge, winged creature that was now towering over him and lashing out at him with its enormous talons. As Anna looked on, desperately assessing what she should do next, she saw the young man finally manage to break away into some space, grab his walking cane in both hands and pull them in opposite directions to unsheathe what looked like a concealed sword! Its blade flashed in the dim lamplight as he took swipes at the hideous beast, which in turn hissed and growled between ear-piercing shrieks, as it lashed out again and again. This time it appeared to lacerate the sleeve of the clothing on the young man's left arm. Despite his sword, surely the young intruder had no chance against such a monster.

By now both Anna and Timmy were running down the stairs in the footsteps of their friends, and Anna noticed the figure of Green in the darkness just beyond the battle. He appeared to be cowering slightly but not running away, as he watched his would-be saviour in his deadly combat. Then, having seemingly steeled himself, he made a move towards the battling pair in an attempt to tackle the huge beast as best he could. He got to within no more than two feet however, before he was batted aggressively away by one of the creature's wings, and he fell painfully to the ground.

"No Davy, stay back!" yelled the young man with the sword, lunging forward once more at the monster. This time he appeared to connect with his blade, causing the beast to let out a terrible roar of pain. Anna knew there was no more time to spare, and leading Timmy she darted from the foot of the stairs and headed in the direction of the fallen boy. Racing past the raging battle, they reached Green, got a hand under each of his arms and hauled him to his feet. "Come on, we've got to leave now," Timmy yelled at him desperately. "We've got to get out of here!"

"No, I can't. He's my brother and we can't just leave him!" responded the boy, half shouting, half crying. Anna and Timmy looked towards the dispersing figures of their friends who no doubt assumed that they were now running after them, and then exchanged desperate glances. Each knew that to intervene in the battle ahead of them would almost certainly end in disaster, but at the same time neither was prepared to leave Green and his brother to their fate in the claws of that monster. "He's right isn't he?" shouted Timmy to Anna. She did not reply, and she did not need to. They both understood as one what they must do.

Turning back and bracing themselves for what was likely to be their final act, the trio moved back in the direction of the beast. At that moment it let out another of its ear-shattering shrieks and lunged forward at the young man again. His sword continued to flash as he strove desperately to fend off the immeasurably more powerful beast, but it was clearly having no effect now. The monster closed its deadly talons tightly around the man's body, leaned forward, beat its mighty wings and then lifted off the ground. Even as

Anna and her companions broke into a run towards them, Anna could feel the wind and dust in the air from the mighty creature's beating wings as it slowly gained height and ascended back towards the roof of the house like some kind of demonic carrion bird, carrying its prey away to its stinking nest. There was a loud clatter as the sword that had been brandished so vigorously by the young man just moments earlier, crashed to the driveway in front of the house, having fallen from his now limp, dangling hand. The dark form soared into the air above the roof of the house, and was gone from sight.

"No! No!" repeated Green, his voice breaking into a terribly cry, as the trio came to a halt again on the drive. They all knew this battle was now lost.

"I'm so sorry," said Anna, taking Green in her arms in an effort to console and comfort him as much as she could. They waited there for a time as Green's initial grief began to sink in, both Anna and Timmy at the same time fearfully aware of the great danger they could still be in if they did not get out of the place soon.

"Come on you two, we've got to get out of here before that thing comes back again!" came a shout from behind them. It was Rebecca and the others, who, having retreated as far as the trees before realising that Timmy and Anna had not followed them, were now running back towards them.

"Come on, there's no more reason to stay in this awful place any longer. Let's get out of here," said Timmy. Sobbing violently, Green now only seemed to be dimly aware of what was going on, and appearing to operate on survival instincts alone he ran with them towards their friends, who themselves were now once again running across the wide stretch of gravel towards the trees on the grassy bank that led up to the main gates.

It was then that all their worst fears were realised. The air behind them was suddenly rent once again by a terrible, deathly scream. Glancing back over her shoulder, her eyes now fully accustomed to the darkness, Anna made out the shadowy form of the beast again, now high up above the house and beating its mighty wings, beginning to swoop back downwards in their direction!

Turning back the way she was running and redoubling her speed, Anna yelled at the top of her lungs to her companions. "It's coming back! The Beast is coming back! Run for it!"

She could see the others ahead of them, who had by now reached the trees and were all looking round desperately as they plunged forward into the cover. All now realised what was happening, and the running became more frantic as the realisation entered every head, that they could be the Beast's next victim. Anna's legs began to burn as she and her two companions ran on in a desperate bid to reach the bank. They were on the brink when something seemed to stop Green in his tracks. He suddenly span round to face the swooping creature above them, opened his arms up in a defiant gesture and shouted at the top of his voice, "Come on then, come and take me if you can! I'll get you for Robbie if it's the last thing I do! I'll have you!" he screamed at the top of his voice, clenching his fists now. At this, the creature appeared to adjust its direction and to begin a steeper dive directly towards him.

Before Anna could do anything to stop him, Timmy ran back to Green, grabbed him against his will and manhandled him forward to the grassy bank. Green tried to fight him off at first, but Timmy was stronger, and helped now by Anna he half dragged, half carried the still yelling boy the remaining feet to the tree cover.

They reached the trees without a second to spare. By the time they darted for cover they could hear the beating of wings and the hissing of the creature in the air above them, so close was it to them. As they reached concealment, they could hear the sounds of the fast-dispersing group ahead of them as they scrambled desperately through the undergrowth.

Grabbing hold of the nearest tree, Anna looked above her in desperation, preparing herself for her final battle should the Beast decide to descend through the foliage onto her or any of her friends. At that very moment the demonic creature clipped the tree she was holding onto as it swept overhead, and she caught a glimpse of it as it passed. It was still clutching the body of the young man, and appallingly sad though that sight was, it was also the one thing that might just save their lives – the Beast could not properly attack anyone else whilst it still held onto its first prey, which it was seemingly determined to do.

The Beast disappeared from view, obscured by the trees again, and the air was filled once more with another of its blood-curdling screams. The powerful sound of its beating wings suggested that it was now sweeping in an arc over the trees, before another shriek, a little further away this time, indicated that it might be heading back in the direction of the house again. Peering back through the trees behind them, Anna could just make out its evil shape against the night sky – and it was indeed moving away from them! Still clutched in its claws was the limp form of Green's brother, which it clearly intended to keep in its possession. The shape finally disappeared from view over the far side of the roof of the house.

"I think it's gone," whispered Anna to Timmy who was by her side, looking as she was into the darkness above the mansion. "I think it was trying to scare us away from the house, but it didn't want to let go of that man."

"You may be right, but it could still come back at any time. Let's get out of here now," was Timmy's response. He was right, and Anna needed no second telling. By now the sounds of their escaping friends running for their lives had gown very distant, each by now surely having lost track of where the others were. As Anna and Timmy were looking back at the creature, Green had also bolted somewhere into the darkness ahead of them. However, now that the immediate danger had passed and he was physically safe for the moment, albeit by now no doubt deep in grief, there seemed no purpose in pursuing him further against his will. "I should think he probably wants to be alone now," said Timmy, and Anna guessed he was right.

All there was left to do now was to run for it themselves. Sticking close together they scrambled up the bank through the trees, panting hard. Reaching the top, they sprinted along the gravel driveway, through the huge iron gates and into the darkness of the road beyond. By now, the acid of fatigue burned painfully in Anna's legs and she thought her lungs might burst at any moment, but she kept running. Even though they were beyond the railings and no more sounds of the Beast could be heard, Anna continued to look behind and above her anxiously for any signs of it. Mercifully, there were none.

Desperately short of breath and their legs on fire, Anna and Timmy continued to pound down the road past the large mansions they had seen earlier. It was only when they reached the junction of the road with the main thoroughfare again that for the first time they allowed themselves to stop for breath, Anna collapsing to the ground, hidden under the trees a short distance from the road. There was no sign of any of their companions, nor the two Marylebone Street boys. They could only now hope that all had made it safely out of that terrible place in one piece, which they presumed to have been the case as Timmy and Anna had been the last to escape, and that all their friends were now executing Rebecca's plan and heading back to the meeting place.

As she rested and the acid slowly worked its way out of her muscles, Anna was suddenly overtaken by a wave of exhaustion, and tears began to well up in her eyes. "That poor man!" she stammered, "if it wasn't for him, the rest of us might have been hurt, maybe even killed."

Timmy drew her close, put his arm around her shoulder

and hugged her tightly. "I recognised him when he was running down the driveway. It was Robbie Green, Davy's eldest brother. He was another of them that was usually up to no good, just like most of the Marylebone Gang's elder brothers. But when it came to it, he did the right thing by his brother tonight. He gave up his life to save him, and he deserves all our respect and more for that."

"Yes," Anna replied, before falling silent again. In the distance there came the sound of a police bell ringing, followed by more bells. Anna and Timmy instinctively moved further into the trees to keep themselves concealed, as the lights of one, then another, then a third horse-drawn carriage filled with policemen skidded round the corner and sped off down the road along which they had just come.

"Someone must have alerted them to what's been happening. More than likely someone heard the sounds of that Beast," said Timmy. "They're too late now though…" he added, his voice tailing off.

After what seemed like a safe time had passed and they had both fully recovered their breath, Anna and Timmy returned to the main road and began their long journey back south and west. It was well into the evening by now, and having only been thinking about the terrible events that had just taken place and whether or not all her friends had made it to safety, Anna's thoughts now turned forward to what might be waiting for her at home. There was no chance she would be able to slip in unnoticed this time, and there was no uncle to explain away her lateness. No doubt her mother and the rest of them would be beside themselves with worry, and no doubt that worry would soon be transformed into anger once they had found she was safe. Still, somehow that did not hold the fear for her that it once would have done. Not after what they had faced that evening. But first, before returning to her home, she had to go with Timmy to the meeting place to make sure everyone had got back safely.

And so it was that Anna and Timmy plunged through the

dimly lit streets of north London, back towards the familiar territory of St John's Wood. The euphoria that would ordinarily have accompanied such a nocturnal adventure with Timmy was all but wiped out by the terrifying and ultimately tragic occurrences that had preceded it, but Anna was nonetheless greatly comforted by his presence. Being with him felt so natural now and so right – she felt safe, and felt as though she never wanted to be parted from him again.

After over an hour they finally reached the familiar street which ran alongside the canal, past Mr. Warwick's shop and down the towpath to the bridge under which the friends always met. As they approached, Anna's heart began to race again. What would they find? Would they all be there? And what news might they have? She hoped against hope that all would be all right. They had been the last to make it off the driveway and into the trees, and they had seen the Beast return to the house, so surely they would all be fine...

As they entered the gloom under the bridge, it was Rebecca's voice that they first heard emanating from the complete darkness.

"Oh thank God you're both all right!" she cried out, rushing forward and hugging first her brother and then Anna. This time there was none of the customary sarcasm in her voice – she was just genuinely relieved and overjoyed to see them. They were immediately joined by the others, and Anna tried to ascertain as fast as she could who was there. Alice, Robert, Charlie, Tilly, Edward, Tessa... they all seemed to be there... apart from Johnny! Plus there was no sign of the two Maryleboners.

"Where's Johnny?" Anna asked over the group's grateful greetings, deep concern returning to her voice.

"He still ain't made it back yet. We all got split up into small groups when that monster came flying back at us. I stayed with Tessa and Tilly to make sure they were all right, and then we all made it back here by different routes."

"All right everyone?" suddenly came a familiar voice

from behind them, and there was Johnny rounding the corner from the opposite direction! They all rushed over to him and Anna was the first to give him a hug, just as she and Timmy had been welcomed moments earlier.

"Everyone here all right then?" he asked, looking around him as eyes slowly grew accustomed to the darkness.

"Yes, we're all here now!" replied Rebecca in a triumphant tone. Anna imagined that Rebecca had been worrying even more than the rest of them that someone might not make it back safely.

Anna remained with the group for a while longer as they all discussed the events of the night, excitedly and then sadly by turns as they recounted their encounter with the Beast and the different scenes that had unfolded. "Who'd have thought we'd actually see the Beast when we set off for Highgate this afternoon?" said Johnny, almost disbelievingly, "and who'd've believed it was actually a real monster? For all my talk, I didn't actually believe there'd be a real beast."

"Did you see that thing?" chimed in Edward. "What was it? Looked like some kind of demon it did. I couldn't believe what I was seeing. And that noise it made? Have you ever heard anything like that?"

"Poor old Robbie Green," added Alice. "And poor Davy. I don't care what that gang has done to us in the past, he must be completely distraught now, poor thing, and I wouldn't wish what happened to his brother on anyone." Anna became aware of a quiet sobbing sound coming from the direction of Tilly and Tessa, and suddenly she had to struggle to contain a similar reaction from within herself.

"You're right, Alice," said Timmy, "Davy was brave all right though. I mean that Beast was fiercer than anything I've ever seen, but he went back to try to help him, even though he had no hope of saving him."

"And you two were even braver for going with him to help him," added Rebecca. "A part of me wants to give you a right scolding and tell you never to do anything so stupid again, my little brother… but in the final reckoning I think we can all look each other in the eye and say we all did the right thing tonight, to help those Maryleboners and to help each other."

There was a murmur of consensus from everyone. The others continued to exchange views about the evening and express their disbelief at what had occurred, but Anna no longer wanted to talk. This was partly because she suddenly felt drained and exhausted, and partly because she did not want to get dragged into any further discussions about certain aspects of the evening's events. She needed space and time to reflect on the battle with the old man, and on what she now suspected the Beast of Highgate to be, but these were not topics she could share with her friends.

As soon as the discussion had started to die down, she said "I'd better go now and face whatever is waiting for me at home." Ordinarily, there would have been banter in response to this, along the lines that battling with the Beast of Highgate would be nothing compared to facing her mother at this hour, but it somehow did not seem appropriate now after the terrible turn the evening's events had taken. The group all bade her farewell, several of them also wishing her good luck for when she got home, and she moved away and started to ascend the steps back up to the road.

"Anna, wait there," came a voice from behind her when she was halfway up. It was Timmy, who had joined her on the steps to say goodbye.

"Anna," he said, "you were really brave tonight. And you saved me back on those steps outside the mansion – again! I thought it was men who were supposed to protect women, not the other way around, but all you seem to do is protect me. I'm not sure my pride is ever going to get over it!"

"But Timmy, you were so brave tonight too, and you didn't hesitate once to act when you needed to, whatever danger we were in. I don't think your pride has anything to worry about. I think you're going to make the best man there ever was. And that's why you're simply going to have to get used to it. I plan to continue protecting you for as long as I'm alive!"

Timmy suddenly looked bashfully down at his shoes again, as was his habit, his long fringe flopping back over his face in the pale light from the street lamp above them. Anna gulped silently, herself slightly stunned at the boldness of her own words once again. What was it that came over her at times like these? Then Timmy looked up again, leaned forward and upwards, and then kissed her on the lips slowly and gently, before beating a retreat back down the steps and round the corner to rejoin their friends without another word.

Watching him go, Anna stood where she was for a moment motionless, looking at the spot where he had been standing and absorbing every last detail of what had just happened. It had been a terrifying night, ultimately filled with tragedy and sadness, but Anna had reached the point where she could no longer take it all in. Right at that moment her heart was full, and only big enough to contain the feelings for Timmy which had just filled it to the brim.

Finally, her head feeling faint and her memory no longer holding any details beyond the brief but stunning occurrence that had just happened there on those steps, Anna turned slowly round, ascended the remaining steps and headed for home.

Joseph Mortlock

The commotion awaiting Anna when she had arrived home had been greater than even she had expected. There had actually been a police carriage parked outside the house, and a police constable inside the house consoling her distraught mother. The latter had at first flung her arms around Anna when she had arrived, and Anna had been genuinely moved almost to tears by the extent of the uncharacteristic emotion that had poured out of her mother, before the far more characteristic scolding began.

When Anna had seen the police carriage, having so recently seen several others her first thoughts had been that maybe its visit was somehow connected with the Beast's attack, and that the police had travelled down from Highgate to obtain information from her. However it had turned out that there was no connection. The policeman was there simply having been called by her mother, and he had just been searching the neighbourhood for any sign of her. Anna felt immediately ashamed for having caused so much trouble, and she felt genuinely upset for the worry, not to mention embarrassment, she had clearly caused her mother. But reflect as she might, she knew that she could not have ignored the plight of those two Marylebone Street boys, and that she had had to do whatever she could to rescue them once the police had decided that they could not help.

The policeman asked her a few questions to confirm that she was all right, quickly satisfied himself that this was nothing more than a case of a child having run a little wild, and then he took his leave of them, leaving said child's mother to dish out the appropriate discipline to bring said child back into line.

The scolding when it had begun was fairly intense, involving a great deal of "worry", and no little "shame". Anna had been certain the others in the house would be able to hear the reprimanding she was receiving, and she could imagine the smug satisfaction on Lizzy's face at hearing all this if she happened still to be there. Anna knew she had to wait for the initial fury to run its course before she would be able to explain herself, and once it had, she did her best.

She had started by explaining that she was genuinely very sorry for having caused so much trouble and grief – and this was true, she really was. Then lowering her voice so that only her mother could hear, she recounted the key aspects of what had happened that day. One thing that had changed between her and her mother was that she could for the first time now talk to her about the Omega World. There had not yet been a chance for a proper discussion about such subjects, but Anna knew from Mr. Warwick and her uncle that her mother knew something of these things. They had had the briefest of conversations about it the day following her discussion with Mr. Warwick and her uncle, but it had been cut short by her mother, who appeared far less at ease than Anna herself. However, brief though it had been, it had still been enough to acknowledge that they both knew of the other's knowledge about The World That Should Not Be.

So, brushing over all but the most general details of the friends she had travelled to Highgate with and why, she gave a fairly accurate account of what had happened once there. The only subject that she did not mention at all was Timmy. Well, there had been no need to raise that!

Anna had explained the plight of the two boys without giving any particular details regarding who they were or why she had already known them. She had explained that once the police had failed to show an interest, she had had no choice but to do what she could to help them. With a sudden rush of boldness, she had even told her mother that this was exactly what she thought Mr. Warwick or her uncle would have done.

"That's as maybe, Anna," her mother had responded, trying but failing to stem the fresh tears that were by now running down her face, "but they are grown men, fully trained and experienced in the world. They are able to look after themselves, although even they sometimes cannot deal with the situations in which they find themselves. But you, you are still only a child. It is simply not safe for you to go out on your own at your age and to put yourself in harm's way like this.

"But it's already starting isn't it? You are already becoming involved in the Struggle, even without any further encouragement from Edmund or your uncle, and without even receiving any training. I can see so much of your father in you even now, and I can see that it is already in your nature to seek out this Struggle and to enter unbidden into battle with the enemy. Oh Anna, just promise me it won't end the same way, please promise me…"

"But mother," she had started to explain, not understanding this reference to her father, "I didn't go looking for the enemy. It's just that we came across those boys and they were in trouble…"

"But Anna, don't you see? What made you slip out from the house in the first place? What led you to Highgate, straight to where they were? I don't pretend to comprehend these matters fully, but it seems to me that we are all mere pawns in a grand game being played by forces beyond our understanding. And they appear to choose certain individuals amongst us to use as they will to meet their ends. And they always seem to choose the good ones…"

"But mother, no-one led me there. I went of my own free will."

"Your father was just the same," her mother had continued, no longer listening to her. "He was subject to those same influences, even though he was older when he became involved. He always understood the right course of action, and he always acted in accordance with it. It was one of the things I loved him for, even though it led him to his death in the end… But you are still a child, and it's happening to you already…"

At that her mother had broken off completely, weeping desperately now. In a reversal of their roles in times past, it had then been Anna's turn to hold her mother and to attempt to console her and tell her that everything was going to be all right. At the same time, she had been desperately trying to absorb what she was being told. So her father had been involved in the Struggle! What was it that had happened to him? But their conversation that evening had gone no further, her mother breaking away as soon as she had regained her composure, telling Anna that she would speak to her further in the morning.

Maybe it was because she was now overtired, but this episode with her mother had stayed in her mind and prevented her from sleeping that night, in spite of her exhaustion. She had lain awake in her bed, reflecting on the conversation. Firstly the reference to her father, which she did not understand and which was tantalising for her. More than ever, she had wanted to learn more about him. She vowed to do just that, although she was already aware of her mother's reluctance to talk about the subject and she sensed she would need to bide her time and pick her moments carefully.

Next she had reflected on what her mother had said regarding her being a mere pawn in the eternal battle between the Energies. She had understood the point, and it did feel a bit like that to her too. But she had then also recalled Mr. Warwick's remarks about the central importance of free will, and she had thought again about the day just passed. While she had certainly felt impulses to act in certain ways at certain times, it had also felt to her that in the end it was through her own free will that she had ultimately decided to act or not. Of course in the end there was no way of knowing, but it had not felt to her as though she were merely acting as a puppet, whose actions were entirely determined by some greater force. As long as she believed in her ability to make decisions through her own free will, even in the face of powerful influences to act otherwise, she would continue to make those decisions in the best way she could, on the basis that she believed would be the closest to the direction of the Alpha World. That was all she could do. However, in doing so, having now seen the anguish she had already caused her mother, she would also attempt to give greater weight to her mother's feelings in those decisions from now on. Avoiding being the cause of grief to her mother did not seem inconsistent with what she imagined the design of the Alpha World to be. The conversation had brought home to her again just how deeply her mother loved her, and in the end no-one cared more about Anna's own well being than her mother. And for Anna's part, she loved her mother dearly too in spite of the difficulties in their relationship, and she never wanted to see her so distraught again, let alone be the cause of it. She had vowed to herself that in whatever lay ahead, for her mother's sake she would not take any unnecessary risks. If her future was indeed to involve any more encounters such as those of that day, there would already be more than enough risks, without her taking any more of her own!

For the next several weeks, Anna resigned herself to returning to her former life. Naturally she longed to see Timmy again, and she also longed for the return of Mr. Warwick and her uncle. But the events in Highgate had also left a deep impression on her. Brief though it had been, most of what she had witnessed had been very violent and distressing, and after her conversation with her mother even Anna was in no hurry to leave the safety of her tall house again just yet. And with regard to Timmy, one thing which that day had given her was a great deal more confidence concerning his feelings towards her – that plus a handful of wonderful memories to accompany her through the long days!

During the weeks that followed, Anna tried on several occasions to engage her mother in conversation about the

Struggle and what she knew of it, and above all about her father, but her mother had proved resolutely determined to avoid both subjects. It appeared to Anna almost as though she wanted to shut out the memories in the same way that she tried to shut out the world outside of that big house of theirs. Anna decided she would continue to bide her time, but she was determined that one day she would hold that conversation and learn the truth about her father, including what his involvement in the Struggle had been.

Then finally, after yet another week had passed and Anna was once again starting to get restless, she received word from her not altogether pleased mother that her uncle was soon to return to London, and that when he did her instruction was finally to begin! This news may not have been welcomed by her mother, but Anna could not have been more ecstatic, and she could not wait.

When she finally saw her uncle again, he had returned to London the previous evening from his trip to Europe, and he looked more tired than Anna could ever remember seeing him. Whether that was simply a result of the arduous journey (he had mentioned "a rough channel crossing"), or whether it was more than that she had no way of knowing, and his mood was such that this was not something she even dared ask. "How was your trip uncle?" and "It was acceptable thank you Anna," had been the extent of the conversation before he had turned away, signalling that he wished to converse no further on that subject.

He had arrived at her house rather than at his own rooms in Kensington, and her mother had confirmed that he would now be staying with them for the foreseeable future. Although Anna imagined that this would be far from ideal from the perspective of her uncle's extensive social life, he appeared determined not to dwell on it. "It will be for the best, Anna. It will be more practical to maximise the time available to us for your instruction, and also to enable me to lend any assistance that may be needed during these increasingly dangerous times." Of course he meant that he was there to protect her, but still she was grateful for his choice of words.

And so the following day, Anna's instruction began. Her uncle explained that after a great deal of deliberation, he and Mr. Warwick had decided that the same back room in his shop remained the best place to hold most of the lessons, with the occasional trip to other locations as appropriate to the specific instruction content. He had mentioned that they knew this was not without risk, but that all things considered, the risk was justified at this point. It had also been decided that the lessons would be held in the evenings as indicated in their last meeting, usually from eight o'clock, after dinner at Anna's house.

"One of our primary considerations in holding these lessons is to make sure that they can be conducted in secrecy, and to ensure that the enemy knows nothing about them," her uncle had said. "Unfortunately, it seems the tentacles of the Opposing Energy have grown long and now run deep – deeper by the day in fact. To keep your instruction concealed is something much easier said than done. So we must remain extra vigilant!"

On the first evening, Anna and her uncle arrived at Mr. Warwick's shop five minutes before the hour of eight. Her uncle ensured that the coast was clear before Anna alighted from their coach, and they entered the shop this time via the back door where Mr. Warwick was waiting.

Upon seeing Mr. Warwick again for the first time in a while, Anna noticed that like her uncle, he too looked more tired than the last time they had met, although in his case it was a little less evident as he retained his customarily jovial air.

"My dear Anna, so good to see you again," he greeted her.

"It is good to see you too, Mr. Warwick," she responded, and she meant every word of it. The excitement was starting to build inside her – the long wait to resume the dialogue with Mr. Warwick was finally over.

"So Anna, I understand from your mother that you had an, ahem, adventure while your uncle and I were away! And from what I hear, it sounds as though some of the things you saw may have been of some significance to the subject we discussed during our last meeting. Would you mind very much if I asked you to tell us what happened?"

"No Mr. Warwick, not at all, I would like to talk to you about it," responded Anna. She had in fact been very keen to raise the events in Highgate herself, since she felt certain that they involved the Omega World. She hoped the information might be of value to them, and she was very keen to learn of their own views on what had happened.

Anna shared all the relevant details (apart once again from certain things relating to her particular friend with floppy hair...), and both men listened with avid interest as she spoke. First she told of the stories she had heard concerning the Beast of Highgate, then of the journey to Highgate and of the sighting of the odious old man in the decrepit old house, then of the struggle outside the mansion, and finally of their encounter with the Beast itself. This time Anna spared none of the details, from the ugly black jewel on the old man's finger and the appearance of his essence, to the physical appearance of the Beast. Neither man spoke throughout her retelling of the story, although she could sense the tension building within them both as they listened. In particular, at the description of the old man with the black ring, Anna's uncle growled audibly and even spat uncharacteristically into the roaring fire. She had seldom seen him so agitated, not even when he had come face-to-face with Higgins in the pavilion at Lord's. For his part, Mr. Warwick had made no sound at all and had just sat motionless, but his eyes had blazed.

As Anna described the battle on the stairs of the mansion, when she reached the point at which the old man had attempted to stab Timmy's essence with his own, transformed into that terrible spike, Anna's uncle again cursed audibly under his breath and he began to pace the room, his hands clasped behind his back, his face a picture of fury. He now looked angrier than Anna had ever seen him, and it was obvious that he knew the identity of this old man, and that what he knew of him he did not like one bit. Her own curiosity was fired still further, but she continued with her story. When she relayed the details of the old villain being unceremoniously thrown over the wall of the stairs into the darkness below, she heard her uncle mutter almost as though to himself, "Good girl, Anna, good girl! Well done!" Anna could tell that both men were storing a mountain of questions, and for her part she was dying to ask a number of her own, but all held themselves in check until her story was over.

It was only when Anna had finished recounting how the demonic winged creature had finally carried the body away over the rooftop of the house and how they had all escaped that either man broke his silence. As usual, it was Mr. Warwick who did so first.

"Anna, that was quite some adventure you had! Not to mention a tragic one in the end. And you really were in the most fearful danger yourself too, though from the way you have described it, it is clear that you already knew that at the time. In fact I believe you even knew that certain decisions you were making might literally have been fatal, and yet you made them nonetheless and you did what you believed, or rather what you knew in your heart, to be the right thing. You certainly put yourself freely in harm's way without support, and I am more relieved than you may ever know that in the end harm did not come to you. A not insignificant part of me wants to scold you for being so reckless and for taking such chances. However I shall resist on this occasion, and I shall not criticise you for your actions. Apart from anything else, I am certain you have already received a full reprimanding from your mother," at that Mr Warwick gave Anna a quick wink before continuing, "and additionally, in the final analysis you acted as the best amongst our Order – the very best – would have sought to do. Although it is my most fervent hope that you do not find yourself alone in such a position again for a very long time, I cannot fault your conduct and your bravery."

"But Mr. Warwick, I wasn't alone, I was with friends who acted just as bravely as me, and they faced the danger just as bravely to try to save those two boys."

"Anna, you are right, and I stand corrected. Please accept my apologies, I was so preoccupied with your situation that I did not pay due respect to your friends. However you are right, you have a remarkable group of companions there, and I am greatly encouraged by that. But rather, to put it more plainly, I meant to say that you faced this situation without the support of people fully trained in the Powers, and specifically in the art of mental combat – the combat of the essences.

"Anna, in the events you described you took on a truly formidable foe in mental combat without even a minute's training, and somehow you were able to emerge victorious. There are precious few within our Order who could have been confident in taking on such an enemy and achieving that outcome. I do not doubt that the element of surprise may have come to your aid somewhat, but nonetheless, the fact that you were able to gain the upper hand before your training has even started quite takes my breath away."

Pausing for a moment to gather his thoughts, a slight look of concern crossed his face as he continued, "Anna, in saving the life of your friend, and make no mistake, the blow aimed at your companion's essence could well have killed him had you not intervened so valiantly, it sounds as though you received a savage blow to your own essence. Would you permit me to view your essence now, so that we might confirm that no lasting damage has been done which might require some healing?"

Mr. Warwick's concern suddenly set new worries running like wild hares in her mind. This was something she had not considered. Was it possible that there might be some lasting effect on her essence from that attack? And if so, what might the impact be on her as a person?

"Certainly Mr. Warwick," she replied quickly, then she watched as the old shopkeeper subtly shifted his focus again, and she waited to hear what he had to say with more than a little apprehension. Mr. Warwick appeared to be examining something in his mind's eye for several moments and her uncle also drew closer and joined him. Finally, having apparently completed his study, his look returned to meet Anna's nervous one and he spoke again.

"Anna, I think it must have been a truly savage blow you received, for your essence still contains visible signs of the impact it made. I can see that the wound made by that wicked strike did indeed go very deep, sufficiently so for me still to be able to see traces of it." At that, Anna heard the sound of fist pounding into palm and another oath uttered, both coming from the direction of her uncle, whose back was now turned again. Mr. Warwick continued, "I can now understand just how painful this must have been for you at the time, and you were remarkably strong and brave to be able to withstand such an attack and to fight back. And to do so with no training or prior experience... once again Anna you surpass all my expectations.

"However, most importantly of all, I do not believe any lasting harm has been done, for although the mark is still visible, the blow has done nothing to discolour your essence; there is merely an area where the blue is more transparent. I can already see that the full colour is returning to this patch from the centre, and I am confident that your essence will be fully restored before too long."

"Oh, thank you Mr. Warwick," said Anna, immensely relieved, and glancing up she recognised a look of equal relief in the eyes of her uncle as Mr. Warwick continued.

"Anna, I am as pleased as you are to find out just how tremendously resilient you are! I'm sure there are many who would not have been able to withstand such an attack, and as with so many things that we are learning about you, this bodes well for what lies ahead of us."

The old man paused again, deciding where to take the conversation next. "Anna, would you mind very much if we now asked you some questions about what happened?"

"No, of course not Mr. Warwick and I hope you may be able to explain to me some of the things that I have been wondering about as well."

"I think we may indeed be able to do that. But first, that house you described in Highgate town, where you first saw the old man with the ring. Can you remember the name of the street?"

The distinctive name came back to her immediately. "Yes, it was called Eagle Street."

"Eagle Street," repeated Mr. Warwick thoughtfully, as though running the name over in his mind. "I don't suppose you happen to remember the house number do you?"

"Um, sorry, no Mr. Warwick, I'm afraid I don't. But you would certainly recognise it if you saw it. It looks completely different from all the other houses there. It is the same design and shape as the rest, but somehow it looks much older and in a much poorer condition than all the others do."

"All right, Anna that should be good enough then. And that old man, you say he wore a ring with a black jewel on it?"

"Yes, that's right," Anna replied.

"Damn him!" Anna's uncle suddenly and unexpectedly broke his silence with a surprising degree of anger. "How dare he wear it so openly, so brazenly!"

Anna half expected Mr. Warwick to rebuke her uncle for speaking up in such a way, but instead he just nodded in silence for a moment. To her surprise, Anna was sure she could read a slight look of sadness in his expression. It was now her turn to ask one of the questions that had been burning inside her right up to that point.

"Mr. Warwick, Uncle, could you tell me who that horrible man was?" she asked, looking from one man to the other and then back again. "It's clear that you both know him. He isn't a Satal is he? From what you have told me before, I don't suppose we would have been able to fight him and survive if he had been."

Anna's uncle let out a brief snort as Anna was speaking, but it was Mr. Warwick who answered the question, after first taking a deep breath.

"Anna, yes we do know who that man is. His name is Mortlock. Joseph Mortlock. And no, you are correct, he is not a Satal, much as he might like to compare himself to one I fancy. But Anna, please make no mistake, although he is not a Satal and he does not possess the power of a Satal, he is still a very dangerous man indeed."

There was a long pause now, as the kindly old man gathered himself for the story he was about to tell, exchanging meaningful glances with Anna's uncle as he did so. Then finally he began, and stunned Anna completely with his very first sentence.

"Many years ago, when I was but a young man of twenty-one and still in the very early stages of my own instruction, I counted Joseph Mortlock as my best friend in the world. Inseparable we were, and two of the finest students of the Powers of our generation they used to say, if you will excuse my immodesty for the sake of recounting the story. Difficult though it is to imagine looking upon him now, Joseph Mortlock was once a fine, upstanding young man, and a very good one. Not to mention devilishly handsome, you know. Very popular amongst the young ladies was Joseph, but he always handled himself in the most gentlemanly way. Perhaps another time when I have more stomach for it, I will tell you more about his younger days, and the adventures he and I had together. But I'm afraid that will not be tonight."

Just as had happened the last time she was with Mr. Warwick and her uncle, Anna found herself gripped now by what was being revealed and she couldn't believe what she was hearing. That foul old man, with such an ugly sneer and evil-looking essence – he had been Mr. Warwick's best friend? And a good man? And handsome? A more complete transformation in a person she could not imagine.

"During your instruction, amongst many other things you will learn more about the nature of our enemy in the Struggle. The Opposing Energy uses a variety of foes against us, and we will teach you much more about these in due course, but amongst the ranks of the enemy that we face, some of the most deadly are what we call 'Turners'. Turners are often people who are strong in the Powers, and who have immense potential to support our side in the Struggle, finally one day to bring about the Alpha World. However, their heads become influenced by the illusory allures of the Opposing Energy, and they turn their Powers against us. Most sadly for me, not to mention for the cause that we all share, Joseph Mortlock is such a case.

"Until we were both around twenty-five, Joseph was still a good man, with a large and predominantly pure blue essence. I say predominantly, although at the time everyone thought him very pure indeed. However, being better able to view people's essences than most, in truth I was aware of the appearance of certain minor flaws in his essence, what appeared to be small blemishes on the surface of its sphere. But at that time I did not understand what they might suggest, or more precisely, what vulnerabilities they might indicate, and I did not give the matter too much thought when through all his actions Joseph had always shown himself to be the most splendid of fellows. And he was a good mental combatant too, he could hold his own with almost anyone in a battle of the essences could Joseph, but he always fought in the most even-handed of ways.

"Things only started to change sometime after his twenty-fifth birthday. At the time I had no idea, but in hindsight it seems that, despite all his many gifts and strengths in the Powers, Joseph also had his insecurities. And, unbelievable though it would have been to me at the time, it also seems that he harboured some kind of jealousy towards my achievements. Now I tell you Anna, and not through any modesty on my part, I do not believe my achievements in the Powers actually outshone Joseph's at all. Certainly we each had our own particular areas of expertise in which one excelled over the other, but in truth I believe we were very well matched, and I would never have claimed to have been the better man. And when it came to courting young ladies, well I can tell you that I lost out to Joseph by a country mile! However, whatever the reason, it seems that Joseph saw things differently. It appears that he was more desperate for approval than he ever let on, and with that came some degree of paranoia about his own abilities, and about what people thought of him. What I now know is that those blemishes on the surface of his essence indicated these flaws in his character, which it turns out left him fatally open to the seductive influence of the Opposing Energy.

"Who can say how the winds of malevolent influence of the Opposing Energy may have blown upon Joseph Mortlock's essence during those years of his early and mid-twenties. Who knows with what strength they bore down upon him, and to what degree he tried to resist them at first. Did an internal battle rage within him against their influence, or was he even aware of them? We cannot know. What is certain though is that the blemishes in his essence would have left him more vulnerable than others to certain aspects of the effect of those winds, like a ship's sails as I mentioned to you previously, unfurled during a terrible storm, and alas he was vulnerable to succumbing and to moving in the direction that those evil winds were driving him.

"If only I had been able to read the signs at the time..." Mr. Warwick was no longer looking at Anna, but into the middle distance in front of him, almost as though he were now talking to himself, "I would have dealt with Joseph entirely differently, I am certain of it. However, to my eternal regret, I did not read them.

"Anna, one of the things you will learn is that the Opposing Energy plays very cleverly and subtly on the flaws that exist within people's characters, and well it might since those flaws are usually a direct result of the very contamination of the universe which the Opposing Energy itself caused. The types of flaws to which I refer are characteristics such as jealousy and greed, which make people hungry for things that they do not actually need, and which ultimately will not even make them happy, but which they crave and yearn for nonetheless. Well, it turns out that Joseph Mortlock had such character flaws, although he did precious little outwardly to reveal them until it was too late.

"The Opposing Energy has ways of luring people to move in its direction by playing on their desires, offering its victims wealth, power, praise, fame... whatever it is that the person most craves from the world around them. But it does so in very gentle and gradual ways which often fail to arouse suspicion at first. Through the many tentacles that the Opposing Power has in our world, it has an almost infinite variety of ways to manipulate situations and to provide almost irresistible temptations to those who are vulnerable. This is how Joseph became ensnared.

"In the period when I was in my mid-twenties through to my early thirties, we experienced another visitation from a Satal in our world, here in this country. That Satal was eventually destroyed in a battle in which I took part, although not before it had wrought immense havoc and had set in motion various catastrophic events, the effects of some of which we are still living with today. Well, it was this Satal and its followers who finally turned my friend Joseph. From being my daily companion, Joseph began to disappear for periods, always with highly plausible reasons mind you, and on the occasions when he did reappear, each time his outward appearance seemed even more... affluent than the last. It was only in subtle ways to start with – a fine watch, a suit from an exclusive tailor and so on – not things which are in any way bad in themselves, or which might create too much cause for suspicion in isolation. However, over time it seemed that he was starting to make a lot of money by some means or other, and apparently he was also starting to become more arrogant with others around him, although he never was so with me in the early stages.

"As the years progressed though, even I finally started to notice the change. Whereas the young man I had known was modest and reserved about his considerable gifts in the Powers, the man he started to become was more boastful, sometimes even engineering situations purely to allow him to demonstrate his power. Worse still, he started to do so at the expense of others. I had heard others speak of his changed behaviour, but I remained loyal to my friend, believing that he was being wronged by gossip. Then one fateful day I witnessed him humiliating another of our Order, a very good man, and doing so purely for his own self-aggrandizement, and finally I understood that something was seriously wrong. Oh how long it took me to wake up and open my eyes!" The old man's face took on a look of sorrow and remorse now, and he stopped speaking for a time. Anna glanced towards her uncle, whose gesture indicated that she should allow time for the old man to gather himself again. Finally Mr. Warwick resumed his story.

"Another of the things you will learn in the practical elements of your instruction is that with training and practice, it is possible to change the way one's essence appears to others, to a certain extent, to disguise it if you will, for example to make it appear smaller, or less blue than it really is, or indeed more blue. Now clearly this is not something that ought usually to be necessary in ordinary life, since most people cannot see essences anyway. However, this ability can become very important for us when confronting the forces of the Omega World, since it is frequently essential for our success that we only reveal our true identities when the time is right for us to face them, and that we retain the element of surprise until then."

This latest revelation brought another of the questions Anna had been harbouring back to the forefront of her mind. "Mr. Warwick, the last time I saw you, and again tonight, your essence has appeared far larger and brighter than I have ever seen it before. I couldn't understand it at the time, but does this mean you have been disguising your true essence?"

"Precisely! My years in the Struggle have taught me that it is better not to attract attention to myself, certainly until I am ready anyway, and I have developed the habit of reducing the size of my essence's appearance. One curious fact is that, to the best of my knowledge, no-one has ever been able to increase the size of their essence through this technique, only to reduce it. Anyway, what you see today is my essence in its natural state, for better or worse."

This whole revelation had hit Anna like a thunderbolt. It seemed fundamentally to undermine what she had always thought to be a completely reliable ability to read people and understand what kind of individuals they were. Until very recently she had not thought that anyone else could even see essences, let alone manipulate them. Nothing was any longer as simple as it had once seemed.

"To continue with the story then," said Mr. Warwick, "I now believe that from his mid-twenties when Joseph Mortlock began to turn, he was already disguising the changes that must otherwise have been obvious in his essence, and I believe that is the reason that I did not detect his transformation sooner. What we now know is that he had fallen for the promise of great wealth and widespread recognition from all whose opinions he most cared about, and we believe that the attainment of these things was being made possible indirectly by the actions of the Satal of that time. It is likely he was not even aware that the Satal was behind such things to start with, as the rest of us did not even know of its existence at first, but over time he became drawn in more and more deeply, and in the end he effectively became that Satal's slave. Certainly the riches promised became a reality, and I have no doubt that he received recognition from some, but at the same time the person he was becoming, as he descended along the twisted path of the Omega World, was turning many more away from him. But for all I know, perhaps the person he was becoming no longer even cared by that time.

"Joseph and I had some very heated arguments in our late twenties, concerning what I perceived to be his dangerous change of personality, once I had finally woken up to it, and he hurled all manner of abusive public accusations at me. I took these at face value at the time, but was considerably hurt by them and did my best to argue against them. Now I know that they were not founded in any truth even in his own increasingly twisted mind, but were merely invented, probably in an attempt to lead me to turn as well. In any event, Mortlock finally showed his true colours when that particular Satal war came to a head… and those true colours were shown to be black tinged with red. By the time we were both in our mid-thirties, Mortlock had committed many heinous crimes on the side of the Opposing Energy, and his duplicitous cover was finally lifted entirely when we came to face each other on opposing sides in a great battle. He had no more use for, nor indeed interest in, disguising his true self, and when I first saw his essence as it actually was, I won't it deny Anna, I was almost physically sick, so disfigured and discoloured had it become. Of course, you know because you have now seen it yourself, but just imagine if you had previously known that person as your closest and best friend, and you had known the blue purity and beauty of his former essence, and had known him to be at heart such a good and true person. To see his essence so completely transformed into that very thing we had both despised so deeply and had sworn jointly to fight against... well I can tell you, it was almost too much for me.

"Without going into the details now, I can tell you that in the end that battle ended up going well for our side, and it led us to the eventual destruction of that particular Satal. Mortlock himself escaped however, and has remained a significant enemy to all those who support The World That Was Meant To Be ever since. We have never been able finally to bring him down or to capture him. He continues to lead a desperate existence, serving one new Satal master after the next, as the best possible living example of the dangers of succumbing to the allures of the Opposing Energy. And the terrible irony is, for all that he used to crave the respect and adulation of others, amongst the Order he is now the most reviled and hated man alive. He has been forced to live a nomadic existence abroad in exile for much of his time since the defeat of his first Satal master, partly I suspect in search of new Satal masters to serve and to gain his twisted gratification from, but mainly I am sure because he knows that if he dwells in this country for long enough he will certainly be hunted down, captured and rendered such that he will never be able to harm anyone else and hinder the cause of the Alpha World again." Mr. Warwick paused again for a moment, and it was clear that recalling this tale had brought many buried emotions back to the surface again. He had started pacing the room as he recounted the final part of the story, but he now resumed his position in his chair by the fire.

"Anna, you will come to learn, although I fervently hope it will not be through firsthand experience, that anyone who spends too much time in the presence of a Satal will experience a tremendous malevolent influence and will come under immense mental pressure as a result. The minds of all but the very strongest tend to end up twisted, even if that person does not realise it at first. However, from what we have subsequently learned, it pains me most deeply of all to say that Joseph Mortlock apparently did not even attempt to resist that Satal when it finally revealed itself. Rather it seems that he embraced it with open arms. He welcomed it with an open heart, and in the end that heart was turned pure black.

"And now your story tells us that he has returned to London, which means that by now he will almost surely have told our new Satal enemies about my true identity as one of the Order, not to mention that of your uncle whom he knows, and of other members of the Order. It is fortunate that Mortlock does not know where I am now, for I did not have this shop when last he left our shores, and of course this shop deliberately does not carry my own name, even though I am its owner. However, we must be doubly vigilant from now on to remain undetected, and I do fear that the time may be approaching when it becomes too risky for us to continue to meet here. Until my arrangements can be completed to remove those volumes of immense importance to the Order that I currently have hidden here for safe keeping though, I cannot afford for the shop to remain unguarded for long periods. During my recent travels I had a most trusted fellow Knight of the Order keeping a watchful eye on the place for me, but he now has other work we need him to do. And we may still be as safe here as anywhere for now, provided we continue to take the right precautions." Then Mr. Warwick paused again in reflection before continuing.

"I suppose it should come as no great surprise to any of us that Mortlock should have chosen now to return to London, for these are times in which we now face possibly the greatest array of evil from the Omega World that we have ever seen – a time such as Mortlock has dreamed of for decades I should imagine. It was inevitable that he would not want to miss the party. There can be no doubt that he will now be in their close service once again."

"Well then he has made the biggest mistake of his wretched, miserable life! We will have him for sure this time!" Anna's uncle almost shouted this through gritted teeth, pounding his fist into his hand again. Anna could not recall ever seeing him quite so angry as this.

Seeing Anna's observance of her uncle's mood, Mr. Warwick added, "There is more to tell about Mortlock, plenty more in fact, including things that are very personal to all of us in this room. But now is not yet the time for that," and at this point he looked directly in the direction of Anna's uncle, who hesitated briefly, then gave a short nod in return, in spite of himself and his agitation. "There are other things in your story that I would now like to explore a little further if I may, Anna."

"Yes, of course Mr. Warwick," Anna replied, "but may I ask just one more question about, um, Mortlock?"

"Very well Anna, yes, please go ahead," Mr. Warwick answered in a kind tone, even as her uncle once again stiffened at the mention of the man's name.

"That ring he was wearing. For some reason I can't explain, my eye was really drawn to it. It was such a horrible, ugly thing... somehow it completely repulsed me. Then Uncle made reference to it earlier. Does it mean something in particular?"

"Yes, Anna, very observant as always, and it does indeed carry a particular meaning. It is actually a very rare kind of ring, containing a variant of the diamond family which is pure black, as you saw. To find such a stone of that size is very rare indeed, but there are a small number of rings such as that which are known to exist. Legend has it that the ring you saw was originally created by the last European Gorgal at a time when jewellery making was not the fine craft that it is today – hence its ugly, vulgar appearance. It was created as one of several, to be given to the greatest of turners who had served the Gorgal beyond normal measure in that era, helping it to achieve its evil ends. As such, from our point of view it is a sign of the greatest treachery and evil that a person can commit in this world. So the significance of the ring you saw on Mortlock's finger was that he received it from that Satal of our youth which I spoke of earlier, before its defeat, in recognition of the valued service that Mortlock had given to the Omega World. When he lined up against us on the side of our enemies on the day of that battle, he wore the ring openly, with such apparent pride, that it shocked me and many others to our very cores. It was your mention of that ring that told us beyond any further doubt that the man you saw was indeed Mortlock. What is most significant though, is the fact that he now feels able to wear it so brazenly once again, in public, right here in London."

Anna sat back in her chair and became aware of the beads of sweat that had spread across her brow as she had listened to the story of Mortlock. Only now did she realise just how rigidly she had been sitting as she had followed her kindly old mentor's story, every muscle in her body tensed.

"I have already described that the man was starting to exhibit a terrible arrogance even during the later years in which I still knew him. However, I believe his flagrant wearing of that ring now goes beyond even the considerable arrogance of Joseph Mortlock. What it tells us is that the Satals that are now lined up against us must be even more strongly established than we had feared. Otherwise I cannot believe he would dare be so bold.

"This to me is yet more evidence that another Gorgal, the direct heir to the creature that forged the very ring that Mortlock now wears, has indeed appeared in the world in our own time. I should imagine that Mortlock now believes his day has come at last."

"Well I shall see to it that it has not, I swear it!" the words burst from Anna's uncle as though he were no longer able to hold them in. "I will bring downfall upon that creature if it takes the final breath in my body to do so. I have sworn it before, and it remains the most important mission of my existence!"

"James, no-one understands better than me the depth of passion that Joseph Mortlock instils in you, and the reasons why he does. We have both suffered immeasurable loss and hurt at that man's hands. You know that in this particular case I do not criticise you for your oath – you have made it in the name of the Alpha World, to move us towards that destination. However, I urge caution nonetheless, for Mortlock is a man who is both cunning and extremely dangerous, open as he is to the worst influences of the Opposing Winds. But most of all I urge caution because if the positive intention which you have to rid the world of this Omega influence turns into unfettered hatred and the lust for revenge, whilst you may succeed in reaping that revenge, you may at the same time do irreparable damage to your own essence in the process, and unwittingly start yourself to descend in the very direction Mortock has gone. It would mean that the Omega World had triumphed over you even in the very moment of Mortlock's demise, which would surely be the ultimate tragedy. I perceive that this danger is great, and one that the Omega forces will attempt to make reality, as they seek to exploit every one of our possible weaknesses." Uncle James stood for a moment longer, before taking a deep breath, nodding in acknowledgement of the point made by his Master, and then resuming his seat.

All the talk of Mortlock had cast a blanket of gloom over the room. That such a foul and treacherous man should now feel rewarded for his evil ways was something for which Anna already felt the injustice, and she could imagine the strength of feeling that he must induce in those that knew him and had witnessed his treachery firsthand. On hearing Mr. Warwick's warning regarding the lust for revenge however, Anna began to perceive for the first time just how cunning and manipulative an enemy they faced, and how difficult and dangerous the terrain ahead might be.

"Now, Anna," Mr. Warwick spoke, breaking the thick silence that had descended, "I would like to ask you some questions about the Beast that you described. Would you mind talking about it in as much detail as you can?"

"Yes, I will try. Although to be honest I could not make out many details as it was so dark. But the monster had long arms, or rather wings, with long claws at the ends of its fingers. The wings themselves looked more like pictures I've seen of a reptile's than a bird's, as though they were made of thick skin rather than covered with feathers of any kind. But I didn't get to see them closely, thankfully. On its feet, at the ends of its toes it had very long claws, large enough to hold the body of Watson as it carried him off over the house. And its body appeared to be slightly shiny in the lamplight. I think it might have been covered in small black scales, again a little like pictures I have seen of lizards, but it was black all over.

"Its head was the most horrible part though. Its mouth was like a long beak, or a snout, and I am sure I saw large fangs when it opened its mouth to let out that awful scream. That was the other part – the screaming. Just as people had said, it really was the most appalling sound I have ever heard. More than that though – it actually sounded like something that was not meant to be heard in this world, if that makes any sense. I don't know, it's difficult to explain…" Anna shuddered as she recalled the appearance and sounds more vividly than she had done since the night itself.

"Don't worry, Anna, you have explained it more than well enough. And your uncle and I know the sound, for we have ourselves heard very similar sounds in the past. And your description was very apt. For I think you already know what that beast was, don't you?"

"Well," Anna replied, her theories seemingly confirmed by Mr. Warwick's words, "I guessed that what we saw was the Beast of Highgate which has been in all the newspapers..."

"Go on," said Mr. Warwick.

"... and, well, I had started to think that the Beast of Highgate might in fact be a Satal..." Although she had had these thoughts since the evening itself, somehow actually putting them into words still had the power to send another shiver through her.

"Anna, it is my belief that you are right, on both counts. Your uncle and I have long suspected that these stories about the Beast of Highgate which have consumed the newspapers of late, if in fact true, did relate to the appearance of a Satal, coinciding as they have with a marked increase in the activities of our enemies here in London in recent times. In response, members of our Order have made certain visits to Highgate since the stories began to carry out our own investigations, although no-one has actually witnessed the Beast until now. But yes, Anna, I do believe it was a Satal that you and your friends faced that night. It would appear that you have come into close proximity with one of our most feared enemies well before you were prepared and trained for it, and you have escaped unscathed, which is something for which we should all be very grateful."

"Mr. Warwick," a thought suddenly struck Anna, "Do we know for sure that this beast was not the Gorgal? It was very powerful, and to be honest it was utterly terrifying."

"Ah, Anna, yes, we may be almost certain of that, for two reasons. Firstly, you may be sure that had it been a Gorgal on the top of that mansion, the consequences would have been far, far more terrible. For a Gorgal is far more powerful and evil, even than the so-called Beast of Highgate, difficult though I am sure that must be to imagine now, having come face-to-face with it. But such is a Gorgal's power, it would have had no difficulty in destroying you all without any chance of escape. And unfortunately, I believe that it would have singled you out first Anna, in a way that this Satal appears thankfully not to have." Anna gulped, reminded again of just how real this secret world was that she was now dealing with. "And secondly, following certain investigations I made after we met last time, I have strong reason to believe that the Gorgal is in fact a very long way away from London at the moment. So rest assured Anna, I feel certain that the Beast of Highgate is not the Gorgal."

Anna was naturally relieved to hear that Mr. Warwick did not believe the Gorgal was anywhere near London, but even that reassurance carried with it another stark realisation. That this Gorgal could somehow be even more powerful and more evil even than that beast they had encountered, "much more powerful and evil", brought home to Anna the full magnitude of the challenge and danger that lay ahead of them. She suddenly felt very small and vulnerable again.

"Anna, there is one more important question I must ask you before we move on. I wanted to ask about that large mansion where you encountered the Beast. Exactly where was it? Please be as precise as you can."

Anna could not give an exact location or name any roads this time, but she described the route they had taken from the centre of Highgate to get there, and she thought that Mr. Warwick understood the area she was describing.

"Thank you Anna, this information is extremely valuable." Then the question returned to Anna's mind again which had appeared throughout all her conversations with Mr. Warwick so far, but which had always missed its chance to take the stage. She had forgotten to raise it last time, but she was determined not to make the same mistake again. "Mr. Faulkner!" she exclaimed.

She was taken aback by the reaction her words caused in the two older men. Both started violently in their seats, Anna's uncle bolting from his and immediately reaching for his cane. "What? Where?" inquired Mr. Warwick, gripping both arms of his chair, a sudden urgency in his tone.

"No, I am sorry, I didn't mean he's here. I beg your pardon, I didn't mean to surprise you both so. I meant that I have been meaning to ask you about Mr. Faulkner and what his role is in all this. It's just that I have heard a lot of rumours about him, that he could be a vampire and such like, and other stories about how he has been conducting evil ceremonies to summon up the spirits of hell, and that in fact it is he who has been summoning the Beast of Highgate. Well my friends believe that Faulkner may own that mansion in Highgate where we saw the Beast. Mr. Warwick, do you think it is Faulkner who is summoning the Beast? He is somehow responsible for the appearance of the Satal, isn't he?

Anna's uncle had slowly returned to his seat while Anna was talking, but he had not sat down and was still holding his cane like a weapon, looking all around him intently as though the very mention of Faulkner's name could have been enough to summon him out of the thin air. Mr. Warwick, however, seemed to have regained his composure far more quickly.

"Well, Anna, another very perceptive question from you. And yes, it is my belief that what you say is in fact correct – that Faulkner is indeed responsible for the Satal's appearance. But there is much we need to explain to you about the nature of Satals, the exact mechanism by which we understand they appear in our world, the form they take and so on, all of which we will cover in your instruction. However there is a logical sequence to the teaching of these things in order for it to make the most sense, and I would ask that you bear with us until that point in your studies. All will become clear very soon, I promise!

"Yes Mr Warwick, I understand," Anna replied. But at last she had had the theory confirmed – the rumours about Faulkner had been right! Her head now filled with further questions about the nature of these ceremonies that conjured up Satals, and where the Satal returned to until the time it was next summoned. She also wondered exactly what the relationship could be between Faulkner and Mortlock.

However she could clearly see that Mr. Warwick was now very keen to move on to her instruction, and she did not want to delay that any more than he did. The way of these discussions seemed to be that everything became clear in the end, so she decided to wait and just to look forward to whatever was coming next.

"So to conclude this discussion before we finally commence your formal instruction Anna, as I said at the beginning, your adventure was very dangerous but also in the end very valuable in terms of the information you have given us. I congratulate you on the way in which you and your friends handled yourselves on this occasion, although I must also most earnestly request that you take all care possible to avoid finding yourself in such a situation again. If ever you do have to face a creature of the Omega World again, it must only be after you have completed your training and you are fully prepared.

"Which brings us back finally to the main purpose of your visit this evening. The time has come for your instruction to begin." Mr. Warwick turned and left the room for a moment, before returning with several large books which appeared to be of great age. Anna's spirits had recovered somewhat at the idea that her studies were finally to start, and she looked on with fascination. She was about to begin that journey which would finally reveal those truths about the world of which she had been shown such tantalising glimpses of late. Her pulse quickened as she waited for Mr. Warwick to begin.

The Book

"Now," said the old man, "down to business, and the introduction to your instruction. There exists an enormous body of thought and practice relating to the Powers and the Struggle, in fact more knowledge than any one person could learn in a lifetime. The purpose of the first stage of your instruction is to equip you with the basic elements of knowledge and practical training in the Powers, and to begin your journey in the cause of the Alpha World – a journey that will last a lifetime.

"It is unfortunate for us all that you are about to undertake this instruction at a point in history when we face a very grave threat from the Omega World, possibly the gravest we have ever faced. How I wish that all in the Order felt this threat as keenly as we do – but it turns out that not all do. In the time since our last meeting, your uncle and I have travelled to meet various leaders of the Order in this country and in Europe to discuss the revelations of your dream. We have been somewhat disappointed, although not entirely surprised, to find many sceptics amongst them who do not fully accept our interpretation of your dream, particularly concerning the Gorgal. Perhaps we should not be surprised, since the idea that Gorgals have ever existed has been increasingly dismissed as mere legend over recent centuries.

"What is most frustrating is that they fail to see a connection between what you saw and what has been predicted by several of our most prominent seers (who are a particular type of scholar within the Order), that the coming Twentieth Century is set to be the most momentous the human world has yet seen, but that it has the potential to be momentous both in the most wondrous ways, and in the most catastrophic ways for mankind. Scholars for whom I have the greatest respect tell us that this future is very precariously balanced, and the world could now follow either path, at a greater speed than ever before. What more important role can we have as the Order of Knights of the True Path than to ensure that the balance of these unfolding events is tipped in favour of the Alpha World, given that the final attainment of the Alpha state has been the very reason for our existence for millennia? The appearance of this Gorgal at this precise moment in history could not be more significant. It could literally presage the most fundamental shift of our world that mankind has ever known towards the Omega state, bringing with it the most horrific events that the human world has seen, within our own lifetimes and those of our children and grandchildren! The gravity of the situation that now faces us, as illuminated by your dream, simply could not be greater – and yet so many in the Order simply do not see it! Anna, it may just be that the Order's complacency turns out to be the greatest weapon our enemies have. It has made me wonder if there might also be other, more sinister reasons for the rejection of our findings now… but that is something that we must discuss further another time.

"What this means for you though, Anna, is that we will conduct your training in a shorter space of time than usual, since the danger is growing all around us and we cannot be sure when you will need to apply the skills and knowledge you are going to learn. We will omit some areas which would ordinarily be taught at this stage and simplify others where we can, but we will always aim to retain the core of knowledge that you need to gain. And your teaching will still cover the five major elements which have formed the basis of instruction within our Order for centuries.

"The first element is 'The Theory', which includes topics such as the nature of the Alpha World which we are striving to achieve, what we know of the Omega World, the winds of influence of the Opposing Energy, the nature of the essence and how it may change or be changed over time, and other related matters. For some new students, The Theory seems a little abstract and obscure, and can sometimes seem difficult to identify with at first." At that point he shot a quick, amused glance towards Anna's uncle. "However, what we must realise is that we defeat the forces of the Omega World not only through our skills in combat, although it is often necessary to engage them in both mental and physical combat, but also through our knowledge. It is by knowing our enemy and understanding who they are, their aims, their modus operandi, in fact everything we can about them, that we can gain the upper hand strategically and maximise our chance of defeating them when the time for combat comes. Equally however, we can only be truly triumphant and bring about the Alpha State if we understand the ideal human state of being, and how to act in accordance with the original design of the Elemental Energy. Thus it is in The Theory that we start to lay out the philosophy of the Alpha World.

"The second element of the instruction is 'The Histories', which cover the known human history of the Alpha-Omega Struggle, and the lessons we can learn from it. We study history not merely for the interest of understanding the key events in the Struggle which underpinned some of the great events in mainstream world history, but because we can draw from it a set of practical lessons which may be applied to the future challenges we will face. There have also been certain battles and confrontations from which we have learned specific techniques and methods for defeating the enemy, which will be applied in your mental combat training in The Practice to come later. The other value to be gained from The Histories comes through finding in it a source of inspiration in the deeds of the great knights who have gone before us, in the bravery that they showed in their time and in the spirit that they displayed never to give in, even in the darkest of times. Having faced one or two such dark times before in my own life, I can say that the determination to persevere and never to be defeated in the cause that we believe to be right is essential, and at the darkest of times I have found great solace and encouragement in the stories of those who have been through the same and far worse before me, and have yet emerged victorious.

"The third element of your instruction will be 'The Nature of the Enemy'. This takes us from the overall Theory already mentioned, into the specifics of the individual forces of the enemies that we face, what we know of how they operate, the kinds of individual missions they tend to run to further the overall cause of the Omega World, and the ways in which we may oppose each one.

"The fourth element is 'The Order of the Knights of the True Path', where we will explain to you more about the Order to which I keep referring. We will explain who we are (and there are not so many of us, even in the wide world), our hierarchy and how we are organised (although I use that term loosely, for it could be said that we are not very organised at all, and indeed that the nature of our mission means that of necessity we never can be). We will also explain something of our history, the different roles and abilities of our members, for example Seers, Healers and so on, and the unbreakable Codes of Honour by which we all live and act.

"Then the fifth and final element is 'The Practice', in which the lessons from the other four elements are brought together and the key techniques in applying the Powers in the real world are practiced. This will involve a variety of aspects of the Powers, some of which you will not even be aware of. The Practice will cover training in reading and interacting with essences, although this may be one topic on which you may also be able to teach us much, Anna! It will also include Seeing, which covers reading the patterns and foreseeing certain things yet to come (although there are few who possess this skill with any real power, and it remains theoretical for most of us), and Healing, which teaches how damaged essences may be healed, and for those who have this power (and again, many do not), the fundamental rules which must be followed in doing so. And then there is the area that appears to excite most new scholars the greatest," another quick, knowing glance from Mr. Warwick at her uncle, "at least that is until they fully understand it and its terrifying implications – and that is 'mental combat'. I believe your uncle here, for example, initially would happily have foregone any and all of the first four elements and probably a good deal of the fifth too, to have launched straight into his mental combat training, such was his nature. However, that training would not have been in any way as effective had I allowed him to do so. James, would you agree?"

Uncle James, who had been gazing into the fire with an air so detached he could have been unconscious, suddenly demonstrated that he had in fact been listening, by responding immediately with a serious and somewhat injured expression, which he turned first on his old Master and then on Anna, before creasing it into a crooked smile and replying, "That is, in fact, absolutely true – but indeed, what else would you have expected of me? Alas I'm afraid it was part of my nature, for better or for worse, and indeed at different times it has turned out to be for both!" His expression then turned more serious. "However, Anna, I now freely acknowledge what my Master has just said, that to be truly effective in mental combat, it is essential to understand the theory and the context. Without this grounding you will always be fighting blindly, and you will be bound for certain defeat in the end." Then turning back to his master he added, "By the way Edmund, did the Order ever give you that medal you said you had earned for persevering with me and finally turning me into the fine mental combatant I am today?"

"No, as a matter of fact, I don't believe they did, although one lives in hope! What I would add though is that since learning this lesson and taking the theoretical elements of the instruction on board, your uncle has in fact become a very fine exponent of the art of mental combat – in fact I do not flatter him (although I do risk feeding his not insubstantial self-opinion!) by calling him one of the very finest amongst our Order at his age. If only he had listened to what he was told a bit sooner..." said Mr Warwick with another quick, sly grin.

"So to conclude, The Practice, including mental combat and defence, will form a critical element of your training, as soon as the theoretical groundwork has been laid. And in The Practice you will learn the techniques of combating and ultimately defeating a Satal. Now, on that topic there is something important that I should make you aware of. To the best of my knowledge, you may be the youngest person ever to receive this instruction – certainly in modern times anyhow. We should not underestimate the toll this may take on you. For of necessity, to practice the techniques and truly prepare you for combat with a Satal, and the emotions that go with such an experience, we must replicate that combat situation. For the training to be effective we have no choice but to do this, but it can sometimes be a terrifying experience even for a grown adult. To prepare you fully there is no way around this, and I do not pretend that it will be without its dangers, but all I ask is that you trust us to conduct this combat practice as safely as we can. You have my word on this, and that of your uncle." A sudden, very quick but equally meaningful nod in Anna's direction from her uncle confirmed his solemn agreement – and also confirmed that he was indeed still awake, having resumed his fire gazing again.

"Mr. Warwick," said Anna, speaking up for the first time since the introduction had started, "I'm afraid I don't feel the same way my uncle did regarding mental combat. To be honest it shocked me greatly to see an essence be used as a *weapon* in such a dreadful way by Mortlock outside that mansion. Until recently I had only seen essences as a reflection of a person's character and personality, and the purer it was the better. It just doesn't seem right to me that an essence should be used to fight other people!"

"A very interesting observation, Anna. You know, in all other cases I have come across, the ability to see essences is one that has only developed as they have reached adulthood – the final stage in their development if you like – and for such a person for whom all this is new, the idea that the essence could be used actively as well as passively is just another thing to learn. But for you, who has been able to see these things since you were a very small child, it is fascinating that you do not see the essence as something to be used actively. And you know, Anna, it is our firm belief that if the pure Alpha state were to be realised, there would be no more need for mental combat. However in the unstable, contaminated world in which we exist today, there are those who would attack us, against whom we must defend ourselves, and then of course there are creatures such as Satals who are not of this world, and whom we can only defeat and banish using mental combat. So, undesirable as it may seem, I am afraid that to achieve the Alpha state finally we have no choice but to learn the art and be prepared to engage in mental combat with our enemies. However Anna, your instincts are nonetheless valid. It is the way in which we engage in mental combat that is absolutely key. There is a right way, one which will not lead to self-inflicted damage of our own essences through our conduct, and wrongs ways, such as the abominable act you saw Mortlock attempt outside the mansion, which will surely only have served to turn his essence blacker and redder still.

"So Anna, for the time-being please take solace in the fact you will learn how to combat your opponents in ways that are consistent with the attainment of the Alpha World during The Practice." Anna nodded at this. There was a lot for her to take in here and she would need more time to adapt her thinking to it, but what Mr Warwick had said had made basic sense to her. Then her uncle rejoined the conversation.

"Anna, do you remember that day at Lord's a few weeks ago, when Gregory Matthews faced down that aggressive bully Higgins? I didn't mention it to you at the time because you had not yet embarked on this journey and it was not something I was yet permitted to speak about, but young Matthews is in fact a student of mine, and I am leading his instruction in the Powers in the same way that Mr. Warwick is leading yours. Now although the cricket field is clearly different from the field of mental combat, I believe you could take a number of lessons from that episode, in how to conduct yourself in a situation of confrontation without compromising yourself and jeopardising the purity of your own essence. I could not have been prouder of Greg that day, not for the century that he scored but for the way in which he controlled his emotions and conducted himself in exactly the way Mr. Warwick is describing. Greg is one of our finest young students of his age, and you will have the chance to meet him before too long. Indeed it is a meeting I very much look forward to, as I believe you will both one day go on to make a truly significant contribution to the cause of the Alpha World in your own ways, in the fullness of time."

Anna was dumbfounded. So that dashing young hero Matthews was in fact possessed of 'the Powers' too, and he was a student of her uncle! Anna was momentarily speechless and did not reply to her uncle, merely nodding wide-eyed to indicate her understanding. But in recalling the gallantry and bravery she had witnessed that day, the fires of excitement in her own instruction were instantly reignited.

"Yes indeed," Mr Warwick rejoined, "young Matthews is indeed one of our finest young prospects, and another who brings us hope for the future of the Alpha World. And not a bad batsman either, by all accounts! However, to return to the introduction to your instruction, Anna. There will need to be one more aspect of the fifth element of your training in your case, one which would never ordinarily be covered at all with most students, regardless of their age. And that is the theory and techniques of combating a Gorgal." Anna's attention was immediately gripped once more.

"It is this aspect that is going to be the most problematic part of your training, not least because we have no way of knowing exactly what it would be like to face a Gorgal, let alone how to replicate the experience, since no-one alive that we know of has ever faced such a creature. However, it is not only that. I'm afraid we have an even greater challenge, which is that at this point in time we do not even know the exact theory as to how a Gorgal may be defeated."

Anna looked up and directly into the old man's eyes for a moment, in response to a sudden jolt in the pit of her stomach. Here was something that she had not anticipated, and needless to say she was less than happy to hear! Until this point, for all her uncertainty and fears the one consistent source of reassurance had been that Mr Warwick and her uncle could teach her all she needed to know, and in particular how to deal with the dangers that lay ahead. But now, on this most important and *personal* point of all, concerning that man from her dream and how to defeat him, it turned out that even they did not know how to do this!

The extent of Anna's concern must have shown itself through her expression, because Mr. Warwick added quickly, "Yes Anna, I am afraid this is true. I deliberately did not mention it last time as we had already given you enough to worry about by that time, but as we sit here, neither your uncle nor I fully understand how a Gorgal may be defeated. And neither for that matter does anyone that we know of in the Order. As I mentioned, there are now many who do not believe that Gorgals have ever existed, and that the legends are based merely on stories of particularly dangerous Satals from times past, which have become embellished over centuries of the stories being told. However, your uncle and I and certain others have strong reasons to believe that the Gorgal is a real phenomenon, distinct from a Satal, and so your concerns that we do not yet know their mode of defeat are fully justified. However, please do not despair! For things may not be quite as desperate as they sound. Well, not quite anyway…

"Firstly, I believe that many of the techniques we will teach you to combat Satals should also be applicable and relevant in facing a Gorgal. For despite the far greater power that a Gorgal possesses, from my studies of the ancient texts I understand that it is still a being of the same fundamental nature as a Satal; it has come into our world at the instigation of the same Opposing Energy with the same ultimate purpose, and it has come to be here through what appears to be a very similar process. This may be borne out by your dream, Anna, in which the Gorgal seems to have appeared at precisely the same moment as the four Satals, following that 'horizontal lightning' that you described."

Mr. Warwick paused and Anna nodded in confirmation. She was struck by the detail with which Mr Warwick had apparently taken in the content of her dream, but then of course at that time she had not understood the particular significance of the dream and what Mr. Warwick was gleaning from it. Great importance was now clearly being placed on what she had said, and Anna felt compelled to add, "Well, at least I think so. I mean, what you say makes sense, because first of all I could only see the shape of the huge stone with no figures, then that strange lightning flashed, then all five of them were stood around the base of the stone. That is what I saw, but I don't really know what happened or how they appeared." The recollection made her shudder again.

"Anna, don't worry, I understand, and I thank you for your honesty, for it is critical that you do try to be as clear and open as you can be on this topic. I intend to return to the content of your dream in the future. But regarding the Gorgal's appearance, it is my interpretation of what you saw that they did indeed all appear at the same moment, and fundamentally by the same means. And despite certain important differences between a Gorgal and Satals, I believe that they are nonetheless the same kinds of beings at a fundamental level, and hence the techniques we will teach you for defeating a Satal should still be useful and relevant to some degree, in defeating a Gorgal. You will learn those methods in the future, but they roughly involve a reversal of the process by which we understand the Satal enters this dimension. That is why the subject of the similarity between the way in which the Gorgal and the Satals all appeared here is so important.

"But there are other reasons to take heart too, Anna. For looking to history again, in the handful of Gorgal visitations that we believe to have occurred, on each occasion they surely were defeated in the end, by the brave and noble Knights of the Order of those times. Clearly I do not mean to understate the immense difficulties and sacrifices that were required, but I do believe we should take encouragement from the knowledge that on each occasion, knights of great bravery, but people essentially no different from ourselves, have risen to the challenge and found a way to prevail. And if we do believe that Gorgals have existed in the past then they surely were defeated, for had they not been, the world by now would likely already be approaching the Omega State, and mankind would have perished entirely as a result.

"And finally, one more reason to keep your chin up, Anna. I told you that we do not fully understand how to defeat a Gorgal, but I did not say that this knowledge does not exist at all. It is one of the ways of the Order, part of our Code indeed, that following each confrontation with a creature of the Opposing Energy's design, by which I mean a Satal or a Gorgal, the details of that encounter are documented as accurately as possible by those who survive it. This is a discipline that has been unswervingly followed by all in the Order for thousands of years, since this is one of the means by which our knowledge of how to defeat these agents of the Omega World has been developed and handed down through the generations. And in accordance with this Code, the encounters with the last European Gorgal and the means by which it was ultimately defeated were in fact captured in a book by the knights of the Order who survived that epic encounter. And what's more, the book in which that information was captured already contained details of encounters with Gorgals from even more ancient times.

"Now as I mentioned, our Order has a Code of Honour by which we are all bound, and in that Code, the most fundamental imperative is that the Order must always remain secret. This is of absolutely paramount importance, both to enable the Order to remain hidden from our enemies so that we might oppose them effectively, and to avoid persecution by the world at large, who know nothing about the Struggle. You yourself have seen the kind of reaction our Powers can create, even when only a fraction of the full Powers are known – and that is in our own, modern times. The persecution for such things by the populace as a whole, even without the direct influence of the Omega World, has been far worse in former times – people burned at the stake or drowned for being witches or warlocks, or treated in a similarly barbaric manner for being possessed, and so on.

"In order to adhere to our Code and minimise the risk of discovery, the Order has always taken every precaution to ensure that our writings are never discovered by anyone outside the Order – and many good men have even given their lives to achieve this. There is an enormous body of writing concerning the Theory, the Histories, the Philosophy, the Art of Combat and much more in libraries, deeply concealed in various locations throughout the world. So, whilst it is important to capture all information valuable to the Struggle concerning the Powers, since ancient times it has been the rule to keep the number of copies of each book to a minimum, to minimise the chances of them falling into the wrong hands. This same principle has been applied in the decision not to translate the old texts from the original languages they were written in, such as ancient Egyptian, Hebrew, Greek, Latin and so on, into the modern languages used today – English, French, German, Italian, Spanish. It has been argued successfully that the texts are all the better protected from discovery by the general populace by having them written in Greek or Latin, which fewer people can read these days, and hence you will only find little concerning the Struggle written in modern languages. The only exceptions made to the translation principle have been for the more ancient or very obscure languages which were in danger of becoming obsolete, but in which some of our oldest texts were written. Some of these have been translated, but only into Latin. And the documentation made in recent centuries has also been captured in Latin, again to reduce the risk of discovery. Furthermore, all our documentation tends to be written in a fairly obscure manner, a particular style containing oblique references rather than direct narrative, so that only someone who is really looking for it will realise what they are actually reading, and understand its full meaning. This helps guard against accidental discovery.

"All these steps and more have been taken to ensure that the secrecy of the Order has been maintained through the generations. Over-cautious you might think, and it has in fact led to the loss of considerable knowledge in various catastrophes that have occurred over the centuries, but the paramount objective, that the Order must remain secret from the general populace overrides all other considerations, even if that means invaluable knowledge is lost on occasion as a result. And the fact that the Order has remained to all intents and purposes unknown to the general population for tens of thousands centuries now is testament to the success of this policy, and has probably been central to our continued existence.

"But, back to the Book of the Gorgals. We understand that in this case, not one but two editions of this book were actually created, the original written in ancient Greek, and a copy later written in Latin. The original came to be held for many centuries in Rome, despite it being written in Greek, as Rome was the major centre of influence and at the heart of many of the key events at the time of the last Gorgal, and was the base for the majority of those from the Order who came finally to defeat it. From what we know, it then appears that exceptional approval was granted for one copy to be created, to meet a specific perceived need for the book to be held in two different locations, caused by one of the many divisions that developed in Europe through the Dark Ages. That second book was copied in Latin and then held in the city of Constantinople, which continued as the Eastern capital of the Roman Empire even after the Western part of the Empire had fallen." Anna did know something of the Roman Empire from her tutor's lessons on history, lessons which had always particularly captured her attention and interest, but those lessons had not stretched as far as Constantinople, and her imagination began to ignite further as the old man continued.

"Alas, in one of those catastrophes that I mentioned, the book held in Constantinople is recorded as having been destroyed, along with almost all the Order's other manuscripts held in that city (including many other invaluable writings from ancient times), during the great fires caused by the destructive conquest of that city in the thirteenth century, during the Fourth Crusade. By the way Anna, a digression, but this destruction of Constantinople caused huge suffering on all sides and a vast loss of art and knowledge, not only that of the Order but of European and Middle Eastern culture in general, with the destruction of the great Library of Constantinople and various other centres of learning that had existed in that great city. This was just one terrible event amongst hundreds that occurred during the Dark Ages, albeit a particularly notable one, and it was one of the many that was influenced by malevolent interventions of Satals in our world. They often acted on all sides at once, both to initiate conflicts and then to exacerbate those conflicts once started. And of course, don't forget that the whole Dark Age period itself was actually the result of the evil works of the last European Gorgal. You will learn a good deal more about such things during your instruction in the Histories, but it is to avoid a descent into a second period of Dark Ages possibly spanning the entire globe, or indeed something far, far worse this time, that we must defeat the Gorgal of our own time before its evil works run their course. Which brings us back to the central importance of the book.

"As I have said, the second book was destroyed, we believe, along with almost everything else in the city, in the sacking of Constantinople. In the meantime we understand that the first book had remained hidden in Rome through the troubled times that followed the fall of the Western Empire, before being transported at various points in history to different locations in Europe, wherever and whenever a perceived severe need arose. That need was based each time on the belief of the Order that the threat of the next Gorgal appearance was imminent, and that the knowledge held in the book would be required. As it turns out though, in each case a Gorgal did not appear, and it may be this fact that has led many to question whether or not Gorgals have ever really existed. Anyhow, my studies have revealed that driven by such events, the book criss-crossed its way through Europe, and came to be held at different times in various important locations during the Struggle in the Dark Ages, including Avignon in France, Prague in the kingdom of Bohemia (which has been an important region in the Struggle at various points in history), and on one occasion in Canterbury here in England. Each time, it was returned to Rome once the perceived threat had passed. Then, just prior to the Renaissance, during which Europe finally began to emerge from the Dark Ages, the book came to be held in Florence, the birthplace of the Renaissance, where our Order maintained a key presence and exerted a major influence during that vital period of recovery of knowledge and the re-flourishing of art and culture. It is my understanding that from that time, Florence took over from Rome as the permanent home of the book, when not being held elsewhere in preparation for some specific Gorgal threat, even after Rome had regained its pre-eminence at the heart of the cultural world later in the Renaissance.

"Once again, it may seem strange to us that only one copy of the book was kept and transported hither and thither throughout the continent rather than having a number of copies made, and especially after the experience of Constantinople. However, on the contrary, from the records I have seen it would appear that Constantinople was actually used as a reason to reinforce the Order's determination not to increase the numbers of our key manuscripts, since they believed that in times of anarchy, our Order faced its greatest risk of being discovered through our written works, or equally that our knowledge might become known to the enemy by the same means, and this merely re-affirmed their belief that no more than one copy of the Book of the Gorgals should exist from that time onwards. Even the risk of losing such knowledge altogether was deemed preferable to the Order being discovered.

"In more recent centuries, those perceived threats of Gorgal appearance have arisen here in London on a couple of occasions, in Paris once and in other important locations where our Order has been involved in the Struggle at key moments in history, and on each occasion the book has temporarily resided in those locations. That trail continues right up to a certain time around a hundred years ago, and then, suddenly, it seems to have vanished! There is no more mention of the book in any of the records we have searched. It is almost as though it suddenly ceased to exist, in reality and even in human memory. The last record we have found refers to the volume having been returned to Florence from

Paris in the second half of the last century, following a period of Satal activity in France, when two Satals appeared in that country in rapid succession, and attempted to negate the positive and exacerbate the negative aspects of the significant events taking place in France during the eighteenth Century. The records indicate that the book was returned safely to Florence after Paris... and then nothing!"

Anna's uncle now joined the discourse. "I paid a visit to our Order in Florence myself just two weeks ago, Anna. However there is no sign of the book in their extensive secret library. At the instruction of Signor Delvecchio, an old friend of Mr Warwick's, the Order there allowed me complete freedom to search through their collection, but although that is still supposed to be the place where this volume is kept, amongst the great many rare and fascinating tomes they hold there, the book we seek was nowhere to be found. It is also absent from their library indexing, which at first led me to believe that it must once more have been transferred to another location. However, I went back through their old indexes, a new one of which is produced every time they have a reorganisation of their library. In the index before last, completed seventy years ago, there is a note in the appendix detailing books that have come or gone since the previous one, which simply logs this book as 'missing', with no further explanation. When I then checked the previous index before that, sure enough it was registered as being present, its receipt back from Paris having been logged.

"None of the Order members I spoke to there could shed any light on what had happened to the book, nor where it could be now. Indeed they seemed as perplexed as I was, and actually quite visibly shocked at the finding when I pushed the point. It seems that no-one in the living memory of the Knowledge Keepers there had inquired after the book – which actually I can believe, given the prevailing belief these days that the Gorgal never in fact existed. However, whether the content is believed or not, it is still very surprising to me that such a famous book could go missing without anyone knowing anything about it. The only advice they could give me was that when books entered or left the inventory, detailed information was usually given, such as 'transferred to the library of the Order in Cambridge, successful receipt confirmed from them on such-and-such a date', or 'received from the Order in Bologna on such-and-such a date'. As the Master has already indicated, the Order places great value on the written knowledge captured by our forebears, and our Knowledge Keepers are always very exact in keeping these secret inventory records. From all that I saw, those in Florence were no exception, and they said that entries with no more explanation than 'missing' were very rare, and only applied when there was simply no information about the book's whereabouts."

"This finding was a great and unexpected mystery," continued Mr. Warwick. "To me it is almost unbelievable that such an important library as that of the Order in Florence, could have allowed such a book simply to disappear without an explanation, and also that such a disappearance could go unmarked and hence unknown to the rest the Order. I know that there are many in our number who no longer believe that Gorgals have ever existed, and hence that there is no need for such a book, but even as a historical artefact and record of events from times past it is a significant volume. I find it most remarkable that its disappearance should not have created a greater stir. It is inconceivable to me that it did not warrant any greater investigation or reporting – and yet it appears that it did not. To me this simply does not ring true, it is just not the way the Order in such established places as Florence works. In fact," and his voice now lowered as though he were starting to reveal his innermost fears, "I would venture to say that this could only have been achieved through a conspiracy to keep this information from the outside world..." Mr.

Warwick's voice then trailed off completely and he fell silent for a time, as though the very sound of his voice had been smothered by the weight of his musings. "It is my intention, as soon as time permits, to follow this up myself with my old companion Signor Delvecchio. He is one of the best men I have known, one of the very best, and his family has a long and proud history in the Order of Florence. I must discuss this further with him and see if he can somehow help make sense of it.

Mr. Warwick's voice had tailed off again momentarily, before he reined his thoughts back in and continued once again in his full voice, "Anyhow, as you have now heard, the specific knowledge of how to defeat a Gorgal, written by those who had actually themselves achieved such a feat, did exist until relatively recent times. And it is my fervent hope that it still does today, and that we will still recover the book. It may simply be that it has been lost or that it has been concealed for some purpose… either of which would mean that it can be found again. Certainly until we find out the truth and get to the bottom of this mystery, we must make it our mission to recover that book. It is essential if we are to complete your instruction and to prepare you, and indeed all of us, for the battle with the Gorgal of our own time that I am certain lies ahead."

Anna and her uncle nodded in agreement. Even Anna with her very limited knowledge of anything that had so far been discussed could confidently concur with this. Whatever had gone on, there was no-one keener than her for the knowledge in that book to be recovered!

Mr. Warwick examined his pocket watch in the firelight. "The hour is growing late once more, and we have covered a lot of territory this evening, so I suggest we draw this session to a close. There are certain letters that I would like to write before the evening is at an end, including one to my old friend Signor Delvecchio I think. If you are both still in agreement, I propose that we recommence tomorrow evening. I would like to continue to hold the sessions here for just a short while longer, and at the same time of the evening. Would that be acceptable to you both?"

Anna and her uncle responded simultaneously that it would. Although she had been slightly alarmed to learn of the missing book, for Anna's part she would have been happy to continue there and then and go on all night, so bright were the fires of curiosity that had now been lit inside her by the historical scale of what she was learning. That this was going to be a fascinating journey was now abundantly clear to her, and she resolved to absorb every ounce of knowledge that she could.

Secret Liaison

The early days of Anna's instruction had been amongst the happiest she could ever remember. A whole new world containing unbelievable revelations had started to open up to her, and she had felt freer than she had for as long as she could remember – both physically, with actually being able to leave the house most evenings now for her instruction, and mentally, with her imagination being well and truly captivated by all she had been learning. Having spent all her life feeling like an outsider, she had now found herself on the inside of something apparently of the highest importance, and she had been spending time with people who, although far older than her, she liked and respected very much. For the first time in her life she had been able to see a future for herself, a life ahead of her that was worth living, in which she might actually be able to achieve something significant. At first, all these things had represented a complete transformation, both of her life and of the way in which she viewed herself.

Possibly the biggest change of all that had made those days so happy though was the way in which things had developed with Timmy. While possibly not beyond her wildest dreams (after all, she had had a lot of dreams on this subject!), it had been more than she had ever imagined could become a reality. In truth, not all that much had really happened, just two meetings in which they had finally managed to express to each other something of how they felt, plus of course a first, brief kiss… but they had been the most magical moments of her life. And at first, in particular during the early days after that harrowing trip to Highgate and the subsequent emotions of her conversation with her mother, this had been enough and she had been content to wait and bide her time.

As the weeks of her early instruction had progressed however, whilst one side of her imagination had been getting nourished beyond belief, the other side had started to yearn again for Timmy. At the times when she had had no instruction or homework to occupy her full attention, she had sometimes felt a yearning in her stomach to see him again which verged on physical pain. What was this thing, love? How did it grow so powerful, able almost to take possession of her body and command her thoughts? There had been no question that it had the potential to make her feel happier than she had ever felt, but she had also begun to see that it could be double-edged. It had reminded her of one of those addictions she had read about – if she did not feed it, oh how it started to hurt! The passions that had overcome her at these times had been strong, to the point that she had sometimes no longer been sure she could trust her own judgement. And worse, the yearning had increasingly been followed by those more familiar, darker clouds of self-doubt. By following her mother's and her mentors' instructions and remaining safely indoors indefinitely, had she been making him wait too long? Would he grow bored of waiting? Who else would he be meeting? Might his feelings for her be superseded by those for another? Had she been letting the best (and maybe only) chance she would ever have of happiness slip through her fingers while she did nothing about it?

Late October came and went, and Anna had felt as though she could bear it no longer. Her fifteenth birthday was approaching, and she had known that Timmy's birthday was two weeks before hers, so she had decided it was time to act. Even if it was only possible for a short time, she would arrange to meet with Timmy, to celebrate their birthdays together.

More than once she had hesitated before trying to set it up. She had reflected heavily on Mr. Warwick and her uncle's endless warnings about the dangers that lay outside the door these days, and even more deeply on the internal commitment she had made to avoid unnecessary worry to her mother. She had vowed that she would be extremely careful. Was this going to be an unreasonable risk? Was she going to walk straight into unknown dangers? More than once she had talked herself out of it. But each time that she had come face to face with the alternative of not seeing Timmy, the idea of not knowing when she might see him again had served only to feed those evil twins who dwelt inside her – the pain of yearning to see him, and the even more painful paranoia that she might lose him. She had needed to do something or she thought she would go mad. She had decided to put her plan into action, vowing as she did so that she would be as careful as humanly possible and take no unnecessary risks.

But how to put it into action? Anna had grown increasingly wary of Lizzy, whose attitude if anything had grown even colder towards her the last few times they had met in the house. And then there had been that veiled warning she had received from Rebecca the last time, which she had never managed to get to the bottom of. Her instincts had told her to avoid using Lizzy this time, and at first she had followed those instincts.

The problem was that she had not exactly been overwhelmed with other options. As far as she knew, Lizzy had been the only person working in the house who knew Rebecca and Timmy. She had thought of simply slipping out of the house without making any arrangements, and just waiting outside Rebecca and Timmy's house. But what if Timmy had not been there, or what if other family members had been with him? She had felt as though she could not afford to risk leaving the house more than once, so she had needed certainty that she could meet him when she did slip out. No, there had to be another way to get a message to Timmy and to be sure he would be there to meet her. But how?

Of course everyone in the house had known full well that she was not allowed to leave it unaccompanied, so she would have been taking a big risk in asking any of them to help her, not to mention probably putting them in a very difficult position themselves. The more she had thought about it, the more convinced she had become that there was only one viable alternative to Lizzy whom she might try – and that had been Jim. She knew Jim to be a very straight and completely dependable type, and what was more, she had had reason to believe he might understand her feelings and situation. After all, his situation with Emily had not been so different, and Anna had kept that secret faithfully for him.

However she was to be disappointed. Having managed firstly to engineer the time alone where no-one could have heard the conversation, she had also managed to overcome the extreme embarrassment of telling Jim about Timmy – well, in as much detail as he had needed to know anyway. It had been the first time she had told anyone about Timmy, and it had been one of the most difficult things she had ever made herself do, but the goal had been so important to her that she had seen it through. And Jim for his part had seemed to understand fully, and to her eternal gratitude he had not treated it like some silly schoolgirl infatuation, but with due and proper seriousness. He had told her how incredibly sympathetic he was and how much he had wished from the bottom of his heart that he could help her, but that unfortunately he just could not. He repeated the message she had already heard on a thousand occasions that there was "danger all around now", and had told her that he was under the strictest instructions to ensure that she was safe. He had told her that as much as he truly sympathised, he simply could not break his commitments and betray the trust that had been shown to him. Looking at his beautifully pure essence, Anna had known he had been speaking absolutely from the heart, and she had understood that for someone with Jim's admirable character there had really been no other response he could have given. So by the end of that conversation she had given up and told him that she understood, and for his part he had promised her that he would not tell a soul about Timmy. That at least was something for which she had been hugely grateful.

But none of this had helped her fend off her impending madness. After another day of trying again to follow the guidance of Jim and all the others, a day spent wrestling futilely with her emotions in a state of complete inner turmoil, she had returned finally to her plan again and the only alternative left open to her – Lizzy.

When she had finally managed to engineer the opportunity to catch her alone, Lizzy had at first been her usual recent prickly self. She had pointed out in no uncertain terms that she had already done more than enough to help Anna and her friends, that Anna shouldn't be putting her in that position any more, and that anyway she didn't know why Anna wanted to flout the rules, why she didn't live up better to the position that she had been born into, and so on. However once Anna had weathered all of that, Lizzy's attitude had started slowly to change. Whether it had been due to the extent of Anna's pleading (and frankly her obvious desperation) or something else that had been ticking over in Lizzy's mind Anna had not been able to tell, but finally and a little unexpectedly, Lizzy had agreed to pass on the message, which was for Timmy to meet her in the usual place the following Tuesday to celebrate his birthday.

Lizzy's expression had once again become unreadable by the time she had agreed to meet Anna at the same time the next day in the drawing room, which was usually deserted at that time, to update Anna on Timmy's response. However, complex and unreadable had become the standard of Lizzy's expression by then, and all Anna had been able to do was to hope that she turned up. And turn up she did.

When they had met up again the following day, that day had so far been going well. Anna had successfully managed to negotiate the baking of a couple of small cakes with

Maggie the cook, whom she had always liked (and who she had occasionally even secretly wished had actually been her mother), under the rather pathetic pretext of holding a secret solitary midnight feast ('Well, only a white lie really, and it seemed to make Maggie very happy!' Anna had rationalised to herself). Of course in reality those cakes were to be smuggled out of the house and to be shared with Timmy as a small surprise to celebrate his turning fifteen.

But the day was about to take a turn for the worse. As soon as she had met Lizzy in the drawing room, Anna had been able to sense that something was not right. Lizzy had been looking a bit awkward and smiling even less than usual. "Did you manage to speak to him?" Anna had asked urgently.

"Yes, I managed to speak to him, but we only had a short time before his parents turned up and we had to cut it short. But I asked him what you told me to."

"And?" Anna had pressed impatiently, "Did he agree?"

"Well," Lizzy had responded, now looking down at the carpet even more awkwardly, "actually no, he didn't."

"What?" Anna had asked with a sudden sinking feeling in her stomach.

"Well that was it," Lizzy had by now managed to look up at Anna again, "he just said he couldn't see you."

"But..." Anna's head had now been scrambling to take on board what this might mean. "Did he say why?"

"No, he didn't. Well no sooner had we started talking than his parents appeared, so obviously we had to cut the conversation short. But before I left he repeated it again. He said 'Look, just tell her I can't see her, all right?' And with that he was gone. I got no more explanation than that."

"Did you tell him it was to celebrate his birthday?" Anna had asked, desperate now, her voice becoming faint.

"Yes Anna, I told him that to begin with, but he just said he couldn't see you. I can't tell you no more than that because there ain't no more to tell. It was only a very short conversation, he said what he said, and that was it." She had looked again at Anna, and her stare had softened and a look of genuine sympathy had appeared. "Look, I'm sorry Anna. I suppose this ain't what you were hoping to hear, but I'm just telling you what he said. I did try, I promise!"

To say Anna was crestfallen would have been the understatement of the century. She had thanked Lizzy as best as she could, then retreated rapidly to her room to think through what this could all have meant.

In all her desperate planning of how she would arrange things and engineer her exit from the house, this had been the one outcome she had not planned for at all. On the face of it, Timmy had rejected her suggestion to meet up, and not even given so much as an explanation. At first she had been desperate not to believe Lizzy, and her behaviour had become so unusual lately that she had had reason to be suspicious. But she had looked genuinely awkward at having to pass on the information, and she had not in any way appeared to be revelling in Anna's disappointment. Maybe there had been a different explanation. Running the words through her head again and again, she had wondered if she had been reading too much into them. Maybe there had been a perfectly reasonable explanation as to why Timmy had said he was unable to meet with her, and he had just not had enough time to explain any more to Lizzy as his parents had arrived. And not wanting to talk about this in front of parents had been one thing Anna could understand very well.

But there had been another worry in her head that she had not been able to shake off. What Lizzy had said had resonated just a little too strongly with other fears that Anna had already been harbouring for her to be able to safely dismiss them as untrue. The fears that she had left things too long, that Timmy had not been able to wait indefinitely for her any more, that it had become too much and that he had decided to move on. And behind that had lurked the even worse fear, that in moving on he had actually met someone else. In her more rational moments she had known that she was now jumping to huge conclusions based on very little that had actually been said, but in those times that were less rational she had quite been able to believe that Timmy could have come across someone far more attractive and more interesting than she was, someone else who had liked him and deserved him more than she had. And apart from anything else, someone that he could probably actually have met up with from time to time! Each time, with a great deal of effort Anna had been able to slam the door shut that led too far down this path, for Timmy had not actually said anything about someone else, but that door had still remained there in her mind, drawing her back towards it. Later that troubled afternoon, Maggie had appeared smiling in her room with the two cakes Anna had asked for, and had then been taken aback and concerned in equal measure when Anna had burst into a flood of tears at the sight of them!

It hadn't helped that this turn of events had coincided with a break in her instruction, as Mr. Warwick and her uncle had both had to leave London for some time, leaving her with nothing else to distract her from her endless speculation. There had also been no progress regarding the location of the missing book before they had left, which had started to add to her general level of tension and concern about the future as their discussions had progressed. And now, whatever the reason had been, she was not going to get to see Timmy after all. That night she had the most troubled night's sleep she had had for a very long time, and when the first light of dawn had begun to filter through her window, she felt as though she hadn't really slept. In the cold light of that new day, Anna had steeled herself and decided enough was enough, she could speculate as to what the message had meant all she liked, but with almost no facts to base it on she would never find the answer, and she simply could not go on like that. She had needed to find out one way or the other what the situation really was, whatever it might have been. And hopefully there would be a perfectly reasonable explanation and things would be fine again. Putting her former caution to one side she had resolved that, arranged or not, this time she would go to Timmy and Rebecca's house and wait around until she was able to speak to one of them. Rebecca might have been able to help shed some light, even if Anna couldn't speak to Timmy. And if Anna could speak to Timmy... well, she would just have had to cross that bridge, wherever it might lead, when she got there.

Buoyed by the idea that she would now be able to find out the facts of Timmy's refusal to meet, and by the fact that she was now going to do something about this for herself, she had been able to eat a full meal at breakfast time much to Molly's relief, unlike dinner the previous evening. And it had been then, on her return to her room to make final preparations for her mission, that she had encountered Lizzy again.

"Morning Anna!" Lizzy had said in a voice brighter than any Anna had heard from her in a long time. "Actually I was on my way up to see you. I've got a message for you from Timmy!"

No amount of iron plating that Anna had attached around her heart since their last conversation could have prevented it from leaping at these words. "Says he wants to meet you and explain things. It was another real quick conversation, so I've got no idea what it is, but at least you can see him now, eh?" She had looked genuinely encouraging as she had said this.

"Did he say when to meet him and where?" Anna had asked immediately.

"Usual place, this afternoon at four o'clock. Now Anna, you know I don't really approve of you sneaking out of the house an' all, and you know I shouldn't be helping you. But I could tell you were right upset yesterday, so I hope it all works out well for you this time."

These kind words had finally melted any remaining metal plating around Anna's heart, and she had replied, "Oh thank you Lizzy!" and given her a quick hug of gratitude. The messenger had reacted a little stiffly at first, but had then relaxed and returned the embrace more warmly. 'I knew I was overreacting and that there would be a rational explanation. How things can turn on their head in the space of a day!' Anna had thought to herself, the smile finally having returned to her tired face. 'Or perhaps they're just turning back the right way up again!' And it had warmed her heart still further to see her smile returned by Lizzy. Friends again at last.

She had not, however, seen the very different, venomous smirk that had crossed her new friend's face the moment her back had been turned!

It had been before four o'clock when Anna had reached the usual meeting place, and she had sat there alone on the ledge under the bridge in a state of horrible agitation. The minutes had dragged by, and the feelings of elation at hearing that Timmy had asked to see her had started slowly to ebb away. The first dark clouds of self-doubt had soon begun to drift across her mind again as she began to re-examine Lizzy's latest message for clues.

He had said that he wanted to meet her 'to explain things'. She had assumed this had meant to explain why he had not been able to make Anna's previous suggested meeting time... but what if he had meant something else? What if there had been other, different things that he had needed to explain to her? Things more along the lines of her worries of the previous day? She had slammed that door shut again, but once again the door had not gone away. Whatever this explanation was going to be though, at least she was now going to find out, and she would finally have something factual to build on for once instead of the endless spiralling speculation she had been putting herself through. Speculation that had tended to spiral only downwards of late.

There she had sat, cold and alone, waiting – waiting for

fate to do to her what it would. More time had passed, and she had reached the point where Timmy could have said anything to her and she would have accepted it. Anything would have been better than that waiting. She had looked up the canal and been struck by how different the scene now looked compared to those heady days of the summer. They were now deep into autumn, closer to winter than those distant summer months, and a cold mist had started to descend all around her. Straining her eyes, she had just about been able to make out the shape of a barge moored to the bank somewhere in the vicinity of Mr. Warwick's shop. She had wondered idly if it might have been the cheerful yellow Canal Queen owned by the Rileys. Whether it had been or not though, it had appeared then the same as everything else, just another shade of dull grey in the gathering misty gloom. There had been nothing to brighten the darkening landscape. And still he had not come.

Paranoia had started to snap at her from all sides. Timmy wasn't going to come. What did that mean? Was it the final evidence that he no longer cared, regardless of how he might have felt when the sun had still been high and the trees still full of leaves? Or had Lizzy lied to her? Had there been no message? How was she possibly supposed to tell? But if it had been a lie, then that would have meant Timmy had not even contacted her at all, and that she would never get to the truth about what Timmy had felt, whatever that had been. She had not given up completely on Timmy, not yet. It had still been possible that there was some explanation that would clear up her confusion, and that everything might still have turned out all right. But even in that increasingly unlikely event, in the meantime she would be left alone with only her speculation again, and she simply couldn't face that. Where had her uncle and Mr. Warwick gone? Where had all the hope gone from her life which had shone so preciously but so briefly just weeks before? Now there was nothing but cold, thickening fog and fast descending darkness – both outside her and within. This spot had once been such a happy place for her, but now she couldn't remember ever having felt so alone.

Anna had waited there for well over an hour, which had felt more like a year, and Timmy never came. She had taken one last, long look at the cold dark waters of the canal, before steeling herself again for the longest walk home of her life. The worst part had been the ascent up the stone steps to the road – those same steps on which Anna's world had exploded into the most dazzlingly beautiful colours when Timmy had kissed her. Where was he now? Her mind had been torn in two as to whether to go and camp outside his house as she had originally planned, or just to accept that things had changed now and to make her way home again. And this time her fatalistic side had won out. There had been enough signs now, things must have moved on, well for one of them anyway, and she had been a fool even to have come out today and to have sat under that stupid damp bridge on her own for so long. She had broken all the rules laid down by those who had cared about her most by coming here, and she would not rub any more salt into those wounds now by staying out even longer. Whilst she hadn't given up all hope, she had for the time being at least given up trying to find out any more for herself. She had taken enough risks, and she had had to move on. For the time being she would now focus all her mind and energy instead on her instruction and studying. When were Mr. Warwick and her uncle going to come back? She had needed them more than ever now, to help her fill her mind, and the gaping hole that had opened up in her life.

And with those thoughts, Anna had begun her long, lonely way home, heavy darkness falling all around her.

The Second Lamp

The nights had well and truly started to draw in as Anna made her lonely way back northwards, along the streets that led to her home. It was not yet very late, but soon the darkness was like ink, rendered all the more impenetrable by the fast-deepening fog that was now starting to swirl all around her, like an enormous blanket engulfing London. Anna looked up at the gas-lit street lamps and found that she could no longer even clearly make them out – just fluorescent halos emanating from where the burners were presumably located. It was becoming a grim and eerie night indeed.

Pulling her cloak around her she pressed on, eager now to forget the day's crushing misadventure, to get out of the threatening night and to return to the warm safety of her home again. Until recently it had been most unusual for her to think about her house with such longing, but times had now changed. Following the searing disappointment of not being able to see Timmy after all, she started to regret having been so foolish as to have ventured out at all. Her home now seemed like a safe haven, and especially on a night such as this, it was infinitely preferable to being out in this haunting mist.

Suddenly, as she passed a narrow side street she heard her name called out. She froze to the spot instantly, senses immediately sharpened. Her initial reaction was to hope that maybe Timmy had turned up late and had caught up with her, but a second's reflection told her that it had not been his voice. She peered into the swirling, foggy darkness in the direction from which it had come.

"Anna, over here," called out the voice again. It was familiar, a boy's voice, but she still could not place it. Then, through the dense fog that the gaslight could only penetrate for a short distance, Anna started to make out the form of someone just slightly taller than she was. She immediately took a step back and braced herself, ready to fight or flee if necessary, as the figure stepped forward.

"Anna it's me, Billy Gillespie. But don't worry, I don't mean no harm. I just want to talk to you. I really need to talk."

This was the first time Anna had encountered Gillespie since the canal incident, and she had long been wondering when their paths would cross again. Whenever it was to be, she had been certain their next meeting would not be a kind one. Immediately anticipating some kind of trap, she looked behind the emerging form of Gillespie, then quickly all around her, to check for other Maryleboners lurking in the gloom. She could see no-one, but of course that didn't mean they weren't there somewhere, obscured by the fog and darkness.

"Stop there," replied Anna. "Don't come any closer, Gillespie."

The figure stopped obediently. Its form was slightly slumped with drooping shoulders. Gillespie's demeanour certainly did not appear threatening, if that meant anything.

"Anna, please, I don't mean you no harm. I want to ask for your help. If I meant you any harm or wanted to get revenge for that dunking you gave me, well I'd have jumped you wouldn't I? Not called out to you to let you know I was here."

This may or may not have been true, but Anna was taking nothing for granted. She did not particularly believe that Gillespie had the wits to think of bluffing to create a false sense of security – he had never seemed the type able to think any more laterally than a dog fixated on a bone, and left to his own devices subtlety was unlikely to have played a leading role in his planning. What worried Anna more, and had set her senses on full alert, was that Gillespie was more likely to be someone else's pawn, either one of the Fletchers who were the Marylebone Gang leaders, or far worse, someone altogether more cunning and more dangerous. But nevertheless, Anna had developed a pretty good sense for people and their intentions, and Gillespie's manner appeared to her sufficiently sincere, at least to suggest the possibility that he might be telling the truth.

Instinctively she shifted her focus to view Gillespie's essence. Although looking at essences used some sense other than regular sight, Anna's ability to see them still depended on her visual sense, and the extent to which she could see them at any given time was roughly in proportion to her ability to see normal objects at that moment. She could not see a person's essence when her eyes were closed for instance, nor if the person was obscured behind a solid obstacle like a wall. In Gillespie's case, her ability to see the detail of Gillespie's essence was hindered by the fog, but although it was somewhat obscured she could still make it out sufficiently to make a number of observations.

She noticed that its appearance had changed since their last encounter, and in most respects this change was for the worse. There seemed to be even more scarring on the surface – no doubt the result of further unsavoury experiences since they had last met, Anna thought. But at the same time, Anna had the overall impression that its owner was now somehow less open to seeking trouble. There was unquestionably less red in Gillespie's essence than there had been, but it had been replaced by something else – a yellowish hue. Anna recognised it as fear, but she knew that it took more than the short-term fear caused by a specific situation to create such an effect in someone's essence – this required a long-term, deep-seated fear that had almost become a permanent part of that person's make-up. It seemed to Anna that something had happened to Gillespie since they had last met, and whatever that was, she sensed that it was somehow connected to his approaching her now. In spite of herself, Anna's curiosity was starting to grow.

"What do you want?" she asked shortly, all the while keeping an eye all around her, taking a step neither forward nor back.

"It's my brother," replied Gillespie. "He's in real trouble, and I don't know what to do. You're the only person I can think of who might be able to help."

To Anna this immediately sounded ridiculous, but it nonetheless captured her interest further. What circumstances could possibly have befallen Gillespie's no-good brother that would make Anna the only person who he thought could help – even if she was minded to help that nasty ruffian? The idea was so unlikely that again in spite of herself, Anna wanted to hear a little more, and the truth was that anything right then would have been a welcome distraction from her desperate thoughts of Timmy.

"How did you know I'd be walking this way at this time?" Anna asked.

"I wanted to speak to you, so I caught up with that Lizzy who works in your house and asked her if she could arrange for us to meet. She looked right down her nose at me she did, but in the end she told me if I was to wait around here this afternoon I might catch you. Been here a long while I have, but you came past in the end."

So Lizzy had told him to be here. At first that news set her nerves on edge even more, but when she thought about it, it did in fact sound like a plausible explanation – Lizzy had been one of the very few people he could have found this out from, and Anna knew that Lizzy was acquainted with some of the Marylebone Street Gang. However then Gillespie continued, and his next words sent shivers straight down her spine.

"There's this man, a realy evil man, and he's got his hooks into my brother. I'm certain he's going to kill him if someone doesn't help. I mean this man is really evil, Anna. He goes by the name of Faulkner."

Even though she had started to fear what was coming as Gillespie was speaking, Anna still felt an inward jolt at the mention of Faulkner's name – the very person that she had most of all feared could be behind Gillespie's sudden appearance. But Gillespie's voice had tailed off slightly as he had completed the sentence, and Anna could clearly hear a deep desperation and sadness in his tone. This had sounded entirely genuine to Anna, either that or Gillespie was in a whole different league of cunning, not to mention acting ability, than Anna would ever have given him credit for. Then there was the change in Gillespie's essence, which was consistent with the desperate plea for help that he now seemed to be making. And the mention of Faulkner's name had clinched it for her. Anna simply did not believe Gillespie would have introduced that name upfront if he were in fact acting on Faulkner's behalf. She now had a strong desire to hear what Gillespie had to say, and to understand what her supposed part in the story might be. There might just be some vital information here that she could convey to Mr. Warwick and her uncle.

However, her belief that Gillespie might be sincere had not reduced one bit her sense that she was in danger. In fact the mere mention of Faulkner had caused quite the opposite effect. She needed to think fast. Continuing the conversation here in this place of Gillespie's apparent choosing, or at least where he could easily have been followed to, was clearly too risky. On the other hand she did not want to lead him to her own house. She somehow needed to manoeuvre him to a different place, one of her choosing and without being followed, and one where she knew the terrain better than him or anyone else. That way she could still hear what he had to say whilst at the same time avoiding any possible trap that may have been set. She looked all around her again into the foggy gloom. There were no human forms to be seen, but who was to say that there was no-one there nonetheless, lying just beyond sight? She shifted her focus once again to search out any essences that might be glimpsed amidst the swirling fog, but again there was nothing to be seen. Somewhat reassured, she made up her mind.

"If you want to talk, then you will have to do exactly as I say," she instructed him in the sternest tone she could manage.

"All right Anna, yes, anything," was his quick reply.

"Right. Walk in front of me up the street. I will be behind you and tell you where to go. But if you make any sudden movements or try to talk to anyone else, then the agreement is off, and you will have to pay the full consequences. Remember what happened the last time you crossed me!" She had no more idea than he did quite what those full consequences might be, but she hoped that there was still a sufficient residue of fear remaining in his system after their previous encounter to stop him from taking any chances.

Gillespie uttered not a word of protest, and simply set out just as Anna had instructed, walking past her and then proceeding up the street ahead of her. They walked for half a mile through the dense, swirling fog with Gillespie ahead of Anna, as far ahead as she could let him get without losing sight of him altogether. Anna continued to peer all around her using both her visual senses, but saw no-one. 'That's one blessing of this eerie fog,' she thought to herself, 'even if anyone did try to follow us, they'd have the devil's own job trying to keep track of us.' No sooner had those words flitted across her mind than she wished she had come up with some different expression!

As the pair continued their peculiar procession, Anna suddenly tensed up as she became aware of the muffled sound of hooves coming from somewhere in front of them. Then she started to make out a dim light approaching on the road ahead through the all-encompassing blanket of mist. Senses heightened, she moved right to the wall-lined edge of the pavement away from the road, and looked all around her again. Gillespie was continuing to walk ahead unchecked, and although now divided deeply into two minds, Anna decided it better not to let him leave her sight as the light approached.

'Stop there Gillespie,' she hissed, and he immediately did as instructed.

The sound of the horses' hooves on the cobblestones of the road was now clearly audible, and the silhouette of a horse and carriage slowly emerged from the mist. Tense as a coiled watch spring, Anna crouched motionless against the wall, ceasing even to breathe as the carriage drew up alongside... and then continued on its way, without any change of speed or direction. The cloaked silhouette of the driver did not appear to look around or notice her at all as far as she could tell. Hunched forward, he appeared to be exerting all of his attention on peering into the fog and trying to keep his coach on the road. Whether or not the carriage had any passengers, Anna simply could not tell as the interior was entirely obscured. The carriage slid once more into the all-enveloping fog behind her, and was gone. After a further pause, a deep breath and another look all around her again, Anna looked forward and hissed to Gillespie to continue once more. He obliged instantly.

Anna had thought ahead, and she knew exactly where she would direct Gillespie. There was a large house down one of the other residential roads that adjoined her own street, which had now been deserted for some time. Its generous but by now overgrown garden was lined by a high wall, but one section of this wall had almost completely fallen into the garden, at the end furthest from the house. Anna had often sneaked in there on her own to play in the large garden when she was younger, on the occasions she had been able to escape from her own house. She had shown it to Rebecca and a couple of the others, but no-one knew every inch of it in the way that she did, and she was sure that none of the Maryleboners would ever have set foot in there before. This was her territory not theirs, and it was the perfect place to continue her strange conversation with Gillespie.

Having turned into the road in question, Anna finally saw the opening created by the partial collapse of the wall, lit up faintly by a gas street light that stood next to it. She hissed again to Gillespie, "Right, stand under the lamp, and don't move until I say so."

Through the swirling mist, Anna saw Gillespie stop and nod. Taking one more look all around her to make sure she was not seen, she climbed over the remains of the wall and the pile of fallen bricks that lay within, and moved into the garden. On the other side of the wall was a very overgrown lawn, lined with large, equally overgrown bushes. The bush nearest to her was one that she could partially walk through – and one in which she had played on numerous occasions – with a low branch where she could sit and still clearly make out the shape of the gap in the wall and the mound of old bricks, dimly illuminated by the street lamp. It was near the broken part of the wall, and if it had been normal daylight Anna would probably have been partially visible from it at this vantage point, although still partly obscured. However, in the current conditions Anna knew that she could no more be seen there than if she were hidden behind a wall of solid granite. It struck her that she was probably being ridiculously cautious, but ridiculous caution was the order of the day now, especially if what she was about to hear was in any way connected to Faulkner.

"All right Gillespie," said Anna again, slightly louder than before, "walk in a straight line towards me, and step just inside the wall where you can't be seen from the street. When you're inside the wall, sit on the pile of bricks facing the direction my voice is coming from. I want you to stay in the light of the street lamp so that I can still see you."

Gillespie did exactly as he was told. Stepping over the low remnants of the wall, he sat himself atop the pile created by the bricks that had collapsed into the garden.

"Is here all right?" he asked in a low, slightly shaky voice.

It was actually perfect. She could now clearly see his figure silhouetted against the light of the gas lamp. She was confident in the knowledge that she was as invisible to him as the night around them, and she would also be able to see if anyone else entered from the street. "It'll do," was all she said to Gillespie though.

Anna allowed a feeling of excitement to rise inside her now, sufficient for the first time to match the nervous apprehension she had been feeling since the moment Gillespie had called out her name. Her plan had worked like clockwork so far, and she was certain she was about to learn something new and unexpected that might just prove to be of great importance. She also could not help but notice the slightly tremulous tone in Gillespie's voice, and she wondered briefly what this episode must be like for him. Whilst she herself had been understandably nervous up to this point, the thought crossed her mind just how nerve-wrenching for Gillespie this whole scene, might be, unfolding as it was in this dense, ominous fog. Unexpectedly she found herself for the first time empathising and feeling for him slightly, before snapping out of it and reminding herself that in these particular circumstances, his feelings were not her first concern.

"Right, speak slowly and quietly, and tell me what it is you have to say," she instructed him.

There was a pause, and Anna could see Gillespie's form hug itself in the now increasing chill of the damp night. This time it was Gillespie's turn to look all around him and to make sure that no-one was listening. Anna felt sure she was right, both about his sincerity in wanting to talk to her without any trap in mind, and about the fact that he was by now scared quite out of his wits. Visibly bracing himself, Gillespie began to speak.

"You know my brother, Kenny?" he started. Anna certainly knew about Kenny Gillespie, a friend of Archie Knowles, and what she knew she thoroughly disliked. However she withheld reply, instinctively sensing that the less she spoke, the more she retained the upper hand in the situation.

Gillespie continued, "Well he's been working for that man I mentioned, Faulkner, for some time now. Not one specific job though – Faulkner has him doing all kinds of things see, and he pays him a wage to keep him and a number of others around and available whenever he needs something doing." In other words he's a paid-up full-time member of Faulkner's gang, thought Anna to herself. "And Faulkner pays very well, too," added Gillespie, reinforcing her view.

"At first everything was all right, seemed like easy money. I even helped him with some of the errands he had to run, like delivering packages, that kind of thing. A lot of the early work seemed to be getting hold of rare books, some of them very old-looking, usually written in strange languages no-one could read. Someone reckoned they were written in, what's it called, Latin? And old Greek, but most of the gang can't hardly even read English so that theory didn't go too far. No-one could understand what Faulkner could want with a bunch of old books, stolen or otherwise, but the talk started that the books were about devil-worshipping rituals, evil spells and such – you know, black magic and that kind of thing. But at first this just seemed like talk, and the work seemed harmless enough.

"But then things started to change. Some of the work began to get a bit, well, closer to the edge of the law if you know what I mean, and, well, you know, a bit rougher. But my brother thought he could cope with that though because, well, you know, he's a pretty tough type."

From what Anna had seen with her own eyes, she thought she understood all too well what he meant. His brother was a ruffian who didn't mind breaking the law, or for that matter hurting people, provided there was a profit in it for him. He seemed like exactly the kind of person who made the world worse for everyone else who lived in it, the kind of person who stopped things from being as they could and should be.

Her dislike for Kenny Gillespie hardened. What surprised her slightly though, was that from his words, his younger brother seemed to think that Anna would understand what he meant, find it all right and sympathise with him. That showed just how little Gillespie understood about the person he was talking to – and that was also to her advantage. Again she said nothing, and waited for the silhouette to continue its story.

"So, he could deal fine with the work he was asked to do for a while. But see, the man he's working for, Faulkner, well, he ain't no normal man, and he ain't up to no normal business neither. And he has some others working for him too – not like Kenny and his mates they ain't, not just a bit close to the law, but right cruel, vicious types. And in particular there's this one evil old man who seems to be closest to Faulkner – old, but real strong and a right nasty piece of work he is – the kind of person who hurts people just for the fun of it." 'Mortlock,' thought Anna immediately to herself, as she focused on Gillespie's words with every ounce of her attention now. "Like I say, my brother's a tough one, and he'll do a job for you if the pay's right, but him and his mates didn't like these other men of Faulkner's.

"Now rumours were going round amongst the gang about what Faulkner was up to, and what was in some of them parcels and boxes that he was sending and receiving. There was serious talk that Faulkner was into that occult business and doing black magic, and that sinister objects were being sent to use in his evil ceremonies... all manner of wild stories were going around, even that some of the boxes might contain parts of bodies! And they reckoned that the other older man was part of it as well – some even thought it was him that had corrupted Faulkner and turned him evil. But most of the talk was about the true identity of Faulkner. Who was he? Where had he come from? What was his real game? Where did he get all his money from? None of their theories ever stopped them from doing his work, mind – as long as he kept paying them well, they were still happy enough to continue doing as he asked them."

Gillespie paused at that point, and drew his shabby coat around him more tightly. As Anna sat on her low branch, she peered intently at the silhouetted figure of the storyteller. The dense fog all around him seemed if anything to be intensifying, almost as though it had become a living thing which was beginning to envelop its prey. In spite of her undoubted advantage in every aspect of their current situation, a chill slowly began to spread through her body. Sure enough the night was growing colder by the minute, but the chill that Anna was beginning to feel inside was altogether colder, and it was not because of anything that had yet been said. It was where this was all leading. And what was more, try as she might to rationalise to the contrary, she could not escape the irrational and yet persistently nagging fear that by divulging Faulkner's secret business, Gillespie was somehow almost invoking his dreaded presence.

Poor Gillespie was clearly suffering now. Anna could see him shivering inside his coat, both from the hardening chill around them and, she suspected, from the same inner chill that she was now feeling – although in his case she imagined it could be far worse. She really started to feel for him, she almost wanted to go over to him and put her arm around him. However, she resisted. There was no doubt that Gillespie certainly felt the risk he was taking by sharing this information with her. But for what purpose? With slightly fearful concentration, Anna spoke in the most commanding tone she could still manage, "Continue."

"Well," continued Gillespie, after a deep breath that sounded more like a sigh, "then all those stories started about the 'Beast of Highgate'." Anna had not thought it possible that her state of tension could have gown any more severe, but it did now. "You must have heard the stories – made all the papers they have. Well there was them in the gang that reckoned they'd seen and heard this beast, always late at night in the area around Faulkner's big old house up in Highgate. Reckoned it looked like some kind of demon they did, huge, like one of them old gargoyles statues you see on them old churches. And the awful sound it made they said was like something only the devil himself could make." Anna shuddered and hugged herself tightly, recalling for herself the terrible, inhuman sound that the Beast had made. Once again she looked all around her as the storyteller continued. "And always there were stories of people disappearing around the same time as the Beast had been sighted. Well, you can imagine the theories about just what kind of business of Faulkner's they were involved with, and what his connection with the Beast might be – they just grew wilder and wilder. And more and more of the gang started to believe that it was Faulkner who was summoning the Beast from the pits of hell through his occult ceremonies, although others still thought this was only drunken talk. But it made all of them more curious to know what was in them boxes they were carrying for him, and what the contents might be used for by Faulkner, in his ceremonies or otherwise – and you can probably imagine the kinds of theories they were coming up with by now."

Until just a few months before, as dictated by her nature Anna would not have believed any such stories involving demonic monsters and the like, but that had all now changed. She had now seen with her own eyes that there were things in this world which were not of it, which should not be here but which had nonetheless come forth. Beings which came to bring about a very different world, one in which all people would ultimately, certainly perish. Anna knew from her conversations with Mr. Warwick that the Beast was just such a being – a Satal. She had not yet learned exactly how Faulkner summoned Satals in his ceremonies, nor where they existed when they were not summoned, but whatever it was that drove Faulkner to conjure up their presence, it must surely be somehow connected to the hideous state of that essence she had seen in Mr. Warwick's shop. She considered the disappearances that Gillespie had mentioned, and wondered just how many victims of this beast there had been, beyond those who had made the papers. She shivered as she continued to listen.

"Well, Kenny's best mate, Archie Knowles, him that my brother ran all his errands with, well, his curiosity started getting the better of him. He wasn't for leaving Faulkner's employment or nothing, the money was too good for that, but he reckoned that no-one paid the kind of money Faulkner was paying without having something serious to hide. Archie wasn't complaining about that, but he wanted to know what Faulkner's business was – probably thought there might be even more money in it if they knew what was going on, knowing Archie...

"So, early the other morning, after Faulkner gave Kenny and Archie their next errand – more boxes to deliver – Archie said he was going to open it and take a look inside. Kenny warned Archie against it, said they shouldn't look a gift horse in the mouth and should just deliver the things as they were told to. But Archie wasn't for changing his mind. Never was one for caution, wasn't Archie.

"So they picked up the package from Faulkner from a house in Highgate, and they were to deliver it to an address south of the river in Lambeth. Well, Archie decided they should make a quick detour to one of the rail warehouses by Marylebone Station on the way, where no-one would see them, and take a look inside the box. He said it couldn't do no harm, and that no-one but them would know. Anna, you know we know that area real well, so it was no problem for them to find an empty spot with no-one around to open the thing. The box Archie was carrying was wooden and about a foot and a half long, with the lid nailed shut with small tacks – easy for someone who knew what they was doing to open up, and then re-seal again without much sign of what had gone on.

"So Archie sets about opening it. He prizes the lid partly up and peers inside. And it sounded like he was disappointed with what was in there. 'Just more stupid books!' was what he said. But before he'd had time to get the lid fixed back on again, Faulkner was suddenly there! Now there's no way Faulkner could know the Marylebone warehouses like Kenny and Archie did, and there's no way he should've been able to find them there without them knowing. But there he was, and his rage was terrible!"

Gillespie paused again, as though the words were now getting harder to come by. The living fog slowly tightened its grip around his form in the dim lamplight.

"Like I said, Kenny and Archie are pretty tough, two of the toughest around, and they know how to look after themselves all right. But they didn't know how to deal with what happened next. Faulkner screamed at Archie that he should never have tried to cross him, and that now he was going to pay for it. Archie tried to fight him off with his stick, but Faulkner just smashed it aside like it was made of paper."

Gillespie stopped again, and now Anna herself shuddered. Suddenly this carefully chosen place did not feel so safe after all – nowhere did. By now Gillespie was starting to breathe very heavily, almost as though the fog that enveloped him was crushing the very air out of him with its swirling grip. Anna felt a shiver of fear at what was coming next. Impossible though she would have believed it to be even minutes earlier, she now started to feel for that undesirable duo, Kenny and Archie. She hoped fervently that they would somehow escape from this tale unscathed, that their rough, underhand natures would somehow help them to find a way to escape the undoubtedly far greater evil that was Faulkner, and the Beast he could summon. "Go on," she said simply, in the most deceitfully calm tone she was capable of.

"Well..." Gillespie hesitated again, hugging his knees to

his chest as his voice almost seemed to dry up completely. "I reckon you ain't going to believe what I'm going to tell you next. But this ain't just another tale Anna, like what I may have told in the past. I swear this is the truth. And I can swear it because I saw it with my own eyes. And I ain't mad Anna – at least, not yet, although I reckon that's maybe where I'm headed.

"See, I wanted to go with them on this errand that day, same as I had on other ones. But I heard Archie explaining his plan to Kenny, and then they both turned on me and told me I couldn't join them. Archie threatened me with a hiding if I didn't leave them to it, so I left them. But I was also burning to find out myself what it was we'd been carrying for Faulkner, so I secretly followed them. And I know the warehouses round Marylebone even better than they do I reckon – maybe better than anyone. They was much too focused on that box and where they should open it to notice me trailing them, and it was no problem for me to get to a good spying spot behind some old cargo trucks. From where I was, I couldn't see the direction that Faulkner approached them from myself, but Kenny and Archie should've been able to see him. But they didn't see nothing until it was too late.

"When Faulkner appeared and started going for Archie, I thought I'd better get nearer, in case I could help them out somehow. So I made my way down the side of the trucks I was hiding behind, and I lost of sight of them all for a while as I was moving. But when I got to the end of the trucks and was able to see them clearly again, it wasn't Faulkner that Archie was fighting with no more – at least, not as you'd recognise him. Faulkner the man weren't there no more. But in his place there was this huge creature, a demon just like the stories, but even worse! And it was closing down on Archie who'd tried to make a run for it."

Anna was momentarily dumbstruck. "You mean..." she asked, trying but failing to retain the calmness in her voice, once it had returned to her, "… that Faulkner *is* the Beast?"

"Yes, Anna, that's what I'm saying. I didn't actually see him change on account of being behind them trucks an' all, but one minute Archie was fighting with Faulkner, and the next it was the Beast!"

Anna was now shaken to her core by what she was hearing. "Gillespie, are you absolutely sure? Couldn't it just be that you didn't notice Faulkner any more once he'd summoned up the Beast?"

"No Anna, it ain't no mistake, it's true. The torn remains of his clothes were on the ground where it stood, and the last strips of his shirt were still hanging off its arms! I tell you Anna, Faulkner *is* the Beast of Highgate!"

Anna was gripping the branch she was sitting on now with both hands as this started to sink in. So when Mr. Warwick had bundled her into that secret room in his shop, he had actually been saving her from the Satal itself! And when they had faced the Beast up in that Highgate mansion, that creature that had swooped down at them from the roof had actually been Faulkner, transformed into that unearthly monster. Did Mr Warwick know this, Anna wondered. When he had confirmed to her that Faulkner was responsible for the Satal's appearance but that there was more he needed to explain, was this what he had meant? Of course Gillespie could be lying, but the thing above anything else which told Anna that what Gillespie was saying was true was her recollection of that essence. From its size to its shape to its colouring, it had been like nothing she had ever come across before – it had looked utterly inhuman! And it had given her a greater impression of evil than anything she had ever before seen, with the sole exception of the man in her dream…

Gillespie had stopped again now, gasping for breath and beginning to sob slightly. The freezing fog, which seemed to be drifting slowly but ever more thickly into the garden through the hole in the wall, already had Gillespie held tightly in its sinister grip, and now it was starting to envelop Anna too. Gillespie's form was growing more difficult to make out as the gas lamp grew even fainter. But Anna continued sitting motionless, almost unable to move, gripped with grim fascination. Somehow, with what must have been close to superhuman effort on his part, Gillespie continued with what he had to say, his voice little more than a croak now, as if he believed his life depended on finishing his piece.

"Like in the stories I'd heard from those who'd claimed to have seen it, this demon creature was covered in some kind of shiny black scales. It had a long, pointed tail and huge claws where its fingers should've been. And its head was long and sharp with horns, and it had huge teeth. Its head was the same kind of shiny black as the rest of its body. And its arms were long, black wings – I swear it was just like a creature from the pits of hell, which is the only place I reckon it could have come from!

"This beast, or demon, or whatever it was that Faulkner had turned into, well it set about Archie in a real furious frenzy. He tried to run away from it, but it was on him again in seconds. And the noise the creature was making… Anna, I tell you it was like nothing I've heard, like this terrible, shrieking sound – I can still hear it now in my head, clear as day." Gillespie shuddered visibly at the recollection, and so did Anna.

"At the same time Kenny was also trying to run away in the other direction. Now you know Kenny ain't no coward, and normally I reckon he'd have done whatever he could to save his mate. But see, faced with something like that, well there was nothing he could have done – nothing anyone could have done. And I don't mind telling you, I was terrified myself an' all. I ducked back under the truck and hid. I couldn't watch no more – I hid my face, but I couldn't block out the terrible screams…"

By now, Gillespie was in floods of tears. "Poor Archie,"

he continued, "he could be a hard one he could, and he gave me the odd hiding or two when he thought I'd warranted it, but I don't reckon he deserved that – no-one deserves an end like that!"

Gillespie clearly didn't want to give any more details regarding Archie's demise, and for her part Anna did not wish to ask him. She was now wondering what had become of Gillespie's brother, but from Gillespie's opening remarks that evening about him being in trouble, she knew that he must somehow have survived this episode at least. "So what about Kenny?" she prompted, still trying to keep her tone stern.

The question seemed to help refocus Gillespie's mind. He started again. "While Faulkner was setting about Archie, Kenny had made a run for it. Like I say, he would normally have stood by Archie and tried to help him out, but there was just no point with a monster like that. There wasn't nothing he could have done, and he knew it. So he tried to scarper. The Beast was focused on devouring Archie for a while, and it was a bit of time before it turned its attention on Kenny, and he'd almost reached the door by that time. It flung poor Archie's body to the ground, beat those black wings it had and began to fly. Its wings grew real long, and it went up high, up near the roof, before diving down after my brother. Kenny just made it through the metal door and slammed it shut, and bolted it just a second before the diving Beast went crashing into it. Then it let out more of that screaming again, and it started to beat at the metal door. Luckily though it was a strong old door, and it took it a while to smash it off its hinges. That gave Kenny a good head start, and like I said, he knows that area real well, and he was able to get away.

"Well I was scared out my wits. I just stayed right where I was without moving a muscle, hidden under them railway cars for hours until long after the sound of that beast had gone. When I finally decided it was safe to get out of there, I headed straight for Kenny's lodgings south of the river.

Kenny wasn't there, but I managed to find him in another of his hideaways that very few apart from me know about. He was in a right state Anna, like you'd imagine. I told him I'd been there and I'd seen what had happened. He was right shocked, and yelled at me how careful I needed to be, that I'd seen what Faulkner was and what he could do, and he'd be sure to kill me if he ever knew I'd been there. He said he was sure that Faulkner had got his hooks into him somehow, and that he was sure he'd track him down one way or another wherever he was if he stayed in London. So he was going to do a runner, maybe catch a ship and go overseas, somewhere where Faulkner wouldn't be able to find him – if there was anywhere. He told me to look after myself and the family, and whatever I did I was not to follow him. And then he was gone.

"I didn't know what to do Anna. Kenny was real clear that I wasn't to follow him this time, real clear, so this time I did what he said. My dad's in jail, my mother was away at work and I didn't feel safe, so I decided to go and find my mates up in Marylebone. It was several hours later and I was on my way to our normal meeting place, when suddenly he was there, Faulkner, back in his normal human shape, all dressed up like a gentleman again. It was like he'd known I'd be coming and he was waiting for me.

"I turned to run, but he had hold of me before I got more than a couple of steps. He was strong Anna, real strong. I've got a good wriggle on me and I can get out of most holds put on me even by adults, but there was no escaping his grip – I swear it was like iron, and it hurt plenty I can tell you.

"He dragged me off down into a dark side alley. It was broad daylight and there was people about on the main street, but no-one did anything to help me. Well, I suppose the sight of a well-dressed gent like Faulkner sorting out a young ruffian like me… and I suppose I haven't got a great name amongst them shopkeepers that know me around that area… well I suppose they probably thought I'd deserve the good hiding I was about to get. They was probably pleased to see someone taking me in hand. Anyway no-one batted an eyelid and no-one followed us, in spite of me screaming for help."

Gillespie stopped again for breath. He had been talking fast as the memories had come back to him in a rush, but now that he started to recall Faulkner again he began to slow down, as though the words were once again becoming harder to speak. Despite the unseasonably cold conditions, Anna could imagine Gillespie breaking into a sweat as he recalled what happened next.

"Well, he, he dragged me down that alley, and then he pinned me against the wall. Then he slowly lowered his head towards mine and he looked at me with this terrible stare. God Anna, it was awful – he's got these eyes that go right through you. I've heard it said by women that Faulkner has the most handsome of eyes. Well, not to me he don't. I can still see them in me head now, and reckon I always will. He was looking right into me – almost like he was looking right inside me." Anna shuddered again as she understood all too well. This had not been a man but a Satal looking into him, penetrating his heart. The dream she had had all those years before returned to her once again, together with the feelings. Gillespie stopped again, struggling for both words and breath. But he battled on.

"He started asking me where my brother was, and whether I'd seen him. I said I hadn't seen him for a few days, and I didn't know where he'd been or what he'd been up to. I was doing my best to lie, and I rate myself as a pretty good liar too when I need to be, but it was like he was looking right inside my head, inside my heart, and I felt like there was no deceiving him. He started to grip my arms even tighter and he hammered me against the wall. Having seen what I'd seen earlier that day back in the warehouse, I thought that was it, my time was up. I was sure he was going to do for me one way or another right there and then –

probably turn into the Beast again, tear me limb from limb and devour my heart, or something worse.

"But he didn't do me no more harm – no harm to my body I mean. But he did do something to me. I can't really explain what happened next, but he kept staring into my eyes, and I started to feel the most dreadful thing, Anna. I don't understand it and I don't have no words to describe it, but all I can say is, it was like he had his hands round my soul, and he was slowly strangling the life out of it. I felt sick to my stomach, I felt terror right to my core. I felt like I was inches from death. And then I started to feel like I was on the very edge of some terrible other place, like if he pushed me one more inch I would be gone there, wherever it was – and that it would be a place much worse than death."

Anna was now transfixed. She knew that the feelings Gillespie had experienced must have come from Faulkner's contact with his essence, but exactly what evil act had he been performing? This time it sounded like something beyond anything she had experienced or seen before, and by the sounds of it something truly terrible.

"Anna, I've never felt nothing like it in my life, I didn't know that feelings like that existed. But Faulkner was somehow inside me, and he had my whole being in his grip, ready to snuff out me life, or doom me to far worse forever if he wanted to.

"If he'd asked me again where Kenny was, I reckon I'd have told him all I knew. Not even to save myself no more, but because I was completely powerless – completely in his power. But he never asked me. I reckon he'd looked inside me with them damned eyes and seen all there was to know. Then I was no more use to him, so he just threw me to the ground and left. He could have killed me as easy as killing a fly, but I reckon it just made no odds to him whether I lived or not – once he'd got what he wanted, my life wasn't important to him one way or the other. And that's the only reason I'm still here, I reckon. But what he did to me Anna, what he made me feel – Anna, it was worse than anything I've ever known or imagined – worse, much worse I reckon than if he'd torn me apart like what he did with Archie."

Anna could see that Gillespie was now in a terrible state as he relived these events, and she could hold back no more. He was a broken child, shattered by the experiences he had had and he posed no more of a threat to her now than he had when he had stood defenceless in front of her on that canal bridge – in fact he was far less of one. Mustering the considerable effort needed to free herself from the almost physical hold the freezing fog seemed to have on her, she finally laid her caution to one side and moved forward from her place of concealment to sit beside him. She continued to look around them as she put her arm around Gillespie's shoulder to console him, and then she gave him a hug. She noticed again just how dense and frozen the fog had become, especially around him. It seemed to dispel just slightly with her arrival.

Slowly Gillespie lowered his head onto Anna's shoulder, as his tears continued to stream down his cheeks in floods. Anna could never have imagined feeling so sorry for her former enemy. But in the face of the infinitely greater evil represented by Faulkner, their previous differences now seemed utterly trivial. Anna continued to hold Gillespie close until the sobbing began to subside again slightly. She then finally put a voice to the question that had been burning inside her since Gillespie had started all this.

"Billy, why did you come to find me tonight, and why have you been telling me all this? You said something about wanting me to help you – and I really wish I could help you, I honestly do – but why me? What is it you think I can do? I'd have thought you'd be looking for help from your Marylebone... uh... friends."

"After Faulkner had finished with me, I knew there was nothing any of them could do. Even if they believed me, which they might not have, but even if they had, well what could they have done? We're a tough bunch, but not as tough as Kenny and Archie. They'd have just ended up the same way as Archie if I'd got them involved.

"Anna, the reason I wanted to find you and talk to you," and for the first time since she had come to sit next to him, Gillespie raised his head and looked into her eyes, his own glistening with tears in the dim streetlamp light, "is that I reckon you're the one person who might be able to do something about Faulkner and save Kenny... and save me. Or at least help me get over whatever Faulkner did to me. If anyone can..." With that his voice faltered again, and he lowered his head once more.

Anna was stunned at this. What could possibly have led Gillespie to make this connection? "What do you mean, Billy? What is it that you think I can do? I'm really only a child still, and not even hardened grown men seem to be any match for Faulkner."

Gillespie was silent for a moment, then he said, "Anna, you remember that time we fought on the bridge over the canal? When you threw me over the side into the water?

"Yes, of course I remember it. But Billy, I don't really think it's the same as - "

"Well I felt something that day too," continued Gillespie, "something deep inside me – the same kind of place I felt Faulkner had a hold of me I think.

"Anna, I reckon I'm stronger than you, physically I mean – well, I'm a boy after all," Anna's pride bristled briefly at that remark but she let it pass. "But when you walked towards me, you had me completely helpless before you'd even laid a finger on me. You was also looking right into me eyes, real intense like – but right pretty at the same time." This time Anna felt herself suddenly and unexpectedly blush, in spite of herself and the situation!

"But now that I look back on it, you did something like what Faulkner did to me, I'm sure of it. It's like you reached right inside me and touched me, like you were touching my soul or something. But it weren't nothing like the way Faulkner did it. See Anna, when you approached me and did what you did, I felt a huge calm inside me, like all my troubles were being soothed – I felt better than I've ever felt I reckon, really blissful – but also I was completely in your power. When you reached me and pushed me over the side, I couldn't resist your push any more than I could have resisted landing in the water straight after. But I didn't feel no hatred from you Anna, not like with Faulkner, and I didn't feel no hatred for you either." He was looking at her again, his eyes slightly clearer and brighter now in the dim light from the streetlamp.

"What you did was something like what Faulkner did, but the feeling was the opposite, if you know what I mean. What I'm trying to say is that you both seem to have some kind of similar power, I don't know what it is but you're both able to do something, you can reach inside of people and change them, either in a good way, or in the most awful way. Anna, I know everyone thinks you're a loony and strange," again Anna let this pass, "and I don't begin to understand any of this I'm sure I don't, but I'm just desperate. I've got nowhere else to go and I reckon you're my last hope of finding something that might just help me against Faulkner, or at least undo whatever he's done to me, and help me save Kenny, better than any grown man armed with weapons."

Although it was crystal clear that Gillespie scarcely understood himself what he had felt and what he was attempting to articulate, there was no doubt what he was referring to. Here was firsthand confirmation of what Mr. Warwick and her uncle had told her about Satals and their ability to manipulate a person's essence in the most terrible ways. And now he had given her firsthand evidence that the power she possessed also touched a person's essence in a way that was recognisably similar. Although she understood something of the theory now, it was nonetheless still deeply shocking to have it confirmed through someone's real experience, that like it or not, she and Faulkner shared some of the same kinds of powers, regardless of the fact that their intentions might be entirely opposite. The idea that she might have anything that connected her with a monster like Faulkner – a *Satal* – was utterly abhorrent to her. She wanted to have nothing whatsoever in common with that beast, and with a power which had such evil potential. But at least Gillespie had explained that the effect of each had felt entirely different. She held onto that thought.

Now that they were sat close to one another, Anna was able to see Gillespie's essence in detail for the first time. Although she had already noticed the increased scarring on its surface when she had looked at it earlier from some distance away, now that she could see it more clearly, what she saw made her gasp.

The scars on the surface of the essence, thought not wide, ran far deeper than she had at first realised – they were deeper and also redder. It looked almost as though this essence had undergone some kind of frenzied attack, leaving its surface deeply lacerated. Although the overall hue of the essence was still yellow as she had previously observed, the colouration in and around the scars themselves was all dark red and black. It was clear that this was the essence of someone who had undergone a brief but quite ferocious mental attack. The image of Faulkner's savage essence, the colourations of which were exactly the same as those around the wounds, returned to her mind. The damage looked very severe. This was not good, and it was unlike anything Anna had seen before. 'So this is the kind of damage that can be inflicted by a Satal attack,' she thought, gasping inwardly.

Looking again, she felt an irresistible urge to try to mend some of the harm that had been done, to heal him and to restore his essence at least a little way back towards a pure state. Visualising her own essence, she reached out and began gently to massage Gillespie's. This was something she had never attempted before, but she found that, little by little, she was able to smooth out the surface of the essence ever so slightly, and to reduce the extent of the red and black colouration, if only to a small degree. Given more time, training and practice, she hoped that she might one day even be able to restore an essence as damaged as Gillespie's to a more healthy state – if that was something that Mr. Warwick's teaching confirmed she was permitted to do.

Gillespie had certainly felt the effect of her touch. Looking up at her as she paused, he said "Yes Anna, that's it. That's the first time I've felt anything like peace since Faulkner got to me. I knew you could help – I knew it! Thank you Anna."

Encouraged, Anna looked back to Gillespie's essence again, ready to try to soothe it some more. But at that instant, the deep scars in its surface suddenly flashed momentarily with a terrible, bright scarlet colour, before returning to their former dark red and black! Anna looked on startled as Gillespie winced visibly with pain. Then another scarlet flash and another gasp from Gillespie. This time Anna jumped. She had never seen anything like this before, but all her instincts told her one thing – somehow it must be Faulkner causing this to happen. And she was filled with a sudden chill of fear... was he somewhere near? Whilst she could not fully comprehend what was happening to Gillespie's essence, what she was sure of was that she no longer felt safe in this place. In fact she had the sudden and growing sense that staying in any one place too long now might be a fatal mistake. They had to move, and move right now!

With a suddenly heightened sense of urgency, she told Gillespie that they needed to get away from there, and she helped him slowly to his feet. "But Anna, I don't think I can move no more," Gillespie croaked – not surprisingly, given all that he had been through and was now experiencing again.

But Anna was not taking no for an answer, and Gillespie continued to sob as she began to lead his stumbling form slowly away from the pile of rubble. She needed to think fast. Back onto the road, where anyone might be waiting in ambush for them? Or deeper into the garden, where at least she would know the terrain better than anyone else would, although from which it might be more difficult finally to escape? With no more time to think, she chose the latter course.

As hurriedly as Gillespie's almost immobile legs would allow, they passed through the long grass of the lawn, through the swirling mist to the far side of the garden, which was also lined with tall bushes, then moved some way up the garden away from the point where they had crossed. Having put some considerable distance between themselves and the spot where they had just been, Anna led Gillespie through the low branches of a large bush there, sufficiently deeply to be concealed from all but a few feet away. Anna stopped and looked urgently back through the leaves, across the lawn to the spot from which they had just come. Their leaving had coincided with a slight thinning of the fog – or had it been their movement and increased energy that had actually caused it to disperse a little? There was something supernatural about the fog that night that made anything seem possible.

Then, out of the corner of her eye, below the gas street lamp which was just visible through the fog, Anna thought she glimpsed another, fainter light, moving slowly on the pavement side of the broken wall. As she peered harder through the foggy darkness, there was no mistaking it – there was definitely a second lamp! It came to a halt at the point where the lowest part of the wall was located, and Anna was suddenly gripped by absolute fear. She knew this garden almost like the back of her hand, and she also knew that all means of escape other than the way they had come were equally difficult, requiring either the scaling of high garden walls or else breaking into the old house itself. Her worries began to attack her. Had this been a trap all along? Had Gillespie in fact somehow outsmarted her after all and distracted her with his stories until his accomplices could arrive? She suddenly heard his intake of breath next to her as he too noticed the second light, and she felt him reach for her hand – however not in a way intended to capture her, but rather with a grip that articulated only his own, intense fear.

"Oh my God Anna, we've got to get out of here!" Anna could feel Gillespie now physically trembling, and she put all further thoughts of his possible deception out of her mind, once and for all. He could already have given her away by now had he chosen to, and his condition showed that he was clearly in a state of absolute terror.

They both stared in silence across the misty abyss towards the far side of the garden. The light had slowly started to move again, slightly upwards in a motion that suggested its bearer was now climbing over something. The lamp lowered again, before once more moving gradually forward and upward, and then stopping. The swirling fog cleared slightly, and just for an instant they were both able to make out the dark, silhouetted outline of a tall man stood astride the rubble mound where they themselves had been sat just moments before. The figure, wearing a top hat and a long cape that reached almost to the ground, appeared to be brandishing a walking cane in his right hand whilst holding aloft a lamp in his left. He was immediately enveloped once more by fog. It had been no more than a glimpse, but it had been unmistakable.

"It's him!" Gillespie breathed, almost inaudibly into Anna's ear. "Oh my God, it's him. He's here, Anna. We've got to get out of here!" Gillespie was now in the grip of complete and utter panic.

"Don't worry, Billy, I have a plan – you must trust me," said Anna, lying desperately and gripping his hand, no longer worried by the possibility of his treachery so much as the danger that his fear might give them away. "Don't move or make a sound unless I say so!" Trembling from head to toe, Gillespie fell silent.

Anna fought desperately to control her own, crippling fear, which was now slowly creeping up her body. This had been the one situation above all others that Mr. Warwick and her uncle had most feared – the very one which they had urged her at all costs to avoid. Her training had barely begun, she was entirely unready, and not only did she not have anyone there from the Order to protect her, she did not even have any of her own friends with her. The thought of Timmy returned to her mind. She had felt so safe in his company when they had fled from the Highgate mansion together; she had felt that they would always be all right as long as they were together. But what had happened since then? Where was Timmy now? He had seemingly gone from her life. Mr. Warwick and her uncle were miles away and now there was no-one to help her when she needed it most desperately.

As she stared into the fog which had become impenetrable again, she could see nothing but she could sense the figure they had glimpsed now slowly approaching. She started to feel physically sick to the pit of her stomach. How could she have let this happen? How could she have been so stupid? She had been trapped after all – and in a trap of her own making! Seven words from Mr. Warwick returned to her: 'The malevolent influence of the Opposing Energy...' Was this where her short life was to end, right here in this garden that she had once loved, her potential unfulfilled, and despite all Mr Warwick's hopes, nothing in the end achieved in the name of the Alpha World?

For she knew that Gillespie was right. Faulkner, Satal of the Omega World and the dreaded theme of Gillespie's harrowing tale just moments earlier, was right there, inside the garden with them.

The Hunter and the Prey

Anna fought desperately to regain control of her emotions and to resist the tide of raw fear that had already consumed her companion. She had to think clearly, and very fast.

There was no way that Faulkner could have known in advance that Anna was going to lead Gillespie here, as even she had not known that beforehand. And if he had somehow managed to follow them unseen through the fog, surely he would have arrived at the garden far sooner than he had. She did not understand how, but she felt sure it was something to do with the effect she had seen in Gillespie's essence – those red flashes in the scars on its surface. It seemed as though Faulkner had some kind of contact with Gillespie's essence that had enabled him to locate Gillespie and then hunt him down. And if that were true, presumably he would be able to do so again even if they did somehow manage to escape from that garden. Their only chance was to find a way to break the connection that Faulkner had established with Gillespie's essence.

Trusting entirely to her instincts, Anna began slowly to move her own essence over that of Gillespie, mentally picturing it gradually engulfing and finally surrounding it entirely. Of course she could not actually see it to know whether or not she had been successful, nor whether or not what she was attempting would actually have any kind of positive effect, but she could feel the contact with her companion's essence and it did feel as though she were now 'containing' it. No sooner had she done so than she felt a strange sensation in her own essence, like a prickling feeling all over its surface. She was certain that this was somehow connected with the scarlet flashes she had seen in Gillespie's essence. It was as though Faulkner was somehow sending out some kind of signal, presumably from his own essence, which was making contact with Gillespie's and enabling him to know Gillespie's location. Anna wondered desperately if this might mean Faulkner could track her essence as well in the same way. Somehow she imagined not though. She felt certain that the connection between the two of them had been created during the encounter Gillespie had described with Faulkner, when it had felt as though Faulkner had 'had his hands around his soul', and presumably when Gillespie had received that terrible scarring on his essence. Faulkner did something to Gillespie's essence at that time, somehow got some kind of hook into it that had enabled him to trace Gillespie. But this time, although Anna had felt that prickling sensation on her own essence, the scars in Gillespie's essence had not flashed red! Was it possible that she was now successfully shielding Gillespie from Faulkner's reach by surrounding his essence in this way? She had no way to be sure, but the first glimmer of hope appeared in her heart.

Holding the trembling hand of her silent but terrified companion even more tightly and quietly whispering words of encouragement, she peered intently into the foggy darkness. Another wave of the prickling feeling swept over her essence more forcefully than the first, and now she braced herself for an onslaught, imagining Faulkner's snarling face suddenly emerging from the fog right in front of them, or worse still, that of the Beast. But once again Gillespie's essence did not flash, and nothing appeared.

As the moments passed, Anna noticed that the haunting mist was beginning to part again as it swirled in the night, and straining her eyes in the direction from which they had fled, once again she glimpsed it – the distant, cloaked figure of Faulkner, palely illuminated by the lamp he still held aloft, inside the garden but thankfully still a considerable distance away from them. His head was moving slowly from one side to the other as he peered intently into the darkness. From their concealed position in the bushes, Anna instinctively shifted her focus to see if she could make out his hideous essence through the fog at this distance – and to her relief she could not! 'That might just mean he won't be able to make out our essences either, at least as long as he stays at that distance,' she reasoned desperately.

The mist parting had coincided with a third wave of the prickling sensation, and then suddenly the figure let out a terrible, anger-filled growl and he began to swipe violently at the air around him with his cane, just as the fog engulfed them once again. Whilst the image had only been momentary, it had been enough to send a jolt of terror right through Anna. But once it was gone, faint hope once again returned – a hope that their archenemy's anger might actually be born out of frustration at having lost track of Gillespie.

Anna now focused desperately on holding Gillespie's essence entirely concealed within her own. Wave after wave of searching probing played upon her essence and another muffled roar of frustration reached their ears, but Anna remained motionless, maintaining the positioning of her essence. At her side, Gillespie if anything seemed to be breathing slightly more easily, as though her were finally feeling some respite from Faulkner's continual presence, but he did not move and he did not lessen his tight grip on Anna's hand.

Several minutes which felt like hours passed, and then they heard the angry growl of rage again – and if anything, the noise of their hunter sounded closer this time! Anna could not see anything through the fog, and neither could she make out anything of Faulkner's essence, but once again her fears began to get the better of her. She had visions of their nemesis wading through the long grass, snarling and thrashing at the misty darkness with his cane, seeking out their essences and hunting for any trace of his prey. And if he were to find them, every instinct in her body told her that it would certainly spell their end. Then, suddenly, the prickling sensation on her essence intensified, becoming positively painful as it now bore the brunt of the Satal's most penetrating search yet. Anna braced herself for the final attack.

The longest snarling growl of rage yet reached them, but as it continued Anna could have sworn that it was beginning to grow slightly more distant, as though the face of their enemy had now turned away from them. Anna held her breath, barely daring to believe it could be true: was their hunter finally abandoning his murderous quest? Yes, as the moments passed there was no mistaking it – the sound of Faulkner's anger was definitely growing more distant! Not for one second did Anna let down her defences, the evening's experience having taught her all too well that any further lack of caution on her part might be the last mistake she ever made.

There came one more angry growl, this time much more distant, followed by silence. Perhaps most tellingly, the frequency of the prickling sensation on her essence also subsided then stopped altogether. However Anna remained absolutely motionless, a brief whisper to Gillespie not to speak a word or to move a muscle until she told him otherwise being the only sound she made. She would take no further chances and she would wait there as long as it took to be certain that Faulkner had truly left. Deep down inside, that intuition which sometimes spoke to her told her that this time the danger had indeed passed – at least for now. They had been incredibly lucky to escape with their lives, but that same sense also told her with certainty that this was only to be a temporary reprieve, and that the time was now very close when she and Faulkner would indeed come face-to-face in battle. Whether or not that encounter would bring with it the still greater menace of the man from her dream, the Gorgal, she could not sense – she could only hope with all her heart that it would not. But whatever lay ahead, Anna was determined that the encounter would not take place that night at least, and she and Gillespie remained silent and motionless in their place of concealment, safely hidden in the bushes of the old garden.

Several hours deeper into that same, ominous night, many miles across the great city and its mighty river, Billy's brother Kenny Gillespie desperately stuffed the meagre possessions that came to hand into his battered old bag, together with the hidden money he had come back to collect. He dashed down the stairs of the dilapidated building where his lodgings were housed, opened the back door and slipped silently into the unholy fog that had gripped the city that night. Escaping to the docks and finding a ship that might take him as far away from London as it was possible to go was now the only thought in his terror-stricken mind. In recent days he had witnessed things more terrible than he could ever have imagined, still less have explained, and he had spent every waking moment since in quaking fear for his own life. Kenny Gillespie had done many bad things in his time, some of them very bad, but that road had now brought him face-to-face with evil in its purest form, and it had been far more than he could deal with.

It had taken until now for him to dare risk a return to his rented lodgings from his previous place of concealment, to pick up the small amount of money he had managed to accumulate from his various 'work', and he had known full well he could not afford to linger a moment longer than absolutely necessary. Gillespie was no stranger to the London night, indeed it had become his natural habitat over the years, but the fog that night was denser and more sinister than on any other he could ever remember. It seemed possessed of an eerie, almost living quality, which sent shivers right through him more vigorous than could have been induced by the mere cold alone. Through wide, frightened eyes, time and again he was convinced he had made out a snarling ghostly face in the swirling mist through which he ran, dimly illuminated by distant gas lamps. 'It's just the troubled state of my head... my mind's playing tricks on me... it's this damned fog... I'm seeing things because I haven't slept for days... it'll all be all right once I'm safely out at sea...' Gillespie rambled desperately to himself as he hurried down the cobbled backstreet, past the back yards of the terraced houses that adjoined his lodgings, sticking close to the wall for fear of losing himself forever in the haunted sea of mist that stretched out away into the blackness.

Then he heard it. It was the sound that he feared most in the world, the sound that had haunted the scarce moments of sleep he had managed since the awful events in that Marylebone warehouse. It was an inhuman, blood-curdling scream, completely filling his ears and echoing around his head. He could not tell from which direction it had come – it had seemed to come from all directions at once – and his head began to spin as the tricks played by his eyes in that infernal fog intensified. Gillespie stumbled once to his hands and knees on the freezing cobblestones, before immediately regaining his feet and lurching forwards again into the foggy soup in front of him. By now he was seized by sheer and utter blind panic, and the most basic animal survival instinct was the only thing driving him forward. On he plunged through the thick darkness, until his wits began dimly to return as he became aware he was finally approaching the better-lit main road which adjoined his own back street. A vague flicker of hope and the remembrance of his plan to reach the docks re-entered his consciousness. There was no way to convince himself that he had imagined that terrible sound moments earlier – no way that his imagination could have conjured up such a sound – but maybe, just maybe its owner had not yet spotted him through the all-consuming fog.

On reaching the corner he scrambled straight around it... and there it was. Perfectly silhouetted against a bank of thick, ghostly white fog that was palely illuminated by a large gas streetlamp somewhere behind it, was the large black outline of a horned creature at least seven feet tall, with wings outstretched at either side, each tipped with long, deadly talons. Gillespie froze dead in his tracks, the final remnants of hope now draining from his tired body, and for a moment neither figure moved. The thought of turning and trying to escape crawled across Gillespie's numb and exhausted mind, but the futility of such an attempt was apparent even to him. All hope now gone, he stood rooted to the spot as the monster before him slowly arched its head upwards, let out a scream that was to be the last sound he would ever hear, a sound so unlike anything from this world that it would be spoken about in the folklore of the area for generations to come, and then it struck.

The end for Kenny Gillespie when it came was mercifully swift, even if the damage inflicted on his physical body was truly horrific, shaking to the very core even the most hardened of policemen who saw it. 'Beast Strikes South of the River!' screamed the newspaper headlines the following day, stories of demons spread like wildfire, and London lay gripped in mortal fear.